TONI BLAKE

*One
Reckless
Summer*

AVON
An Imprint of HarperCollinsPublishers

This is a work of fiction. Names, characters, places, and incidents are products of the author's imagination or are used fictitiously and are not to be construed as real. Any resemblance to actual events, locales, organizations, or persons, living or dead, is entirely coincidental.

AVON BOOKS
An Imprint of HarperCollins*Publishers*
195 Broadway
New York, NY 10007

Copyright © 2009 by Toni Herzog
ISBN 978-0-06-142989-7
www.avonbooks.com

First Avon Books paperback printing: June 2009

Avon Trademark Reg. U.S. Pat. Off. and in Other Countries, Marca Registrada, Hecho en U.S.A.
HarperCollins® is a registered trademark of HarperCollins Publishers.

Printed in the U.S.A.

10 9 8 7 6 5

"Now be the good little girl you are and go home."

He placed his large hands on top of her and physically began to turn her around.

And that was it! It was the straw that broke the camel's back. She wouldn't be manhandled. She wouldn't be bossed around by one more person. She was tired of being "good" Jenny, obedient Jenny, tired of letting men make her decisions for her. All the anger, fury, and disgust boiling inside her over the last few months finally overflowed.

"Get your hands off me and get out of my way," she spat, and started to push boldly past him . . .

Only Mick didn't let her pass—his arm shot out to block her path. His hand closed firmly over her hip, the length of his arm stretching down over her breasts and torso.

He bent down, his voice low and menacing, "Listen, sweetheart, you don't want to mess with me, okay? Now turn your pretty little ass around and get back to your side of the lake while you still can."

She sucked in her breath, raised her gaze—frightened but bold. "Or what?"

She remained in his grasp, their faces but an inch apart. Mick's potent gaze drifted from her eyes to her mouth. He didn't answer, or maybe his answer was what he did next . . .

By Toni Blake

ONE RECKLESS SUMMER
LETTERS TO A SECRET LOVER
TEMPT ME TONIGHT
SWEPT AWAY

*This book is dedicated to the teachers
who most encouraged me to pursue
my dream of being a novelist:
Sandra Lillard Adams,
the late Dolly West,
and Dr. Peter Schiff.*

Acknowledgments

My deepest thanks to Renee Norris, first reader extraordinaire. Your insights were vital in helping me make this book the best it could be, and I appreciate your time, input, and enthusiasm more than words can express. Thank you, as well, to Joe Roberts of Rocket-Roberts.com for so kindly taking the time to answer all my questions about astronomy—and I hope I got everything right. Thank you to Lindsey Faber for all your wonderful efforts on my behalf—you completely rock! And finally, thank you to May Chen and all the fine folks at Avon Books for being so fun and fabulous to work with, and to Meg Ruley and Christina Hogrebe at the Rotrosen Agency for being the best cheerleaders on the planet.

Prologue

"Meow, pussycat."

Jenny lay sleeping on a lounge chair in the sun when a warm male voice permeated her senses, making her feel hot and melty inside. Was she dreaming? It was the kind of voice that wrapped around her like a blanket and made her want to snuggle down into it, even on a sweltering summer day.

"Hey, wake up—rise and shine."

Wait a minute. Different voice this time. More abrasive—and kind of menacing. Jenny flinched fully awake now, opening her eyes.

At the end of the small dock floated an old wooden rowboat with three guys inside, all of them ogling her in her new bikini. Oh God. Her stomach shriveled—they were older, rough-looking. Where on earth had they come from?

Then she recognized two of them—the Brody boys from across the lake. She'd just never seen them this close-up before.

She thought of replying, but how on earth did someone respond to "Meow, pussycat"? Her cat, Snowball, currently meandered across the dock, a few feet away, and in her sleepy haze, Jenny honestly wasn't sure if the greeting had been for her or for Snowy.

"Cat got your tongue?" This came from Wayne Brody, the older of the brothers—he had to be at least twenty-one—and it turned out the abrasive voice belonged to *him*. And apparently the "Meow" had been for *her*, even if he hadn't been the one to say it.

"What do you want?" she finally managed. She tried to sound mean, scary. But that was ridiculous, she realized as quickly as she spoke—how scary could a sixteen-year-old girl in a bikini be? Vulnerable was more like it. Yet attempting to sound mean was her only defense at the moment.

"What's your name?" asked Mick Brody, and she realized *he'd* been the one to say, "Meow." Now his voice poured over her, deep and enveloping, like a guy older than nineteen. But she still guessed that to be his age—he'd been a senior when she was a freshman. A senior who skipped class and got caught drinking and "raised every kind of hell there is to raise," according to her father. Mick Brody held a beer can in his hand right now, and all three boys were smoking cigarettes.

She just sat there. She didn't *want* to tell them her name, or let herself be pulled into conversation at all—somehow that would make her even *more* vulnerable. But her silence also made it seem like she was simply too frightened to talk. Her heart beat too hard.

"Fine," Mick Brody said. "Guess I'll just have to call you pussycat then."

God, why did that make her pulse skitter? The word *should have* sounded dirty—a word you would see in pink neon outside a sleazy strip club or something—

but instead it seemed to caress her skin. Or maybe that had to do with the way Mick Brody was looking at her right now. Everything about him made her feel threatened, yet at the same time his blue eyes shone on her like two shimmering stars in the night sky, captivating her. Yeesh.

Suddenly, she rethought the skimpiness of the bathing suit. She'd been comfortable in it with her friends, even with the guys in the group, when she'd worn it the other day—but she wasn't comfortable *now*. Now she felt practically naked, like Mick Brody could see *all* of her.

Just then, Snowball padded to the end of the dock, where the boat had pulled up.

"Want something to drink, cat?" asked the third boy, who Jenny now recognized as Lucky Romo, a long-haired guy who frequently sped through town in his souped-up car. She happened to know her father had given him a ticket just last week.

Lucky leaned over to spill a puddle of foamy beer out onto the wood in front of the cat, and as Snowball bent to taste it, fresh anger surged through Jenny, pushing her to her feet to barrel toward the edge of the dock. *"Leave my cat alone! Get out of here!"*

The white cat darted away, clearly much more frightened of Jenny at the moment than of anyone else—while the boys in the rowboat laughed. Rage burned through her, and she wondered if they could see her face turning red beneath the color she'd acquired from the sun. She also wondered if her nipples showed through her bikini because of the weird way Mick Brody affected her. She crossed her arms, trying to cover her breasts, but instead only succeeded in heaving them higher. *Ugh*.

And Mick Brody continued to pin her in place with

his dark, wicked grin. "Come a little closer, pussycat. Wanna go for a ride?"

Despite herself, she heard the sexual implication in the question, and even as it repulsed her, she couldn't deny that it also aroused her. *Oh God*.

She took a deep breath, tried to act a little more cool than she'd managed so far, and rolled her eyes. "Um, no thanks." Her tone implied that the very suggestion was ludicrous.

"Aw, come on, honey, we don't bite," Wayne Brody chimed in.

"Unless you want us to," Mick added with raised eyebrows.

Dear God—why did that make her feel so warm in her bikini bottoms? He was . . . dangerous. A guy you stayed away from. It was one thing to be attracted to *normal* boys that way—Adam Becker from school, Jimmy Raines who worked up at the Whippy Dip. But this boy? Something must be wrong with her. "You heard me," she said. "Go away."

"Or what?" Lucky Romo replied. "You gonna sic your big bad daddy the cop on us?" All three boys broke up with still more laughter as if it was the funniest thing they'd ever heard.

Jenny let out an irritated breath. "Fine. You won't go away? Then I *will*."

After all, she was pretty sure they were drunk. And from what she could tell, none of her neighbors along the lake were outside—she was alone here. Her father had always taught her: Get out of a potentially bad situation before it has the chance to escalate; it was better to be safe than sorry.

So she grabbed up her towel and swim bag, along with her Diet Coke, slipped on her flip-flops, and started away from the dock.

"Nice ass," Mick Brody called, making her glad they couldn't see her face anymore—since it was *surely* beet red after *that*. And she continued to feel the three boys' stares on her rear all the way across the narrow road lining the lake and up the front walk to her house.

But especially Mick Brody's.

She walks in beauty, like the night;
Of cloudless climes and starry skies.

Lord Byron

One

Fifteen years later

As dusk fell over Blue Valley Lake, creating texture and shadow in the air, Jenny Tolliver pushed the old green canoe from the grassy bank down into the water. Still in the summer skirt and cotton blouse she'd worn to Mrs. Kinman's mah-jongg party, the only concessions she'd made for the lake excursion were trading in her slingback sandals for a pair of canvas tennis shoes and zipping her telescope and other equipment into a large waterproof bag.

As she climbed carefully into the canoe, using the dock for balance, it felt like stepping back in time. She hadn't crossed this lake in this canoe since she'd been eighteen years old, and back then she'd had Sue Ann for a companion. And Sue Ann probably would have left her mom's party to come with her tonight if she'd asked, but her best friend had different obligations in life now—she had a husband and daughter to go home to.

Besides, Jenny had wanted to be alone. She'd wanted to . . . escape.

Good God—you've only been back in Destiny two short days and already you need to escape? Not a good sign.

But when people had said one too many nice things about her at the party, it had pushed her over the edge. Not that it made much sense to get upset over people being kind to her, but *nothing* about her life made sense lately.

When Rose Marie Keckley had seen the lemon bars Jenny had whipped up for the occasion, she'd said, "That was so nice of you, Jenny." And when Jenny had refilled some iced tea glasses to keep Mrs. Kinman from getting up after just sitting down, LeeAnn Turner had said, "You're so sweet." Then Lettie Gale had added, "You're so good, Jenny," simply because she'd helped old Mrs. Lampton up from her chair. And that was *it*, the final straw—she'd had to get out of there.

Now the words echoed in her head, taunting her. *You're so good. You're so good.* Well, she was *sick and tired* of being good.

So what was she doing about it?

Canoeing across the lake.

Hardly a bold act of rebellion against society.

But at least it had gotten her away from the party and all those people she'd grown up with who thought she was so damn *good*. And now it was getting her away from her old family cottage just across the road, another place she wasn't quite ready to go back to—at least not yet.

So despite knowing that paddling across a quiet lake as the sun set behind the trees wouldn't take her any farther away from her problems than coming home to Destiny had, she pushed off from the dock anyway, dipping the oar in the water. And that old saying came back to her: *Wherever you go, there you are.* Meaning there really *was* no escape. Swell.

Then she knit her eyebrows. *Stop it. This isn't you. You're the girl whose glass is always half-full, the girl who always has a smile for everyone she meets. Where's your smile?*

Glumly, she answered herself. *Maybe I left it in Terrence's classroom with the shattered heads of George Washington and Abraham Lincoln.* The expensive ceramic ones she'd given him for their first anniversary. The same ones she'd sent crashing to the floor when she'd found him lip-locked with Kelsey, the twenty-one-year-old student teacher who'd been working in Jenny's science classes all semester long.

"This isn't what it looks like," he'd said when she'd walked into the schoolroom late that March afternoon.

She'd just stared at him in disbelief. "Seriously?" she'd asked. "That's seriously the route you want to go here?"

"We should talk someplace private, Jenny. I didn't want you to find out like this."

"Then maybe you should have, say, *locked the door.*" That's when George had hit the floor. She didn't exactly remember making the decision to pick up the bust and throw it—it had just happened, and pieces had flown everywhere.

"Jenny, you need to calm down," he'd insisted, his eyes all aghast—like *she* was the one doing something reprehensible here.

"Let me get this straight. I walk into my husband's classroom to bring him a piece of the vice principal's birthday cake, and I find him making out with my student teacher, and he thinks I should be *calm*? Well, how's *this* for calm?" That's when Abe had bitten the dust, as well, crashing down to explode into a thousand shards.

It was the most uncharacteristic thing "good Jenny" had ever done. But cheating on her was the most out-of-character move Terrence had ever made, too. And it was that night at home, when the blind rage had passed, settling into a good old-fashioned gnawing ache, that she'd asked him the question, "*Why?* Just tell me *why*," and Terrence had dealt the lowest blow of all. He'd told her she was the twenty-first century June Cleaver.

June Cleaver! Of all the cultural icons in all the world, he'd had to compare her to *June Cleaver*? Not that she had anything against June, but . . . she didn't want to *be* her.

And it had grown even worse when he'd gotten down to the real heart of the matter. "It's not that I don't love you. It's just that you're too sweet to . . . well, to have the kind of sex I want. The kind I've been craving for *years*."

It had been like a punch in the gut. "The kind you have with Kelsey, you mean."

He'd looked down at the living room carpet they'd picked out together last year. "Well, yeah."

Another punch. Since they hadn't technically established, up to that point, that he was indeed having *sex* with Kelsey.

"You're just . . . so *good*, Jenny," he'd said, his voice pained. "*Too* good." Ugh.

She didn't bother reminding him that not once in all their years together had he let her know he desired anything different. And that he was the only guy she'd ever *had* sex with, so that everything she knew she'd learned from *him.* "So what is it you want exactly?" she'd snapped instead. "Whips and chains? Stripper poles in the bedroom? *What?*"

And just like earlier, he'd had the nerve to look at her like *she* was the crazy, unreasonable one. "It's not about . . . props," he'd said. "It's about . . . heat. Passion."

Since then, Sue Ann had taken to calling him a "rat bastard," and what the term lacked in originality, Jenny felt it made up for in accuracy. Sue Ann also liked referring to Kelsey as "the chippy" and "the tart," and in some odd, weak way, that helped ease a little of Jenny's grief, too.

Although as she got far enough out into the lake to truly start feeling isolated, she suffered a blip of emotion—one that continued to hit her often. It was a fraction of a second when she remembered what life had felt like back when it was normal, back when she'd felt safe, happy, content.

Her life with Terrence had been simple but good— she wasn't a woman who asked for the moon, even if she loved watching it through her telescope. They'd been together since college; they'd taught in the same middle school. He specialized in history, she in science. She'd once had aspirations of becoming an astronomer, working at NASA or doing research at a university, but Terrence had urged her to settle for teaching, and she'd discovered that when you're young and in love, it was shockingly easy to agree to anything—even giving up your dream.

And so they'd taught. And they'd had dinner parties. They'd been active in the community. They'd never had children—she'd just never gotten pregnant—but they loved the kids in their classes, and they were the kind of stable, happy couple people envied. Or they *had* been. Before the tart.

Losing her marriage had been devastating. But the part that still seemed to hang over her now, every day, every hour, was that Terrence had betrayed her because he thought she was *too sweet, too nice.* The dreaded Catch–22: He loved her because she was a good girl, but he secretly desired a bad girl. She could *never* be *everything* he wanted.

So she'd pushed the divorce through quickly, and she'd quit her job—no longer willing to work so closely with Terrence, and now she suddenly found herself back in Destiny, Ohio, where her father was still the chief of police and where the old cottage by the lake on Blue Valley Road sat completely furnished but unlived in since he'd bought a small second home in town. And where she was still the perfect good girl. Like it or not.

She'd come home to think, and to heal. Just for the summer. Partially because her father had insisted, and partially because she hadn't really had anyplace else to go when the bi-level she'd shared with Terrence had sold practically overnight. And she had big decisions to make over the next couple of months. Like where to live. And how to earn an income. And how to come out of this unscarred. Since people in Destiny didn't *get* divorced. And good girls like Jenny didn't, either.

Of course, when people had started asking at the party tonight what she was doing in town, she'd had to tell them. "Terrence and I have split up, so I'm spending the summer here to be closer to Dad." That was how she and Sue Ann had decided it would be simplest to say it. And she'd left out the parts about the rat bastard, the chippy, and not really having any-place else to go. But the whole time, she kept seeing a black-and-white version of June Cleaver's body in her mind—with *her* head placed on top, and she'd felt just as monochromatic as ever.

And now she was canoeing across the lake of her youth, headed toward the darkness, toward the jagged, tangled woods on the other side because it was a clear enough night that she might be able to spot the Hercules Cluster with all its fine, glittering points of light. The skies, the heavens: one more form of escape.

She hadn't been able to see much of *anything* through her telescope in Columbus—too much light pollution, and if she was honest with herself, Terrence had never encouraged her passion for astronomy any more than he'd encouraged her passion in bed—so that was *one* good thing about coming home. She could see the stars again.

Part of her couldn't believe she was back here, in this precise spot on the globe. Crossing this lake without her father's permission, usually with Sue Ann in tow, was the one rule Jenny had broken as a girl. Unlike *her* side of the lake, where well-kept cottages and bungalows lined the shore in pastel colors, the southern edge of Blue Valley Lake was rimmed with steep, rocky hills and untamed woods. No one had ever lived here but the Brodys—in a scary little shack—and back then, coming here had been trespassing, and it had felt wildly dangerous and freeing at the same time.

And maybe a little foolish, too, now that she thought back on it—but the property had possessed a hill with a wonderfully elevated rocky outcropping, perfect for climbing up on and stargazing. Given the proliferation of trees in her yard, some even big enough to shadow the dock—plus the fact that she'd probably been hoping to catch some brief glimpse of scary, hot Mick Brody back then—crossing the lake had seemed worth the risk.

And it still did. But thankfully, there remained no more Brodys here to trespass against. From what she remembered hearing from her father and Sue Ann over the years, Wayne Brody was in prison, the Brody parents were dead, and Mick Brody was just . . . gone.

No one knew where. Or cared much. People in Destiny were just generally relieved that the Brodys were no more.

Thinking back, she could still hear Sue Ann's nervous whispers all those years ago as the canoe floated smoothly across the water. "You realize that if we tip this canoe over and drown, no one will ever know what happened to us."

"No—someone will find the canoe, and then they'll drag the lake," Jenny had explained. She was a cop's daughter—she knew about these things.

"Well, what if some Brody shoots us and buries us in unmarked graves? No one will ever find us."

"Oh, would you just relax?" Jenny would spout. "Nothing bad is going to happen." Even if she hadn't been a hundred percent sure of that herself.

So given the departure of all the Brodys, as the canoe came to a halt against the same small, sandy landing Jenny had used all those years ago, she didn't feel that same sense of nervous excitement about being here— and it was just as well. She'd come here for peace, after all. And as she stepped out and pulled the canoe farther up onto land, then reached in and hefted out the bag holding her equipment, she sensed herself getting closer to it. At least for tonight.

Mah-jongg at Sue Ann's mother's house had been pleasant enough, but right now she needed the stars, the planets, the cosmos—to remind her that in the big picture of the universe, her troubles were small potatoes. She needed the night sky to whisk her away to another world.

She'd brought a flashlight but didn't yet need to use it. Still, as she began the initial ascent up the rocky hillside, the tall trees closed in around her, blocking out much of the remaining daylight. When some low brambles seemed to reach out and latch on to her skirt,

she decided she probably should have changed into
jeans, but she just untangled it and went on. Then
glanced down at the flowered skirt and thought—
oh God, it's true! I am *June Cleaver!* Even June would
have the sense to put on pants for a hike through the
woods!

Of course, June's husband never cheated on her because she wasn't kinky enough in bed, so maybe they
didn't have *that* much in common.

Just then, a fleeting look to the left revealed the old
Brody cabin through the trees. Even more overgrown
than when she'd last seen it, she could barely make it
out through the vines climbing its walls. It sat dark
and desolate, neglected and mysterious, almost disappearing in its surroundings, a part of the forest
now—and yet at the same time, it beckoned her in
some strange way, making her want to explore it, peer
in the windows, now that the Brodys were gone. Had
they left anything behind? Any clues to what they
were really about? She'd always heard there was a
small cemetery behind the house, and now she wondered who exactly was buried there, and why.

And then—dear God, what had she just seen? A
light? Had a small light just come on inside that dilapi-
dated shack? Surely not. Surely she was seeing things.

Old leaves and new undergrowth crunched beneath
her tennis shoes as she plodded on, her head still turned
toward the little house, confused. She didn't see the
light anymore—had only spotted it for a second—but
it seemed to her a question of angles, of having exactly
the right view through all the trees between here and
there.

Still, maybe she truly *had* imagined it. Maybe it had
been the setting sun reflecting off an old windowpane
as it glanced down through the heavy trees.

Trees too thick and billowy to actually *admit* any sunlight at the moment, she couldn't avoid noticing. And actually, hadn't the sun just *set*?

But don't think about that.

Her heart began to pound against her chest.

And it was in that precise moment that her body collided with . . . another body.

No question about it—she knew even before she looked up that what she'd connected with wasn't a tree; it was far too warm, too broad and looming. Uh-oh.

Her gaze darted upward as a sharp blade of panic sliced down through her, and she found male eyes on her. And a male body, still connecting with hers. She couldn't make out much more than that in the dim lighting, other than his white T-shirt. She took a quick step back and tried to breathe. Who in the world . . . ?

"This is private property," he said brusquely, "so I don't know who you are, but you need to get the hell outta here."

Good God. She sucked in her breath so hard that she thought for a second she'd faint. So much for trying to breathe. The man before her was at least six-two and smelled musky, like the woods, like the earth, and his deep voice had run through her like warm liquid, like . . . an old memory.

She wanted to step farther back, put more distance between them, but she'd reached out to press her free hand against a tree trunk and needed it for balance at the moment. "I was just . . . going to look at the stars," she explained, hefting her telescope bag a bit higher to show him. "Up on the rocks at the top of the hill." Now she freed her hand from the tree to point. Apparently talking had helped her breathe better.

"I don't care what you were doing—you're trespassing."

Wow, he still sounded just as mean. She'd sort of thought her explanation would calm the guy down.

Not that she was sure, now that she thought about it, why someone would be so concerned about trespassers on this piece of useless, almost uninhabitable land. Except . . . maybe she really *had* seen a light in that cabin. Was this guy staying there? Who was he? Could he be . . . ?

"I don't mean any harm," she told him. "The rocks are just the best place around here to look through a telescope."

The man towering above her gave his head a derisive tilt and lowered his chin. As her eyes began to adjust to the dimness, she began to make out *his* eyes, along with the dark stubble on his cheeks. He had a full mouth, thick hair, a broad chest. "I don't think you're hearing me. You need to leave, go back to wherever you came from."

She swallowed but met his gaze, aware of the rise and fall of her chest as she continued focusing on her breathing. Then she pointed over her shoulder. "I just canoed across the lake. I won't hurt anything." Normally, on any other night of her life, she'd have turned around and left. But she just couldn't bring herself to do that right now. She wanted . . . hell, maybe she just wanted something in life to be simple, to go the way she'd planned.

"Damn right you won't," the guy groused, "because you're gonna get right back in that canoe and go."

"*Look,*" she snapped, pushed to a breaking point. "What's the big deal? What is it you think I'm going to do that's so terrible?" Maybe it was foolish—no, *certainly* it was foolish—but she was tired of doing what people told her, tired of feeling she had so little control over . . . anything.

That's when she sensed his eyes narrowing on her—and began to think she was right, about who he was. About that voice. Oh my.

"Are you . . . Mick Brody?" she ventured.

He looked stunned—so stunned she knew she was correct—but she wasn't sure why he was so surprised to be recognized, given that this was his family's old home. She'd assumed the land belonged to someone else now, but apparently it didn't.

Instead of answering, he said, "Who the hell are *you*?"

"We . . . met once," she offered, again pointing over her shoulder in the direction of the lake. "At my family's dock. It was a long time ago." *You asked me if I wanted to take a ride. In your rowboat. But I'm pretty sure you really meant* on *you.*

His eyes narrowed further as he said, "You're not . . . that Tolliver girl?"

She nodded. "Jenny. But I don't think you knew my name. You called me—" *Stop! Why on earth are you telling him this?*

"Pussycat," he recalled aloud, his voice a bit softer now, more smoldering than fiery. Something in her womb flinched, contracted. That he would remember. That the word still sounded sexual to her, sensual, as much as it had then.

She stayed quiet, her breasts heaving slightly. Her astronomy equipment grew heavy, weighing down her right arm.

"Well, pussycat," he said, sounding much more matter-of-fact now, "it's time for you to go."

She let out a breath—now *she* was the surprised one. She'd thought once he realized who she was that he'd finally say okay, let her go on her way. "Seriously?" she heard herself reply. "You seriously have a problem with me walking up the hill to those rocks and looking through a telescope?"

"Seriously," he said, unsmiling, his expression as dark as the dusky air. "I know you always get your way, but not this time."

Everything in Jenny tightened. He thought she always got her way? He didn't know her at all; he didn't know anything about her. All she'd wanted was a little distraction from her troubles, a little peace. Was it so much to ask? A lump of anger rose in her throat as she said, "I see you're just as big an asshole now as you were then." A *good-looking* asshole, she was beginning to realize, but an asshole just the same.

"Whatever, pussycat," he said. "Now be the good little girl you are and go home." Then he placed his large hands on the tops of her arms and physically began to turn her around, toward the lake.

And that was it! It was the straw that broke the camel's back, the last bit of opposition Jenny could stand. She wouldn't be manhandled. And she wouldn't be bullied by one more person who thought being "good" meant being *weak*, willing to be bossed around. She was tired of being "good Jenny," obedient Jenny, tired of letting men make her decisions for her—from Terrence insisting she be a teacher instead of an astronomer to her father insisting she come live in the lake house for the summer. And now she had *this* guy— Mick-freaking-Brody—insisting she couldn't go where she wanted? Every bit of anger, fury, disgust, that had been gathering inside her over the past months boiled hotter inside her, finally overflowing.

So as Mick tried to turn her body one way, she turned it the other, silently refusing to go where he was directing her. She faced him again and spat, "Get your hands off me and get out of my way." She couldn't quite believe she'd said it, but she couldn't stop herself, either. Then she started to push boldly past him, tired of this ridiculous game.

Only Mick Brody didn't let her pass—his arm shot out to block her path as she barreled forward, and before she knew it, his palm had closed firm over her hip, the length of his arm stretching down over her breasts and torso. His strength stopped her in her tracks even as his nearness, the solid connection of her flesh against his, made her pool with shocking moisture between her thighs. Dear God.

He bent down, his breath warm on her ear. "Listen, sweetheart," he said, voice low and menacing, "you don't want to mess with me, okay? Now turn your pretty little ass around and get back to your side of the lake while you still can."

She sucked in her breath, raised her gaze—frightened but bold. "Or what?" she whispered, the words coming out far softer than planned. She remained in his grasp, their faces but an inch apart.

Their gazes locked, so close she could barely fathom how she'd ended up in this position. With Mick Brody, of all people on the planet. Mick Brody, who'd once frightened and aroused her all at once, at a time when she'd been far too young and sheltered to understand such conflicting emotions. And now she found herself in the very same situation—only their bodies were much nearer now, touching, and something inside her sizzled with strange, desperate need.

Mick didn't answer—or maybe his answer was what he did next. He used his anchoring arm, and his body, to push her back against a tree trunk a foot away. His potent gaze drifted from her eyes to her mouth. She heard her own breathing. His, too. Oh God. She took in the soft clatter as her equipment bag slipped from her grip to land on a bed of wild ivy at her feet.

She didn't understand.

What was happening.

Or what she wanted.

What her *body* wanted.

It was insane. Unreal.

And when he finally leaned into her, hard, and kissed

her, hard, she struggled against him. Not because she didn't want him to kiss her. But because she knew she shouldn't. Couldn't. Want *that.* Want *him.* He was a virtual stranger. He was . . . forbidden.

So even as she sensed his palms pressing to the thick bark at both sides of her face, more fully trapping her there, possessing her, she lifted her hands to his upper arms, curled her fingertips tight into the muscles, and tried to push him back.

His body didn't budge. But he ended the kiss. Met her eyes again. His looked glassy with lust. A male hardness she recognized pressed firm and insistent at the crux of her thighs. Her lips felt swollen, sensitive.

"Are you leaving now?" he asked. She wasn't sure if he was letting her off the hook or bossing her around some more.

"No," she said on a hot breath, still refusing to back down. Maybe it was crazy, but to back down now would somehow feel like the ultimate defeat. And she didn't need any more defeat in her life.

"Well, you're not going up that damn hill, I'll tell you that much."

"Give me one good reason not to," she insisted, and then made a move to extricate herself from where he pinned her to the tree, knowing full well that he'd stop her, and despite herself, when his hand closed firmly around her wrist, the sensation shot to the crux of her thighs.

Again she wrestled, trying to get free even though she knew she couldn't—and that was the dark temptation of the fight. It made everything okay as long as she tried to resist, right? As long as she let both of them know she wasn't the sort of girl who just gave in to a stranger in the woods without a struggle.

A *little* struggle, anyway.

Because when he spun her around, still holding tight to her, and she ended up with her back pressed to his chest, her bottom plastered to his erection, her breath coming heated and labored, she lost the will to struggle anymore. He just felt too good. Too hard. Too everything. She let him hold her there, let him make her feel . . . captured, hot, ready.

His breath was audible, too, the only other sound besides last autumn's dead leaves being crushed beneath their feet. Her heartbeat pounded in her ears and the whole forest seemed to pulse. Sweat trickled between her breasts in the still summer night air.

That's when his free hand moved across her torso, fingers splayed. Every nerve in her body responded with horrified pleasure. His touch skimmed slowly, roughly upward until he was cupping her breast, fully, firmly—and she gasped. And felt it between her legs. And thought—*just say no, all you have to do is say no.*

As his labored breath echoed in her ear, she sensed him waiting for just that, her protest, the protest that would surely come—but it didn't. Instead, she just bit her lower lip and felt the powerful energy of a stranger's touch move all through her.

As he began to massage her breast, tangled, conflicted sighs of pleasure escaped her. Leaning her head back into his chest, she spotted the moon, beginning to shine down through the heavy limbs from a fading purple sky. She kept her eye on it—something so familiar to her; she'd seen the moon from a hundred different angles, a hundred different magnifications, full, half, crescent, in partial and total eclipse. Right now it was the only thing anywhere around her that felt real, safe. A shame its nearness was only an illusion.

When Mick Brody released her breast only to curl his

fingers into the placket of her blouse and briskly yank it open, she let out a small cry. But she still didn't protest—even as the warm night air caressed her newly revealed skin, even as he flicked his fingertips at the front opening of her simple white bra, as if he'd known without doubt that was where the clasp would be.

The white cups fell away, baring her breasts to the night. She looked down, as stunned as if she hadn't willingly let things get this far. As if she'd tried to stop it somehow. *I only wanted to look at the stars. I only wanted to feel something besides disillusionment and failure.* Well, she was feeling something else *now,* all right.

How is this possible? It can't be happening. Who the hell am I?

When Mick finally released her wrist, it provided one more instance when she could have stopped this—yet still she didn't. She simply stood there soaking up the heat of his body on an already hot summer night. She simply stood there as he closed both rough hands over her breasts from behind. She heard herself whimper as forbidden pleasure arced through her. Oh God, it felt good. To be touched. Wanted. Desired. It was the first time she'd felt . . . truly womanly, sexual, in *years.*

As he molded the two mounds of flesh in his palms, she became still more aware of the column of granite at her rear and the sensation it sent rocketing to every inch of her body. She moaned and sighed. She sank into him as if she knew him.

When he turned her around to press her back against the same big tree as before—and she let him this time, no more fighting—things grew more difficult, strange. Because his eyes were back on her, and this was real. Her breasts were bared between them and it wasn't quite so dark yet that the white flesh and their beaded pink tips weren't clearly visible.

And when he used both hands to pin her arms to the bark, their gazes met and she could have sworn his expression was as pained and conflicted as her own surely was. She saw the same worry mingling with lust that coursed through her own veins. But she had no idea why. What did *Mick Brody* have to lose here?

And, oh God, his eyes. The more she looked into them, the more intoxicated she became. They took her back to that day on the dock all those years ago—she'd noticed them then, blue and wicked. Nothing about them had changed.

Next Mick bent to capture one turgid nipple in his mouth. A strangled-sounding breath left her throat as the intense pleasure permeated her being. He wasn't a gentle man—she'd already gathered that much—and he didn't do *this* gently, either. He suckled her firmly, in a way that seemed to connect squarely with her crotch, delivering mindless pleasure even as the rough tree bark bit into her back and her knees threatened to give way beneath her.

Releasing one breast, he moved to the other, sucking this peak in just as hard, making her whimper, "Oh God," as the pull stretched all through her.

What are you doing? What are you thinking? Stop this, now, somehow.

But she couldn't. She just couldn't. To her surprise, it seemed that, when put up against Mick Brody, she'd been stronger at sixteen.

Or . . . maybe it made her feel stronger now, somewhere inside, to stay, to let this happen. At sixteen, she'd scurried away. He'd tried to make her do that tonight, but she hadn't, wouldn't. Tonight she was holding her ground—sort of. If holding her ground could be interpreted as letting him seduce her.

When he dropped to his knees and pulled her down

with him, it happened in a rush, so that she mostly just fell on him, her skirt up around her thighs, her top and bra open. She'd never felt more brazen, or more like a stranger inside her own body.

He leaned back against the tree on the opposite side of the path, the smaller one where she'd balanced herself when she'd first bumped into him. Grabbing on to her hips, he drew her up into his lap until she straddled his blue-jean-clad thighs. Then he pulled her closer still, pressing her to the hard bulge behind his zipper. Oh God, the mind-numbing pressure. In exactly the right spot. She let her eyes shut, as if that would weaken the sensation. Then Mick's palms slipped under her skirt, onto her bottom, over her underwear, squeezing, molding—in a way that encouraged her to move on him.

She sucked in her breath as a fresh bolt of desire pierced her body. God, how she *longed* to move against him, to writhe with him in the night.

But up to now, it had been all *him*, him *doing* things: holding her, touching her, suckling her, making her respond. So this was different. This was about *her* doing something.

Yet she quickly realized she didn't possess the power *not* to move against him, not to rub her softest flesh against his hardest, and she felt her body give in, felt herself begin to grind against him through their clothes.

For the first time since this had started, Mick began to emit more than just labored breathing—he let out growls of pleasure, heated groans. The sounds were as potent as hands on her flesh, beginning to drive her movements, until she got lost in the motions, almost forgetting where she was and what she was doing and how insane it was.

Yet, perhaps oddly, it was only when he reached down between them to undo the button on his jeans that she realized—dear Lord—this was actually leading to *sex*! This wasn't some backseat in high school, where you fooled around and heated each other up and then finally stopped. This was real lust that *went* somewhere, had a tangible *destination*.

She went still as he lowered his zipper, pushed down his underwear. At this point, he probably thought she was ready and waiting. And maybe he was right about that and she just couldn't accept the truth about herself. She could barely breathe, after all. And her whole body pulsated with want.

Yet when she glanced down and caught a glimpse of his erection in the thickening air, when she saw how big he was, how rigid, and understood what she was expected to do now, she froze. She'd only had sex with one man in her life. And she hated that man for making her doubt herself, making her question who she was, but she surely hadn't planned to move on in her sex life like *this*. With a stranger. On the ground. In the woods.

I can't do it. I just can't.

Even if I want to.

With Mick Brody, it seemed, arousal and fear mixed and mingled until she could barely tell them apart.

Tell him you're sorry, you've made a mistake here. You're not this woman, not someone who can have—or handle— sex in the woods. And maybe he'll be a decent enough guy to let you leave now.

Not that he seemed like a very decent guy so far. But she knew she couldn't do this. It wasn't right. It made no sense.

I can't. She practiced saying it again in her mind, and was just about to break the bad news out loud—when

Mick Brody lifted her bottom with one hand, yanked her panties aside with the other, and situated her body just atop his erection.

Oh! She sucked in her breath at the sensation.

It's now or never. Say it.

But she didn't.

And then he pushed her down, onto him.

Oh God.

Oh my!

It was the end of life as a good girl.

But those with the courage to explore the weave and structure of the Cosmos, even where it differs profoundly from their wishes and prejudices, will penetrate its deepest mysteries.

Carl Sagan

Two

The pleasure was startling and profound. Almost painful, because he was big and because she hadn't had sex in a while, so a stunned cry left her—but it was also amazingly *good*, in a way she felt in her gut, her very soul.

He was inside her—deep inside her—and there was no sense in protesting now, no turning back.

She wanted desperately to be angry at him, to feel she'd been forced, compromised, but—Lord—he felt too incredible inside her. And she knew she'd had a thousand chances to say no and had never once uttered the word. And besides, she was on *top*, for heaven's sake.

And as she began to adjust, to find exactly the right angle where he felt best, as he hissed in his breath sharply, then let out another masculine groan, it occurred to her that she was finally taking that ride he'd invited her on all those years ago. This is what she'd pictured *then* in the forbidden spots of her mind, her on top of him like this, moving. And the very thought propelled her to do just that—to move as she had in those illicit visions, to move and take him still deeper and to moan when their bodies connected in just the right way.

He moved, too, thrusting up into her, powerful plunges that nearly blinded her with pleasure, made her bite her lip, made her curl her fingernails into the thin fabric of his T-shirt.

She felt the urge to kiss him, but resisted, because even though *he'd* kissed *her*, once, earlier, this . . . didn't feel romantic. And even as he moved in her, she found herself not wanting him to think she'd suddenly gone soft. This was not about kissing—this was about need, and hunger, and darkness. This was hard sex, in the woods. This was Mick Brody.

She moved on him more vigorously, felt his hands mold to her ass. She closed her eyes and drank in the scent of the pungent forest floor, the damp earth, the very greenness of it all. But then she *opened* her eyes because it still seemed so unreal, and the pleasure inside her began to tighten and gather in the spot just above where their bodies met so wet and smooth. And she met his gaze again, writhed against him more wildly, let herself feel that—the utter wildness of it—until he whispered, "Come, pussycat," and she did.

The orgasm was rough, as jagged as the uneven land they occupied. Strangled cries left her throat as she tried to absorb the startling sensations that rocketed through her. Her arms locked around his neck; she bit her lip to try to stop sobbing her way through the abrupt pleasure.

When the intense waves of climax finally passed, eased, her mind raced—what to do now? She had no idea.

But she didn't have to ponder it long since Mick was ready to take over again—without a word, he plastered both hands on her bottom and rolled her onto a soft bed of moss beside the tree. Before she knew it, she lay on her back looking up at him as he moved in her in long, deep, thorough strokes she felt all the way to her core.

His eyes on her remained glassy, his teeth clenched. She kept biting her lip to hold in her cries, but that didn't last long—soon sound erupted from her throat with each powerful thrust he delivered.

What had been slow and rough before had turned fast and urgent—and Jenny lay there astounded, soaking in every sensation, every hard drive, surprised to eventually realize her legs were wrapped snug around his back, locked at the ankles.

The darkness was complete now, covering them like a blanket, and a lone cricket began to chirp in the trees. She grunted and groaned as each stroke pressed her farther, deeper, into the moss, and she felt lost to it all somehow—she'd quit worrying, quit thinking; now she did nothing but *feel, feel, feel* each hot plunge.

"Aw . . . Aw, shit," he whispered, and she knew he was coming even before his guttural groans echoed up into the night air. She watched him, unduly pleased to see it happen, unduly pleasured to know she'd *made* it happen.

When he pulled back, rolled off her, she felt the hollow space he left behind, the physical awareness of losing that connection, even as she hurried to sit up beside him, anxious to act like a woman who had casual sex all the time.

"You okay?"

For some reason, his concern surprised her. "Yeah, fine."

"I, uh . . . didn't mean for that to happen," he admitted, surprising her further—but she wasn't sure how to take it.

"Regrets?"

"Damn—no. I just meant . . . I don't usually yell at a woman and then . . . do *this*." Up to now, he hadn't been looking at her, but even in the full darkness that had fallen around them, she felt him turn toward her. "You wanted that, right? I didn't, uh . . . ?"

She let out a breath she hadn't realized she was holding, then swallowed nervously. "I must have," she whispered. "I never said no." So much for sounding like a hip, modern, casual-sex-having sort of girl. To her own ears, she sounded like exactly what she was—a woman who'd never done such a thing in her life and was probably going to be irreparably scarred by it. Turned out *this* was the time to worry about what to do afterward—and she knew she would suffer later for knowing it meant nothing. She'd never *had* sex that meant nothing, so the emotional aftermath sure to come would be painfully new.

"Okay, good," he said in response. But she thought he didn't sound quite as comfortable as the words implied. Then he got to his feet and held down a hand to help her up, too.

Standing left her unsteady, and aware of the sticky flow around her upper thighs. She turned away, using the same tree as before for balance as she reached awkwardly up under her skirt to pull her dampened panties back into place.

"You can't tell anyone you've seen me here," he said, suddenly gruff again.

She flinched. So much for postcoital cuddling. "Why not?"

"Because I said so."

She flashed an annoyed look in the dark. "How very parental-sounding. Well, guess what. You're not my dad."

He turned abruptly toward her, his eyes glimmering in the dark. "Don't worry, pussycat. After what we just did, I'm not confused about *that*."

She sucked in her breath, thankful now for the heavy trees blocking out most of the moonlight and hiding her blush.

"I'm serious," he went on. "You can't tell *anyone* you saw me. Got it?"

She was tiring of his attitude, especially *considering* what they'd just done. "Sure," she said, rolling her eyes.

"You're not convincing me."

"Fine," she snapped. "I *told* you—I won't tell anyone I saw you. Happy now?"

"And you can't come back here again, either."

She let out a quick, short gasp, truly stunned. "What on earth is your problem? All I wanted to do was look through a telescope at the sky, not steal state secrets!"

"I told you before, I don't care about any of that—I just need you to understand this is private property."

"So I can be on your property long enough to have sex with you, but not long enough to look at the stars?"

"It's not like that." She sensed him shaking his head.

"Then what's it like?"

"It's got nothing to do with me, or you. And it's none of your business. And you'd do well to just forget you ever saw me here or that this night even happened."

"That sounds like the best suggestion you've had yet," she assured him, her voice thick with sarcasm.

"Good," he said—and this time he actually sounded like he meant it.

Jenny stood there for an uncertain moment longer,

but quickly realized there was nothing left to say. That feeling of emptiness she'd anticipated started setting in sooner than she'd expected. She'd thought it would require getting away from him first, being alone. But being *with* him, she realized—apart from when they were having sex—was a lot *like* being alone.

So without another word, she began to walk away, back through the woods toward the downhill descent that led to the canoe landing.

"Hey," he called behind her. "You, uh, want me to walk you down to the lake?"

"Go to hell," she tossed back over her shoulder.

And it was only when he didn't answer that she realized that, just like the first time they'd met, she was hurrying away from him. And that, in the end, she still hadn't gotten what she'd wanted—she hadn't gotten to see the stars. And that if this was a game of some sort, he'd won—again.

Go to hell.

"I probably will," Mick muttered to himself as her footsteps grew more distant.

He stood unmoving in the woods, listening, carefully listening, to faint and still fainter sounds of her walking through the brush, of a boat being pushed into the water, and could almost feel her getting farther away each second.

Around him now—stillness. Perfect, blessed stillness. As it should be. As he *needed* it to be.

But—*shit.*

Shit, shit, shit, shit, shit.

What had he done here? *What the holy hell had he done?*

At a time in his life when he most needed not to be found, at a time when he most needed to be as non-existent as possible—*he'd screwed the police chief's daughter.* What the hell had he been thinking?

Well, he *knew* what he'd been thinking. That she was still just as pretty—only grown-up now, which was even better. And that there was still something between them—the same thing he'd felt the first time he'd met her, that invisible something that moved between a guy and a girl and drew them together whether they liked it or not.

The stupid part had been giving in to that.

For God's sake—he'd really just had sex with her. With Jenny Tolliver.

He'd known her name *then*, and he knew it now, too. He wasn't sure why, either time, he'd acted like it was such a mystery. He just hadn't wanted her to know, he guessed, that he'd even realized she existed. That he'd seen her, when they were teenagers, cheering at high school basketball games in that little red-and-white skirt. *Go Bulldogs—ruff, ruff, ruff!* That he'd seen her back then hanging out at the Whippy Dip, with guys who were much cleaner-cut than him but who were still probably talking her out of her panties on hot summer nights.

He blinked, still shocked to remember that *he'd* just talked her out of her panties. Well, not talked—no, not that at all. But the result was the same, and something he would never forget. The police chief's daughter, who had provided him with more than a few teenage fantasies, who he'd been certain would never look twice at him, had just done it with him in the woods.

The wonder of that—and the horror of it—made him drop to his knees on the forest floor and close his eyes. He ran his hands back through his hair, frustrated.

She couldn't possibly understand what was at stake here, why what he'd just done could possibly be the biggest mistake of his life—and he'd already made more than his fair share. And—realistically—she probably couldn't be trusted not to tell people she'd seen him, not to tell her father. Mick emitted a huge groan of defeat at the very thought.

Then again, maybe she *wouldn't* tell her dad. To tell him the whole story would mean admitting to having sex with Mick without having hardly exchanged a word. And why that had happened—why she had let it—he'd never know.

He'd never consciously made the decision to start kissing her, touching her—it had just happened when she'd tried to get past him. It hadn't resulted from thought—but mere instinct.

He truly hadn't recognized her at first, but once he'd figured out who she was, something about her had brought out the animal inside him. And there'd been moments when he'd been sure she'd stop him, and other moments when he'd been much more sure she wouldn't—but he still couldn't believe the latter had turned out to be true.

Although even if she didn't tell her dad, she'd surely tell *someone*. She just didn't have any reason not to.

And then word would get around. And *then* her father would find out. And then everything Mick was trying to do here would fall apart. And he might go to prison, for all he knew—something he should have thought about before he'd agreed to this, but he hadn't. He might go to prison, and that was only *one* lousy aspect of being found here.

I shouldn't have let myself be talked into this. I should be at home in Cincinnati, having a beer at Skully's on the corner, or watching a little TV before bed.

But it was too late for the shoulda-coulda-woulda thing.

He supposed he should get back to the house. He'd only intended to take a short walk, get some air, clear his head from the troubles between those walls. And then he'd seen someone on the property and his body had gone on red alert—he'd closed the short distance between them without even thinking about consequences, his only thought that whoever it was couldn't be here. And the truth was, he hadn't been overreacting. The last thing he needed was a woman trotting around the woods with a telescope that could just as easily be pointed in a window as at the sky.

Which was when he realized the big clear plastic bag she'd been carrying lay right next to him on the ground—she'd been so pissed at him that she'd walked off without it.

And that gave him an idea.

Since he didn't think Jenny Tolliver could be trusted to keep his presence a secret . . . well, it might be wise to pay her a visit, remind her that he was deadly serious about the promise she'd made.

And in the meantime, maybe he'd sleep worse than usual in that hot little house tonight, because he had brand new problems to worry about.

Or . . . maybe he'd sleep better, because he'd be taking even hotter memories back inside with him.

Jenny awoke the next morning to someone banging on something. Slowly, she realized it was her door. And that she had lunch plans with Sue Ann, but it surely couldn't be *that* late—could it? And as she dragged herself out of bed and felt the ache between her legs— she gasped.

Oh God. Oh God, I had sex with Mick Brody in the woods last night. Mick Brody! It felt as surreal the morning after as it had when it was happening.

She practically fell going down the narrow staircase, her white nightgown flowing around her, and she suspected her hair pointed in all directions as she yanked open the door, saying, "Can you stop that incessant banging?"

Sue Ann, looking perky and pretty in a yellow sundress, just blinked. "Why do you look like the crazy wife in the attic in *Jane Eyre*?"

"Well, good morning to you, too."

Sue Ann tapped her watch. "Um, sorry, sunshine, but it's almost noon." Then she blinked again. "What the heck is going on? Are you sick or something?"

"Don't I wish."

"You *wish* you were sick?" Sue Ann asked, brows knitting as she pushed her way inside.

"It would be better than the reality of why I look crazed."

Sue Ann took a seat on the same couch that had occupied the living room in this house for thirty years, complete with a big white doily over the back next to a folded afghan crocheted in a zigzag pattern. "Start talking."

Jenny, on the other hand, began pacing the hardwood floor, not quite meeting Sue Ann's eyes. They'd known each other forever—since the first grade—so she could tell Sue Ann anything. But this—this was . . . big.

"Well?" Sue Ann said, her shoulder-length blond hair bouncing as she spoke.

"Well—it would seem . . . that last night . . . I crossed the lake to look at the stars."

Sue Ann smiled reflexively at the memory. "Oh, like we used to in high school." Then her smile faded. "Why is that bad? Apparently you didn't drown, and there are no more Brodys left to kill you, so what's the problem?"

"That's just it," she said, now stopping in place to meet Sue Ann's gaze. "There *are* Brodys left."

Sue Ann's gasp filled the house. "*What?*"

Jenny resumed pacing and, without planning it, started talking very fast. "I was walking through the woods and I ran into Mick Brody—literally—and after he told me I was trespassing and had to leave, I had sex with him."

Jenny waited for another gasp, but instead, Sue Ann looked at her like she'd just asked her to solve a difficult math problem. "Wait, stop. I completely misunderstood you, because it almost sounded like you said you had *sex* with *Mick Brody*."

"That's correct," Jenny said.

And *then* Sue Ann gasped. "Wh-wh-what . . . why . . . how . . ." She finally gave up. "Oh hell, I don't even know what it is I want to ask."

Jenny stopped pacing again and joined her on the couch. "I do. You want to know what I was thinking. And how the hell something like that happened in the first place. Frankly, so do I. One minute he was yelling at me and I was yelling back and refusing to leave, and the next, he was . . . you know . . . inside me."

Sue Ann bit her lower lip, suddenly looking fascinated. "How was it?"

A chill ran down Jenny's spine at the memory. "It was . . . the hottest, most amazing sex I've ever had. Which," she added, holding up one finger, "may not be saying much considering that I only have Terrence to compare him to, and that he thought I was too sweet to actually have good sex with."

"The rat bastard," Sue Ann said.

"But . . . it was pretty freaking phenomenal."

"Dare I point out that you, uh, aren't usually the sort of person to have sex with, um, a guy we don't know at all, not to mention a guy who always scared us? And when the hell did he get back in town anyway?"

Jenny slapped a hand to her forehead. "Oh God—I

forgot! I wasn't supposed to tell anyone he was here. I mean, he was really forceful about that. So you can't tell anyone." She shook her head to reinforce the point.

"Not even Jeff?" Sue Ann's husband.

"Not even Jeff. Sorry. I know it's awful to invoke the keep-a-secret-from-your-husband rule, but it's necessary this time around. I'm only telling you because I have to tell *somebody* and—well, like I said, until right now, I sort of forgot it was a secret. But you seriously can't say anything. It's not too late for a Brody to shoot me, you know."

"Or, say, give you a disease. Or get you pregnant," Sue Ann added, eyebrows knitting critically. "Please tell me you used a condom."

Jenny let her eyes fall briefly shut, then let out a tired sigh. "Oh boy." She shook her head in regret. "There are moments in life when it's not as easy as they made it sound in health class. I mean, we were in the *woods*. On the *ground*. Panting and stuff."

Sue Ann looked livid. "That's no excuse!"

"Well, I started taking the pill to regulate my period a few months ago. Once I realized I didn't *want* to have a baby with Terrence. So at least I've got *that* going for me."

"Okay, no babies fathered by the scary dude in the woods—that's good. But what about disease?"

Jenny could only let out yet another sigh. "I'll . . . get checked. Again. Like I did after I found out about the tart."

"Wow, who'd have thought *you* would need two AIDS tests in a three-month period?"

"Who indeed," Jenny replied dryly.

Sue Ann took a deep breath, then blew it back out, clearly trying to process it all. "I'm, like, so freaked out right now."

"Try being me," Jenny said matter-of-factly.

"Well, hey, this is one sure way to get your mind off Mr. Rat Bastard and Little Miss Chippy."

"You can say that again." In fact, neither party had really crossed Jenny's mind since she'd paddled over to the south side of the lake last night. And then *she* gasped.

"What? What is it?" Sue Ann asked, brown eyes gone wide.

"My telescope! I left my telescope there!"

Sue Ann's eyes fell shut. "Oh geez. This is bad."

What a nightmare. A nightmare that kept getting worse, even though it was daytime now. "I can't believe I did that."

"I can't, either. That thing cost two thousand dollars! How on earth did you—wait, stop, I can answer my own question here. You forgot it because you were too busy having *sex* with *Mick Brody*! Oh my God, I still can't believe it!"

"Neither can I. And I also forgot it because we argued some more before I left."

"So you argued *before* you had sex, and you argued *after* you had sex. Sounds like a charming evening."

Jenny pursed her lips. "I never said I was proud of my actions. But that aside, we have to go over there and get my telescope back." She pushed to her feet, ready to move on this.

While Sue Ann peered up from her spot on the couch. "Um, we?"

"Yes. Right now. I have to get it back."

"What about lunch? I have on a new dress." She motioned down at it in Vanna White fashion.

"And it's lovely," Jenny assured her. "But my telescope is very dear to me, as you know. I spent a long time saving up for it and researching to pick out just the right one. And all my star charts and notes are in the bag, too. We have to go get it right away, so I can forget this ever happened and move on with my life." *Just like Mick said.*

Sue Ann sighed, surrendering. "Do you have some jeans I can wear?"

Jenny nodded. "Good thought—I can tell you after last night that a skirt in the woods isn't a good idea." And upon reading Sue Ann's immediate thoughts, she held up one finger, adding, "And *not* just because it's so easy for a guy to push up, either. But because it gets tangled on things."

"Do you promise to give me all the juicy details on the way over?"

Jenny sighed, rolling her eyes. "Sure, fine, whatever."

"And can we go to lunch afterward? If we make it out alive, I mean?"

Again, Jenny nodded. "I'll even buy."

"Then you've got a deal."

Two things are infinite: the universe and human stupidity; and I'm not sure about the universe.

Albert Einstein

Three

$\mathcal{F}$or the first time in her life, Jenny actually sympathized with the criminals her father had caught over the years because they'd been stupid enough to return to the scene of a crime. It was strange being back here, in these overgrown woods, so soon. And also strange seeing the place in the daylight—she bit her lip as she glanced over at the cabin through the trees, then said to Sue Ann, "Keep your head down and move quickly and quietly."

"You sound like we're in a war zone," Sue Ann whispered from behind.

"No, just a 'no trespassing' zone, but I still don't want to get caught. Mick Brody was seriously intent about this being private property."

And when she reached the spot where she was pretty sure the sex had occurred, it felt even *more* surreal.

She remembered the scrape of the tree bark against her back, along with the much *better* sensations of his hands on her flesh, her breasts, her rear. She halted in place and let out a heavy *whoosh* of breath as fresh heat overcame her.

Sue Ann drew up beside her and said, "You're flushed."

Jenny began waving her hand up and down, fanning herself. "It's hot out here."

Sue Ann spoke matter-of-factly. "Not *that* hot. In fact, it's a lot cooler under these trees than it was crossing the lake."

Jenny turned in a rush toward her friend, suddenly alarmed. "What if someone saw us in the canoe? What if they tell my father?" It hadn't even occurred to her 'til now. She'd been too focused on getting her telescope back and too occupied with answering Sue Ann's questions about sex with Mick, which had mostly resulted in short, sheepish answers including words like *big, intense, hard, rough,* and *hot.*

"Okay, relax," Sue Ann said. "We're not teenagers anymore. We can canoe across the lake without anyone's permission if we choose."

"Good point. I'm flustered and not thinking straight."

"We'll just say we decided to take the old canoe out for a spin, for old times' sake or something."

"Okay, good, that's good," Jenny replied. "Old times' sake." That sounded much better than being on a mission to retrieve a valuable possession lost in the woods while having wild sex with a scary guy no one has seen in a dozen years.

"All right," Sue Ann said. "Since you've stopped and since the brush here seems sort of matted down, I'm guessing this is where you did the deed. So where's the telescope?"

Jenny scanned the ground, particularly around the

big, wide tree trunk where she was pretty sure she'd abandoned the waterproof bag. Only she didn't see it. Damn it!

She kept looking, though, because it had to be there. It *had* to. Where *else* could it be? "I don't see it," she said to Sue Ann, not bothering to hide her distress. She pointed to the ground. "I dropped it right here when he started kissing me."

Sue Ann perked up. "There was kissing? You said nothing about kissing. Kissing sounds more . . . romantic or something, than the rest of it did."

"There wasn't *much* kissing. It's just how things got going."

Sue Ann sighed, clearly disappointed, then got back to business. "And you're sure this is the right spot?"

Jenny took in the area again. "It has to be. I remember this huge tree. He pinned me to it."

"Yowsa."

"You can say that again." Then she pointed to the ground a few feet away. "And you're right about things being mashed down here. This is where I was, you know, actually . . ."

"On top of him," Sue Ann provided.

Jenny swallowed. "Right." She still wasn't comfortable with the memory. What sort of person did this make her? She was just barely starting to get over Terrence and the divorce, for heaven's sake. She lifted her gaze to Sue Ann. "How did I let this happen?"

"Sounded to me like it was some unstoppable force of nature," Sue Ann said as if this made it okay, and also as if they had these sorts of conversations all the time. "So do you think your lover boy took the telescope?"

Oh God. The nightmare grew worse still. "He must have." She closed her eyes, sighed anew, then met Sue Ann's wide eyes. "What am I gonna do *now*?"

"Well . . . I suppose we could always go to the cabin and ask him."

Jenny's eyes flew wide. "Are you crazy? He forbade me to even be on this land, let alone come knocking on his door. He's got some kind of secret he doesn't want anyone to know about, remember?"

Just like when kissing came up, Sue Ann's gaze widened. "And you aren't dying to know what that is?"

Jenny simply let out a heavy breath. "Well, I'm curious, sure. Okay, more than curious—I'm worried. About what it could be. But like I said earlier, it's still not too late for Mick Brody to shoot me. I don't want to agitate the guy any more than I already have. And—" Jenny stopped and let out a huge gasp as something new and even more horrible hit her. "We have to get out of here!"

"Why? I mean, why more now than thirty seconds ago?"

"Because he told me not to tell anyone, and if he were to find me here again, that's bad enough, but if he were to see *you* here, too, he'll obviously know I told someone! Which will get us both in hot water, and God knows what he'll do *then*." For heaven's sake, she really *wasn't* thinking straight here. Bringing Sue Ann had seemed like the natural thing to do, but it was probably the *worst* thing to do. Although sex with a scary stranger could confuse a girl that way, she supposed.

"This really *is* like sneaking over here in high school," Sue Ann said. "Dèjá vu all over again."

"Only worse now. Before, we just *assumed* they wouldn't want us here. Now we know it for sure. We should go. *Now*."

"What about your telescope?"

Oh God, the telescope. She shook her head. "I'm not sure. I'll have to figure that out later."

Within five minutes, they were back in the green canoe, pushing off from the sandy landing and back out into Blue Valley Lake. And Jenny felt positively childish. She *should* be able to march up to his door and ask if he'd found her bag. *Should* being the key word. The fact was, despite the brief concern he'd shown for her just after sex, she really didn't know how dangerous Mick Brody might be.

She supposed Sue Ann was thinking pretty much the same thing when she said, quietly and seriously, "You know, maybe you should go to your dad about this."

"And tell him what? I lost my telescope when I was having sex with Mick Brody in the woods?"

Sue Ann appeared to be thinking it through as the hot mid-day sun beat down on them. "Maybe you could just leave out the sex part. Just admit you were going over there to stargaze. Say you ran into him and had an argument and he insisted you leave and somehow you ended up without your bag."

"But don't you think that if my father goes out to that cabin to interrogate him, the sex part might come up? And don't you think that if Mick's probably illegal secret isn't obvious to my dad upon getting there, and that even if he gets my telescope back, Mick Brody will then promptly come to my house and kill me?"

Sue Ann slowly began to nod. "Both excellent points."

"Besides which . . ." Something churned in her stomach at the thought just edging its way into her brain, and she was beginning to sweat from the summer heat.

"Go on."

"I . . . had sex with the guy."

"Yeah, we've established that."

"And, I mean, it wasn't *sweet* sex, God knows, but . . . but . . ."

"Uh-huh?" Sue Ann rolled her hand in circles, motioning for Jenny to get to the point.

"But he was . . . you know, interested in my pleasure. At least to a degree. He wanted me to have an orgasm."

"Oh *my*." She hadn't shared that part before—actually just divulging as little as possible based on Sue Ann's prying questions. They were best friends, but having both been married for years now, they didn't sit around talking about the details of their sex lives. "And did you?" Sue Ann inquired.

"*Oh* yeah." She suspected her tone pretty much said it all.

"I see. That good, huh?"

"Intense," she said—probably the tenth time she'd invoked that particular word to describe sex with Mick Brody. "And anyway . . . I know it wasn't sweet or romantic or anything like that, and I feel kind of . . . blah now because I've never had sex with a guy while knowing I'd probably never see him again. But at the same time . . . he made me feel . . . desired. Which is nice after the whole Terrence fiasco. Because . . ." She trailed off again, suddenly feeling emotional and not wanting to get weepy.

Sue Ann sat across from her, facing her—even though it required the person in front to paddle backwards, it made talking easier, so they'd always done it that way—and she stayed quiet, silently supportive, waiting for Jenny to go on.

"The thing is," Jenny said, once she swallowed back that teary feeling, "after I found out Terrence had cheated on me and why, it made me feel . . . so horribly undesirable. So . . . dispensable. And she's *twenty-freaking-one*, Sue Ann!"

"Tart," Sue Ann tossed in, never one to miss an opportunity.

"So I also felt . . . past my prime, or like I never *had* a prime. And I know thirty-one is hardly old, and the thirties are the new twenties and all that, but compared to Kelsey, I felt boring and frumpy and like . . . like something he'd just put out with the trash. And those feelings just kind of burrowed down inside me and got stuck there—and they were *still* there . . . until last night.

"So . . . I really hope Mick Brody didn't steal my telescope, and I really hope he's not doing anything terrible in that cabin—but at the same time . . . maybe I don't really want to be the one to get him in trouble since, if nothing else, he made me feel attractive. That's probably why I did it. Because he made me feel desirable."

Across from her, Sue Ann looked thoughtful, then frank. "That's all very nice, Jen, and I'm really glad this made you feel good about yourself again, but . . . could the reason you had sex with him also have been, just maybe, because he was *hot*?"

Jenny blinked. Clearly, Sue Ann thought Jenny was working too hard to justify what she'd done. But the bigger shock to her was, "You thought Mick Brody was hot back in the day?" She squinted her surprise beneath the bright sun.

Sue Ann shrugged. "In that rough-and-tumble kind of way, sure."

"You never said anything."

Another shrug. "It never came up. And maybe I worried you'd think I was gross for thinking so. The Brodys were so . . . socially off-limits."

"Well, actually, *I* thought he was hot, too—at least the one time I saw him up close—and I never told you, either, for the same reason."

"Wow. Small world. Maybe *every* girl secretly thought he was hot and was just afraid to say. So—is he still? Hot?"

Jenny nodded. "As much as I could tell. But it was nearly dark, so I couldn't see him very well."

Sue Ann's jaw dropped. "You had sex with a guy you couldn't even *see*?"

Now it was Jenny's turn to shrug. "Sort of."

"Wow. It's fun to hang with you these days. You've had more excitement since yesterday than I've had in five years."

"And it only cost me my peace of mind."

Sue Ann sighed. "You didn't have that anyway. So cheer up. Maybe it only cost you a pricey telescope."

Jenny worked in the living room, listening to the clinking and clanging of tools on the other side of the wall as her dad tried to fix the air conditioner. It wasn't broken completely, but when she'd gotten home after lunch with Sue Ann at Dolly's Main Street Café in town, the house wasn't cooling well. And after last night, the last thing Jenny needed was to be overheated.

When she heard her father grumble and cuss under his breath, she called, "Sorry about this, Dad." If she wasn't here, after all, it wouldn't matter if the A/C was working or not. Even if her father *had* pretty much insisted she stay in the house when hers had sold so quickly.

"Don't apologize," he called back to her. "You know how happy I am to have you here."

The words made her feel a little guilty—the same guilt she'd felt upon settling in Columbus after graduating from Ohio University. It had meant leaving her father alone. But she'd always come home for every holiday and for long summer weekends, and given that he'd lived here his whole life, he had plenty of friends.

Pushing aside her guilt, she continued unpacking.

She'd put all of her furniture and most of her other belongings in storage for now, but she'd brought along some magazines and books to make the place feel like home—like *her* home. Mostly astronomy reference books and some of her favorite coffee table books featuring good visuals of planets, galaxies, and nebulae. From the moment she'd let her dad talk her into coming here for the summer, she'd planned on doing a lot of sky-watching.

Which, of course, brought back thoughts of Mick Brody. Not that they'd been far away—"the Brody incident," as Sue Ann had taken to calling it over lunch, had continued to dominate their conversation. In fact, Jenny had planned to use the lunch to catch up with Sue Ann and ask about some of her old friends and neighbors, but casual sex clearly superseded catching up.

So now she officially had Mick Brody on the brain. Which was better than having Terrence and Kelsey on the brain. Maybe.

And what was up with her telescope? She was trying not to think about that part—somehow hoping it might magically appear somewhere, on her doorstep, or on the dock. In fact, when Sue Ann had driven her home, they'd both carefully scanned the whole area, just in case, and after calling her dad about the airconditioning, Jenny had sat in the front porch rocking chair, watching the lake and the steep shore beyond for any sign of Mick.

If the telescope *didn't* turn up, if he didn't bring it back on his own, would she return there? Would she *dare* go up to that cabin? Her stomach pinched just thinking about it.

He'd been angry enough just finding her in his woods—how angry would he be if she came to his door, even if she had a perfectly valid reason? And how weird was it that she was so scared of a guy she'd actually allowed to penetrate her with his penis, for heaven's sake?

Oh my—the thought brought another wave of heat over her in the already too-warm house. But what a penis it had been. Not that she'd gotten a really good look at it—but good enough. And she'd certainly *felt* the full impact of it. She bit her lip, remembering the pleasure of being filled that way. The pleasure of being filled a whole *new* way, by a whole new man, a man who was driven to seduce her at the precise time he was trying to get her off his property.

That part hadn't escaped her. He'd been so determined to make her leave—he must have wanted her pretty badly to have forgotten about that for a while.

Or . . . maybe it just meant he was a typical horn dog guy.

But even if so, to her surprise, the forbidden excitement of the event, the sensation of being wanted, was beginning to override the horror and emptiness of having meaningless sex. In fact, maybe—for her anyway—those things alone, coming at this particular moment in her life, were enough to *give* it meaning.

When her father grumbled again, following the loud bang of some tool or other, Jenny flinched—at how violently thoughts of what she'd done with Mick Brody clashed with thoughts of her dad. She instantly likened it to what happened when two stars collided— a scorching explosion that dwarfed anything we could comprehend here on Earth.

Her father had always disliked the Brodys, as most people did—he'd warned her to stay away from them as a child, and she knew he'd had several run-ins with them in his job. He'd arrested the older boy, Wayne, at least twice, once for a bar fight, and once for breaking into McMillan's Hardware, right next door to

Dolly's Café. He'd made the long, twisting drive out to the isolated south side of the lake when people on their own side had heard gunshots and yelling, and he had arrested Harlan Brody, the father, on a domestic charge. And she recalled that *both* Brody boys had been suspected in a liquor store robbery in the neighboring town of Crestview while she'd been away at college.

That's when it hit her. Wow. Had she just had sex with a guy who robbed liquor stores? The very thought made her shiver.

And what *was* he hiding in that old cabin? What was his big secret? With his reputation, she imagined it could literally be anything!

Oh boy.

She blew out a long, slow breath, absorbing the revelation.

She supposed when she'd argued with Mick, and when she'd allowed him to seduce her, she'd been thinking primarily of that boy she'd met at her dock as a teenager. Gruff, and from the wrong side of the tracks—or the lake, in this case—but that was a far cry from being a guy who really broke the law, who robbed places!

She bit her lip, wondering: *Did you do that, Mick? Did you rob that liquor store with your brother? And what else have you done?* Maybe she *was* lucky just to leave there unhurt; maybe a telescope was a small price to pay.

Except she still wanted that damn telescope—badly. Not to mention her star charts and the journal where she recorded notes on all her sky-sightings.

She unpacked a few more books, then found a spot to stack some of them—on the small bookshelf below the shrine to her mother. She stopped then, unwittingly kneeling before it, and stared up. Atop the waist-high shelving unit sat an array of framed photos of Judy Tolliver—some with Jenny as a child, others with Jenny's dad or by herself. A Bible sat among the photos, as did a framed copy of the little tribute program from the funeral home given out to everyone who'd come to pay their respects that winter day eighteen years ago. *Beloved Wife and Mother. God's daughter. At rest now, in His arms.*

Two dusty, never-lit pillar candles sat on candleholders at either side of the display, and above it all, on the wall, hung an enormous photo of Jenny and her mother when Jenny had been only five years old. Her mom had been a bridesmaid in Aunt Carol's wedding and Jenny had been the flower girl, so in the picture they stood together before a grouping of pine trees wearing matching rose-colored dresses, with wreaths of pink rosebuds and baby's breath adorning their heads. Jenny's father had loved the picture and insisted on ordering one in gargantuan proportions, and it had hung in their living room ever since.

Of course, the rest of the shrine had come later, when Jenny was thirteen. While other girls had been worried about periods and first dances and crushes on boys, Jenny had juggled all that *and* her mother's death from cancer.

Pillar of the community, always helping with this fund-raiser or that bake sale, if there was a cause in Destiny, Judy Tolliver could find it and fix it. She'd been a perfect police chief's wife. When someone's house burned down, Judy Tolliver had handled the clothing and furniture drive and made sure the family had a place to stay. When the school system threatened to take away music and art classes, Judy Tolliver had organized the PTA and the whole community to combat it. When a real estate developer tried to buy the land where the tidy little Pinewood Mobile Home Park sat, ready to rush the mostly elderly residents from the only housing they could afford, Judy Tolliver had gone door to door with a petition, finally convincing the town council not to approve it.

But while the rest of Destiny had lost a kind, loving woman always ready to lend a helping hand, Jenny had lost a mother. Someone to talk to about school and boys and bras . . . and stars. Indeed, it had been her mom who had first introduced her to the mysteries and majesty of the night sky, who had bought her that first telescope—not much more than a toy, but it had been enough to turn Jenny into a hard-core astronomer at an early age.

And with a mom like Judy and a police chief for a dad, could Jenny have turned out any *less* than utterly pure and wholesome? She'd been taught to care about good and bad, right and wrong. She hadn't drank underage, or had sex before falling in love, and to this day she'd never even smoked a cigarette. She'd been the ultimate goody two-shoes, willingly, all her life.

Until last night.

And when her father had moved out of the lake house and into town a few years ago, Jenny had been surprised he hadn't sold the old cottage—until now. Because only now, upon actually moving back in here, did she truly realize that *everything* in the house was exactly the same as when she'd grown up, right down to the dishes and the doilies. Right down to the shrine.

And as she rose to her feet now and backed away, she found herself wishing she could take down the huge photo in its gold gilt frame. Not that she didn't love the picture—she herself had kept a five-by-seven version on her dresser in Columbus—but this one was just . . . too big. For the room. And for Jenny's life now. Losing her mother at such a young age had been the tragedy of her existence, but she'd long since moved on, and something about the huge presence her mother still held in this room took her back there, to the loss, to the desperate disbelief and denial and sorrow, to the memories of her mother lying in a bed upstairs, withering away to a shell of her former self.

Whoa. *You're back to being "not you" again—being pretty darn morose, in fact.* How had *that* happened?

"It's this picture," she muttered under her breath.

"D'you say somethin', honey?" her dad called from the utility room just off the kitchen.

"No, Dad. But how's it coming in there?"

"Think I pinpointed the problem. With any luck, we'll have 'er cooled down in no time."

Jenny smiled. Her dad sounded more chipper now. And unless she was imagining it, the house might be cooling by a few degrees already. As for the picture of her mother in rose taffeta, she still found herself wanting to take it down and feeling guilty about it at the same moment. *Wow, for a girl who's spent her life doing nothing wrong, you sure keep finding a lot to feel guilty about.*

But the picture would have to stay. The house belonged to her father—she was a temporary visitor here. She'd just have to get used to it again, and then she'd probably quit seeing it, just like most things you passed by every day.

Returning to the couch, she situated her favorite astronomy coffee table book right where it should go—in the center of the coffee table. *In case this is the only way I get to see the stars this summer.*

She looked up just as her dad walked in the room in his beige police uniform, wiping his hands on a rag. He'd come over as soon as his shift had ended, but he kept his police radio on his belt at all times, and it buzzed unsteadily even now. "Feelin' cooler to ya yet?" he asked.

She nodded. "Much better. Thanks, Dad."

"By the way, I saw Miss Ellie and Linda Sue in town at the drugstore this mornin'. Miss Ellie's havin' a garden party Sunday afternoon—it's her eightieth birthday. She asked me to invite you."

Jenny lifted splayed fingers to her chest. "Miss Ellie is eighty? Oh wow, I had no idea she was that old." Miss Ellie had lived in the house to the right of the cottage for Jenny's entire life, and she kept a lovely English garden in her big side yard, complete with a small gazebo.

"Of course, it'll mostly be Linda Sue and Mary Katherine throwing the party, but Miss Ellie said she'd seen you were staying here at the house and she'd love for you to come."

"Did she ask why I was here?"

He shook his head, fully aware that Jenny didn't look forward to telling still more people she'd gotten divorced. "Nope."

"Well, I'll be there, of course."

"Tell ya what—I'll pick you up and you can be my date." He winked.

And she said, "Dad, can I ask you something sort of personal?" They'd grown close after her mother's death, but this was a topic they'd never covered.

He suddenly looked a bit uneasy, but said, "All right."

"Have you ever dated anyone since Mom died?"

He looked like she'd suggested he take his squad car on a wild rampage through Miss Ellie's garden. "Why, no—of course not."

She'd pretty much figured that, but had felt compelled to ask anyway. "Do you ever think about it?" After all, he was only in his early fifties, he had a respectable job, a pleasant home, and he was a nice man.

"Well, no, can't say that I have. I mean—who could ever replace your mother?"

She tilted her head and tried to look cheerful. "I wasn't suggesting you *replace* her, but . . . wouldn't it be nice to have someone to go out to a movie with on a Saturday night up at the Ambassador? Or to take to the annual Fourth of July cookout at Betty and Ed's house?"

Her father stayed quiet for a moment, then said, "Don't you worry about me, Jennygirl—I'm fine just as I am. I've got plenty of folks to be with and you know that."

"I know. I was just thinking that . . . well, it's been a long time, Dad. And I'm sure Mom would want you to be happy."

"Then she's already got her wish," he said with another big wink. "You let me know if this air-conditionin' gives ya any more problems, and otherwise, I'll see ya Sunday—about one o'clock?"

She relented and let the matter drop. "All right—see you then." After which she pushed to her feet and gave him a small hug while planting a kiss on his cheek, the tip of his big gray mustache tickling her lip.

As she listened to his car drive away a moment later, she realized she was looking forward to Miss Ellie's party. Sort of.

A lot of people in Destiny, especially the older residents, were . . . weirdly stuck in another time. A comforting time. But also a time when . . . divorce was frowned upon, for any reason—even a cheating husband, she suspected. And she was pretty sure most of them would have heart attacks if they knew what she'd done in the woods last night.

By ten o'clock that evening, Jenny felt . . . almost content. Still aggravated about the whole telescope situation, but she'd spent the day making peace with herself over the sex. Mostly. And as the evening had passed, she'd quit seeing that huge picture of her mother. Mostly.

She'd cooked herself a hamburger and a baked potato on the gas grill on the back patio and sat outside at the picnic table to eat, despite the remaining heat that hadn't waned at day's end. Afterward, she wandered over the soft grass in bare feet to an old swing hanging from a maple tree in the side yard, and from there, she'd peered out across the lake, quiet and smooth as glass at that time of the evening, appreciating the peaceful view. She'd glanced over into Miss Ellie's garden, across the empty green space that sat between their homes, and drank in the profusion of color. She'd listened to birds singing in the trees.

As night had begun to fall, she'd thought longingly of her telescope, but pushed it aside, telling herself that maybe he'd . . . mail it back to her or something. Of course, that would require him going to a post office. Being seen. Just as bringing it here to leave on her doorstep as she'd hoped earlier would also do. But . . . maybe he'd be decent enough to get it back to her some other way. She *had* to keep telling herself that, since she just couldn't accept losing it the way she had.

Now she sat curled on the couch in a butter yellow cami and jogging pants, the old afghan pulled half over her since the air was going full force again, eating a chocolate chip cookie, and watching some crime show on TV.

Just as the guy on TV, a detective, crept through a dark warehouse where he suspected a crazy burglar was hiding out—a knock came on Jenny's back door and sent her nearly leaping out of her skin.

Catching her breath, she set her cookie aside and rose to answer, except—who on earth would come to the *back* door?

A serial killer, she thought.

Or maybe her father, she decided more realistically. He'd come to the back door *today*, after all.

So she flipped on the outdoor light, then pulled open the door—to find Mick Brody standing on the other side.

The next best thing to a killer. Or the worst.

She nearly lost her breath—from shock or pure animal magnetism, she wasn't sure.

That fast, in an instant, she knew Sue Ann was right about why she'd had sex with him. Because he stood in the light now. And he was hot as hell.

His thick, dark hair needed a trim, and the sight of the stubble on his jaw made her remember how it had lightly abraded her chin when he kissed her, and later, grazed across the sensitive flesh of her breasts. Her nipples were already hard—she just knew it—and she wasn't wearing a bra. Oh God.

"Why are you at my back door?"

"I didn't want anyone to see me. I'm not in town, remember?" His dark eyebrows knit. "You haven't told anyone, have you?"

"Of course not," she lied. Then dropped her gaze to see with huge relief that he carried the waterproof bag containing her telescope. *Thank goodness!*

"Can you get out of the way?"

"Out of the way?" she asked, taken aback.

But it wasn't enough to keep him from arrogantly pushing past her into the house. "I'm coming in."

Oh boy. This wasn't good. This was . . . scary. She was thrilled to get her telescope back, but . . .

"Um, wait," she said, yet it was too late for that, since Mick Brody was already standing in her kitchen. "*Why* are you coming in? I mean, I see you brought my telescope, which I appreciate, but . . ."

He spoke low but potent. "I'm just not sure you understand, pussycat, exactly how important it is that you keep my little secret."

She blinked up at him, aware that he now stood dangerously close to her. She felt his nearness in every cell of her body, all of which began to tingle in response. "I do. I promise. I really do."

He replied simply, surely. "I don't believe you."

She let out a sigh, part of her drinking in the well-defined muscles on his arms, a tattoo she couldn't quite see because the sleeve of his T-shirt hid it, and the lock of wayward hair arcing down onto his forehead—but another part of her thinking, *I have to get him out of here!* In fact, she suspected she was almost as anxious to get him off *her* family's property as he'd been to get her off *his* last night. "Well, I can't help that," she argued. "And what exactly is it you think you're going to accomplish by coming into my house late at night anyway? Uninvited, I might add."

Still standing agonizingly near, Mick Brody used one bent finger to lift her chin, bringing their gazes together. "I'm going to convince you."

Sometimes I think we're alone. Sometimes I think we're not. In either case, the prospect is staggering!

Arthur C. Clarke

Four

Mick looked around the small but tidy home as he lowered the big plastic bag gently to the kitchen table. It was pretty much what he expected—it felt warm, cozy. Not too much bigger than his old family house across the lake, but it felt a world away. It *was* a world away. The décor wasn't modern, but that didn't matter—somehow he sensed *safety* between these walls. Something he hadn't had too much experience with.

When he turned to face Jenny Tolliver again, she looked a little afraid of him. It wasn't a surprise—he'd gotten that look most of his life, and for a good long while, he'd earned it. And he *needed* her to be a little afraid of him right now, so this was probably good. Still, for some reason, it bothered him. That he was making such a pretty woman look so troubled. He didn't usually care much what people thought of him,

but right now, Jenny Tolliver was making him feel like
an ogre.

Of course, not all of his thoughts were so honorable.
Her nipples jutted prettily at the little top she wore,
making him remember having them in his hands, his
mouth.

By the time he lifted his gaze from her chest back to
her face, he was half-hard and burning up inside, despite the air-conditioning in the house. Her eyes said
she'd seen where he'd been looking, and that she *felt*
his heat.

It was almost enough to make him forget why he
was here and close the distance between them and do
what he'd done last night. He'd never been so physically drawn to a woman on sight, and at the moment
all he could think of—that fast—was taking her back
into his arms, pressing into those sweet, soft curves,
and doing what came naturally.

Yet that's when Jenny Tolliver broke the spell, looking nervously away to say, "Would you like some
iced tea?"

Damn—he was barging into her house late at night,
and she was offering him tea? He almost said no, but it
had been a hot, muggy trip across the lake in the metal
rowboat he'd found still stashed in a half-fallen-down
shed behind the old house. "Uh, sure," he said.

"May as well have a seat," she suggested, motioning
to the table, her tone reminding him that despite the
tea, she hadn't invited him here. And that got him back
in his right mind.

Pulling out a chair, he settled at the small wooden
table, taking in the quaint wicker basket of napkins to
one side, along with the ceramic salt and pepper shak-
ers designed in the shape of mallard ducks. "Listen,"
he said, still not quite sure how to convince her, but he
knew he had to. "I know I was a hard-ass last night."

"Yeah, you could say that," she replied, not looking at him as she reached in the refrigerator to pull out a glass pitcher with lemon slices painted on the side. It gave him a chance to notice her round ass, softly hugged by a pair of sweatpants. And just like with her breasts, the sight made him remember having that ass in his hands, molding it, using it to pull her into his lap. God, they'd been hot together.

"Thing is," he made himself go on, "I didn't have a choice. And when I say you can't tell anybody about me . . ." He stopped, out of words, and the truth was, he just didn't *have* any good way to convince her, damn it. And though his early life had taught him to convince people by threats, he didn't think that had worked last night, so it probably wasn't the best way tonight, either.

Desperate but not letting it show, he tried a different appeal—honesty. Plain, blatant honesty. "It's *important*, pussycat, that no one finds out I'm here. *Really* important. I can't tell you why, and I know you don't have any reason to help me, but it's almost . . . a matter of life and death."

This made her turn to look at him, pitcher in hand. "Yours?"

He gave his head a slight shake. "Not exactly."

"Whose?"

"Don't ask any more questions about it, okay? I can't answer them."

Looking wary, undecided, she passed him a tall, narrow glass painted with flowers and filled with iced tea. Their fingertips touched as she handed it off. "Look, I said I wouldn't tell. But the fact that you felt the need to come all the way over here to make sure I don't . . ."

She trailed off, and he could read her thoughts. He was making such a big deal of it that it fueled her curiosity. Yet just trusting her not to say anything after last night hadn't made sense, either. "Well, I brought your stuff, too," he pointed out, even though that had mostly been an excuse.

"Thank you for that." He thought she might sit down at the table with him, but instead, she leaned back against the counter across the room. "I was worried about it when I realized I'd forgotten it. It's important to me."

He just nodded, then broached a topic he'd been curious about since last night. "I thought you moved away."

"I did."

"Why are you back?"

She bit her lip, still looking wary and like she didn't want to answer the question. Finally, she said, "I got divorced."

"Oh." He hadn't even known she'd gotten *married*. Then, without considering it, he asked, "Why?"

She took the sort of deep breath that made her chest rise and fall visibly, which he enjoyed—but he tried not to stare directly at her breasts this time.

"He, um, cheated on me. With a younger woman. Who I worked with closely. It was pretty awful." She finished by biting her lip and looking like she wished she hadn't said so much.

"Damn," he murmured. Why the hell would any sane man cheat on someone so gorgeous? He'd never been married, never even thought about it, but he heard himself mutter what he was thinking. "Stupid guy."

To his surprise, the words softened her expression just slightly—although she lowered her gaze to whisper, "Thanks." Then she looked back at him. "I thought you'd moved away, too. I thought your whole family was gone."

"We were. Are," he corrected. "Except me."

"What are you doing back?"

"None of your business."

She tilted her head as if trying to tempt him. "I told you *my* secret. You can't tell me yours?"

"Nope. And I didn't exactly twist your arm—you didn't *have* to say why you were back. You could have told me to go to hell, like last night. Or just lied about it."

She shrugged. "It didn't occur to me. I'm not the lying type."

That worried him. "Well, you'd *better* lie—about me being in town." The words came out harsher, louder, than he'd intended, more like the guy he'd been before leaving Destiny.

But she didn't seem startled, only said, "Relax. That's not lying—it's just not bringing something up. I'm much better at that."

"Good." He took a long drink of iced tea and let it calm him down. There'd been plenty to worry about *before* Jenny Tolliver had shown up in his woods, and now it seemed multiplied. This whole damn thing had him on edge.

But not so on edge that he didn't notice when she suddenly started looking uncomfortable again. "Something I *do* need to bring up, though, since you're here . . ."

Damn—what now? "What is it?" he asked.

"Um, about last night." A pretty blush spread across her cheeks, and he supposed that meant this had something to do with sex. "We didn't use . . . you know, a condom."

Oh yeah, *that*. It had hit him after she'd gone. In the moment, though, he'd been . . . blinded. By Jenny Tolliver. And hard, hot lust. "Yeah, I know. Afraid I didn't have one on me. Wasn't expecting to find a girl in my woods."

She blushed some more and ventured, "Are you . . . safe? Should I worry?"

He felt stupid for not realizing until this moment that *of course* Jenny Tolliver would worry about being with a guy like *him*. He hadn't worried about her *at all*, having an instinctive feeling that she was as clean and pure as any snow-white virgin. "Pretty safe," he told her. "I mean, I can't say I never slipped up before, but not since I was young."

She nodded. "Good. And so you know, I got checked out after I found out Terrence was cheating and I'm fine."

He'd already known that without asking. That she'd have dashed out to get checked. And that she was fine. "Thanks," he said anyway. "And . . . thanks for not telling anybody about me. Because you're not going to, right?"

Now she planted her fists on her hips and rolled her eyes, clearly trying to appear irritated, but looking cute as hell instead. "I said I wouldn't, didn't I? How many times do I have to promise?"

He felt himself wanting to smile at her, just a little, but he held it in. "Until I completely believe you."

Another huff of aggravation left her. "When will *that* be?"

"I'm not sure yet. So . . . I might be back. Just to check in. Just to make sure. To remind you how serious I am."

At this, she crossed her arms and let out another disbelieving sigh. "I *got* that already—trust me."

He couldn't help it this time—it made him laugh. "Am I that rotten to be around?"

She'd been rolling her eyes some more, yet now narrowed her gaze on him. "Not really. Not tonight anyway. But this is just like fifth grade all over again."

He raised his eyebrows, still mildly amused. "Fifth grade?"

"When I was in the fifth grade, I stumbled upon three scary girls in my class smoking behind the school at recess one day. To make sure I didn't tell on them, they decided to stick to me like glue—at recess, lunch, gym class—anytime they could. An intimidation tactic."

Despite himself, he cast a soft grin, thinking of innocent little Jenny being forced to hang with the tough girls. "Did you ever tell on them?"

"No."

"Then I guess it worked," he said, pushing to his feet and stepping close to her. "Don't tell anybody about *me*, either, pussycat. I'll be seeing you soon."

And with that, he used one bent finger to lift her chin, then brushed his mouth ever-so-lightly across hers, just before walking out the door.

"Stay close to the dock, honey," Sue Ann called to her little girl, Sophie, a miniature version of her, now floating in Blue Valley Lake surrounded by a blow-up inner tube decorated with Disney princesses.

Then Sue Ann stretched out in her lounge chair next to Jenny's and said, "Wow, this is just like old times. Except that there's another one of us now, and she's short."

Jenny laughed, then laid her head back, soaking up the sun in last year's two-piece swimsuit, the one she'd bought for the trip she and Terrence had taken to the Bahamas. But her mind wasn't on Terrence, or the Bahamas. Her mind was on Mick Brody.

In fact, just glancing across the lake to the woods that hid his home, to the trees that shrouded the place where they'd had sex, made her hot in a way she couldn't attribute to the sun.

"By the way," she said, "crisis averted." This was the first time they'd had a chance to chat privately since Sue Ann and Sophie had shown up a few minutes ago.

"Which crisis exactly?"

Good question, Jenny supposed—depending upon

how you looked at it, there *was* more than just one. "I got my telescope back."

Sue Ann stopped in mid–sunscreen application to stare at her. "How, pray tell?"

Jenny glanced over as if it were no biggie. "Mick brought it to me last night."

Sue Ann tipped her head back. "Ah, I see. *Mick*. So we're on a first name basis now."

"Well, I did sleep with the guy," she said—softly, so Sophie wouldn't overhear. Fortunately, the boom box was playing and Sophie was splashing around in the water.

"It didn't sound like sleeping to *me*," Sue Ann quipped.

And Jenny couldn't help giggling a bit in response.

To which Sue Ann said, "My, aren't we girlishly lighthearted today."

Jenny couldn't deny it. For some reason, she felt better than she had in . . . well, she couldn't remember how long. She wasn't sure why, but decided to credit it to the averted crisis. "Well, I have my telescope back now."

"And I know you love that thing, but I've never seen it make you . . . *giddy*."

Jenny crossed her arms and made a face. "I'm not *giddy*. I'm relieved."

"Uh-huh, sure. So . . . did you get a better look at him this time? Did he look good?"

Jenny ignored the sarcasm and blew out a long breath in reply. "Um, *yeah*."

"Still has that sexy olive complexion?"

"Mmm hmm."

"And that dark, silky hair?"

"Yep."

Sue Ann leaned forward slightly in her chair. "Muscles? Are there muscles?"

Jenny's stomach was getting a little fluttery just remembering. "*Oh* yeah, there are muscles. Not big, bodybuilder muscles. But just, you know, *nice, sturdy* ones. Although I knew that already. You don't have to *see* muscles."

Looking enlightened, Sue Ann shrugged. "Hmm, I suppose you don't. So what did Mr. Brody have to say on his little visit?"

"Well, he was still very adamant about me not telling anyone, so I had to promise again. So we both have to keep our mouths positively *shut*."

"Any clues about what the big freaking secret is?"

Jenny shook her head. "Nope. But the good news is that he claims he's usually into safe sex."

"Good," Sue Ann said on a nod, adding, "Of course, you'll still get checked out."

"Of course." She was still "good Jenny," after all— one romp in the woods didn't take away a lifetime of safety training. "I thought I'd see if there's a clinic or something in Crestview, where people won't recognize me."

Sue Ann lifted one finger in the air. "There is. Jeff's little sister had a . . . misadventure on spring break last year and I got to be the lucky one she confided in. Anyway, I went with her, and I can get you the address. What else did he say?"

Jenny shrugged, sighed—then spilled the beans. "That he's coming back."

Sue Ann's jaw dropped. "Say that again."

"He's going to come back over, to check on me, to make sure I don't feel the need to suddenly go telling anyone."

"Damn, he's serious about this."

"I told you that."

"And it doesn't concern you? That he's hiding something? Or . . . hiding out *himself*? What if he's . . . on the run for committing some crime? What if he's breaking some serious laws over there, doing something so awful that we can't even imagine it?"

At this, Jenny caught her breath and looked up.

Just as Sue Ann added, "Remember, this is Mick Brody we're talking about."

Oh God, it *was*. Mick Brody. Maybe she'd somehow forgotten that. She'd been so caught up in the sex and all the confusing feelings it brought over her, about herself, about her feelings for Terrence, about everything inside her. But Sue Ann was right—any sensible person would be worried about this. She felt utterly foolish to have let the sex aspects of the situation fog her brain even for a minute. "My God," she murmured, "I let him in my house."

"Well," Sue Ann reasoned, "he did have your telescope. And you probably didn't want to make the guy mad by telling him he had to stay outside."

That was true—he *had* pretty much barged his way in. "But I . . . offered him iced tea. I made small talk with him." She cringed. "And sure, I tried to act belligerent and irritated, but I didn't even argue when he said he might come back."

Sue Ann bit her lip, looking pensive. "Was he . . . scary about that? Threatening?"

"Not really." She sucked in her breath, remembering. "He sort of . . . kissed me good-bye."

Sue Ann blinked. "What *kind* of kiss?"

Jenny tried to explain. "Just a soft, tiny, little one. I barely felt it." *Except for the fact that it vibrated all through me.*

"Holy crap."

"Yeah, it kind of confused me, too."

At this, Sue Ann sat up a bit taller, suddenly looking mischievous. "Maybe this means you'll get to have more sex with him."

And Jenny gasped. "No way! I mean, really—*no way.*"

"Why?"

Given the discussion of the last few minutes, she couldn't believe Sue Ann had to ask. "Um, because he might be a criminal, as you just so aptly pointed out? Because I don't even know him? Because even if he didn't act totally scary last night, he still is?" She hadn't been planning to have sex with him again *anyway*, but after being reminded that he was keeping some big, bad secret from her on his side of the lake—it was out of the question.

"And did any of those things stop you in the woods?" Sue Ann asked.

Jenny replied by pointing a threatening finger at her friend. "I was in a bad mood and he pissed me off."

"And you really taught him a lesson by riding him to orgasm the way you did."

Jenny let her mouth drop open and her eyes go wide. "Stop it already." Then she motioned toward the lake, where Sophie was still having a good time swimming around by herself. "There's a five-year-old present."

Sue Ann swiped a hand down through the air. "She doesn't know what *orgasm* means."

"Well, she will soon if you keep discussing it like it's the weather."

"Weather, shmether." Sue Ann at least lowered her voice again, though. "Despite my misgivings about this guy, it was still mind-blowing sex, which counts for a lot in life. So . . . why not consider having *more* of it if the opportunity arises?"

Jenny pursed her lips. "Mind-blowing or not, what happened the other night was a . . . *weird, crazy* aberration in my life. It was . . . freeing, momentarily. But then it was also kind of scary. Because I lost my telescope. And because now I have to go slithering over to Crestview wearing dark sunglasses to make sure

I'm still healthy. And because what do we really know about Mick Brody—besides that he comes from a scary family and has some reason he doesn't want me on his side of the lake? Plus, as you well know, I hold sex as a special thing. I don't do it with strangers for mere physical pleasure."

"Unless they really piss you off."

Jenny rolled her eyes and leaned back in her chair, ready to end this conversation. "Will you pass me a Diet Coke from the cooler?"

"Fine, be that way," Sue Ann said lightly, and after they'd both popped the tops on their cans, only music from the radio mixed with the sounds of Sophie splashing.

Though as Jenny lay soaking up the sun beneath cotton clouds floating in the expanse of blue above, she couldn't stop remembering the way Mick had kissed her last night. She wouldn't have dreamed he could deliver a kiss so soft, and what she hadn't dared tell Sue Ann was that it had tingled on her lips long after he'd gone. It had made her wish she'd kissed him during sex like she'd wanted. And it had made her less afraid of him.

That was stupid, though—she knew that now. She should still be *plenty* afraid. He was still a guy who might have robbed a liquor store and God knew what else. He was still a guy who had a secret he wouldn't tell her, and she knew it couldn't be good, since secrets seldom were.

And that was why she *absolutely, positively* would *not* have sex with him again, no matter what happened. It was the only sensible way to play this.

And yet, as the scent of Coppertone and the sound of Aerosmith's "Livin' On the Edge" took her back to her youth, she glanced across the lake toward those woods, half-frightened of when he would come back and what his secrets were—and half-frightened that he *wouldn't* come back and that the mystery of Mick Brody would be just that, forever. A mystery.

Walking into Miss Ellie's garden on her dad's arm felt a little surreal. Festive yellow streamers festooned tables spread with food as well as the crisp white gazebo in the center of the garden, and colorful balloons sprang up here and there. But, of course, it was mostly the people she noticed.

She knew all the faces, only they were older now. Except, that is, for the children running and playing among the flowers and shrubbery—and it felt strange to realize she'd moved away so long ago that these little kids were now more a part of the community than she was. And the fact that she was literally *on her dad's arm* felt . . . well, a little pathetic under the circumstances.

It was mere seconds before people started recognizing her, saying hello. Caroline Meeks, another neighbor from up the road, and Reverend Marsh, who had officiated at her mother's funeral and wed her to Terrence. Moments later, as she handed off a plate of lemon bars wrapped in cellophane to Linda Sue, one of Miss Ellie's daughters, she heard herself explaining, ever-so-vaguely, as she had to the others who'd greeted her, "Just here to visit with Dad for the summer."

Ugh, maybe she'd been wrong in what she'd told Mick—maybe she *did* lie.

And what was wrong with these people? Had the ladies from the mah-jongg party *not* done their social duty by spreading the word that Jenny Tolliver was indeed Jenny *Tolliver* again, no longer Mrs. Terrence Randall?

After a few long minutes of greeting still more Destinyites and complimenting dresses and saying things like, "Could you *ask* for a prettier day for a party?" she was finally rescued by a tap on the shoulder from Sue Ann.

She turned to find her best friend in a pretty white eyelet dress, saying, "Fabu frock, Jen," about Jenny's pink-and-white-print sundress. Jeff stood behind her, handsome and clean-cut as ever, holding Sophie—in an equally lovely dress—on one hip.

"Good to see you, Jen," Sue Ann's husband said with a broad smile, and she loved him all the more for not mentioning anything about her being back in town for the summer, or why.

"You, too. And hey, thanks for letting the girls hang out with me yesterday, on a Saturday. It was fun."

He shrugged. "No thanks necessary. I managed to entertain myself just fine on the golf course."

Jeff had been a year ahead of them in school and now did administrative work for the highway department. He still looked like the varsity basketball player he'd once been, with trim, light brown hair, and the shirt and tie he wore told Jenny they'd just come from church.

And despite herself, she found herself *envying* Sue Ann a little. She had a perfect family and a perfect Destiny life. They lived in a nice Victorian in town that they'd renovated themselves, and Sue Ann worked part-time at Destiny Properties, also doing admin work. They served on community committees, Jeff was thinking of running for town council in the fall, and as Jenny looked at them standing there smiling and greeting people, she realized that they had . . . well, something like the life she'd had with Terrence, except that they were probably happier. *Truly, deeply* happy.

With Terrence, she was beginning to realize, she'd felt . . . content, but Sue Ann was supremely *happy* with her life. And Sue Ann could act as fascinated with the Brody incident as she wanted, but Jenny knew good and well from little things Sue Ann had said that she was still in mad, passionate love with Jeff.

"Jenny Tolliver, is it really you?"

Jenny spun toward the friendly voice to see her old friend, Tessa Sheridan—and she couldn't hold in a small squeal. Tessa, a dainty blonde, didn't look much different than when Jenny had last seen her, the summer before college. Back in high school, Jenny and Sue Ann had hung out with Tessa and *her* two best friends, Rachel and Amy—but Jenny hadn't kept in touch with them the way she had with Sue Ann.

After giving Tessa a hug, she drew back to give her friend a thorough once-over, taking in her long, flowing skirt and gauzy blouse—inexplicably pleased to see that not every female in Destiny dressed exactly the same. "I had no idea you were back in town," Jenny said.

Tessa looked surprised. "Sue Ann didn't tell you?"

No, we've been too busy discussing the illicit sex I've been having in the woods. "Um, I guess she forgot to mention. How long have you been back?"

Tessa rolled her eyes confidingly, then lowered her voice. "Too long," she replied, then let out a small laugh. And in response to Jenny's unspoken question, she added, "A lengthy story for another time. But the upshot is—after years in the city, I have to admit that Destiny holds a . . . certain charm."

Looking around the garden party, Jenny couldn't really deny that—but she was still surprised to hear it from adventurous Tessa.

Just then, Amy bounded up between them, naturally curly hair bouncing around her face, eyes bright and wide as ever. "Oh my God—Jenny! It's so good to see you!"

Jenny felt almost overwhelmed—so many old, familiar faces, and now suddenly both Tessa and Amy were here. After giving the always-sweet Amy a hug, she said, "All we need to make the party complete is Rachel."

In reply, Tessa and Amy exchanged looks and Tessa said, "Then you'll have to go with us to Chicago in September to see her. She hasn't been back to Destiny in the fourteen years since we graduated from high school."

Somehow, though, Jenny wasn't surprised. She remembered Rachel wanting to leave Destiny far behind, and it sounded like she'd succeeded. "Well, thanks for the invitation, but you'll have to give her a long-distance hello for me instead. So what is she up to these days?"

Amy sighed enviously. "She's in Italy right now. She's traveled all over the place."

"She's an advertising bigwig," Tessa said. "She runs herself ragged if you ask me, but she's as sassy and full of energy as ever, so I guess that kind of life suits her."

"Tessa and I take a trip to see her every fall, and we can barely keep up with her the whole time we're there," Amy added. "But I guess a small-town way of life has always just been more my cup of tea."

For the first time, Jenny had a chance to wonder what Amy did for a living—or if maybe she was a homemaker with kids, a role that Jenny thought would probably make Amy happy. "So what have *you* been doing with yourself?" she asked.

Amy beamed proudly. "You haven't heard? I own the bookstore in town—Under the Covers."

Ah—while it wasn't what she'd predicted, it was another bit of news that didn't surprise Jenny at all. Amy had always wanted to be a librarian when she grew up—and it sounded like she'd come close. "Wow—color me delighted to hear Destiny now *has* a bookstore."

"Times, they are a changin'," Tessa quipped, adding, "I work there part-time, so stop in and say hello."

Jenny was still talking with Tessa and Amy when she felt two hands clasp her own. She looked up to see Miss Ellie's other daughter, Mary Katherine, who *had* been the town librarian Jenny's whole life but—according to her father—had just recently retired. Jenny turned to the older lady with a smile. "It's great to see you, Mary Katherine," she said, truly pleased.

They exchanged pleasantries for a moment until Mary Katherine said, "Now you must come over and say hello to Mother. She doesn't get around so well anymore, so we've got her sitting in the shade in the gazebo, and she's dying to see you."

After promising her old friends they'd get together soon, Jenny let Mary Katherine lead her by the hand up into the gazebo, complete with gingerbread trim, to find Miss Ellie seated in a patio chair in a yellow dress sprinkled with blue flowers, looking as bright and chipper as a woman her age could.

Her aged eyes lit up when she spotted Jenny. "Why, as I live and breathe, if it isn't sweet Jenny Tolliver."

Jenny had mentally braced herself for all the *sweet* and *good* comments, and especially given that this was beloved Miss Ellie, she let it roll off her back. She took Miss Ellie's withered hands in hers, having been reminded by other greetings, both here and at the mahjongg party, that this was how Destiny ladies expressed affection. "Hello, Miss Ellie—it's so wonderful to see you again."

"What's that you say, dear?"

Oh my—poor Miss Ellie's hearing must be starting to go. Jenny leaned closer and spoke louder. *"Hello, Miss Ellie—it's wonderful to see you again."*

Miss Ellie nodded in understanding. "You, too, sweetheart—you, too." Miss Ellie still held one of her hands and now squeezed it. "Your father tells me you're here for the summer."

"That's right," she said, nodding. She'd forgotten to speak up, but Miss Ellie seemed to understand.

It was then that Miss Ellie began to peek around behind Jenny, and then around the gazebo in general, as if looking for someone.

"What is it, Miss Ellie?" Jenny asked, remembering to project her voice this time. "Can I get you something?"

"No, no—I was just looking for your Terrence. Where is he?"

Oh dear.

On one hand, it would be easier to fib to Miss Ellie than a lot of people. Jenny could just say he was busy today and it would suffice—and probably not *technically* be a lie. But on the other hand . . . *hell, why not just get over this madness and tell it like it is.* So, for the first time ever, Jenny didn't mince words or try to choose the best way to say it. "We're divorced."

Miss Ellie lifted a palm to cup her ear. "What's that, dear? My hearing's gone bad. Can you say again?"

Jenny took a deep breath and leaned nearer, but didn't raise her voice overmuch. "He's gone, Miss Ellie. We're no longer together."

Miss Ellie knit her brows. "Oh my—where did he go?"

Oh crap. Hell. *Just say it.* "He . . . left me for a twenty-one-year-old chippy."

"What's that, Jenny? I'm afraid I still can't hear you."

Jenny raised her voice, just slightly. "I said that he left me for a twenty-one-year-old."

But Miss Ellie still clearly wasn't hearing her, squinting and shaking her head, and cupping her ear more tightly. "Again, dear?"

So Jenny tried again. *"I said that Terrence left me for a twenty-one-year-old chippy!"*

When a hush fell over the garden, she realized that anyone in Destiny who hadn't known why she was here before definitely knew *now*. She met Sue Ann's gaze across the garden, and her friend delivered a tight-lipped smile, as if to say, *Oh well, at least it's out now.* She caught looks of sympathy from Tessa and Amy, as well.

Then, at a loss, she looked back down at old Miss Ellie, who said, "Well, just between you and me, I never did think that boy had much sense—and now he's proven it if he's stupid enough to give up a sweet girl like you. Although . . ." she added, clearly puzzled, "I wonder why he was attracted to a hippie."

The rest of the party was awkward, no two ways about it. But Jenny survived.

And in the days after, she began to realize she was glad the news was completely out—it took a lot of pressure off when she stopped into the police station to meet her dad for lunch a couple of days later. And when she stepped into the Daisy Dress Shop on the town square, no one asked her a thing—she chatted with the owner, Mary Ann, about normal topics like the weather and fashion, then bought a pretty cotton skirt suitable for other upcoming Destiny summer social occasions. When she ran into Tessa on the same outing, crossing the square, they *did* briefly discuss the divorce, but Tessa was supportive and didn't dwell on the topic. "According to Sue Ann," Tessa said, "he's a rat bastard and you're better off without him."

Running into Tessa and Amy at Miss Ellie's party

had reminded Jenny that she had more here than she remembered—more than just Sue Ann and her dad. She, in fact, had a lifetime of friends and other people to get caught up with. And sure, she'd seen a lot of those other people even before Miss Ellie's party, but despite her faux pas in the gazebo, something about those reconnections was starting to seem more like a comfort than something to avoid.

Jenny spent the rest of her time that week . . . rediscovering herself.

She read astronomy books and turned to the Internet for more recent information, since new findings were being made in space all the time. She downloaded some of her favorite pictures taken by the Hubble Telescope and created a slide-show screensaver. She put on garden gloves from the shed out back and tidied up the perennials in the front yard. And a couple of times she took a chair back down to the dock to soak up the morning sun—and let her eyes stray across the lake to wonder if Mick Brody was still there, what he was doing, and if he'd changed his mind about coming back.

That would be best, of course. A guy like him could bring nothing but trouble into her life. And yet—the more time that passed, the more she couldn't deny to herself that she'd never experienced such deeply *pleasurable* trouble.

In the evenings, she took walks, and once stopped in to see Miss Ellie and drop off some oatmeal raisin cookies after a visit to the bakery in town. She grilled out some nights; other nights she whipped up light salads. She started watching reality TV competitions, which Terrence had frowned upon, and soon began to understand the national indulgence. Twice she took her telescope down to the dock, but the first night turned out to be too cloudy, and on the next, although she did spot Saturn and Jupiter, she found that, as she'd suspected, the taller trees on the shoreline tended to get in her way, which quickly became annoying.

Of course, that led her thoughts back across the lake, as well. It was frustrating to have this new freedom, freedom to do whatever she wanted, accountable to no one else, but *still* not be able to do what moved her the most: exploring the cosmos one-on-one, through her telescope.

On that particular evening, she briefly considered throwing caution to the wind, climbing back in the canoe with her equipment, and paddling across the lake. Because surely he wouldn't be out walking again. Surely she could sneak up the hill to the rocks without being noticed.

But then sense prevailed. He might be able to kiss more softly than she'd first thought, but he was still potentially a criminal. And though he'd never directly threatened her, he'd made it very clear she wasn't welcome there. And sure, the wild, feral sex had sent a *blatantly* mixed message—but she had to remember: *He does not want you there. He told you repeatedly to stay away.*

So a week after their sexual liaison in the woods, she stood on her dock, let out a sigh, and started dismantling and packing her telescope carefully back in its case, accepting that it would be foolish to go back over to the Brody property and that maybe she just wasn't meant to see the stars like she wanted to right now.

Though as she trudged back to the house and stepped in from the hot June night, she couldn't help feeling a little . . . let down. Because even if she was enjoying the freedom to do whatever she wanted—or nothing at all—she still wasn't quite used to spending so much time alone. Or maybe it was disappointment over the stargazing, not being able to reach out to the universe and find that sense of peace it always gave her. Or . . . was it because Mick Brody apparently wasn't coming back?

Uh-oh, bad thought. Because it was *good* he hadn't come back, she told herself again as she stashed her telescope in the coat closet. And a soft kiss doesn't make him any less dangerous, she reminded herself as she went upstairs to change into a pair of cotton drawstring pajama pants with little slices of watermelon on them, topping them with a mint green tank. And as she headed back down to do a little reading before bed, she decided that disliking the "good Jenny" label was one thing, but abandoning her good sense was another.

She was just about to curl up on the old sofa with Brian Greene's *The Fabric of the Cosmos* when she remembered she'd left some gardening tools on the back patio today and there was a slight chance of rain overnight. Rain that would be very welcome, given the unrelenting heat that had been building since her arrival in town, but she didn't want to be responsible for letting her dad's tools get rusty.

So she tossed the book on the couch and went to the back door, pulling it open and starting through—only to find herself face to face, chest to chest, with Mick Brody. His warm hands curled around her wrists to keep her from barreling him over as his deep voice washed softly over her.

"Hi there, pussycat."

Our feeblest contemplations of the Cosmos stir us—there is a tingling in the spine, a catch in the voice, a faint sensation, as if a distant memory, of falling from a height. We know we are approaching the greatest of mysteries.

Carl Sagan

Five

Jenny sucked in her breath and tried to get hold of herself. "Um, hi." She felt how wide her eyes had just gotten, felt even more how close she stood to him. Then she summoned the strength to take a step back.

"You look surprised to see me," Mick said, voice low, even.

She swallowed, wishing she could hide it. Damn it, she'd just never been very good at disguising her feelings. "I . . . thought maybe you'd changed your mind. You know, decided you could trust me."

Now that she'd moved back over the threshold, into the house, he came inside, too. "Can I?"

As the words turned her indignant that fast, she crossed her arms—and realized that just like once before, all those years ago, the move shoved her breasts higher beneath her already low-cut tank. But she ignored that. "What difference does it make how I answer? You won't believe me anyway."

He shrugged, then smiled lightly as if conceding the point, and it made his eyes sparkle in a way that nearly paralyzed her. "Tell me enough times and maybe I'll start believing, pussycat."

So she pursed her lips and spoke matter-of-factly. "For the twentieth time, no, I haven't told anyone about you, and no, I don't intend to." She really no longer even counted Sue Ann because she trusted her implicitly.

"That's good," he said, that small, sexy smile still playing about his lush mouth. *But, oh God, stop looking at his mouth already.*

She watched then, a bit surprised, as he moved with ease from the small kitchen into the living room. Taking a deep breath, she followed, yet stopped in the doorway. It seemed important to keep some distance between them, and she was pretty sure her nipples were showing through her top again—though there was nothing she could do about it but try to at least *act* unaffected by him. "I was just getting ready to go to bed," she said—then immediately wanted to bite her tongue. What if that sounded like . . . an invitation?

"Sorry, pussycat," he told her. "I won't keep you up long, but how about another glass of iced tea? It's still hot out. And it's a lot of work rowing across that lake."

She stood up a little straighter. She hadn't even thought before now about how he was getting here. But it only made sense, she supposed, since the road around the other side leading to the Brody place was a long and twisty one. Which, she *further* supposed, is what made it such a good place to hide . . . whatever he was hiding. *Remember that. He's hiding something. Something big.*

"Sure," she heard herself say, heading back into the kitchen—then berating herself as she poured the tea. *Why did you say sure? Why didn't you tell him no, you're sleepy, or that you'd put it in a plastic cup for him to take with him?*

But as the cold air from the fridge hit her skin, she *knew* why. It was the mystery of Mick Brody. She hadn't solved it yet, and she wanted to. No matter how she might try to deny it to herself, deep down inside, she was glad he'd come.

When she returned to the living room, he'd taken a seat on the couch. She noticed he'd placed her book on the coffee table so as not to sit on it. "Here," she said, passing him the glass, then sat down across the room in her mother's old easy chair.

"That you?" he asked, motioning to the giant photo of her and her mom in the rose-colored dresses.

She nodded succinctly, watching him take a sip from the glass, noticing his Adam's apple and the bottom edges of his hair, damp with sweat. They curled slightly, and she found herself wanting to run her fingers through them to straighten them. "When I was five."

He leaned his head back, appearing to study the large image closer. "That's a really big picture."

True enough, it was way too large for the room, overpowering. "I'm thinking of taking it down," she admitted, "but this is still technically my father's place, so I'm not sure if I should."

His gaze shifted to hers. "You don't like it?"

She shrugged softly, crossing one leg over the other. "It's like you said—it's too big for the space. And it makes me think about my mother's death too much since I got home."

He nodded. "You look like her." It wasn't the first time she'd heard that. "When did she die?"

"When I was thirteen."

To her surprise, he flinched.

"What?" she asked.

He shook his head lightly. "I guess I just . . . figured it was more recent."

Because of the shrine, she presumed. "That's why I want to take the picture down. Dad doesn't seem quite able to get over it, even though it's been eighteen years."

"Wow," Mick murmured, still studying the portrait, and looking shockingly . . . reverent. "That's something. A guy that crazy about his wife."

She couldn't help being reminded of the "domestic calls" out to the Brody cabin when she was younger and bit her lip. "I guess it's pretty rare," she mused, thinking, too, about her *own* marriage.

So she was relieved when Mick's gaze drifted from the shrine to some other old pictures on the wall—until she realized they were of *her*, in her teenage years. In one, she hugged Snowball to her chest. "I remember your cat," he said.

Why did that please her? Probably the same reason it pleased her that he'd remembered calling her "pussycat"—it meant he remembered that day as well as she did. Still, she tried to act annoyed. "*I* remember your friend trying to get her drunk."

He shrugged, as if she'd over-reacted to that and was *still* over-reacting, and she supposed a guy like him couldn't really grasp how protective a girl could be of her cat. "Whatever happened to that cat anyway?" he asked.

Jenny cringed at the unpleasant memory. "She got hit by a car." God, it still stung. It had happened the weekend before she'd left for college. She'd had Snowy since her kittenhood, when Jenny was nine, so it had been a blow.

"Sorry," he said, sounding like he actually meant it—and as usual, she knew she wasn't camouflaging her pain very well. Then he took another drink of his iced tea and shifted his gaze slightly down the wall to a photo of her in her cheerleading uniform, holding her pompoms overhead while doing the splits. "I used to see you," he ventured. "Cheerleading."

Her chest tightened. To think Mick Brody had been watching her then, *aware* of her then—when she'd been aware of him, too. Only vaguely before that day at the dock—but even then she'd been drawn to study him across a parking lot or the gymnasium, drawn to his lean, lanky boy's body, his dark looks. And after the dock encounter, she'd sometimes found herself actively keeping an eye out for him on trips to town, especially in summer when people were out and about more.

She didn't know what to say, so she just bit her lip, then drew her gaze down, afraid he would see the sex in her eyes.

"What's that one?" he asked, pointing to a photo of her in a formal gown, standing next to Adam Becker— they both wore crowns on their heads. Then he lowered his chin, casting another slightly accusing grin. "Don't tell me you were the prom queen?"

She tilted her head to one side, thinking how silly something like that must seem to tough Mick Brody. "Guilty as charged."

He laughed softly.

And she couldn't help saying, "What? What's so funny?"

He pinned her in place with those blue eyes of his,

even from across the room. "Let's just say . . . you're my first prom queen."

Heat climbed her face—and it also invaded down below, in her panties. In her mind, she saw harsh, dark images of them writhing together on the ground.

He chuckled a little more then. "Hell, I've never even *been* to a dance."

"Really?" She wasn't sure why it caught her off guard, but it was just one more reminder of how different they were, how different their lives had been.

Instead of answering directly, he tilted his head slightly and said, "What's that like, pussycat? To do all that high school stuff—the sports, the dances, everything else?"

She thought back, tried to encapsulate it in a way he would understand. "It's not for everybody, I guess. But I liked it. It . . . made me feel good about myself."

He laughed. "I guess I'd like it, too, if I had a pretty cheerleader to dance with." Then he shook his head again. "Damn, I wouldn't have the first idea how to even do it."

"Do what? Dance?"

He gave a slight nod, then looked like maybe he was sorry he'd said it.

She decided to put his mind at ease and share the truth of the matter. "*No* boy knows how to dance in high school. It's more like . . . hugging on the dance floor."

He looked skeptical. "There's no moving? Just hugging?"

A soft laugh escaped her. "Well, you kind of rock back and forth and sometimes turn in a slow circle, but trust me . . . for seventeen-year-old guys, it's mostly hugging."

Mick shrugged and said, "Now that I could probably master," making her giggle yet again.

When her laughter faded, her gaze had dropped from his, but she found herself lifting it back to his face. "I could teach you."

He raised his eyebrows matter-of-factly. "How to hug? Thanks, but I've already got that part down."

"No. How to dance." She knew a guy like him would never admit to wanting to learn, and—feeling a little sad that he'd missed out on all the things that had made her youth special, more bearable, after her mom's death—she couldn't help the urge to make it easier on him.

He looked doubtful, lowering his chin. "I don't know, pussycat. Not sure I'm the dancing type."

She'd never seen him even come *close* to looking sheepish before, and "good Jenny" continued wanting to relieve his discomfort. "Come on," she said. "It's painless, I promise." Then she pushed to her feet and moved to the old stereo across the room. She didn't have any of her own CDs with her, but it was just as well since the stereo was circa 1980s anyway, pre–CD player. So she opened the built-in cabinet and pulled out the first record she found: The Honeydrippers, Volume One. Lifting the cover to the turntable, she carefully lowered the vinyl onto it and set the needle on the second track, "Sea of Love."

As the slow, dreamy music filled the room, Jenny stepped near the couch and reached out her hand. When, after a short, tentative look, he took it—that's when she realized what she'd put into play here. Closeness. With a guy she hadn't even meant to make more small talk with. It had just happened. *What are you doing? Stop this! Stop it now.* But she only bit her lip as she drew him to the open center of the room, realizing there was no turning back.

"The proper way to dance," she said, nervous but trying to hide it as she looked up into those crystal blue eyes, "is like this." She placed one of his hands on her hip, then closed the other in her own and assumed the common slow-dance position. "But in high school, it was more like *this*," she added, situating *both* of his palms at her hips and easing her arms around his neck.

"And then you move," she said, but that part came out in a whisper, because his hands were on her now and she could smell the musky, woodsy scent of him.

Stupid, stupid, stupid—what were you thinking inviting him to dance? What a horrible *idea!*

Except for the fact that it felt so darn good.

She looked down, no longer quite able to meet his gaze as they began to sway slowly to the music. His movements were awkward at first, but she concentrated on easing them back and forth, and whispered into his chest, "Shift your weight from one foot to the other, in time with the music." His motions grew smoother, more comfortable—as her body grew hotter and more sensitive.

As he caught on, she changed her focus from teaching him the moves to being sure she kept a couple of inches between their bodies. Even though it would have been easy to lean into him. Easy to show him how much slow-dancing could feel like sex when you wanted it to.

They didn't speak for a while, the music seeming to cocoon them. They swayed and turned ever-so-slowly, and Jenny got a little lost in the moment, in the simple effortlessness of it, dancing with a man, not thinking very much, just listening to a romantic song her mother had once loved and letting it build a pleasant memory for her.

"This isn't bad," Mick said low and soft near her ear. "Now I can see why guys bother going to dances."

Without forethought, she smiled up at him, and realized how close his eyes were to hers, how close their mouths were, that somewhere in the last minute or so their bodies had grown closer, too. She'd forgotten to keep concentrating on the separation, and now her breasts brushed against his chest.

He gazed down on her with heavy-lidded eyes. "So, did you lose your virginity after the prom, pussycat?"

She blinked up at him and knew she looked surprised.

"I've just heard that's how it happens a lot," he explained.

"Oh. Well . . . no." She glanced down. Despite everything that had taken place between them already, she hadn't expected to suddenly be talking about sex with him again.

"Before that?" he asked, clearly curious.

She couldn't help laughing. "No again."

"Why not?" He sounded sincerely curious.

And she bit her lip, peering back up at him. "He tried, but I said no."

"The guy in the picture?"

Adam. Her first real boyfriend. She nodded quietly.

And Mick raised his eyebrows slightly. "You didn't want to?"

She didn't know how to answer except honestly. "I . . . did, but I wanted to be in love, and I wasn't. I wanted sex . . . to mean something."

He drew back slightly, clearly caught off guard. She understood why, after their encounter in the woods. "Time changes things, I guess," he offered.

Jenny couldn't help feeling a little embarrassed. By all of it. "What happened with you . . . wasn't normal for me."

"Why'd you do it then? I would have stopped if you'd told me to."

They still moved to the music, swaying gently. "I . . . can't explain it."

"It was *good*, pussycat. *Really* good."

She felt his words in her chest, and lower. She felt how close their bodies were now, closer than before, almost pressed together. And—dear God—was he getting *hard*? *There? Against her belly?* She bit her lip once more and cast her eyes down.

A few seconds later, he spoke again. "Thanks for teaching me to dance. It's . . . kinda nice."

More than kinda. Her whole body tingled, almost pulsing with heat. Feeling a little lost again, to more than just the song, the dance, she lifted her eyes back to his face once more to murmur, "Yeah."

Those sexy eyes were fully open now, burning on her like blue flames. "So, back in high school, did people ever, you know, make out on the dance floor?"

She laughed, nodded. "Yeah, but then a teacher would always come along and separate them."

He smiled—yet it quickly faded to something much hotter as he said, "No teachers here *now*, pussycat."

She didn't answer—too busy trembling inside. Her whole body ached for him. How had she gotten back in this position—*aching* for Mick Brody?

You asked him to dance, that's how! Oh brother, she couldn't believe she'd done that.

But she had. And now he was leaning forward, tentatively, as slowly as any boy on a first date, lowering his mouth to hers.

She sank into the kiss readily—there was no stopping it. She pressed her lips to his, drinking him in, the warm, salty taste of him laced with the flavor of iced tea. As one kiss turned into two, he parted his lips, let his tongue push through, and she instinctively met it with her own. She surged with moisture below just to kiss him that way, that intimately. Strange, she'd had *sex* with him already, but something about this, licking at each other's tongues, felt even more up-close-and-personal.

Warm, powerful waves of longing washed over her as Mick's kisses grew deeper, longer. He massaged her ass and drew her to him tight, his hardness pressing into her where she longed for it most.

She sighed and panted beneath the weight of the passion. Every fiber of her body seemed to stretch taut with needing more, needing to touch him, move against him. She kissed him more deeply, found her hands in his hair, on his neck. She pressed her chest to his and got lost in the animal hunger inside her, a hunger she hadn't known she possessed before Mick Brody. And to think she'd been afraid to kiss him in the woods. To think she'd thought he didn't know how to kiss a girl the way she wanted to be kissed.

She was disappointed when his mouth left hers— until it sank to her neck. A soft moan left her as the first kiss there set her whole being ablaze. Oh God— amazing. Just like in the woods . . . except different. That had been hard; this was definitely softer. This was more like she was accustomed to. Only better. Much, much better.

She sighed her pleasure, tilting her head to give him easier access—and that's when she spotted the too-big portrait of her mother over his shoulder. *Oh, damn it.* Strange shame shot through her. And it was silly, she knew that—illogical, because she was a grown woman. But she was also "good Jenny." "Good Jenny," through and through, to the core of her soul.

The very sight of her mother forced her to press her hands to Mick's chest and push him back.

Then she turned away—away from *him* and away from everything that reminded her she couldn't do this. Not with Mick Brody. Not here.

He said nothing, but she felt his presence behind her, felt him waiting for her to say something. "I can't," she finally managed. "I just can't."

He sounded utterly reasonable when he reminded her, "You did before."

Jenny lifted her gaze only to realize she now faced the room's small fireplace, and the wide mirror that hung above it. She could only see herself from the chest up, but more importantly, she saw Mick behind her, looking gorgeous and hotter than the night. When she found words, they came out too soft. "I told you—what we did in the woods wasn't normal for me. When I have sex with a guy, I want it . . . to matter."

Yuck. She hated herself in that moment, hated what a good girl she still was deep down inside, hated how much it showed. She wanted to be like other women, the ones who could have casual sex and not care where it led—but she didn't think she ever *would* be. Some things ran deep.

And maybe she should have given him *other* reasons: *Whatever your secret is scares me. I'm afraid you're still a bad guy, someone I should run from.* But despite herself, in that moment, that wasn't the reason. What she'd *told him* was the reason.

She waited for Mick to say something that confirmed her worst fears, that he thought she was acting like a little girl, that he didn't need to waste time with someone like that; she waited for that sting of pain and embarrassment to come.

So it shocked the hell out of her when he stepped up behind her, closed his arms around her from behind and whispered in her ear. "You might not be in love with me, pussycat . . . but I want to make you feel good. Doesn't *that* make it matter?"

God help her, she wanted to make him feel good, too. She wanted to prove to them both that she *could*, just like in the woods.

Yet she didn't answer, because she didn't know what to say. She loved being wrapped in his arms right now.

She loved gazing in the mirror and seeing how they looked together, his muscular arms folding around her. He looked so much bigger than her, stronger, and she suffered the urge to be taken by him—taken hard and urgently.

But she couldn't tell him that. Good girls didn't say such things.

You'd think after what happened in the woods, you'd be tougher now. Yet she wasn't. The woods seemed a world away at the moment. This was her *house.* Her *parents'* house. Where she'd lived for the first eighteen years of her life. For some reason, being here with him felt as forbidden as if she'd snuck him in when she was sixteen. And despite how warm it felt in his embrace, everything she knew about him still scared her to death.

"I want you, honey," he nearly purred in her ear, a sound like velvet that closed around her warm and snug. It made her close her eyes.

So she didn't see it in the mirror when he began to caress her, when he grazed his roughened fingertips over her arms. She didn't see when one hand moved softly to her shoulder, the other molding, squeezing her hip.

When his touch drifted from her shoulder down to her breast, she let out a breathy sigh, but still didn't open her eyes. And as his other palm moved daringly low on her belly, she still didn't look.

But when his hard-on pressed bold and undeniable into her from behind, *then* her eyes shot open to meet his, and to see the erotic reflection they created in the glass. The juncture of her thighs pulsed at the sight.

"You're so pretty, Jenny," he breathed. The first time she remembered him actually using her name. But she still couldn't reply. She could only watch in the mirror. As his hand molded more fully to her breast, cupping and caressing through her thin top. And at the passion that etched itself across her face when his other hand sank between her thighs.

Oh God oh God oh God. She never decided to part her legs for him, but it happened. She never decided to move against his touch, but that happened, too. His kisses returned to her neck, and every time she met his caresses in front, it meant meeting his erection in back a fraction of a second later.

She shut her eyes again, not because she couldn't bear to watch but because the pleasure was too consuming. Her knees went weak and she feared she would collapse, yet he must have sensed that, too, since he released her breast in order to anchor that arm more tightly around her.

A moment later, his fingers were at her waist, finding the drawstring on her pants a moment before they *whooshed* to her ankles. She sucked in her breath, but he simply kept kissing her neck, holding her tight, making her feel . . . precious in some way.

"Come here," he murmured, releasing her from his embrace, but taking her hand. And lost in the fog of desire, she let him lead her to the couch.

He lay her down across it, then reclined gently on top of her to resume kissing. Jenny wasn't sure she'd ever been so intoxicated by a man. Sure, she'd been hungry for sex before, but this was different—this was about the guy, about Mick Brody. About his mouth, his eyes, his hands, his body.

They exchanged more kisses as the Honeydrippers moved from one song to another, and soon Mick reached down to slowly begin rolling her tank up over her torso, and then finally over her breasts. A low groan left him when he saw them, and she realized there was more light here than in the woods. "So pretty, baby," he murmured just before he molded both work-roughened hands to them, then bent to lick one turgid nipple.

She gasped as the stark pleasure echoed through her body, then watched as he drew the same pink peak into his mouth.

She didn't try to hold in her moans—she couldn't. And she didn't close her eyes now, either, because he was so nice to look at, and because she still couldn't quite believe this was happening and seeing it made it more real.

As he moved from one breast to the other, suckling, licking, the pleasure echoing outward and arcing through the small of her back, she found herself wondering—*did* this make it matter? Did pleasure really, truly *matter*? Enough? At the moment, it felt like plenty to validate her actions, but would it feel that way later?

She stopped thinking, though, as Mick moved downward, kissing his way across her lightly tanned stomach, then past her belly button, to nibble her skin at the edge of cotton polka-dot panties. Her stomach contracted, and the flesh between her legs tingled madly. It felt like a storm you could see coming in the summer sky: She couldn't stop it—she could only watch it growing nearer and nearer while bracing for the impact.

When he placed one small, solitary kiss directly between her legs, she flinched, gasped, lifting—and he used that opportunity to ease his hands under her, beginning to pull down her panties.

She met his gaze over the slender expanse of her body and said nothing, but she knew her eyes were saying everything. *Yes, I'm letting you do this. And yes, that must mean I want it the same way you do. I'm afraid, but I want it.*

As Mick removed her panties, she found herself reaching for his white T-shirt, pulling upward, needing it off him. When he looked up at her, clearly taken aback by the most sexually aggressive move she'd ever made with him, she whispered, "I feel more naked than you."

His eyes softened on her and he took over, ripping the tee off over his head, and then rising on his knees to undo his jeans. She watched as he kicked off his socks and shoes, then shed the blue jeans, letting them hit the hardwood floor a moment later—and taking in his body was . . . almost overwhelming. Maybe feeling like the only naked one had actually been easier, because his body was . . . beautiful.

He hovered above her in a pair of gray boxer briefs that hugged his hips and rear—and erection—perfectly. Above, his chest was broad and muscular, with a light sprinkling of dark, curling hair narrowing into a line that headed straight down into his underwear like an arrow pointing the way to the really good part. She let her eyes return there, linger—she bit her lip, yearning.

And as Mick reached down to remove the tangled tank top over her head, to leave her completely and truly naked, she knew she wanted to be here with him, like this. It didn't matter how dangerous he was. It didn't matter what he was hiding. She wanted him like she wanted to breathe. "Please," she heard herself whisper without planning.

"Please what, honey?" he whispered back, leaning down over her.

Then she took a deep breath and asked for exactly what she desired. She glanced down in between their bodies and said, "Please kiss me. There."

The universe is unfolding as it should.

Edwin Hubble

Six

*M*ick responded by moving down her body and parting her legs. She let him. She was nervous, but she *did* want this. She *did* believe her pleasure mattered. It *was* enough. At least right now. And right now was what counted.

As he sank his mouth over her, she let out a soft moan. The bliss was thick and scintillating, spreading through her whole body in an instant. Terrence had done this sometimes, of course, but already, with Mick, it was different. Mick, she instantly understood, really *wanted* to be doing it. It showed in how deeply he moved his tongue over her, how slowly and thoroughly. It showed in the way he touched her, using his hands to caress her as he delivered the mind-numbing ministrations, eventually using two fingers to enter her wetness below where he kissed.

She quickly forgot herself. She forgot this was the same couch where she'd watched cartoons as a child.

She forgot her bare foot was anchored on the same coffee table where she'd done homework. She knew nothing but the pleasure being delivered by the mysterious Mick Brody, so very different from the *harsher* pleasure he'd given her in the woods. She sobbed her delight as each lick and kiss vibrated through her; sometimes she closed her eyes, but other times, like before, she had to watch, because he was amazing to look at, and because he was really *here*, doing *this*, with *her*.

Before long, she found herself clutching at the couch cushion beneath her, simply needing to hold tight to something as she lifted herself against his mouth, felt the sensation rising, rising, toward that glorious peak. Her movements became faster as moments passed, the whole thing less gentle, but she needed it that way now, and was soon clenching her teeth, writhing against his giving mouth—until she tumbled into the abyss of ecstasy, low, hot moans leaving her throat as everything in her world but Mick disappeared for a long, heavenly moment.

And then the waves of orgasm receded and it was a little like in the woods, coming back down to earth to remember where she was and what was happening—until Mick rose above her, looking so masculine and pleased that she forgot all her worries again and said, "Oh God, I want you." She even reached for the elastic at his hips and pushed downward.

When his erection burst free, she gasped at the sight, then worked to get his underwear all the way off.

"Wait, I have . . ." he trailed off as he reached down for his jeans.

A moment later, he produced a condom and she said, "Hurry." She'd never once told Terrence to hurry—never, even back in college. But Mick she needed *now*.

She watched as he sheathed himself, a little sorry

when he was hidden beneath the rubber, but she forgot all that when he spread her legs again.

She tensed, trembled, looking up at him, pressing her palms to his chest. Their eyes met briefly until his dropped below as he reached down to position himself. She parted wider, instinctively, wanting him deep inside.

And then he was. And she was crying out, "God, oh God!" then arching into him, accepting his full length at the same moment as she wondered how she could take his size so willingly.

"So tight," he whispered.

She bit her lip. Said the obvious. "So big."

And he sank a little deeper and they both groaned.

He began to move inside her, gentle, thorough, rhythmic. She met his thrusts. It was the closest Jenny had ever come to total abandon. It felt like hurtling through space and time, like nothing mattered but existing, and feeling.

Every thrust made her whole body pulse with pure pleasure like she'd never known. She clawed into his chest and shoulders, simply trying to touch him as much as she could. She wrapped her legs around his back.

Soon Mick moved harder, faster, and she cried out at each powerful stroke. She curled her arms around his neck and held on for dear life. She felt *his* abandon, along with a certain feminine pride for having taken him there.

She had no idea how long he pumped into her accepting body, how long she met each hard, welcome thrust. She only knew she'd completely surrendered to him and that she never wanted it to end. She loved his groans, loved the low growls that left his throat. She loved being beneath him, feeling his strength, everything hard and masculine about him.

And she loved it when he came, just as much as she had in the woods. When he said, "Aw . . . aw, now," she could have sworn she felt him emptying inside her, and she sensed the tension leaving his body when he collapsed gently onto her a few seconds later.

They lay quietly that way a long time, neither talking. The music had long since quit playing, leaving the room quiet and softly lit. But still light enough for her to be reminded once more where she was, and to catch sight of the rose-colored dresses on the wall across the room. *Don't think about that.*

And yet somehow it reminded her. Not only that she was a good girl, but that Mick Brody was still dangerous. Probably a lot more dangerous than he'd been as a boy. It just hadn't felt that way when he kissed her. And as for whether it felt that way when he was inside her, well, maybe he *did* feel dangerous in those moments, dangerous and hot and tough, but she couldn't deny liking it *then.*

After a long, still moment, Mick reached up to brush his thumb gently across her breast, then lean in to kiss her on the cheek. "Am I crushing you?" he whispered in her ear.

Figuratively or literally? she almost asked, but held her tongue. Then laughed lightly and said, "A little," and together they rolled to their sides, facing one another, bare legs intermingling in a way that made her think of that tangled forest across the lake.

"You okay, pussycat?"

He'd asked her that last time, too, and she'd lied. This time was better. "Yeah," she said. Even if she was starting to remember again that she *didn't have sex with guys she hardly knew.* Or she didn't used to anyway. "Although *I* should have separated us."

"Huh?" he asked, understandably confused.

She explained. "*I'm* a teacher. So *I* should have separated us when we were, you know, making out while we danced."

"Really? You're a teacher?"

Oh God, did that make her sound boring? Even naked on a couch with Mick Brody, she was still "good Jenny," like it or not. "Yeah," she said.

"Well, you *tried* to separate us," he reminded her, his voice warm, slightly teasing.

A sheepish smile claimed her. "*That* didn't last long."

"No, and I'm damn glad." He smiled sexily into her eyes, gave her a short kiss, then asked, "What do you teach?"

"Middle school science." *Yep, just pass me my nerd glasses and pocket protector.*

She was pleased when he didn't seem to hear it the way she feared and simply said, "So that's why you're all into looking at the stars."

"Or the other way around. I loved the stars before I started teaching about them."

"I saw your books about it, too." He motioned to the coffee table, where the Brian Greene book lay next to a bigger one. "You're really into that sort of thing, huh?"

How could she explain the majesty of the universe to him? "Have you ever looked through a telescope?"

He gave his head a light shake against the throw pillow they shared.

"Once you start to grasp how . . . *vast* it all is, and that the whole earth is just a tiny pinhead in space, well, let's just say it can put things in perspective, make your problems seem smaller."

The expression on his handsome face gave the impression he was actually thinking about what she'd just said, absorbing it. "Hmm, smaller problems," he finally murmured. "I could go for that."

"Maybe . . . I can show you the stars some night," she

heard herself say unplanned. *Oh God, did I just ask Mick Brody out on a date?*

Apparently she had, so relief flooded her as he smoothly replied, "Maybe so, pussycat." But wait—*should* she be relieved? Or terrified?

No time to examine that now, though—instead, she bit her lip and lifted her gaze to his in playful challenge. "Of course, given all the trees in my yard, it'll be difficult since you won't let me on your side of the lake."

He winced, grinned, as if to say, *Touché.* "Sorry about that."

So did that mean she was welcome now, to show him the stars on his side . . . or not? She was about to ask, when he said, "I gotta take off, honey," and sat up, reaching for his underwear.

Hmm. At least she'd gotten a *little* snuggling this time.

Followed by an abrupt departure.

But I guess that's how it is in casual sex. Wham bam thank you ma'am. She'd had sex with him twice now without hardly knowing him at all, so she had no right to complain that he was leaving, even if it tugged at her emotions a little.

As he pulled on his boxers, then his jeans, she finally got a good look at the tattoo on his arm—a rather menacing-looking skull and crossbones. "Interesting tattoo," she said.

He glanced down at it as he zipped up.

"So why'd you pick that," she asked, "out of any tattoo in the world?"

The look on his face said he found her inquisitiveness cute. Or maybe silly. He winked and said, "I didn't think a butterfly or heart would suit me."

She giggled softly, then said, still smiling, "Seriously. Why that?"

He looked down at his arm again, his expression reflective, and honest. "I got it a long time ago. Guess maybe I wanted people to think I was a bad-ass."

"Are you?" Her heart beat a little harder at the question.

Yet he only answered with another wink. "Probably depends on how you see the world, pussycat."

Maybe he was right. The tattoo didn't mesh with the Mick Brody who'd just made love to her. And though she knew he'd never call it that, that was what they'd just done—made love. But maybe it made sense for the Mick Brody she'd known as a girl, and even the Mick Brody she'd had sex with in the woods.

The part she couldn't figure out was: Who was the *real* Mick Brody?

As he pulled his T-shirt over his head to hug the muscles in his chest and arms, he looked down at where she still lay naked on the couch. "See ya soon."

How soon?

No, stop, don't ask that. It's so stage-five-clingy. "Does this mean you still don't trust me to keep your secret?" she came up with instead.

A wicked little grin made his eyes sparkle once more. "Could be. Or could be I just want to get in your panties again."

Walter Tolliver pulled his cruiser into the gravel lot peppered with pickup trucks and a few souped-up cars to park right outside the front door of the Dew Drop Inn, a dive bar along a lonesome stretch of highway skirting the Destiny city limits. The building was a flat, drab, one-story establishment with low ceilings that left the smell of stale beer hovering in the air. Neon beer signs hung in windows lined with strings of Christmas lights, many of the bulbs extinguished. Behind the building stood a small dingy white house with tilted green shutters that had also seen better days.

Walter knew Digby Woods had sold the whole place recently and headed off to parts unknown, but he hadn't yet met the new owner. Since he'd broken up more than one fight here over the years and figured he was apt to break up more, he'd thought he should stop in and introduce himself.

It was nearly midnight when Walter pushed through the door, mostly unnoticed, and he was pleased to find the place quiet. A few slightly rough-looking characters shot pool in the corner, but no one was causing any trouble. Bruce Springsteen's "Cover Me" filled the room, echoing from an old-fashioned jukebox near the door, as peanut shells on the floor crunched beneath his shoes.

The bar itself was empty of customers, so he ambled to a stool at the end nearest the entrance. He didn't see anyone tending bar, but he wasn't in a big hurry—he dug his fingers absently into a dish of peanuts, shelled a few, and popped them in his mouth.

When his eyes landed on a folded newspaper a couple of stools down from him, the horoscopes on top, his thoughts turned to his daughter. She didn't follow astrology, but she did look to the stars for solace. When he'd asked her a couple of days ago if she'd gotten out her telescope yet, he could hear the disappointment in her voice when she'd explained that the trees around the house and road were just too tall. They'd been *nearly* too tall when she was a teenager, but time had passed and they were even bigger now. So he'd offered to call up his friends Betty and Ed, who had a big, empty meadow on their farm across town, and ask if she could bring her telescope over, but even as he'd said it, he knew that wouldn't meet Jenny's need to look at the sky in private. Ed would come out and want to look, too, and Betty would come rushing out with cold drinks.

And though most of the time, his daughter was a vivacious, sociable girl, she'd always had a strange sort of communion with the sky. There was something about it that made her quiet and introspective, like it was her . . . religion or something.

And maybe it was. God was up there, after all. Somewhere. Looking down on them. Maybe when Jenny looked through her telescope, she was looking for God.

He'd been working hard not to smother her since she'd returned home. The truth was, he wanted to check in with her every day, every night, but he was resisting the urge. Still, it was nice just to have her back around, just to know she was in the old lake cottage a few minutes away. She was his only family—and even if it seemed crazy, he could have sworn he somehow *felt* her physical nearness. They'd always been close *emotionally*, but having her close *physically* gave him a different sort of comfort.

He hated what her ass of an ex-husband had done to her, but rather than letting himself get as enraged as he wanted to, he tried to be thankful that something good had come out of it—and that good thing was having her back home. He'd never told her this, but he'd never totally trusted Terrence—despite being a clean-cut, dependable sort, he'd always struck Walter as being a little self-absorbed, even selfish.

And it cut him to the bone to imagine if Judy could see Jenny now. His daughter wasn't . . . broken. No, nothing like that. But he knew her sense of security, and maybe her sense of self, were shattered. He could look in her eyes and see that part of her was missing now.

Although he hadn't brought it up because he knew people had to work through that sort of thing on their own. He knew because *he'd* been working through it for the last eighteen years.

He'd grown used to life without Judy—and yet, if he was truthful with himself, he probably thought of her too often, almost imagining she was with him sometimes when he was alone. It was easy enough to do for a man who spent ample time by himself. *You just start imagining what you'd say to her if she were here—and in your mind, you say it. You imagine what she'd say back to you, and you hear it.* He could still hear her voice, same as if he'd heard it yesterday.

But Jenny had gotten him thinking. Not about dating other women like she'd said—Lordamercy, who would *he* date, for heaven's sake? Yet Jenny had him thinking that maybe it wasn't . . . *healthy* to cling to his memories of Judy the way he did.

Only problem was, now it was habit. Now it was impossible to imagine life any other way.

When he'd eaten enough peanuts to realize they'd made him thirsty, he looked around and spotted a woman bent over a table across the room, loading empty glasses and dirty napkins into a tub. He could see enough of her to tell she had red hair and a curvy body. Her jeans were too snug—"painted-on" he'd heard it called when women wore their jeans that way—and the bold print of her top hugged her flesh just as tight.

Just then, as if she'd sensed someone watching her, she looked up. Met his gaze. Set down her tub and rag and walked around behind the bar. He guessed her to be in her mid-forties, the lines on her face making her no less pretty—she struck him as a woman who'd lived hard but aged well. She greeted him pleasantly without going so far as to smile. "What can I get you, Officer?"

"A Sprite'll do."

"On duty?" she asked, turning to reach for a glass.

"Yes, ma'am," he replied softly. Not that he drank

much anyway. He didn't think it wise for an officer of the law to engage in activity that could impair his senses. He didn't begrudge those who indulged, so long as they didn't overdo, but other than sharing an occasional bottle of wine with Judy when they were young, alcohol had never been his thing.

"Here ya go," she said, lowering his glass to a little square napkin on the bar in front of him. She flipped long, bouncy hair over her shoulders, and Walter couldn't help noticing that her top was just as form-fitting in front, showing off plenty of cleavage.

"Can you tell me if the new owner's around?" he asked, then took a sip of his Sprite. Despite the A/C, it was too warm in here.

Now she smiled. "You're looking at her. Anita Garey." She held out a hand, her fingers tipped with long, pointy red nails, to shake his.

He returned the gesture gingerly, not wishing to be stabbed, a little surprised to hear she was the owner. But he knew he was . . . well, pretty behind the times in ways—these days, he reckoned a woman could own a bar if she wanted. And he was equally surprised when he felt the handshake in his groin—just a small, tender pull, but the first such sensation he'd experienced there in . . . a very long time.

He hoped to high heaven, though, that none of that showed on his face. "I'm Walter Tolliver, Destiny Chief of Police," he said as their hands parted and he lost the ability to make eye contact. His gaze dropped—first to her chest, then hurriedly to the bar before him. Hell and damnation, he felt like he was twelve—which made him remember he was actually fifty-four and raise his gaze back to hers. "I, uh, just wanted to drop by and introduce myself. I try to work close with local business owners to let 'em know we're there if they need us."

"Well, that's comforting to know, Officer," she said,

and something about the deep tone of her voice got him in the groin again, that fast, a feeling he wasn't at all comfortable with. *Cripes.*

Drawing in a deep breath, he struggled to think of something else to say. "You . . . from around here?"

When she shook her head, her mane of red hair bounced on her shoulders. "Moved down from Cleveland, to the little house out back." She pointed over her shoulder. "Decided I'd had enough of city life—figured I'd try country living for a while."

"And . . . does it suit you?"

She shrugged and sent a soft trill of sarcastic laughter wafting over him. "It's peaceful enough. Not sure I really fit in, though."

Aw, for heaven's sake, *now* what did he say? He didn't want to hurt the woman's feelings, but the truth was, he couldn't envision her making too many friends in Destiny. She was just . . . different than small-town folk. From the overt confidence in her eyes to the fact that she wore tighter clothes than most women her age—or at least most women her age around *here*. Other than her bar patrons—who likely lived outside of town on the way to Crestview given the location of the place—he wasn't sure he knew anyone who would want to spend social time with Anita Garey.

"Might just take a while," he finally offered as a toss-off, a space filler. It was the only alternative he could think of besides maybe inviting her to church, and *that* didn't seem like a good idea.

Anita Garey smiled knowingly and said, "Probably a *long* while," concluding with a wink.

Again, the gesture traveled straight to his groin—and he knew it was time to go. He reached in his back pocket to extract his wallet, tossing a couple of bucks on the bar. "I, uh, need to get back to my patrol. But it was nice meetin' ya, Miss Garey."

"Call me Anita," she said. "And it was nice meeting you, too—Walter, was it?"

He nodded again.

"You be careful out there, Walter."

For some reason, the words echoed in his head as he turned to exit the Dew Drop Inn, and he had the perplexing feeling that he would somehow be safer *outside* the place than in it.

Mick stood outside the old cabin, digging.

He'd started early, as soon as he'd gotten up. He needed to beat the heat. But it was discouraging when he stopped to rest, leaning against the shovel, wiping the dirt and sweat from his forehead, to look down and see what little progress he'd made so far. Thank God for the tall trees all around the house—at least they kept the sun out most of the time. Along with any prying eyes across the lake.

He'd been putting this off, but now that he realized how long it was going to take, he was glad he'd gotten started. He'd thought about renting a Bobcat for the job, but had decided that even if he drove to Crestview or farther to get it, it would be a bad move. A guy in an average blue pickup wasn't all that noticeable, even if someone were to see it turning off the quiet stretch of two-lane highway that led back to his family's land. A guy in a blue pickup *pulling a trailer with heavy machinery*—more noticeable. So he'd have to do this work by hand, no matter how long it took.

He didn't like thinking about why he was here, what this was all about, so when Jenny Tolliver entered his head instead, he didn't push the thoughts away. She was pretty, clean, sweet—everything his life was not.

He'd never planned to kiss her in her kitchen on that first visit—it had been pure instinct, and it had kept his body tingling for the whole walk across her yard and down to the rowboat. Even now, standing dirty and sweaty, wiping his hands on the thighs of his jeans, he could still remember the feeling. He hadn't known one little kiss could do that.

Then again, he guessed he hadn't had many occasions in his life to give a girl just one little kiss. From the start, his life had been full throttle, very go-after-what-you-want-while-it's-there-or-it-might-be-taken-away-from-you.

That was more how he'd felt kissing her while they danced. That tiny kiss had stayed with him, taunting, teasing his brain, and his body, and he'd felt like if he didn't have her again, right then and there, while she was in his arms, he might never get another chance. It had been worth pushing for, convincing her. He'd needed to be inside her more than he'd needed anything in a long time.

It seemed like a good enough arrangement for the summer. Checking up on her to ensure—as much as was possible anyway—that she was still keeping his presence quiet. And taking some pleasure with her while he was there.

Was it using her? Maybe. Sure. Whatever. Who didn't use people in this world? It didn't mean he didn't like her. The truth was, he did. The prettiness and sweetness was more than skin-deep. Normally, that would make her a girl who was far too good for him, even in his own mind. But this summer was different.

This summer was . . . the darkest of his life. Darker than beatings as a kid. Darker than his mom and dad screaming, fighting, hitting each other. Darker than the way people looked at you when your last name was Brody. Darker than the fear and shame that came from stealing, taking what other people had worked for and he hadn't. Darker than being trapped in a life he couldn't escape.

So if Jenny Tolliver could carry the darkness away for an hour now and then, how could he not take that? How could he not take the little bits of light a girl like her could inject into one long, dark, thankless night of a summer? At the moment, it was the only thing in the world he had to look forward to.

He just hoped to hell that she wouldn't betray him.

Shit, she *had* to be the police chief's daughter, didn't she? *Typical Brody luck. The girl you can have is . . . the one girl you can't have.* He almost laughed—but didn't. There was nothing funny about digging this goddamn hole, or the fact that—for another month or two—his fate lay in the hands of a girl he hardly knew, a girl who would probably have a damn heart attack if she knew what he was doing right now and why.

Returning his gaze to the ground, he got back to work, stabbing the shovel into the hard dirt, feeling the muscles in his shoulder and back stretching as he added another bit of dark earth to the pile behind him. Then, mopping his brow with his forearm, he stopped and looked at that pile. *Gonna take a lot more dirt. A lot more dirt.*

Three nights after she'd had sex on her couch with Mick Brody, Jenny found herself feeling antsy, bored. No wonder she'd left Destiny—there was nothing to do here.

But then, this had nothing to do with where she was—it was about . . . oh hell, being lonely. Lord, it was hard to admit that to herself. *Is this what your life is now? Pathetic and sad? Is this how divorced women all over the globe feel?* She sat looking around the living room, bored with TV, bored with her books, bored with the night. Days were better—there was shopping and people in town, there was lunch with Sue Ann, there was garden work, which, despite the heat, was better than sitting inside a little house staring at her past on every wall, in every framed photo. The nights were starting to feel long.

Except for the nights Mick Brody had shown up.

She still couldn't believe that Mick Brody, of all people on the planet, had become such a force in her life.

Sue Ann had squealed aloud when Jenny had told her over lunch yesterday about her most recent—and satisfying—encounter with him. At first she'd been excited. "You're having an illicit affair, Jen! Wow, how does it feel?"

"Weird," she'd answered simply. "And . . . really good," she'd added, "when it's, you know, actually happening."

Yet then Sue Ann had changed her tune, turning reproachful. "But on the other hand, now that I think about it—how can you have sex with a criminal and not be totally freaking out about it?" Sue Ann had always had a bad habit of flip-flopping on issues, but this was getting ridiculous.

"We don't know that he's a criminal—we just suspect it," Jenny had quickly reminded her.

Sue Ann had only rolled her eyes. "Okay. How can you have sex with someone we *think* is a criminal and not be totally freaking out about it?"

Jenny had sighed. She supposed Sue Ann wasn't flip-flopping on this any more than she herself was. It was just easy to forget he might be a criminal when he was kissing her and touching her and turning her insides to molten lava.

More than anything in this moment, she wanted to look at the stars. Not through tree limbs and leaves. And not with Betty and Ed or anyone else looking over her shoulder. Damn it, she just wanted to do . . . *what she wanted to do*. Why was that so hard to accomplish?

Letting out a sigh, she pushed to her feet and walked

out on the front porch. The warm night air hit her like a brick, but somehow in this moment it felt better—more real—than the cool, artificial air inside. She glanced across the lake in the darkness. The moon was out and shining bright—a glowing crescent just big enough to help her differentiate between the tree line and the sky. No lights shone in those woods—but of course they wouldn't, the trees were too thick. Lights from the Brody house had never been visible when she was young, either.

What if I went back over there now?

It was late, so surely Mick wouldn't be out walking like last time. In fact, he was probably asleep. He'd never know she was there.

And, well, even if he did see her, weren't they . . . friendly enough now that it would be okay? Surely he trusted her now; surely he knew she meant him no harm. And she truly didn't. She was still concerned over what he was hiding, but she had no intention of announcing his whereabouts. Hadn't she proven that by not telling her dad about him—or anyone else, except for Sue Ann. And she still didn't think Sue Ann counted.

She bit her lip, remembering how he'd felt moving inside her, groaning his pleasure. How could a guy question her loyalty after she'd done *that* with him?

Of course, he'd questioned it after the first time she'd done it with him, too, but hadn't things changed after the other night? She'd taught him to dance. He'd kissed her so tenderly. He remembered her cat, for heaven's sake.

All tiny things, but didn't they add up to something?

And damn it, she just wanted to look at the stars. She just wanted to—*finally*—feel that sense of peace and acceptance that only the night sky gave her. That sense that there was something so much greater, grander out there than her or her problems.

Surely Mick wouldn't mind anymore.

Surely.

And with that thought in mind, Jenny went back inside, put on a pair of jeans and tennis shoes, packed up her equipment, and headed for the canoe.

The sky is like water—on this side, the bright, familiar world; on the other, the mysterious depths. Look through the sky, and into the starry depths, and you'll find more out there than anyone has imagined, or *can* imagine.

Timothy Ferris

Seven

As Jenny paddled quietly across the lake, even more serene this late at night, she asked herself an obvious question. *Why is this so important to me that I'm risking his wrath again?*

Then she leaned her head back and took in the expanse of stars above, like a blanket of diamonds lighting her way, and knew the answer. *It's all I have left that's completely mine right now.* There was no more husband, no more home. There was no more job or students or classes. There was her father, and Sue Ann, of course— but they had fully developed lives here already, jobs to go to, places they needed to be. And sure, she'd started to rekindle a friendship with Tessa and Amy, but not well enough yet that she felt really close to them again. So despite an existence here that was slowly growing a bit richer as time began to pass, she still felt adrift in many ways.

Which had been bad enough before Mick Brody had entered the picture—and now, added to all the other uncertainty in her life, she found herself having crazy, wild sex with a man she didn't know, and worse, a man who had something to hide.

So she needed—desperately—to find something to grab hold of right now that would make her feel solid, grounded, like everything was okay, like the world would keep spinning.

And as the canoe slid up onto the small stretch of sand at the foot of the trail to the rocks, she felt calm, sure, like she was right where she needed to be in this moment—and, well, if Mick caught her here tonight, he'd just have to understand.

Yet as she began trudging up the hill, waterproof bag in hand, her heart beat too hard, and she felt thankful that darkness had brought with it the loud trill of crickets and other night sounds in the woods—to hide the noise of her steps through the brush and old leaves.

A long glance over to her left revealed no lights on in the Brody cabin tonight—thank goodness—and actually no sign of any cabin at all through the heavy blackness created by the tree cover. *I'm alone here. It's all right.*

Despite her assurances to herself, though, reaching the outcropping of boulders felt like having survived a gauntlet. Relief flooded her when she stopped in her tracks and realized that, indeed, the only sounds belonged to crickets and tree frogs.

The next two hours were wonderful. The night was clear as could be, and to see the sky without the "fog" created by city lights was simply . . . amazing. With each new object she studied in the sky, she felt a little more at peace, a little more relaxed.

She hadn't seen Saturn's rings so clearly since her girlhood. She stared in wonder, studying the planet at 200x magnification, thinking about the 746 million miles that separated her from it. Like always, the very thought dwindled her troubles to a size so small they couldn't be measured.

Ready to look deeper into space, she changed her lenses and filters and soon found the Ring Nebula. Most people described it as looking like a sugar donut, but Jenny had always seen more of a tilted halo hanging in the sky, perhaps forgotten by an angel who would come back to get it soon.

A few nebulae later, Jenny felt like she suspected most people did after getting a massage. She hadn't been this relaxed in months. And part of her was tempted to stay—to keep looking at the sky all night long while she had the chance. Although Mick had agreed to let her show him the sky, she had no idea if that would really happen. Yet she'd grown tired— it was the middle of the night now—so she simply rolled over on her back on the flat boulder where she sat and studied the Milky Way with her naked eye for a last few minutes, flowing like a wild river of stars above her.

By the time she headed back through the woods toward the lake, she felt almost carefree. She *so* hoped Mick would let her show him the stars. She wasn't sure why exactly, since she usually preferred solitary star-gazing, but somehow she wanted him to see what *she* saw up there—the vastness, the majesty of something so immense and inexplicable. Maybe she thought if Mick could appreciate the sky the same way she did that it would . . . give them something in common. Besides sex. Not that sex was a bad thing to have in common. She just needed . . . more. Even from Mick Brody, even if it was only about pleasure, she needed a little bit more of a solid connection with someone she was sleeping with.

At just that moment, her eyes were drawn to her right, and she immediately knew why—a light had just come on in the cabin.

It wasn't much larger than a candle's flame at this distance, but she stopped in place as soon as she saw it, not wanting to lose sight of it through the trees. Her heart beat faster not with fear now, but with . . . rank curiosity.

What the hell could be going on in that house?

Jenny took a deep breath and told herself to just keep walking. It didn't matter what was going on—it was none of her business.

Except that maybe it was.

If she was keeping his secret . . . wasn't she entitled to know what the secret *was*?

And she so fervently yearned for that connection-that-went-beyond-sex now. The more she thought about it, the more she knew to the marrow of her bones that she just wasn't a woman cut out for casual sex. His memories, their dance, had shown her just enough of Mick Brody to leave her *certain* there was more to him than the gruff guy she'd met in the woods. And having him *inside* her had made her *need* to know more of him, need to dig deeper, to understand what made him tick.

Whatever's in that cabin makes him tick.

And that light in the window, that tiny, burning light in the night, was drawing her like a proverbial moth to a flame.

You're crazy, she told herself as she took the first tentative steps in that direction. *You're out of your freaking mind.*

Yet the cacophony of insects around her made her feel safe—undetected and silent—as she walked, drawing slowly nearer. And as the light in the window got bigger, brighter, it seemed to beckon her. All she wanted was one tiny peek inside. To see what he was hiding. Was it drugs? Or maybe guns?

If either of those was the answer, she'd know to run, run, run as far away from him in the other direction as she could. She'd know she couldn't let him seduce her again—no matter what. And . . . maybe she'd even have to tell her dad. Because drugs and guns were serious business.

And she didn't want to see those things when she looked inside his house, but maybe that's why she felt she *had* to look, why she suddenly couldn't be this close and *not* look—because she longed to see . . . something wholly innocent there. Or nothing at all.

Of course, seeing something innocent seemed unlikely at this point, and seeing nothing at all would only mean that whatever he was hiding wasn't in plain view; it wouldn't exonerate him. But at least she'd have one more piece of the puzzle. And given that the light had just come on and that it had to be at least 2:00 A.M., she knew in her heart that she wouldn't see nothing. *Something* was going on in that house right now and she was about to find out what.

As she crept silently into the small clearing that surrounded the cabin, though, her blood ran cold. What would Mick do if he caught her out here?

Well, that probably depended upon what exactly he was hiding.

Now would be a smart time to turn around and leave. And yet, she'd come too close now—she had to look.

So with trembling breath that she tried to hold inside, Jenny bit her lip and took careful, quiet steps toward the run-down cabin. She watched her feet in the light now illuminating the area from inside to make sure she didn't trip over anything. As she got closer, her heart rose to her throat.

The first window she reached was filled with a big, square electric fan, the blades turning, humming—but a few feet away stood an old screen door, the inside door wide open. Sweat seeped from her pores—from the heat, and from fear. But she had to look, so she stepped up near the door and leaned to peek cautiously inside.

What she saw made her jaw drop and she completely forgot to try to hide herself.

Mick sat next to a bed, shirtless and beautiful in the heat—but that wasn't what took Jenny's breath away. In the bed lay a man with Mick's general coloring and features, also shirtless, but he was gaunt, hollow-looking. A small, scraggly beard adorned his face and varied tattoos ran up and down his arms. She knew this had to be Wayne Brody—except that he was in prison. Wasn't he?

She also knew instantly why he was there, what was wrong with him. He looked pale, drawn, smaller than he had as a young man. He looked just like her mother had lying in that bed upstairs. He was dying.

Mick leaned over his brother and said softly, "Doing better now? Getting better?" He spoke gently, but his eyes looked strained.

The man in the bed gave a slight nod, but looked too exhausted to answer as he managed, "Just tired."

"Go to sleep," Mick said. "Get some rest."

The sight made Jenny want to collapse. Or run. She wished she *hadn't* seen, *didn't* know. This was too awful, in too many ways to even sort out at the moment.

Just then, Mick raised his eyes, in her direction.

She sucked in her breath and turned her body quickly away from the door, placing her back against the cabin's outer wall. Damn it, had he seen her?

But when nothing happened, she began to breathe easier. She stood there feeling the weight of the telescope in her hand—heavy now after carrying it for so long—and wondering when it would be safe to move.

That's when a large shadow came out of the darkness on the other side of her and two large hands pinned her shoulders to the wall, hard.

Her breath flew out of her in a gasp and the handle of the waterproof bag slipped from her grip to hit the ground below. She met Mick's eyes in the dark, although he looked surprised to see her, like maybe he'd been expecting someone else.

Not that it lessened his anger any. *"What the hell do you think you're doing?"*

Her words felt strangled; she could barely get them out. "I'm sorry. I just . . ." *Just what?*

He lowered his voice, but still managed to growl at her, his expression no less than ferocious. *"Doesn't matter—whatever the answer is, it's not good enough."* Then he locked his fist around one of her wrists and pulled her away from the house, across the small clearing and into the woods, toward the lake. Her heart pounded so hard it hurt and she could barely breathe. Where was he taking her? What on earth was he going to do to her now? The power of his anger echoed through his grip, through the very way he moved, and she felt like a rag doll being dragged along behind him.

Oh God, oh God, what have I done? To him? And to me?

He finally stopped in another small clearing, a tiny bluff that provided a view of the lake—she caught sight of a thin strip of moonlight glancing across the surface, and of a few porch lights across the water, one of them her own.

When he turned to her, even in the dark she could see his expression—he looked like she'd just slapped him, and a hard pit of guilt gathered in her stomach. Not that she was sure she was the one doing something wrong here. She wasn't sure of anything at the moment.

"Sit down," he said.

She did, surprised to find a soft blanket of green grass beneath her—this must be the one spot on the whole Brody property, besides the rocks, where the sun hit the ground.

Mick sat next to her but didn't look at her—he *couldn't* right now. Instead, he let his gaze fall vacantly over the lake. Only, in his mind, he still saw what *she'd* just seen. Wayne. Lying in a bed, fighting off pain.

How the hell did I end up in this god-awful situation?

"Go ahead," he snapped. "Ask me whatever it is you want to know, whatever was so damn important that you snuck up to my house in the middle of the night."

When she started to speak, she sounded a little frightened, and the part of him that needed to protect his brother was glad. "I . . . I just . . ."

Damn it, he never should have softened toward her, never should have been anything but a bastard. He should have *kept* her scared and she'd have never come back here.

"I just wanted to look at the stars," she finally spit out. "Like before."

He turned to glare at her. "Looks like you took a detour."

He heard her gulp, audibly. "I didn't . . . mean to."

"Bullshit," he bit off before she could go on.

"I just . . . saw the light. And you were so secretive,

you made such a big deal out of whatever you were hiding, that . . . I couldn't help myself."

"Well, now you know."

"Not exactly."

Yeah, he knew what she'd seen left a lot of question marks. That's why he'd told her to ask him whatever she wanted to know. Hell, at this point, why not just tell her and get it off his chest. "My brother is dying," he began gruffly, and he wanted to *continue* just as gruffly, but something about his own words took the steam out of his voice. He'd never said them out loud before.

So he went on more quietly, trying to think where to begin. "A couple of years ago, in prison, he was diagnosed with a brain tumor. He did chemo and went into remission. But then it came back, and it brought leukemia with it, and at that point they told him there wasn't any reason to treat it because there wasn't any hope."

Next to him, he sensed her swallowing nervously. "But . . . how did he get *here*?"

Somehow, the next part was even harder to say, because he knew what she'd think of him and his family. The same thing people *always* thought. "He . . . broke out, with some other guys he knew, and he came here to die. He called me and asked me to come here and help him. Die. So that's what I did. I gave up my job, pretty much gave up my life, to come back to this godforsaken place and help my brother die someplace other than a prison cell."

He stopped, looked at her, tried to read her face in the dark, but couldn't. So he decided he'd better keep talking, better get to the business of trying to convince the police chief's daughter that he wasn't actually doing anything wrong here. Unless you counted harboring a fugitive. And giving him the painkillers that Wayne had brought with him and that were surely stolen. *Shit, how had this happened?*

"I'm sure you think my whole family was trash, and you might even be right—but Wayne is my brother. The last family I have left and the only one of them I ever really gave a damn about. I don't want to be here, believe me. This is the hardest thing I've ever done. But my brother asked me. I couldn't say no."

Finally, next to him, she spoke, more quiet than usual. "I don't think you're trash, Mick."

Despite himself, despite how fucking *angry* he was with her right now, somehow the words sank down inside him and rested there, in a good place.

"Can I ask you a question?" she said.

He let out a sigh. "Hell, why not. You know all the important stuff now anyway."

"What was Wayne in prison for?"

Mick swallowed back his disgust over what Jenny would think. "Armed robbery."

He sensed her drawing in her breath. "What . . . did he rob?"

"The time he got caught, a quickie mart. And he would've been out by now, but he, uh, wasn't a model prisoner. He has a way of getting himself in trouble. Always has." He stared back out over the dark water below them, to the perfect cottages on the other side. He couldn't see them, but even now, in the dark, he could feel them—and feel how far away they were, how far away they'd *always* been.

"Were . . . *you* there? When he, um, got caught?"

She sounded nervous again, and the question burned in his chest. She might not think he was trash, but she also apparently knew the truth about him, a fact which stung. "No," he said softly, "or else I'd have probably gone to prison, too. But I'm getting pretty damn tired of keeping secrets, so you might as well know—I . . . I haven't exactly been an angel.

"The thing is, though," he went on, "the thing I want you to know about me is . . . Wayne going to prison changed my life, changed *me*. I . . . don't do those kinds of things anymore, Jenny. I haven't for a long time."

She stayed quiet too long, the silence wrenching his gut, before whispering, "Did you ever rob a liquor store in Crestview?"

His shoulders slumped forward in automatic response, and he pushed his hands back through his hair, unable to answer, hating his life. He knew the fact that he didn't tell her no right away pretty much said yes—but still, somehow, he couldn't spit it out. Finally, he asked her, "Does that make you afraid of me?"

"A little. All of this does."

His next words came out in a rush. "I'm different now, Jenny. I live in Cincinnati, and I work as a bricklayer and stonemason. I had a job there, a decent job contracting for a big homebuilder, and I had an apartment."

She turned to look at him in the dark. "Had?"

"I had to give that stuff up to come take care of Wayne. I had a little money saved—but not enough that I could pay my rent for a few months with no job. So I put my stuff in storage, drained my bank account, and came here, for now. I wish I was back there. I wish I wasn't waiting for my brother to die."

He felt more than saw her eyes on him, but was glad for the dark—glad it meant she couldn't see him very well, either. "How much . . . time does he have?"

Mick shrugged. "Another month or two, maybe three, according to the doctors he saw. Right now, he's mostly tired, but he can take care of himself, get up and out of bed and all that. Tonight," he stopped, sighed, remembering and feeling awful about it, "I forgot to give him his pain medication. So he woke up in pain. That's why we were up in the middle of the night. But usually, I'm able to keep him comfortable, and he mostly lies in bed and watches TV, or sleeps."

"Where did you get . . . pain medication?"

He drew in a breath. Despite how shaken she'd seemed initially, Little Miss Pussycat kept coming up with hard questions, sounding less and less afraid to ask them. "He brought 'em with him. I didn't ask where they came from. But he found out what he'd need, and he got it before he came here."

At least she sounded calmer now, more curious than freaked out. "So . . . what do you do with *your* time? When he's sleeping or watching TV."

He peered out over the lake. "I go out for the things we need—I drive over to Crestview to get groceries and do laundry to make sure no one recognizes me. I go fishing with an old rod and reel I found in the shed. I come across the lake and see you." *And I dig.* But she didn't need to know about that part. The uglier parts. That a man had to have a grave. And that a grave took a damn long time to dig.

"You've only come to see me twice. But you said it like it was a regular thing."

I think about you a lot. Our sex. Your face. While I give Wayne oxycodone and slap duragesic patches onto his skin to take away his pain, I use you to take away mine. "Guess it seemed like more," he murmured.

Beside him, she lay back in the grass and looked up at the sky, so he did, too. Damn, there were a lot of stars here—way more than in the city. He supposed he didn't see them much, living under the trees the way they did. He hadn't noticed them on the nights he'd crossed the lake to her, either, but he was noticing them now. "Tell me what's so special up there, pussycat," he requested quietly.

"The sun is one of literally trillions of stars," she began, "in the Milky Way galaxy. And the Milky Way is one of more than a billion galaxies. We are . . . so small, Mick, as to be almost non-existent."

He kept looking up, trying to wrap his mind around the scope of what she'd just relayed to him. "You say that like it's a good thing. To be non-existent."

"That's not how I mean it. I mean that, if we're that small, how big can our troubles really be?"

"Mine feel pretty damn big right now, honey."

"Look up for a while and think about everything else out there and maybe it won't feel that way so much."

He did. He tried. And he felt it. Just a little. Not a lot. His brother was still going to need another pill in the morning, and his seventy-two-hour patch with the fentanyl in it would need to be changed, too. And at some point soon, in a month, or two, the meds would quit working and things would get much worse. But thinking about all those stars, all those worlds out there, did take him away from it all, just for a few minutes, just like thinking about Jenny always did.

Only then, like a freight train, Mick's big problem came roaring back into his mind, nearly mowing him down, zapping his strength. Jenny knew about Wayne now. *Jenny knew about Wayne.*

And maybe when he'd asked her to keep his presence a secret it had been easy for her because she hadn't known why. But now she did—now she knew he was breaking the law, hiding an escaped convict, for God's sake.

Could she keep *that* a secret? From her *father*? Would she?

Everything depended on it. Wayne's death. And Mick's life—his freedom.

Fear and fury gathered inside him and, without warning, without planning, he rolled toward her until he was on top of her, clamping his hands around her arms as he brought his face down close to hers. *"You can't turn me in, Jenny! Tell me you won't, damn it. Promise me."* The words came out harsh, hard, angry—he felt them in his chest, pounding there. *"Damn it, tell me!"*

That was when he saw one glistening tear slip from her eye. That was when he saw the look on her face. Oh God, he'd just scared the shit out of her.

And he should have *wanted* that—God knew that had been his goal in the beginning, that night in the woods. And from a practical standpoint, it was a damn smart goal.

But a bigger part of him hated himself for this, for what this situation made of him, for letting it take him back too close to his old life, back when all he'd wanted was to please his big brother, no matter what it took. He hated making Jenny Tolliver cry.

And so he released her arms from his grip and moved his hands gently to her face, pushing her hair back off her forehead, stroking her cheek. "I'm sorry, pussycat," he whispered. "I didn't mean to scare you. Please don't cry. I'm just . . . really fucking afraid here, you know?"

Beneath him, he felt her nod, and he used his thumb to wipe away that lingering tear on her cheek.

She moved to sit up, so he helped her, kept his arm around her afterward, wanted to make her feel better—somehow.

"I won't tell, Mick," she said, her voice soft as the dark night. "I promise."

"Really, pussycat?"

She nodded.

But it wasn't enough. "Because I know you're tight with your dad, and I know it might be tempting . . ."

She let out a heavy breath, yet shook her head. "I won't tell."

"Why?" he whispered.

"Because I don't want you to get in trouble."

"Thank you," he said, then leaned his forehead over to touch hers.

A few minutes later, Mick walked her down to the canoe. And he believed her, he really did—but it was still hard to let her go paddling back across that lake. He believed her, but he hardly knew her, and now he had to trust that she was as good and kind as she seemed most of the time. Damn, she was a nosy little thing—yet kind at heart, he reminded himself. He was depending on that kindness.

"Goodbye, pussycat," he said, low and soft.

"Bye," she murmured, but as she turned toward the canoe, Mick's instincts made him grab on to her hand.

"Wait."

"What?"

"Come here," he breathed, and pulled her to him, close, tight. He hadn't planned it, but he wasn't quite ready to go back to that stuffy cabin where death was coming. "I just . . . need to hold you a minute. That makes it better."

Her arms had closed around his waist now, yet she pulled back slightly to peer up at him. "Makes what better?"

"Everything, honey. Everything."

He never meant to kiss her, either, but before he knew it, his mouth was on hers, and her lips were so soft—*everything* on her was soft. He went hard in the space of a heartbeat as she kissed him back, kissed him back even now, even knowing his darkest secrets—and *that* made him kiss her even more hungrily.

Oh God, he needed her—*bad*. He hated admitting that to himself, but he knew it—he needed her now, to take all the rotten stuff away.

Shit, he'd let that happen too fast, *way* too fast—he

wasn't a guy who got attached to women often—but this was different. This was about slaking the pain, about finding a way to feel good when everything around him was bad. And Jenny made him feel *damn* good.

Her hands were in his hair, his on her sweet, round ass. He got lost in the kissing and touching, and soon couldn't keep from moving, driving himself against her through their clothes. Her breath grew ragged, which he loved. It excited him to make a girl like her lose control.

But when he reached for the button on her blue jeans, he realized—oh God, oh shit—he was trembling. What the hell? His hands shook, and inside . . . inside he suddenly needed to be with her so bad he could barely get her out of her clothes. God, what was happening?

He didn't know, but he quit thinking and pressed on, urgently now, unzipping her pants, tugging to get them down. She reached for his, too, and they worked feverishly. And despite how much he'd loved her breasts that last time they'd been together, he didn't bother removing her tank top—by the time both their pants were lowered, he couldn't wait another second.

He moved behind her, instinctively needing her in a whole new, rough way. He used his hands to press hers to the rough bark of the nearest tree. Then he closed one palm over her hip and wrapped his other arm full around her waist, and plunged inside her.

Oh God—yeah.

They both cried out at the firm, deep entry, and all he wanted to do was fill her, fill her, fill her, over and over. He still quivered a little, but nothing mattered in this moment but thrusting into her sweet wet warmth, again, again.

He soon let the arm that supported her dip between her thighs, let his fingers sink into her slick folds to stroke the little nub there, swollen beneath his touch. When she began to move more rhythmically, he knew he was hitting the right spot.

Sweat rolled down his temples, his chest, and he felt it gluing their bodies together below, too. The dark water looked like black glass beside them, reminding him how alone they were here. Turned out there were one or two things this godforsaken land was good for, and just now, he was *glad* the other side of that lake was so damn far away.

"I want to make you come, pussycat," he murmured in her ear. He wanted to feel her convulse against him, wanted to hear her sobs of pleasure. In front of him, her breath grew labored, rough, beautiful. She moved more intently against his hand, saturating his fingertips with moisture.

Come, he willed her, *come for me.* He'd always enjoyed bringing women pleasure during sex, but with Jenny, it was different. It was as if . . . making her come made him worthy. And despite himself, he wanted that, he wanted to be worthy of Jenny Tolliver.

"Come, baby," he whispered in her ear. "Come hard, just for me."

"Close," she breathed, the word barely audible. "So close."

And then her body jolted in front of him, and she let out a hot little cry, and she moved against his hand harder for a few amazing seconds, whimpering her pleasure. And she started to go still after that, limp, clearly weak, but he couldn't let her. He anchored his arm back around her to keep her upright, and as blood gathered below and heat shot through his veins, he said, "Damn, honey, I'm coming, too."

His head fell back, his eyes shut, as he drove into her welcoming body, groaning his release again, again, again. He kept plunging inside her, to the very last, grabbing on to every ounce of pleasure he could take—because he needed it so bad.

He could never let her know that, of course, how bad he needed what she gave him. And now that the waves of orgasm were passing and sanity was returning, he knew he'd come too close to that tonight already, too close to letting her see the power she suddenly held over him. He didn't want to scare her anymore, but he also didn't want to appear weak. To her, or to himself. He'd had a few moments of weakness with her here tonight, but he needed to be strong for Wayne, strong for what was coming. So he said nothing when it was over, simply pulled out of her and tried to forget that the girl had actually made him tremble in her arms.

It was as they both drew their blue jeans back up that she said, "We didn't use a condom again."

He let his head drop back, releasing a huge sigh. "*Shit.* I wasn't expecting to find—"

"I know," she cut him off. "A girl sneaking around your house in the middle of the night."

"That about sums it up. Sorry, pussycat."

"Well, it takes . . . two to tango, as they say."

She stood before him, biting her lip, looking innocent and wild all at once. And he wanted to kiss her some more, but decided it would be a bad idea. So instead he just said, " 'Night, honey."

"Goodnight."

Be careful on the lake. He wanted to tell her that, too, but held it in. It was too much, too much like caring.

Yet she'd never know if he stood on the shore, watching the dark shadow of her canoe glide across the lake's surface, creating the tiniest of wakes in the moonlight, until she'd reached the other side. And that was exactly what he did.

We're going to the moon because it's in the nature of the human being to face challenges. It's by the nature of his deep inner soul . . . we're required to do these things just as salmon swim upstream.

Neil Armstrong

Eight

I've lost my telescope again." It was an embarrassing admission, all things considered, but at the moment it didn't seem as important to Jenny as it had the first time.

"What?" Sue Ann gasped, turning to face her. "Where?" They sat side by side atop a picnic table in Creekside Park, watching Sophie play on the swings.

"Outside the Brody cabin."

Sue Ann blinked. "Outside the *what*?"

Jenny gave her only a short, sheepish glance. "You heard me."

"Well, I hope you're not planning to drag me back over there with you to get it this time."

Something inside Jenny felt somber, sad. She just

kept watching Sophie's swing glide back and forth as she said, "I don't think that'll be necessary. I'm pretty sure he'll bring it back to me again. Because I'm pretty sure he's going to feel the need to check up on me again."

Clearly, Sue Ann began to comprehend the enormity of the situation, since her voice dropped an octave and she grew more somber herself. "I guess this means you know what he's hiding now."

She nodded succinctly. "Yep."

"Well?"

Of course, Sue Ann expected to be told. And it was the first time in her life that Jenny had seriously considered keeping something from her best friend. In the end, though, she'd decided, just like the whole *first* Mick Brody incident, that she *had* to tell her. They were practically sisters. How could she not?

Before she spilled the beans, though, she turned to Sue Ann and took both her hands, because this wasn't just any secret—this wasn't just sex in the woods. "This is some serious shit, Sue Ann, so you have to swear you will not breathe a word of this, and if you think you can't make that promise, tell me now. I mean it."

Sue Ann looked appropriately worried, even gulping, and took a minute to think. Finally, she bit her lip and said, "Okay, I promise. I swear."

Jenny let out a deep breath—one that it felt like she'd been holding all night since leaving Mick on the southern shore of the lake—and told Sue Ann about Wayne. It had been eating her up since she'd found out, and she'd never felt so caught between a rock and a hard place in her life.

Thankfully, they were in a quiet area of the large park, so at least she could talk with Sue Ann without worry they'd be overheard. She concluded with, "So, as you can see, this is freaking *serious*. There is an *escaped convict* across the lake from me, and Mick is *harboring* him. It's so illegal that I can barely fathom it. And now I *know about it*, Sue Ann—I *know about it*." Then she gasped. "Does this make me an accessory?"

Next to her, Sue Ann looked understandably horrified. "Now I'm kinda sorry you told me."

Uh-oh. "Why?"

"Because maybe now I'm an accessory to the accessory."

Jenny winced. "Oh damn, sorry—I didn't think of that."

Just then, Sophie stopped her swing, digging small tennis shoes into the sand beneath it, and yelled over to Sue Ann. "I'm going to the castle," she said, pointing. Apparently, this was what Sophie called the big plastic apparatus just beyond the swings consisting of numerous tunnels, ladders, and slides.

"All right, honey. Be careful," Sue Ann called, then turned back to Jenny, lowering her voice. "And that goes for you, too. Be careful with this, Jen."

Jenny bit her lip. She'd been turning it over and over in her head. "How do I not tell my father? I mean, he would be *so* deeply disappointed in me if he knew I was keeping something like this from him."

Sue Ann watched Sophie climb up a ladder, then disappear into a small towerlike structure, and Jenny could almost feel her friend's maternal instincts kicking into high gear. "Maybe you *should* tell him, Jen," she said, turning back to face her and looking much more serious than usual. "I mean, he's a freaking *escaped convict*."

"Who's not hurting anybody," Jenny couldn't help pointing out. "He's just . . . dying here."

"That doesn't make breaking out of prison any less against the law. This is . . . big, Jen. Like you said, serious shit. And your father *is* the chief of police. I think that really obligates you to tell him."

Jenny let out a huge, draining sigh. "I know. That's what's killing me. It was one thing to keep quiet when I didn't know Mick's secret, but now that I know, it feels like I'm . . . breaking a sacred trust not to tell my dad."

"That seals it then. If it feels wrong not to tell him, then you should tell him."

"Yet in another way, it feels just as wrong *to* tell him. I mean, all my life, I've had a pretty clear understanding of right and wrong—my parents made sure of that. But this, Sue Ann, this straddles the line for me. And . . . this isn't just about Wayne. If I tell, Mick might go to jail, too."

"Well, *yeah*," Sue Ann said, eyes wide. "He's harboring a *fugitive!*"

Despite Sue Ann's theatrics, Jenny only swallowed, trying to get rid of the lump in her throat. "Wayne didn't look much like a fugitive lying in that bed."

Sue Ann sighed in return, as if seeing Jenny's point, but then she simply shook her head. "This is bad, Jenny—really bad. I don't like it. I don't like you being in the middle of this."

She tried to play it off a little. "Well, I don't know if I'm in the *middle*, exactly. Just sort of . . . on the side."

"Still, this is your *dad* you're not telling. Your *father.* If he knew you were hanging out with someone who's harboring a fugitive, he'd have a heart attack. And if he knew you were having sex with the guy . . . *and* protecting him from the law . . . *oh my God.* You really *have* to tell."

Yeah, she knew that. She'd already told herself the same thing. "Except that . . . I can't see what good it serves. And . . . then there's Mick."

"Who is sounding like a very scary guy the more I

hear about him. He robbed a liquor store, for God's sake."

"A long time ago. And he's changed since then."

Sue Ann's eyes flew wide once more. "Would you listen to yourself! Justifying it!"

Wow. At that moment, Jenny suddenly realized how awful it all sounded, like she was some dumb, enabling sort of woman—but for some reason, after last night, she really believed Mick, deep down inside. She really believed he wasn't that guy anymore. "I just . . . don't want to get him in trouble," she tried to explain.

"Why?"

Good question. "Well, we . . . have sex. We . . . had sex *last night.*"

Sue Ann's jaw dropped. "You know, I keep thinking I'm going to quit being surprised, but congratulations, you got me again. You had sex with him *after* the whole Wayne thing?"

Another sigh left her. "Guilty as charged, officer."

"Um, outside again?"

It was almost a relief to get Sue Ann on a topic that held more prurient interest for her. "You got it. Standing up. Against a tree."

"Holy God," Sue Anne breathed.

"I really didn't mean to. I know it was a bad idea under the circumstances, but when he starts kissing me and touching me, Sue Ann, what can I say—I turn to putty in his hands. Complete putty! And you should also probably know—" She stopped, swallowed. Crap. "There was no condom."

Sue Ann slapped her hand against her forehead. "All right, that's it. I'm driving you to Crestview myself tomorrow to get that damn test."

"Fine, you're right, I'll go—I know I need to do that." *Since I still really don't know him very well, after all.* But she kept that part inside, given that she felt more on the defensive with Sue Ann here than she ever had in all their years of friendship. They were usually like-minded on important things, but maybe it was hard to make *anyone* understand who hadn't seen the expression on Mick's face last night.

"So, wanting to protect him," Sue Ann began, her voice a little softer. "Is this about sex, or is it about . . . something more with Mick?"

Jenny took a deep breath, trying to think through her reasoning. "I just . . . hate that he's going through this."

"He chose to."

"He felt he couldn't say no," Jenny countered. "He loves his brother. If you could have seen the pain in his eyes, Sue Ann . . ."

But Sue Ann was having none of it. "They're criminals, Jenny. *Crim-i-nals*. They break laws. They're bad dudes, scary guys. You can't go on like this, having sex with him, and protecting him."

"You thought it was fine a few days ago. You said good sex was worth a lot."

"Well, that was before I knew for sure he was breaking a law. Before, it was all . . . mysterious and sexy. Now, it's just . . . illegal."

"You can't tell anyone," Jenny felt the need to remind her, then let out a sigh. "I'm really starting to think I shouldn't have told you."

Then Sue Ann looked wounded. "I'm just scared for you, Jen. You're my best friend."

"I know. I'm sorry. I'm a little stressed-out right now."

"So what are you going to do about this?"

"I don't know. Think, I guess. And try to figure it out."

Sue Ann took back on a scolding look. "And in the meantime, wait for him and his penis to return your telescope? I sure hope that penis is worth it, Jen."

But Jenny didn't answer. How could she make Sue

Ann understand that it wasn't just the penis—it was the whole darn scary guy. The truth was, despite believing all he'd told her, she did remain a little afraid of him—maybe more now than she'd been yesterday.

Yet the *really* scary thing here was that she wanted him more than she feared him.

Jenny poured iced tea into two glasses on the picnic table in the backyard, the scent of the pork chops her father grilled nearby making her hungry. Other than the heat, which seemed to grow worse every day, it was a lovely evening—birds chirped, flowers bloomed, and butterflies fluttered their way across the expanse of lawn that stretched between her place and Miss Ellie's. It could have been a scene from *Snow White*. A shame her hands were shaking when she poured the tea.

"D'you hear about the big housing development going in on the old Ashcraft farm?" her dad asked, spatula in hand, eyes on the grill.

Jenny sat down at the picnic table, trying to calm herself. *Relax. It's not really a lie unless he asks you a question and you don't tell the truth, right?* "Um, no, Dad, I didn't." Then suddenly focusing on what he'd said, she felt confused. "A housing development? Here?" Things like that didn't happen in Destiny.

"Yep, sure enough. And even though it's not right in town, or near the lake here, sure is apt to change things a lot."

Oh, of course it was still a lie. Everyone knew lies of omission were just as bad—sometimes worse—than regular lies. But stop this! Focus on the conversation. "So who are they building these houses *for*?" Destiny's population had held almost steady her whole life, and the only new housing had been three or four homes built by individual families and a nice apartment building near the railroad tracks that ran parallel to Main Street.

Her father looked just as baffled. "Who knows? But according to Johnny Fulks, the developer thinks folks'll buy, and the town council thinks it'll draw new business." Johnny Fulks had been the head of the Destiny Town Council for twenty years.

Jenny tried to wrap her mind around that, but it was difficult since her mind remained wrapped around Mick Brody's secret and how awful she felt not telling her dad.

"Hard to imagine that much change comin' to town," her father said. "Not sure I care for it much."

She nodded, looked down at the wood grain in the table, and wished she didn't know Wayne Brody was lying across the lake waiting to die right now.

"But I reckon you can't stop such a thing," he went on. "Towns change. They sort of . . . grow up, I guess. I just thought that sort of change had passed Destiny by, and I liked it fine."

She barely heard him. *Don't feel so guilty. You're doing what you think is right, aren't you?* The fact was, from the moment Mick had told her, she'd known she couldn't rat him out. She knew she couldn't make a man's death harder than it already was.

But she'd never kept anything of any magnitude from her father—ever. He was a good man, and she'd always felt comfortable telling him things going on in her life. Even when she'd had to suffer the shame and embarrassment of Terrence cheating on her—although she'd first called Sue Ann, she'd phoned her dad right after. Now Mick Brody had her keeping all *sorts* of secrets from her dad. Secrets about what she did at night. Secrets about who she was seeing. Secrets about *escaped convicts*, for heaven's sake.

Just then, she looked up to see her dad arriving at the table with a platter of pork chops and ears of corn that had come straight from his friend Ed's corn patch. He lowered it onto the table next to the baked beans she'd whipped up and took a seat. "Honey, are you feeling okay? Is something wrong?"

She swallowed nervously. Oh crap, she'd let her worries show. "I'm fine, Dad."

He looked unconvinced, his mustache twitching uncertainly. "Are you thinking about Terrence—is that it?"

"Um . . ."

"You can tell me—it's only natural he'd still be on your mind."

She hated to give Terrence the Rat Bastard credit for her mood, but it was a good excuse. "All right then, yeah—I guess I'm thinking about Terrence." *Oh hell, another lie.* This one straight out and verbal. It hurt. To lie to her dad. But she could see no other way.

"Well, I can't pretend to know how you feel, but my only advice is that you gotta keep busy and think toward the future. What'd you do today?"

Went to Crestview with Sue Ann and took an HIV test. Which had come back blessedly negative, hallelujah. "Sue Ann and I . . . hung out a while." *Good, not a lie. Well, except by omission.* She was still trying to make herself believe those didn't count.

Her father smiled. Poor guy, if he only knew. "It's nice, you girls getting to spend so much time together again."

She couldn't argue that—it really was. Without Sue Ann, she wasn't sure how she'd be getting through this. And thankfully, Sue Ann had been more relaxed and fun today, in spite of why they were driving to Crestview, and she'd even made a point of digging for more dirt about sex with Mick.

"What else ya been up to?" her dad asked as he forked a chop onto her plate, then another onto his.

She could only sigh. *Having sex with Mick Brody. Find-*

ing out his escaped convict brother is living right across the lake from us. Or . . . would that be dying right across the lake? "Um, well . . . I've been doing some reading. And I tidied up that old perennial bed on the side of the house. The dianthus will have more room to spread, and I bet the gladiolus will come up better next year."

Her dad nodded, smiled some more. She tried to focus on peeling back the husk on her corn and running a small slab of butter over it. "Things are lookin' real nice in the yard," he said. "I meant to comment. I noticed you've been doin' some work on the place."

"Well, Mom always did like a nice yard." *Mom? What the heck was she doing bringing up Mom?* That was her *dad's* department, and she was usually the one trying to lead him down a different path. Of course, maybe it was that nearly large-as-life reminder in the living room, looking down on her day and night. It made her feel stuck somewhere between the ages of five and thirty-one at any given moment, on an unpredictable sliding scale. "And I figured it would help you out," she added, not wanting to get *stuck* on the subject of Mom.

"Well, only if you want to. You know I generally hire Adam Becker's landscaping outfit to do the upkeep on the place in summer. Just haven't called 'em lately since we haven't had enough rain to make the grass grow—no need to mow."

She smiled. "They can mow, whenever it rains—I'll do the flowers."

He grinned in return. "Sounds like a fair deal." Then he raised his eyebrows. "Have you seen Adam since you've been back in town?"

Adam, the boy who stood next to her wearing a crown in that picture on the living room wall. "No, can't say that I have. He's married now, right?"

"Recently got divorced," her dad replied matter-of-factly. Hmm, maybe divorce wasn't quite the dirty word in Destiny that she'd feared. "Real shame, too, cause him and Sheila have the cutest little twin boys, and I hear it's been rough on 'em."

"That *is* a shame."

"Maybe you oughta . . . call him up or somethin'. Just for old times' sake."

She smiled knowingly. "Dad, it's too soon. Probably for him, too." *And besides, I'm having heated sex with Mick Brody in the woods. And in your house.*

Her father shrugged. "Figured it was worth a try. And he's a decent enough fella, in case you change your mind."

She got back to eating. There for a minute, she'd had Mick off her mind—but now he was back, and she was feeling guilty again.

"By the way," her dad said, "Stan Goodman from the school board stopped by the department the other day. He heard you were in town and wanted to know if it was true."

Okay, now she stopped eating, corncob balanced between her fingertips. "Uh . . . *why*?" She knew Stan Goodman, had all her life, but not in any close way.

"There's a teaching job open at the high school. In the science department. One of the teachers had a baby and decided not to come back. Stan wondered if you'd be interested."

Her first thought? No way. She hadn't come home to *stay* home—she'd just come back to figure out her next move. She had no intention of settling here.

But she bit her tongue, flattered that they would seek her out. And she did need a job.

And she could see the stars here a lot better than in Columbus.

Well, *sometimes.* At least when she had the Brody property at her disposal.

Oh hell, she clearly couldn't think straight about a job right now. So she said the only sensible thing. "I'll . . . keep it in mind, Dad. I, uh, don't know if I want to make a decision this fast."

"Well, fall's right around the corner—but you take your time. I know all this change hasn't been easy on you."

Yeah, she'd thought the divorce and quitting her job and leaving her house had been hard—she'd had no idea what other bizarre ways her life would change by coming home. A vision of her and Mick, beneath the stars, moving together like animals, filled her head. Then came another much *worse* vision, one that seemed to be haunting her the past couple of days—Wayne Brody in that bed. She closed her eyes to shut it out.

"What's wrong, honey? You okay?"

Damn it, snap out of it already. Get hold of yourself. "I think it's just the heat getting to me—giving me a headache is all. Nothing to worry about."

Her father reached out to touch her hand. "You sure? You'd tell me if it was something worse than that?"

Oh God, he was concerned about her health. Because she was *lying*, making stuff up to protect herself. *And* her lover. *Oh Lord, she had a lover. A law-breaking one.* She couldn't quite stop being shocked over it, no matter how much she thought about it.

She took a deep breath, reminded herself to be cool. "I'm fine, Dad, I promise. It's just . . . the stress of it all getting to me, I guess."

"Well, you're home now," he said, patting her hand across the table. "Safe at home where nothing can hurt you anymore."

Oh Dad, if you only knew.

Later that night, Jenny stood in the living room, staring at the shrine to her mother. And even as guilt ate at her, she walked slowly to the wall, closed her hands around the edges of the large frame, and carefully lifted the picture from the screws it hung upon. Carrying it to the steps, she maneuvered it upstairs and into the spare bedroom which had once been hers—she'd been sleeping in her parents' old room since coming home because it looked the least like it had when she was a girl.

Walking back down the steps, she couldn't deny that the wall looked positively empty—a big, blank space staring at her, a tidy square of blue paint, darker than the rest of the room—but she wasn't going to be deterred. If she wanted to take a picture down, she could. If she wanted to keep something from her father, she could. She was an adult and had a right to make her own decisions.

Even if they hurt someone? she asked inside as she carefully gathered the smaller pictures below in her arms, one by one. Taking the pictures down *was* going to hurt her dad whenever he noticed it. And the fact that she was keeping Mick's secret would probably kill her father if he ever found out.

But she had to do these things, both of them. Because her heart and her gut told her they were right. And that was all she had to rely on right now. And getting tougher about it—not getting sad or distraught-looking every time she saw her dad—would be necessary. This was the first step toward feeling like the thirty-one-year-old woman she was, not the little girl who had once lived here.

After stowing the rest of the shrine upstairs in her old room, she went into her parents' room—no, *her* new bedroom—and with much pushing and pulling and grunting, rearranged the furniture. She put the bed against a different wall, trading spots with the chest of drawers. Then she tossed a sheer, colored scarf over the lampshade. Tomorrow she would buy a new comforter for the bed, and maybe some new curtains, too. Even if she was only here for the summer, she needed to make this place her own. She had to. Or she would drown here.

She felt much stronger by the time she went back downstairs. The only way to deal with the things happening to her right now, she'd suddenly realized, was to take control. She'd taken control when Terrence had cheated on her. Yet, somehow, coming here had made her weak. But no more. She couldn't *afford* to be weak. Not with her dad. And not with Mick, either. She'd had enough of being "good Jenny" lately.

Later, she sat on the couch with the radio on, looking through her coffee table book of photos from the Hubble telescope when a knock came on the back door. Mick. She knew it.

Setting the book down, she didn't hesitate to go answer, pulling the door open wide.

And still the sight of him caught her off guard. Because he looked so sweaty good in a dark tee and blue jeans, a lock of hair dipping down onto his forehead. "Hey," he said, but his eyes said more. Things like *I want you*. And *Can I trust you?*

She bit her lip, mainly wrapped up in the *I want you* part. "Hey."

"You forgot this again." He held up the waterproof bag holding her telescope case.

"Not exactly forgot," she pointed out, taking it from him and lowering it to the kitchen table. "More like figured you'd kill me if I went back up the hill for it."

"Good," he said gruffly, but then his tone—and expression—changed, softened. "So, pussycat, are we still cool? About what you know?"

"Yes," she said, but she was going to be totally honest about it, come what may. "Although it's hard for me not to tell my father. In fact, it's sort of feeling like . . . the worst thing I've ever done."

He tilted his head, his eyes looking unusually blue, and lowered his chin. "Maybe it's the *best* thing you've ever done."

"Yeah," she answered quietly. "I'm a little confused on that point. But the reason I haven't told him is because to do that would feel even *more* wrong than keeping the secret. So you can relax. I don't have any intention of spilling the beans."

She could almost see the relief move through his body.

And she couldn't help asking, in her new, stronger mode, "Why do you seem so calm about this? Normally, you'd be yelling at me anyway, telling me I'd better not tell him. And last night you were all *'Don't turn me in'* and everything."

Standing in front of her, he simply sighed. "The truth? Maybe I'm just tired. Too tired to try to scare you. Or maybe I just figured out that if you really wanted to tell, there's nothing I can do to stop you."

There *were* things he could do to stop her, of course. She remembered her earlier words to Sue Ann: *It's still not too late for a Brody to shoot me.* But apparently Mick wasn't willing to go so far as bodily harm to keep her quiet—which made him a lot less scary. Maybe if Sue Ann could see Mick's eyes, she'd understand that he wasn't as bad as he sounded. Maybe she'd understand why Jenny couldn't seem to tell him no—to anything.

"Tea?" he asked, using the back of his arm to mop the sweat off his forehead. "Damn, it's hot."

"Sorry, no tea—I've been too busy to make any. How about a Coke? I've got regular or Diet."

"That'll do fine. Regular."

She pulled a can from the fridge and watched as he pressed it to his forehead, then his neck. He was the only man she'd ever known who she didn't mind being a little sweaty.

"Do something special today?" he asked, glancing down her body. "You're all dressed up." She wore a yellow print cotton skirt and coordinating top.

"Actually, I had an HIV test. I'm clean, by the way."

His eyes narrowed in confusion. "You got dressed up to take an HIV test?"

She couldn't help laughing. "No, this is just what I wore. This is . . . how women in Destiny dress. We still think it's the 1950s or something, I suppose."

"Well, you look pretty," he said, popping the top on his Coke, then asked, "Did you still dress like that when you moved away?"

She'd never much thought about it before, but said, "Yeah, a lot of the time. It's appropriate 'teacher wear,' and I guess I'm just a Destinyite to the core."

The corners of his mouth turned up just slightly. "I coulda told ya *that*, pussycat."

Without talking about it, both walked through the wide doorway to the living room. "Whoa," he said, his eyes gravitating immediately to the big blank spot on the wall. "You took the picture down."

"Just a little while ago, actually."

He shifted his gaze to her. "Does it feel better that way?"

And she nodded without hesitation. Already, the room felt more like a *normal* living room, where people lived, laughed, relaxed.

"Wall looks pretty shitty," he said on a chuckle, "but if it makes you feel better, that's good."

He took a long drink of his Coke but kept watching her, and again, she felt it, his look—this time it held lust, and if she wasn't mistaken, actual . . . concern for her well-being.

They'd come a long way since that first night in the

woods, but . . . taking control of the house was a first step to taking control of her life, and that meant taking control of her relationship with Mick, too.

And that meant she couldn't have sex with him anymore. She just couldn't.

Because every time, she could feel it pulling her in a little deeper, into his web of mystery that wasn't so much of a mystery anymore. She could keep his horrible secret, but she couldn't risk having . . . *feelings* for him. And—okay—she knew she'd *already* had feelings for him, related to their sex, but she couldn't risk *more* of them. She was freshly divorced, just starting to get past the shock and pain of it all. And he was . . . well, he was trouble. Even if it was trouble not of his own making.

They stood a few feet apart, looking at each other, which made her glance down and start fidgeting with the hem of her top. John Cougar sang, "Ain't Even Done With the Night" low on the radio—on a retro station from Crestview, the only signal that reached Destiny.

"You want me to go, don't you?" Mick asked.

How could he tell? Well, didn't matter—it made this easier. She looked back down, but then forced her gaze up to his. *Keep being strong—get your life back in order here.* "Yeah," she said softly. Then shook her head. "I can't . . . keep sleeping with you."

"It's not sleeping, pussycat. It's sex. Really *good*, *hot* sex."

She drew in her breath, felt a familiar flutter in her panties, and resolved not to let it deter her. "No matter what you call it, I can't keep doing it. Because you're dangerous, Mick. Do you understand what I mean?" He'd *felt* dangerous before, because she didn't know his secret. Now that she knew it, danger was a certainty. Even if a part of her wished it wasn't that way.

Even if sex with him had been the most amazing thing to happen to her in a long time.

Slowly, Mick nodded. "Yeah, honey, I understand." It was killing him inside, wrenching his guts into a knot, but he understood. She wasn't the sort of girl who fooled around with criminals. And he wanted to argue the point, remind her how damn good they were together. He wanted to be selfish as hell, because her touches and kisses had become a balm to him over the last few weeks, and they were—more than anything— what had drawn him here tonight.

But Jenny Tolliver had been so . . . untouchable for his whole life that he was just amazed she'd ever let him touch her at all. And she had morals. And people to please. He'd gotten a few morals as life had gone on—but he'd never had anyone to please, anyone who expected something of him. Maybe if he had, things would've been different.

So, sure, he wanted to argue, tell her she was crazy to give up what had been the best damn sex of his life, and probably of hers, too—but maybe the time had come to start showing his pussycat some respect.

He was still mad as hell at her for sneaking up to the cabin—if she hadn't, they'd both have a whole lot less weighing on them. But that aside, if she wanted him to go, he would go.

"Before I leave, though . . ."

Her eyes widened prettily. "Yeah?"

He tried to find the words he was seeking, then finally realized they were simple. "Thank you, pussycat, for keeping my secret. And for not hating me." Then, setting his soda can aside on the nearest table, he stepped toward her, lifted his hands gently to her face, and lowered a kiss to her forehead.

And he meant to step back then, he really did—but God, it felt good to be this close to her, so he stayed that way, smelling her hair, touching her soft cheeks, feeling frozen in time and just wanting to stay this way for a while. If he couldn't have any more of her, this was better than nothing.

It was then that he realized she'd begun to tremble. Same as he had with her the other night.

Still touching her face with his fingertips, he drew back slightly to peer into her eyes, to try to understand what was happening.

She looked anguished. "I can't," she whispered.

"I know," he assured her. "I get it, honey. It's okay."

"Only it's not."

Hell, he was confused. "Huh?"

"I can't, but I just . . ."

Oh. He got it now, from the look in her pretty green eyes—and warmth flowed through him. "But you want to."

"And I can't, unless you . . ."

"Unless I what, pussycat?" he breathed.

"Convince me," she said.

The reason why the universe is eternal is that
it does not live for itself; it gives life to others
as it transforms.

Lao Tzu

Nine

Jenny stood before him, horrified by her own
words. It was like that first night in the woods. She
wanted him like crazy, her skin tingled for him, her
body ached for him, and she felt that if he walked out
that door right now, she'd die.

But she couldn't let herself have him. She couldn't
convince herself it was okay. "Good Jenny" strikes
again. "Good Jenny," who can't be with a guy like
Mick Brody. Yes, it was just like before—except the
stakes felt much higher now.

His eyes were filled with as much lust as her body.
She felt her heartbeat between her thighs. "What'll it
take," he whispered warm, his voice heavy, "to convince you, Jenny? Just tell me and I'll do it."

"I . . . don't know." *Don't break any laws. Don't have
your brother hidden away across the lake. Be the kind of guy*

who fits in my life. All of them were impossible right now, and the irony was, if they were true, she'd have never met him again anyway.

He peered down on her, his eyes going darker as he said, "How's this?" and lowered his mouth to hers.

The kiss was soft yet firm. She felt all the power he possessed shrouded in tenderness. She sighed in response and melted against him. And mmm, he was hard for her. Beautifully, wonderfully hard. She yearned for more.

But she also yearned for old Jenny, the Jenny who wouldn't give a dangerous guy the time of day when he flirted with her from the end of her dock. *That* Jenny stayed safe. That Jenny lived in a prettier world than this one did at the moment.

When he kissed her again, deeper this time, it consumed her. His lush mouth moved over hers, his tongue pushed its way between her lips, and she couldn't resist meeting it with her own. Kissing him right now felt like kissing the devil, like taking an apple from the serpent. This was her chance to say no, to convince them both that this had to stop, even if she'd practically begged him to seduce her.

So tell him no, say you can't.

You'll sleep better tonight, feel stronger—once and for all.

But, oh God, she couldn't. Because she wanted to be with him. And God help her, maybe Sue Ann was right—maybe it was about more than sex, and more than right and wrong. There *was* no casual sex—at least not for her. She'd tried to make it that way. *But how do you take a man inside you without feeling something afterward? How do you become that intimate, let him see the wildest parts of you, without feeling connected to him?*

And despite herself, she wanted to be connected *again. Deeply.*

So when he took her hands and led her to the couch, she let him. When he lay back and pulled her down on top of him, she didn't protest. When he reached up to cup the outer sides of her breasts and stroke his thumbs across her nipples, she didn't ask him to stop. Instead, she kissed him madly. And considered herself fully convinced.

He pushed her top up over her bra—a yellow lace one, because she'd felt like wearing nice lingerie lately—and groaned at the sight. "So damn pretty," he growled, then drew her down for another kiss.

She quickly got lost in them, those kisses, barely aware that they were undressing each other as they made out. They stopped just long enough for him to pull her top over her head, then stopped again to get rid of his T-shirt. She ran her palms down his chest, the muscles of his stomach, as he massaged her rear, then reached underneath to pull her panties down.

"Unzip me, pussycat," he told her.

She hadn't done that before. The unzipping part. But she wanted to. So she worked at the buckle of his brown leather belt, then undid his jeans. It was impossible to lower the zipper without feeling the hard bulge there, and wanting it. She'd been trembling before and now she trembled again. He made her crazy with desire, crazier than she knew a guy could make her.

A moment later she took him in her hand and they both gasped. She looked in his eyes and he held her face in his hands. "That feels so good, baby," he told her, and she squeezed lightly and listened to him moan. Then bit her lip, realizing that she did still retain *some* control here. Control over his pleasure. And she wanted more.

So she massaged and caressed him as he reached up to push her bra straps from her shoulders, letting her breasts tumble free. She watched him hiss in his breath as she worked harder, then leaned forward, urging him to take one beaded pink nipple in his mouth.

He licked gently, firmly, making her surge with moisture beneath her skirt—then he pulled deeply on her breast, making her cry out.

She pushed down his jeans and lifted her skirt and pressed her softest flesh against his hardest and they moved together that way, slowly, while the rough, dark unshaven stubble on his chin abraded the sensitive flesh of her breast.

She needed him inside her. And she wanted to show him, so she used her hand to position him, then thrust down.

Sounds of deep pleasure erupted from them both. "So big," she whispered. "So perfect and big."

"All for you, pussycat," he murmured. "Every inch."

She bit her lip as her body spasmed with fresh sensation, then moved on him rhythmically, like an instinctive dance, one a woman is born knowing. He held her hips, watched her move, and she felt freer than the last time they'd been here, in this room, on this couch, freer to seek her pleasure, freer to let him watch her every sway and undulation.

The orgasm came quickly, furiously, accompanied with high-pitched whimpers she didn't try to hold in. She felt them echo off the walls around her, felt the raw, stark intimacy wrapping around them both—the same as what they'd shared before . . . but different somehow.

"You're so damn beautiful when you come," he growled up at her, and she breathed in the rawness of it, of him, took it into her lungs and let it settle there.

And then he began to pump up into her harder, rougher. Her breasts bounced with the movements; he penetrated her more deeply. They looked in each other's eyes as she met each hard stroke. More rawness. More starkness. It made her wild inside.

So she moved harder against him, too, and she cried out at each plunging upward drive. He held her ass; she clawed at his chest with her fingernails. She reached a point where she felt almost overwhelmed and wondered how much more she could take, felt tears of intensity gather behind her eyes but held them back—and considering that she was on top, she'd never felt more taken by a man, not even in the woods. She grunted with each thrust; she bit her lip and leaned her head back, closing her eyes—and finally he said, "Aw, God, Jenny—I'm coming in you!" and the last few strokes nearly lifted her off the couch.

Afterward, they lay that way, him still inside her, her head nestled against his chest. She felt her bra still half-falling around her, felt her skirt gathered between them, felt the disarray.

Damn it. She'd truly meant not to do this, truly meant to say no. Now that the insanity of full-on lust had passed, she remembered why. Danger. It hung all around him. And she couldn't live that way. *Could* she?

"Oh God, why do I keep doing this?" she murmured into his chest. Then shut her eyes—she hadn't meant to utter the words out loud.

His voice came soft, calm, tired. "Relax, pussycat. It's just chemistry. We have it. A lot of it. Nothing wrong with feeling good."

Unless the guy who makes you feel good is the opposite of everything you ever thought you wanted. Unless he confuses the hell out of you about what's right and what's wrong.

And despite the truth in it, the word *chemistry* stung. She'd told him sex meant something to her, but maybe he hadn't heard that part. And if this kept on . . . oh God, Mick Brody could *not* mean something to her, something *serious*. She had to stop this!

Except that, clearly, he already *did* mean something to her. She kept trying to tell herself he didn't. But she'd kept his deep dark secret from her father, who she loved and cherished and respected. And she craved his body. And she wanted to know what went on in his mind.

Oh hell, she *cared* for him. Mr. Danger. Mr. Scary Lover in the Woods. She *cared* for him! Like a woman cared for a man. This was bad.

She didn't need a man in her life at all right now, let alone a dangerous one. *You. Must. Stop. This. Once and for all.*

She lay there against him, berating herself for her feelings even as he remained inside her, until he gently used his hand to lift her face, to make her look at him. "Listen to me, pretty pussycat," he said. "I might be all kinds of trouble for you in every other way—but me and you, like *this* . . . it's good, honey. *Real* good. And there's just nothing wrong with good, hot, wild sex."

And that's when it hit her—like a ton of bricks.

Good, hot, wild sex. That's what she had with Mick. Truly *passionate, intense, untamed* sex.

The kind that . . . Terrence thought she couldn't have.

She could scarcely believe it had taken her this long to realize it.

Terrence was wrong! Wrong, wrong, wrong. And maybe she'd known that all along in her heart—but not in her head.

I can do it. I can be wild! I can be uninhibited! I can be good in bed!

Take that, rat bastard! Shows what you *know!*

"Um, what's going on?" Mick asked, and she realized she was lying there suddenly grinning at him like a fool.

She tried to form an explanation. "I . . . I just . . . think you're right. There's nothing wrong with good, hot, wild sex."

He blinked, clearly surprised. "*That* was easy. Except for the other times I said that and you didn't believe me."

She couldn't explain that she'd just had a major revelation. She couldn't tell him that what had seemed morally heinous to her a few minutes ago suddenly felt exhilarating and amazingly *right.*

But she felt it deep down inside her, in her soul. A new freedom. A new sense of victory over the world. It was just like taking down the picture. She was a grown-up and she could do what she wanted. She could have all the wild sex with Mick she desired.

And . . . she could do it, she resolved, *without* caring about him. At least in any serious I'd-be-lost-without-you sort of way.

As for all the gooey, girly emotions she'd just been wading through . . . well, screw those. She just wasn't going to feel that way anymore. She was going to be tougher, stronger, more like a guy.

And as for the bad parts, the scary stuff, she just wouldn't think about those. Those were . . . across the lake—far, far away.

Because the revelation she'd just experienced was . . . deep, serious, transforming. It changed . . . everything. Or it would if she let it.

And she was ready to let it.

No more mushy emotions. No more fear. From now on, she would only think about the good stuff with Mick. And maybe that wouldn't be so hard, because the good stuff was *very* good indeed.

It was at Caroline Meeks's bunko party the next evening that Jenny found a chance to pull Sue Ann down an empty hallway while the other ladies were gathered around a fondue pot complimenting Caroline on her new drapes.

"I've had a major breakthrough," Jenny said.

Sue Ann spoke low, to make sure the ladies down the hall of the big Victorian house didn't hear. "You're telling your dad?"

Jenny shook her head. "No—I'm having rockin' sex with Mick."

Sue Ann blinked. "Um, where's the breakthrough? I already knew this part."

Jenny held up one finger. "But the point is, it's rockin'. It's wild. It's crazy."

"Yep, yep, and yep. Still not getting the newsflash."

"Terrence didn't think I could *have* wild sex."

Sue Ann's eyes lit up as she leaned her head back to say, "Ohhhhh." *Finally*, she got it. Then she added, "Rat bastard," for good measure.

"So I'm feeling kind of . . . elated about it all," Jenny said.

Sue Ann blinked. "Just between you and me, Jen, I didn't realize that *you* didn't realize you were having wild sex with Mick, or I'd have told you."

"I realized it—it just hadn't hit me how much it totally contradicts Terrence's stupid explanation for why he cheated on me."

"Stupid is right. That dumb asshole."

Jenny drew back in slight surprise. It was the first time Sue Ann had ever varied her name-calling. "No rat bastard?"

Sue Ann's reply was matter-of-fact. "I'm getting a little bored with it, so thought I'd go a new way." She shifted her weight from one dainty kitten-heeled sandal to the other. "Anyway, I'm really happy for you, I mean it. I hate that that jerk made you feel so bad about yourself. But, uh, now I need to know—exactly where *do* things stand with lover boy Mick these days? Besides the rockin' sex part."

Jenny had thought through this even more since her eye-opening revelation and had an answer prepared. "I'm officially having a wild affair. And I've decided it's okay for me to do that, because I *deserve* some decent sex, don't I?"

"Amen to that, sister." They shared a quiet, mini-high five.

"And I'm just not going to think about . . . you know, the negative aspects of the situation."

"The escaped convict he's harboring," Sue Ann said with a shrug, as if it were any other common relationship impediment.

"And even though I will admit to being a little emotionally involved from all the drama that's led up to this, I've got my head on straight about it now. Figuring out that I'm entitled to some good sex after the crap Terrence pulled has helped me to put this in its proper perspective—it's a summer affair, nothing more."

Unfortunately, Sue Ann didn't look entirely convinced. "I'm truly happy for you if you can, uh, do the deed with the guy without getting all wrapped up in him and his problems. And I'm trying really hard to forget the, um, legal dangers blowing in the wind here. But . . . how are you feeling about not telling your dad?"

Jenny sighed, and her stomach dropped just a little. "Well, that's the hardest part. But I'm doing what I truly feel is right. Surely he would respect that, don't you think?"

Sue Ann looked *wholly* skeptical now, but still said, "Um, yeah, sure he would." Even though they both knew good and well that Walter Tolliver was a lawman to the bone—for him, the law was the law, and there was no gray area, only black-and-white. "But back to the sex," Sue Ann said.

Jenny lowered her chin. "Is that all you think about? Since when did you become such a sexmonger anyway?"

"Since I have a child who's an amazingly light sleeper and also gets scared anytime Mommy and Daddy close the door to their room."

"Oh." Jenny hadn't known that. And back when she was married to Terrence and having *boring* sex, she wouldn't have thought it was such a big deal, but now that she was having sex with Mick, she felt Sue Ann's pain. "Sorry to hear that."

"Thus, whether or not I remain totally on board with this affair of yours, if you're gonna have it, I want to hear about it. So entertain the old married lady—what's new in Mick Brody's bag of sex tricks? Did you do it in the woods again? Against a tree? Standing up? Hanging from a chandelier? Spill."

Jenny couldn't stifle her laugh, but she still managed to keep her voice down when she answered. "It was on the couch this time."

Bitter disappointment colored Sue Ann's voice when she said, "Really?"

"But it was still totally hot," Jenny assured her. "As hot as any sex we've had."

"Compared to the woods? Honestly? The couch is just as hot?"

"With Mick—absolutely." She couldn't hold in the dreamy sigh that came with remembering.

"Wow," Sue Ann replied, sounding a little in awe. "You really *have* spiced up my life lately, girlfriend." Then she looked down the hall, toward the party, so Jenny did, too—in time to see both Tessa and Amy coming in the front door. "Now come on—I'm gonna kick your ass at bunko like only a true Destiny lady can."

And as she grabbed Jenny's hand and pulled her into the large room where the games were set to begin, Jenny couldn't help thinking that Destiny was indeed holding for her many things she'd missed but had perhaps not realized how much: Sue Ann's friendship, her father's love, and sex that rocked her world.

Mick sat next to Wayne's bed watching a Reds game on the TV Mick had brought from his apartment to set up in what had once been their family's living room. It was the eighth inning on another scorching afternoon and Jay Bruce was up to bat. The electric fans in the windows hummed, and Mick never stopped being thankful that the trees surrounding the house blocked out most of the sun, or the heat would be unbearable.

Mick hadn't followed the Reds in years, and he was pretty sure Wayne hadn't, either, but as kids, they'd been fans—watching the games on TV or listening on the radio had been a nice distraction back then. So on a hot afternoon with nothing to do, it had seemed like a good enough distraction now, too.

After Bruce got on first and the game went to a commercial, Mick pushed to his feet. "I'm gonna make a sandwich—you want anything?" Not that Wayne ate much these days. But at least his pain had been under control lately.

Wayne appeared to think about it for a minute, his answer glum. "Peaches, maybe."

Wayne's lack of interest in food was one more constant reminder that they were both sitting there waiting for him to die—for a while, he'd eaten regular food, then it had dropped off to just soft stuff, and for the last couple of days, all he wanted were canned peaches. But Mick tried not to feel that as he peeled back the lid on a can, raked some into a bowl—along with the juices, since he'd noticed Wayne actually consuming more of the juice than the actual peaches the last day or so—then walked the bowl to his brother along with a spoon. Still, he felt a little numb as he slapped together a ham sandwich for himself, almost guilty for his hunger, his health.

"So, uh, where do you go at night when you leave here, man?" Wayne asked out of the blue as Mick walked back into the room carrying the sandwich and a can of Coke.

He sat down, popped the top, took a drink, and suffered more guilt. "I didn't know you realized I was gone. I only go when I think you're asleep for the night—or I'd have been here. Sorry, man."

Wayne chuckled softly, even if it came out sounding tired. "I wasn't mad, just wondering. You don't have to be here every second, dude. I'm . . . all right, for now. Mostly."

Yeah, Mick knew that. Despite the fatigue, as long as he kept up with Wayne's pain meds, his brother was on a pretty even keel for the time being—he could change his own clothes, go to the bathroom by himself, and he even occasionally got up and walked outside a few minutes. Although it seemed to Mick like he was doing that less and less the last couple of weeks.

"I've been . . . going across the lake," Mick said, knowing the news would surprise his brother. He hadn't told Wayne anything about Jenny—the notion of telling his brother he was having sex with a gorgeous girl when Wayne would never have sex again had seemed damn selfish. Plus he hadn't wanted to worry Wayne by letting him know someone else knew he was here.

Wayne looked understandably confused. "Across the lake?"

"You're gonna think I'm making this up, bro, but . . . I'm kind of having a thing with Jenny Tolliver. Remember her? Lived across the lake in that little yellow house?"

Wayne blinked. "You're shittin' me."

Mick laughed softly. "I know it sounds pretty fucking unbelievable, but it's true."

"How the hell did *that* happen?"

Mick relayed the story without focusing on the sex, but when he was done, Wayne's focus was on the sex. And he seemed just as shocked as Mick had been before he'd started getting used to the idea. "So you're tellin' me that you're actually doin' little Jenny Tolliver, the cheerleader with the perfect little bikini."

For some reason, Mick wasn't altogether comfortable talking about that part of it—and he didn't know why, since he and Wayne had always been open about what they were getting from who. So he just said, "Yep."

Wayne laughed. "Man, you are one lucky son of a bitch."

Yeah, if you don't count the part about having to take care of a dying brother and keep it a secret from the whole world. But he didn't say that. And he guessed compared to Wayne he *was* pretty damn lucky.

Mick finally asked, "Aren't you even gonna worry about the fact that she's the police chief's daughter?"

Wayne's expression went grim. "Aw, shit—I forgot about that."

In Mick's mind, Jenny had always been tightly linked with her father's profession, so it was hard to imagine Wayne forgetting, but maybe it was the pain meds. "Well, no worries—Jenny won't tell."

But now Wayne looked as doubtful as Mick had felt until recently. "Why wouldn't she?"

"She knows we're not hurting anybody," Mick explained. "She gets it."

His lean body stretched out on the bed, Wayne seemed to refocus on the ballgame for a minute—then he looked back to Mick. "All I can say is—you better keep that chick happy between the sheets, bro, or we're both up shit creek."

Mick chuckled softly. "We haven't actually, uh, made it between any sheets yet, but keeping her happy isn't a job I mind, so I think we're in good shape."

Wayne's hollowed eyes had returned to the TV, but Mick could tell from the pleasant look washing over his face that he was somewhere else in his head. His peaches rested forgotten in his lap. "You ever think about those days?" he asked.

Mick didn't need to ask him *which* days—he knew good and well. The days when they were old enough to get out from under their parents' thumbs, get away from the house in a car, or a boat, whatever was handy. But before they'd started getting in serious trouble, the kind that had sent Wayne away. "Yeah, I do," Mick said. *Too often.*

They weren't the best of times—they'd still had shitty home lives, and they'd been starting to do stuff that got them on the wrong side of the law. But in another way, they *were* the best times, the best times *he* could remember anyway. Lazy days floating around the lake, watching sweet Jenny Tolliver bask in the sun. Carefree nights riding around in Lucky's old Camaro, trying to get their hands on beer, trying to pick up girls.

Just then, Wayne shifted slightly in bed, jostling peach juice from the bowl onto his bare stomach—it was so hot that neither had bothered with shirts today and Wayne wore only a pair of Mick's old cotton shorts. Wayne cursed softly, and Mick reached in the drawer on the old end table he'd put next to the bed for the napkins he'd stowed there.

A moment later, as he went to shut the drawer, his eyes fell on something—two things, actually—that *he* hadn't put inside. Both took him instantly back to his boyhood. One was a gray flint arrowhead, perfectly shaped, that they'd found one summer while plowing for a garden on the other side of the ridge, an area that was as steep as the rest of the land, but it was free of trees and got enough sun to grow things. The other was a wrinkled picture of them as boys—standing down by the lake. Mick had been about seven, Wayne about ten.

"Damn, you saved these?" Mick asked, drawing them both out. Under normal circumstances, Wayne wasn't a sentimental guy—or maybe, Mick thought suddenly, Wayne just didn't normally let it show.

Now, though, he didn't even bother looking sheepish. Whether the change was due to medication or imminent death, Mick didn't know. "Sure," Wayne said simply.

Mick had nearly forgotten about that arrowhead, but now he remembered how excited they'd been to find it, how it had been the first time he'd really thought about things like history, different people who lived in different times. He'd found the fact that some Indian guy had been here before him, on this craggy, dark piece of ground, somehow comforting. Of course, now he knew that the Indian in question had probably been on a hunting trip, but back then, he'd imagined the Indian living here, right on the same spot they had, and it had made the steep, rocky hillside seem a little cooler than it had before.

"You carried this thing with you all these years?" he said to Wayne. "Why?"

"For luck," Wayne said.

And after a second, they both cracked up laughing.

"Good thing I had it," Wayne went on jokingly, "or something bad could've happened to me."

And they laughed some more. And damn, it was good to have something to laugh at around here for a change. Even if the laughter was kind of morbid, it was better than no laughter at all.

"Naw," Wayne finally said when the laughs faded, "it just reminds me of when we were kids."

Mick thought back and realized he'd been wrong— *those* were the best times. Roaming these jagged hill- sides with his brother, playing in the creek that cut through the steep hills, discovering the earth. He remembered Wayne looking out for him, telling him to be careful when they were climbing trees, show- ing him the best limbs to use. And taking up for him with their parents, too. One time Mick had fallen in the creek and ripped a new shirt, and since new shirts didn't come often, he'd been in big trouble. Wayne had stepped up and claimed that he pushed Mick, that was why he'd fallen, and it wasn't true, but Wayne had taken a beating for it, so Mick wouldn't have to.

"Thanks," Mick said suddenly, because he wasn't sure he ever had, and time was growing short, "for that day you took a whipping for me."

In the bed, Wayne only shrugged. "You were little. And they were fucking assholes."

"*Man,* I looked up to you then," Mick mused, lean- ing his head back. "I wanted to be just like you."

The irony in his words, the irony of how things had turned out, hit him only when Wayne said, "I never meant to drag you into bad shit, man. Never meant to turn you into . . . me."

This was no time, Mick thought, to let his brother take the blame for things he wasn't sure were his fault anyway. "I think Mom and Dad are to blame for any bad shit either one of us got into."

"Still, there were times . . . I should've sent you home, not asked you to come—you know?"

That liquor store in Crestview, he meant, and other similar occasions that Mick would rather not remember. But he still didn't blame his brother for it. And so even though he wasn't sure he'd ever said these words to any human being in his life, he figured now was the time—so he got completely honest. "I loved you, man. You were . . . the *only* thing I loved."

In the short silence that followed, a TV announcer declared, "And this one belongs to the Reds!" They both looked up to find that the game was over and fireworks were exploding over Great American Ball Park, although you could barely see them in the daylight.

Reaching for the remote by Wayne's bed, Mick turned off the TV, then reached down and flipped on the boom box he'd brought from home. The radio blared with that Tommy Tutone song from the eighties—about a girl named Jenny.

Wayne hadn't replied, but Mick wasn't sorry he'd said it. And he was about to stand up and take some garbage to the kitchen when Wayne said, "What do you love *now*?"

"*Jenny, Jenny*" flowed from the radio and Mick tried to tune it out of his mind a little—he even reached down to lower the volume. "I don't know. I . . . like my work. I like . . ." What else? What else was big enough for him to put on a list of things he truly loved? He couldn't think of anything.

"The girl?" Wayne asked. "Jenny Tolliver."

Mick blinked, then turned his gaze on his brother. "Do I *love* her? Hell, man . . . it's just . . . you know, sex."

"Liar," Wayne said confidently.

Did it show on his face? His feelings for Jenny, his need for her? "I'm not saying I don't care for her, but . . . *love*'s a damn big word. I haven't known her that long."

"*What*? You've had a hard-on for her since we were teenagers."

Mick laughed. "That's different than knowing somebody."

"It's a good start, though. So . . . you think you could love this girl?"

Still freaked out at the very suggestion, Mick shook his head. "She lives across the lake and her dad's the chief of police. You do the math."

"I didn't ask what the problems were—I asked if you could love her."

Shit. He'd had to go and bring up *love*, of all the damn things in the world, hadn't he? This is what he got for being honest with Wayne, just saying what he felt. But now they weren't talking about him loving Wayne, they were talking about Jenny. His chest tightened with . . . the truth . . . and how hard it was to think about it . . . and how hard it was to admit it. "In a different place and time . . . maybe."

"Thing is," Wayne said, letting his eyes fall shut, looking suddenly like he'd drift off any moment, "I'd feel better dying if I thought I wouldn't be leaving you . . . completely alone."

"Don't worry about *me*, bro. I've been alone awhile now, and I get by all right."

And he waited for Wayne to argue with him, to keep pressing him about this, but he went completely quiet and Mick realized he'd fallen asleep.

Well, good. The medicine was making Wayne . . . unpredictable suddenly. Or maybe, like he'd thought before, it was *death* making his brother that way. Whatever the case, he was glad the subject was closed. He wanted Jenny, he craved Jenny, he fantasized about Jenny whenever they were apart, and he looked forward to the time when he'd see Jenny again. But none of that equaled love. He wouldn't know that kind of love if it slapped him in the face anyway.

And he didn't even want to. What he'd just told Wayne was true—he'd learned to be alone. After their parents had died, after Wayne had gone to prison. And the truth about being alone for Mick was—in his life, it felt safer that way, and he liked it just fine. Jenny was . . . comfort. But whenever this was over, he'd be good and ready to throw his stuff back in the truck and head back to Cincinnati—alone.

Under the Covers occupied an old two-story building painted sage green with cream trim on Destiny's Town Square. A sign in the window announced a book club meeting on Tuesday night. When Jenny and Sue Ann stepped inside, the wonderful smell of books met Jenny's nose.

A large tabby cat bounded silently from a high bookshelf to land on the counter, and Jenny heard Amy scold, "Watch it, Shakespeare," just before she looked up to exclaim, "Hey, you finally stopped by to see the place!"

"Wow, great store," Jenny said, and she meant it. The space immediately felt warm and cozy, dotted with overstuffed easy chairs and braided rugs. "Sorry it took me so long to get here."

"We have an outdoor patio in back, too," Amy boasted with a smile as she rounded the counter to greet Jenny and Sue Ann. "The book club meets there in good weather—although lately it's been so hot we've opted to stay inside."

Jenny's eyes dropped to the cat, who'd made its way to the floor and had just woven through her ankles before hopping up to settle in one of the chairs. "What's with the cat?" The truth was that it had felt oddly . . . comforting simply to have a cat rub up against her, a sensation she hadn't experienced in ages.

"Want him?" Amy asked. "He just started hanging around about a month ago, so I started feeding him so he wouldn't starve, and—of course—now he won't leave. I started calling him Shakespeare because he seems to sleep in that particular section a lot. But he's officially up for adoption, so what do you say?" Amy's eyebrows lifted hopefully.

Yet Jenny quickly balked. "Uh, don't look at *me*. I'm only in town for the summer." Even if, in some way, the idea appealed. Of having a cat around again. Kind of. Except . . . pets never lasted. A fleeting thought of Snowball passed through her mind.

Amy shrugged. "I'm sure he'd be happy wherever you end up."

But Jenny just laughed and shoved the idea aside, because it was easier that way. God knew she had enough on her mind already. "Why don't *you* adopt him? You're a cat person, if I recall."

"No can do," Amy said with complete certainty. "Mr. Knightley would never allow it."

Now it was Jenny who raised her eyebrows. According to Sue Ann, neither Amy nor Tessa had ever married, nor had Rachel. "Mr. Knightley?"

"My cat at home," Amy said. "He's very possessive of me. And he doesn't play well with others."

Just then, Tessa popped out from between two tall shelving units carrying a stack of books in her arms. "You have to forgive Amy," she explained by way of saying hello. "She's *very* into her cat. And she reads way too much Jane Austen—hence the cat's name."

Amy rolled her eyes in protest. "May I point out

that it's technically *impossible* to read too much Jane Austen? She only wrote six books."

Tessa rolled her eyes right back. "Well, then . . ." She shifted her gaze to Jenny and Sue Ann. "She *re*-reads too much Jane Austen."

"I *like* Jane Austen," Sue Ann offered cautiously.

"Sure, we all do," Tessa said. "But do you have pets named after her characters?"

"Well, okay, maybe I see your point," Sue Ann replied, and Amy crossed her arms and tried to look put out.

"Enough about my cat already," she said, "and on to another matter of importance. Jenny, are you going to join my book club?" An encouraging smile spread across her face.

"Oh, gosh," Jenny hedged, "I'd love to . . . except my summer reading probably isn't what your customers would enjoy. Stephen Hawking? Brian Greene?"

Tessa's eyes narrowed. "Brian Greene? Isn't he a science guy, too?"

"Another of her physicist idols," Sue Ann clarified for the girls.

"So you're still all into astronomy, huh?" Tessa asked.

"Afraid so. Even though I know it sometimes makes me hard to socialize with," Jenny said on a laugh.

Tessa shrugged. "We'll still socialize with you—but we just won't read with you."

"It's a shame, though," Amy added, "because I've even gotten some guys to start coming to the book club lately."

And at this, Jenny let out a harrumph. "Well, then all the better reason for me to stay away. Guys are the last thing I'm interested in this summer." *Other than a criminal I met in the woods, that is.*

Amy responded by lowering her chin and looking as if she knew all. "But have you seen Adam Becker lately? He's looking very fine. And he promised me he'd come next week."

"Because you browbeat him," Tessa pointed out.

Jenny let her eyes go wide with exasperation. "What is it with everyone wanting to fix me up with Adam Becker? I'm *so* not interested."

"Logan Whitaker then?" Amy asked. Jenny searched her memory and remembered Logan being Amy's neighbor when they were growing up—sort of like a brother to her.

"No thank you," she said with a smidge of extra emphasis. "Nothing against Logan, but . . ."

Yet Amy would not be quelled. "How about Mike Romo? Though he's a little older than us, he's a cop and works for your dad, so you probably know him."

"No, I don't know Mike Romo. I mean, I remember him a little from when we were young, but—"

"He's majorly *hot*," Amy informed her in a voice designed to entice.

Which made Tessa roll her eyes. "And he'd never darken the door of your book club in a thousand years, and that's probably good, because most people think he's a jerk."

"Jerk schmerk," Sue Ann said. "He looks good on the softball field." She glanced to Jenny. "He and Jeff play on the same team."

Despite the unwelcome topic of conversation, the more they talked, the more it felt like old times to Jenny—in a good way. Amy had possessed a matchmaking streak even back when they were young, and it reminded Jenny that, at heart, most people didn't change very much, which was kind of reassuring.

Except for Mick, of course. He *had* changed. She truly believed that, more and more each day. And maybe that was healthy for her in more ways than one, because she *needed* something good to believe in this summer.

And the more they talked and gossiped and giggled, the more she reimmersed herself in the simple ease of being one of the girls, there rose a tiny, immature part of her that wished she could just tell Amy and Tessa everything about Mick, just as she'd told Sue Ann. But she couldn't, of course.

Such was the hell of living . . . well, almost a double life. By day she was "good Jenny" Tolliver, and by night she was Mick Brody's lover. She tingled a bit in her panties just thinking about it, about *him*.

"Why the wicked little grin?" Tessa asked suddenly, and Jenny flinched, wanting to smack herself for it.

"Grin? What grin?" She blinked nervously.

Then Amy narrowed her gaze and lowered her chin, looking a little like Sherlock Holmes about to solve a case. "You've got a secret," she said slowly, surely. "A secret . . . man."

Holy God. "What?" she gasped. "That's crazy." Next to her, Sue Ann made a choking sound, then broke into a light coughing fit.

Tessa, who had long since set down the books she'd held, stepped over to slap Sue Ann on the back, laughing a bit at the whole situation—then turned her eyes back on Jenny. "You know, I'm not usually one to dig for this sort of thing like Miss-Jane-Austen-is-my-life over here," she said, motioning to Amy, "but if I do say so myself, you look completely suspicious right now. Your face is even turning red."

"It's the sun," she said quickly. "I'm overly sensitive to it. Ask Sue Ann."

"It's true," Sue Ann said, finally getting her voice back. "It comes over her very suddenly sometimes, just from as little sun as you'd get, say . . . walking here from the café, like we just did."

Jenny became aware that she and Sue Ann were both nodding, so she *stopped*, in an attempt to look natural. As if there was a prayer of that at this point.

"It's okay," Amy said, sounding sly. "You don't have to tell us if you don't want to. But I'm sure we'll figure out who it is eventually."

And Jenny's stomach churned. She didn't think it was *possible* they could find out, but she didn't even like the idea of anyone snooping around the topic. "Amy, my husband just dumped me—what on earth would I want with a guy right now?"

"Um, I think you just answered your own question, Jen," Tessa said. "Your husband just dumped you. Why *wouldn't* you want another guy right now?"

"Because I'm *so* not ready to date." *But I am apparently ready to have a lot of sex.* "And because I'm still recovering." *And sex, it turns out, helps a lot with that.* "And . . . who in the world could I possibly be seeing in Destiny who you wouldn't know about?" *Besides the scary guy across the lake who no one knows is here.*

Thankfully, that last argument seemed to hold some water with Amy and Tessa. "You *do* know everything that's going on with everyone," Tessa pointed out to Amy.

"True," Amy agreed, then looked to Jenny. "So I guess that lets you off the hook—for now. But I still think you've got a secret."

Swell. Just what she needed. It was bad enough to *have* a secret—much worse when people started figuring that out and wanting to know what it was.

Jenny felt good.

Mostly.

Okay, so Amy's accusations this afternoon had made her nervous. Now she knew a little something about how Mick had felt when *she'd* been prying into *his* secret. But by the time she'd left the store, they'd talked about lots of other things and Jenny was hopeful that Amy had forgotten all about it.

And except for the fact that it was too warm in the house—the A/C was acting up again. As her dad worked on it some more, she sat in the living room, reading—and wondering when Mick would come again.

That was part of why she was feeling so good. Since deciding it was okay to have a wild affair with Mick, she truly felt . . . all grown-up about it, in control of the situation, and like a woman of her own. Even if Mick *was* technically breaking the law.

And she was starting to enjoy socializing again. Catching up with her old friends had been good for her soul. Even if Amy was too intuitive for her own good.

At home, she'd taken more control, too. She'd followed through on getting a new comforter set on the bed, along with coordinating curtains, and the place felt much cozier to her, much more like her own little summer bedroom. She'd planted some of the last impatiens available at the garden store under a tree in the side yard, and she was thinking of repainting the rocker on the front porch. If she got really ambitious, she might update the living room a little, too. The truth was, dismantling the shrine had given the whole house new life in her eyes, a new beginning, something she thought both she *and* the cottage needed.

"Feelin' any cooler in there?" her father yelled from the other room.

She contemplated the question. "Maybe. I think so." Whereas a few minutes ago she'd been on the verge of sweltering even after changing into thin cotton shorts and a tank, now she only felt slightly too warm.

"Think I got her fixed again," he said, and when she heard him shut the door to the laundry room, went to meet him in the kitchen. She found him wiping his hands on a rag, yet looking doubtful. "But if this keeps up, I may have to call somebody to look at it who knows what they're doin'. I'm just tinkerin' around and gettin' lucky, but for all I know, we need to put in a whole new unit."

"Oh Dad, no," she said instantly. Because she knew that would cost a lot. And her father wasn't made of money, especially given that he owned two houses without having a particularly good reason, other than not wanting to part with the one he'd shared with her mom. "I'm only here for the summer—I wouldn't want you to go to all that expense."

But her dad was shaking his head. "Doesn't matter how long you're here for—a house has gotta have air." He reached in the fridge for a can of Sprite, which she'd taken to keeping on hand especially for him, and at the same time, he changed the subject. "Betty asked me to invite you to the Fourth of July picnic at their place. Comin' up in just a few days, ya know."

Oh. Was it July already? Actually, that had totally escaped her. Her life had been filled with fireworks of a different kind lately, and her focus had been on other things than the calendar. "That sounds nice," she said.

"Most everybody we know goes there now. And I think some of your old girlfriends will be there, too."

Back when Jenny was a kid, her *parents* had hosted the annual Fourth of July get-together. But after her mom's death, the tradition had ended, and Betty and Ed hadn't started having *their* party until after Jenny had left home. "Tell them I'll be there, and please ask Betty to let me know what I can bring."

After a swig of his soda, he smiled. "Knew you'd say that, so I already volunteered your lemon bars."

"Great," she said. "One batch of lemon bars, coming up."

That's when Jenny's dad meandered into the living room with the words, "Think I need to take a load off for a few minutes before I head home."

But he *didn't* take a load off—instead, he stopped dead in his tracks just inside the doorway. "What happened to your mother's picture?" he asked, clearly aghast. "What happened to *all* her pictures?"

We make our world significant by the courage of
our questions and by the depth of our answers.

Carl Sagan

Ten

---

*O*h hell. Maybe she'd gone too far putting them *all*
away. And she'd worried how her dad would react,
but she'd—foolishly, it appeared—hoped he wouldn't
make a big deal of it. She'd already gotten so used to
them being gone that she'd sort of forgotten he didn't
know about it yet. Now she realized she needed to
handle this gently.

"Dad," she said, stepping up in front of him to make
eye contact, "I took them down. They were making
me think too much about her death. So they're up in
the spare bedroom, but I'll put them all back before I
leave."

She thought she'd explained clearly and succinctly
in a way anyone could comprehend, but her dad still
looked dumbfounded.

"Dad," she began again, "please tell me you're not
mad at me and that you understand."

He shook his head, looking a bit helpless for a man who wore a badge. "I'm not mad at you, honey, but . . . I can't say I really *understand*."

Jenny sighed. "Let's sit down, okay?" she suggested, and led the way by planting herself on the couch. Her father followed suit, and she tried again. "I felt like . . . this room was stuck in time, like it needed a change. It was no disrespect to Mom, but I . . . felt her—too much. In fact, I was thinking—this would be a good time for me to paint the walls, since they definitely need it." She pointed to the darker blue square where the big portrait had hung. "And I thought I might buy some new curtains."

He looked to one of the room's windows. "Your mother made those curtains."

In response, Jenny shut her eyes, tried to regroup. She felt like an uncaring ogre, but it had to be said. "Dad, those curtains are worn—they're nearly as old as I am. We can pack them away with her other stuff you saved, but I really think some new curtains and paint would pep up the room. I hope you won't ask me not to do it—I think it's a good idea, for both of us."

And she was trying to stay strong—she was committed to it, in fact—but it was difficult with her dad sitting next to her looking brokenhearted all over again, as if her mom had passed away just last week.

"All right," he finally agreed. But then he peered up at the blank spot on the wall and said, "I just never dreamed I'd walk in this room and not see your mother smiling at me."

The words nearly took Jenny's breath away, because she could feel how much he still loved her mom, and it made her so sad that after all this time he really, truly had not moved on. It made her want to weep.

And it didn't help that her dad was sitting here looking at her like he didn't know who she was anymore.

And . . . oh boy. If he thought *this* was out of character, what would he think if he knew about Mick Brody?

But this is all okay, she told herself. *It's okay if Amy has her little suspicions. It's okay if I have a secret or two my dad doesn't know, too. It's okay because I'm a grown-up and I can have an affair if I want to.* And none of the . . . well, less-than-great aspects of the situation were going to stop her pleasure. *For the first time in my life, I'm breaking rules, and I'm doing what I want, and nothing's going to get in my way. And that's final.*

Walter Tolliver wasn't quite sure what led him to pull into the gravel lot at the Dew Drop Inn the following afternoon. Truth was, he almost wanted a beer. Something to numb his feelings. He wasn't on duty, so he could have one if he wanted. But he didn't think it was good for a lawman to be seen out drinking, especially when he was driving the squad car, so he decided a Sprite would be smarter.

The lot was empty, and now that he thought about it, he wasn't even sure the bar was open at this hour. But the door was open when he pulled on it. Stevie Nicks sang "Landslide" on the jukebox, and the new owner he'd met last time was busy unloading bottles of beer behind the bar in another pair of tight jeans. She looked up when she saw him, and he could tell she was surprised, but she smiled. "Well, if it's not Officer Tolliver—what can I do for you, Walter?"

He couldn't decide whether or not he liked it that she was so quick to use his first name. But she was bold, he'd give her that much. And he guessed you *had* to be bold to be a lady bar owner.

"Sorry if you're not open yet. I was just lookin' for a cool drink."

"We're not," she said, "but take a stool anyway. Sprite? Or something harder this time around?"

"Sprite's good."

Something about that made her smile, but when she set a glass of it before him a minute later, she said, "Something troubling you, Walter?"

That surprised him. "Why would you say that?"

She pointed to the spot between his eyebrows. "You're all pinched up and tight right there. You look like a man with something weighing on him."

He tilted his head, not sure if he was impressed or annoyed. "You a mind reader or somethin'?"

She laughed softly. "No, a bartender." She went back to unloading beer. "So what's the trouble?"

He shook his head. It would sound stupid, be hard to explain. Maybe it *was* stupid to be upset over this—he couldn't figure it out.

"Aw, come on—whatever it is, I bet I've heard crazier."

He let out a sigh, then blurted it out without planning. "My daughter's stayin' at our old house this summer. And when I walked in there yesterday, she'd taken down my photos of her mother—who passed away."

The bar owner—what was her name? Anita, he thought—rose from her task and ran *herself* a glass of Sprite from the nozzle behind the bar. Finally, she said, "Did she tell you why?"

Walter nodded. "Said they made her think about her mom too much."

"How old was your daughter when your wife died?"

"Thirteen."

"Well, no offense, Walter, but that makes good sense to me. A girl losing her mother is a hard thing—I can't think of much harder. And at *that* age—must have been a nightmare for her. How old's your daughter now, if you don't mind my asking?"

"Thirty-one," he said.

If he wasn't mistaken, Anita Garey looked surprised,

like maybe she'd expected Jenny to be younger. Maybe she thought it was pathetic that he still missed his wife after so long, the same way Jenny probably did.

The thought made him add, "She was the love of my life." Only after he'd spoken did it occur to him that it was a damn personal thing to be telling a stranger, a stranger he had nothing in common with. But it was too late now.

In response, Anita set down her glass and touched his hand. It felt odd, moving through him in ways he hadn't expected, in ways that made him feel . . . guilty. They were talking about Judy here, after all.

"It sounds like you and your daughter both suffered a lot of heartbreak, Walter. Thing is, people deal with heartbreak in different ways. If your daughter will feel better, stronger, having the pictures down while she's visiting, what will it hurt?"

He turned the question over in his mind and couldn't deny it was a good one. What *would* it hurt? Nothing. Nothing at all. He sat quietly for a moment, a little sad, a little embarrassed. "Guess maybe you're right. She just got divorced, my daughter, so . . . reckon she needs to feel as strong as she can right now."

Anita cast a pleasant look and said, "I'm sure she does," and was about to turn back to her unloading—when Walter impulsively reached out and covered *her* hand with *his*.

"Thank you," he said. "I know it seems simple, like I shoulda figured that out on my own, but . . . I just couldn't see it from her point of view." And touching her, it turned out, felt even better than when *she'd* touched *him*. So maybe he kept his hand there a heartbeat too long. Maybe he noticed too much the way her tank top clung to her breasts. Maybe he should take his hand away now—so he did.

But Anita Garey didn't look the least bit flustered—

like *he* surely did by now. She just smiled—all confident, sexy, and tough.

"So," she said, changing the subject, "anybody got any good fireworks around here on the Fourth?"

And for a brief moment, he considered inviting her to Betty and Ed's—but he bit his tongue and took another sip of his Sprite instead. "A few different folks set 'em off. And there's a festival up at Creekside Park," he added, not mentioning that it was usually poorly attended because most people went to Betty and Ed's and that this might even be the last year for the park event according to Johnny Fulks.

Was it unneighborly not to invite her? But if he did, would it be like . . . a date, heaven forbid? And even if it wasn't, he couldn't imagine the crowd at Betty and Ed's making Anita feel welcome. So it was just best he left it at that.

Mick knocked on the back door of Jenny's house and waited, anxious to see her. He'd been thinking about her all day while he dug. And dug. And dug. He wasn't totally surprised when she didn't answer—he'd noticed there weren't any lights on—but he couldn't quite bear to leave so easily. The muscles in his arms were tired and sore from all the digging, so rowing across the lake had taken more effort than usual—and to just go home now would be a shitty end to what had already been a long, hot, shitty day.

So he knocked again, loudly. He knew he should feel bad for trying to wake her, but . . . he just wanted to see her. He wanted to see her smile. He wanted to see her long brown hair all tousled from sleep.

But shit, still no answer.

That's what you get for coming so late. Wayne had been awake, more than usual tonight, and they'd found *Butch Cassidy and the Sundance Kid* on TV. Despite the ending, they'd loved the movie as kids—when they'd been roaming the hills, Wayne had been Butch, Mick Sundance, and they'd held up imaginary trains using small broken branches for guns. Given what was to become of them later, the memories probably shouldn't have been good ones, but for Mick they still were. They were . . . the best of being a bad guy. When it was only pretend, it was pretty damn fun. It was when it had turned real that the fun had ended.

Instead of knocking again, he tried the door handle—and it turned, opened. Damn, people here were still so trusting. He couldn't quite decide if that was a good thing or a bad one, but he had a mind to yell at her for it. What if he was someone else? What if he was . . . Wayne, at another time in his life, looking to rob somebody? He shook his head, disturbed by the notion.

He knew he probably shouldn't go inside, but on the other hand, he didn't think she'd mind. All the bad feelings between them seemed in the past now, and he knew without being told that she waited for his visits.

And as much as he wanted her right now, this wasn't so much about sex as it was about just . . . seeing her. Even if she was asleep. Because the mere sight of her always reminded him that there were better, nicer parts of life out there than what he was seeing on his side of the lake these last weeks. Digging a man's grave was bleak work. Digging your *brother's* grave was even bleaker.

And so he walked quietly through the house, guided by the moonlight that shone through the windows. He caught sight of that big blank area on the wall, and the lingering scent of fresh paint told him she must have repainted the room, but he couldn't tell what color. A half-open window across the room meant she was smart enough to let the fumes out of the house, even if some of the air-conditioning went with them.

He'd never been upstairs before, but he found the steps easily enough, and began to slowly climb them. Some creaked beneath his weight, so he tried to move lightly. He didn't plan to wake her—he just wanted to look at her, just wanted to feel her goodness wash over him a little.

He wasn't sure when he'd started realizing how much he valued that in her—the stark, pure goodness that emanated from her—but it had quickly become something he depended on. He thought of it like oxygen, like something he ran out of and needed more to energize him.

For Christ's sake, dude, when did you become such a goofball? He rolled his eyes at his own thoughts as he neared the top of the narrow staircase, glad no one but him would ever know he'd gotten so sappy and cheesy lately. He didn't like being this way. But he told himself that desperate times called for desperate measures, and these were desperate times. Helping his brother die would be the hardest thing he'd ever do. So if it made him a little sappy for a few months, so what?

A narrow hallway that cut through the center of the house led to a small bathroom dead ahead, with doorways at both sides. He checked the one on the right, peeking through, and his chest tingled when he spotted Jenny lying there, looking just as pretty in slumber as she did awake. A ceiling fan turned overhead and the moon shining in the window above the bed cast a square of light across her body. Covers rose to her waist—but her arms were pretty and bare, looking silky smooth. Her lips parted gently, and her hair fanned across the pale pillowcase beneath her head.

God. She took his breath away. He'd thought she was pretty enough awake, but asleep—damn. She looked as innocent as he knew she was. And as sensual as he *also* knew she was. She was that beautiful girl on the dock, a dream girl, a fantasy girl—somehow magnified, multiplied.

What was it like to be the kind of guy who lived on this side of the lake, the kind of guy worthy of Jenny Tolliver? Not just to sneak around with in the night, not just to have sex with, but the kind of guy she would want for keeps. What would it be like to live here with her, in this cute little house, to climb with her into that four-poster bed, to wrap around her in sleep?

The truth was, he couldn't even imagine. It was too far beyond his reality. He had no idea *who* that guy was, what he was about, what made him tick. He didn't know how to *be* that guy.

Not that it mattered. He *wasn't* that guy and never would be.

But he moved quietly closer to the bed anyway, because right now, in this moment, he wanted to know how it felt to share a bed with Jenny.

Walking to the empty side, he quietly stepped out of his unlaced workboots, folded back the covers, and lay down beside her. He rested on his side, watching her some more. He listened to the silence, to the sound of crickets outside, loud and clear even with most of the windows closed. He thought he could like being that guy, that guy she'd end up with someday after all this was over, after her divorce was long in the past, after this summer when they both needed some comfort and gave it to each other.

Whatever you do, don't fall asleep. It would be easy in such a comfortable bed after working hard all day, but he couldn't leave Wayne alone all night, and he sure as hell couldn't be seen in the light of day heading home.

Still, he reached down to pull up the covers on his side—and she awoke with a gasp.

Shit. "It's only me, pussycat—didn't mean to wake you."

"Oh. God. Mick." He hated having scared her, but he loved the sound of relief in her voice. People around here weren't usually *relieved* to see a Brody.

"You didn't answer the door," he whispered. "But I just wanted to lie here with you a while."

Next to him, she sat up tall in bed, revealing the pretty white sleeveless nightgown she wore, looking like some kind of angel hovering above him, gazing down. And then she crossed her arms over herself and drew the gown smoothly up over her head, leaving her beautifully topless before him in the moonlight.

The sight stunned him—because Jenny never made the first move. And he suddenly felt as if helping himself into her bed had been pushy. "We don't have to," he said quickly. "Just resting here is nice." And he meant it. He was tired, after all.

"But . . . I want to," she replied.

She wanted to. God help him. And somehow, just the way she looked at him felt . . . different. Like she was more sure. More ready. Than ever before. He might be tired, but he couldn't even think of saying no. Instead, he simply reached for her.

Jenny's body hummed with electricity. She felt bold. And beautiful. And a little bit naughty, just naughty *enough* for a guy like Mick Brody. A part of her couldn't believe she'd taken off her gown that way, but this only proved it was true: She *was* wild, and she *could* have an affair. She could be a seductress, a temptress. She could initiate sex. And she wanted to make him feel good. The same thoughts from earlier flowed through her veins: *Nothing is going to stop me here, from taking what I want, from finding pleasure with this man.*

Biting her lip, pleasantly aware of her nakedness, she

bent over him, ran her palms over his chest, stomach,
through his T-shirt—this one a dark color she couldn't
clearly make out in the shadowy light. Not that it
mattered—all that mattered was that it was in the way.
So she pushed it up to reveal the muscles underneath,
the dark smattering of hair on his chest; she ran her
fingertips through it, then bent to kiss him.

His mouth was warm, moist—he smelled musky
again tonight, like the scent of guy and earth mixed
together. She kissed him harder and savored the feel of
his hands in her hair, the sensation of his tongue snak-
ing between her lips. It stirred her desire deeper, made
the crux of her thighs tingle, and a soft moan echoed
from her mouth against his.

Lifting from the kisses, she helped him free of the
shirt, then took in the scintillating sight of him in her
bed. She couldn't have dreamed this as a girl—she
couldn't have known then the raw, gut-wrenching
appeal of a man's hard body, or that having such a
specimen in her very bed would make him feel like . . .
a confection, something decadent and delicious for her
to feast on.

And something inside her, something dark and a
little feral, sent her bending back over him to kiss his
broad chest—she needed to feel that, the hardness of
his body beneath her soft lips; she needed to let it fill
her, with stark awareness, and still more need. Need
to give, and need to take. Still kissing, she pressed her
palm to the firm bulge in his pants.

A low groan escaped him and sounded to Jenny like
sweet, driving music. She kissed his chest again, let her
tongue flick over one of his nipples, loved the sharp
intake of his breath in response.

Beneath her kneading hand, he grew stiffer, larger
still, and her breasts ached with longing, and still kissing him—his stomach now—she reached her other

hand down to work at his belt buckle, then his zipper. She undid his jeans and parted them wide. "Help me," she whispered, and Mick lifted himself from the bed and assisted her in pushing them down. She lowered his underwear at the same time, and felt her utter nearness to that hardest part of him. Her heartbeat pulsed through her whole body like a drum. It pulsed between her legs.

As she leaned down once more to kiss his stomach, her hand curved around his erection, and Mick's breath came louder, and she knew they both anticipated what was coming.

Finally, she lowered her mouth over him and began to move her lips up and down the thick, rigid length. The sensation filled her, and Mick's moans fueled her.

She'd been thinking about doing this, fantasizing about it—and she wasn't sure why, since it wasn't usually one of her favorite things, but she'd just wanted to give Mick pleasure, *amazing* pleasure, like he'd given her. And because her revelation with him the last time they were together had given her license to be daring now. Because they were having an affair. And that sounded lush, racy. It made her feel like a woman who lived life to the fullest. Funny how much her realization—that she could be reckless and wild in bed—had changed how she felt about herself, about the whole summer, and about her encounters with Mick.

"God, honey, that's nice," he groaned. Then, "Aw, God yeah," when she took him even deeper.

Continuing to pleasure him that way, she grew aware of how in control of their sex she felt in this moment. In the woods that first time, she'd wanted *him* to take control, make the decision for her—but now *she* was making the decisions, doing what she wanted to do deep down inside, not letting anyone's ideas about her being a good girl color her actions.

She'd taken down a picture, painted a wall, put up curtains, chosen to protect a man who she didn't feel was doing anything wrong—and now she was choosing to pleasure that man as deeply as she could. She'd never felt more vital, alive.

She was completely, vigorously into her task, loving the way Mick ran his fingers across her scalp as she worked—when suddenly he rasped, "Stop, baby," and gently pulled her up, off him.

She blinked her surprise at him in the moonlight. "Why?"

His voice dropped lower. "I'm about to explode here."

She didn't understand. "Isn't that the idea?"

Their gazes locked in the near darkness, and his moved all through her. Her lips felt swollen, her breasts too, as she waited for his reply. Finally, he said softly, "I want more. Of you."

"Oh," she breathed, and despite the rawness of what she'd just been doing, she'd never felt more . . . beautiful.

"Always," he added then. "No matter where I am or what I'm doing, I'm wanting more of you."

She nearly clambered up his body to get to him, to kiss him some more, and they made out like starved lovers, his mouth devouring hers again and again. And only when he let his kisses drop—over her throat, onto her sensitive neck—did she realize she wasn't yet done wanting to be in control here. She knew what she wanted in this moment, and she remained ready to take it.

Kissing his mouth once more, then touching his face, she met his gaze, sensually bit her lower lip, and whispered, "Take off my panties." Her whole being seemed to pulsate as she drank in the heavy way he breathed as he pushed her underwear down, far enough for her to kick them off. After which she moved her body higher up on his, straddling his torso—and then his chest.

A hot sigh left him as his hands closed firm over her ass and she realized he understood exactly what she was doing. So she kept going, until she was sitting fully upright, her hands clamped around the wooden headboard, her parted thighs balanced over his mouth. It was, by far, the most aggressive thing she'd ever done with a man, but she didn't feel shy—she felt adventurous, and truly worthy of being Mick Brody's lover.

When she gingerly lowered herself, Mick's tongue sliced through her, delivering a pleasure so intense that she gasped and had to clutch tighter to the bed to keep her balance. "Oh God," she murmured, letting her eyes fall shut.

Mick's mouth on her was scintillating, and each stroke of his tongue sent a fresh frisson of tingling heat through her whole body. *Oh God, yes—so hot, so good.* Without exactly planning it, she soon began to move against his ministrations, unable not to clench her teeth against the permeating pleasure. "Yes," she heard herself whisper. "That's so good, Mick. So good."

As the sensations threatened to overwhelm her, she realized her position allowed her to peer out the window above the bed, across the dark lake, the moon and stars showing her a silhouette of the tree line. Looking into the vast heavens teeming with a zillion stars, she realized it was perhaps the first time she'd gazed into them without yearning for something more than she had in that moment. It was the first time looking into those stars made her thankful to be exactly who and where she was. Because she didn't feel so small or meaningless right now, and she didn't have any troubles to escape right now—right now she knew the greatest pleasure she'd ever experienced: physical, emotional, all of it. She was right where she wanted to be.

"Oh Mick," she murmured as his mouth lifted her closer and closer to the precipice of orgasm. It would happen soon. "Oh God, yes, good."

Her gaze dropped down into the dark trees below the stars then, and she realized that a place which had always seemed mysterious and forbidden before felt . . . much less so now. It was Mick's home. And even if he'd once made her feel endangered, now the opposite was true—now being with Mick made her feel safe. And so, so alive.

"Oh God, Mick, now!" she cried as the climax broke over her, vibrating through her body in hot bursts of sensation that echoed through every limb. She'd never before in her life announced when she was coming, but she liked when Mick did that, liked knowing the precise moment she'd taken him there, so she'd returned the favor. "Oh Mick! Oh God, Mick! Oh God!"

When finally the pleasure faded to normal, her whole body went weak, limp, and she moved to collapse on the bed next to him. Meeting his eyes reminded her of what she'd just done, how bold she'd been, and she sighed a dreamy, "Thank you."

A wicked smile formed on his handsome face. "Trust me, pussycat—it was my pleasure."

And the next thing she knew, she was under him, his hard body covering hers as he firmly kissed her, rubbed his erection between her legs, massaged her aching breasts in strong, work-roughened hands. She tasted the remnants of his affections on his mouth, tongue, and it made her feel even headier, wilder. She kissed him back fiercely, and thrust upward against his hard-on. She'd just come, of course, but his sudden urgency, the roughness that reminded her of earlier couplings, drove her now, exciting her all over again.

A moment later, he pinned her arms to the bed on both sides of her head, his grip tight on her wrists. And his gaze on her was downright feral. "I want to give it to you so hard, pussycat."

Unh. The words moved through her like liquid heat. "Let me have it," she whispered.

And then he was plunging inside her, deep, slick, making her cry out, and soon nailing her to the bed in brutal, unyielding strokes. She rose to meet them, hungry, reckless with lust, no thoughts in her head about anything except how her body felt right now, how there was no room in her brain for anything but consuming pleasure, raw and unbridled.

He kissed her lips hard, then dropped to kiss her breasts, harder. He suckled first one, then the other, the pull of his mouth so intense that he turned her nipples sore—in a way she relished. She lay beneath him, soaking up every slick, gliding thrust—until Mick pulled back slightly to slip one hand between their bodies, between her thighs.

She gasped at the fresh pleasure, stunned, a little confused. "But I already . . . " she began helplessly, trailing off.

His gaze on her shone dark, hungry. "I'm gonna make you do it again."

She sucked in her breath. And knew she probably looked surprised by the very notion. She'd always heard about multiple orgasms, of course, but she'd never experienced them. She'd somehow imagined them being reserved for other women, the kind of woman bold enough to proposition a guy in a bar, the kind of woman who'd never had a sexual inhibition in her life, the kind of woman she . . . was not.

But Mick raked his thumb across the sensitive nub there over and over as he continued to drive into her, and she realized her upward thrusts were becoming more pronounced, rhythmic, that her breath had gone shallow, that everything inside her was growing hot and feverish and a little bit frenzied. She kept her eyes on his the whole time, gazing up at him even as she moaned, even as she gritted her teeth, even as she heard herself whisper to him, "Oh . . . oh God. Almost, almost . . ."

She sobbed as the second orgasm exploded through her, more intense than the first, more intense than anything she'd ever experienced. She cried out over and over as the waves of pleasure buffeted her, making her feel as if she were drowning in them, being swallowed by sensation. *Oh God, oh God, oh God.*

Oh wow. She truly hadn't known she could do that. She lay beneath him, spent and astonished.

"Damn, pussycat," Mick whispered, looking gratified and sexy as hell—just before he held her down once more and began to pound into her again, hard, hard, hard. And it was in that moment when she realized: *Oh God, I'm suddenly not so in control here anymore.*

When had *that* happened? But then, maybe it didn't matter. As good as it had felt to be the one orchestrating their sex for a while, she couldn't deny that perhaps, at some moments, control was overrated.

"Aw God, baby, I can't hold back," Mick said, voice heated, breathless, just before delivering the last and most powerful, punishing strokes—and as Jenny willingly absorbed them into her body, she loved knowing she'd just made Mick lose control, too.

Mick woke up with her in his arms, naked, soft, warm. She felt so good that he never wanted to leave—but that thought forced him to glance around the room until he found a digital clock on a bedside table. Okay, good—he'd only been here about an hour, so he could stay awhile longer. He refocused on the woman in his embrace.

He hadn't woken up like this often—he usually ended up with women who . . . didn't inspire him to sleep over. He liked his sex quick and easy—like he wished he could have kept it with Jenny. But his secrets and the need for her trust had complicated things from the start.

Of course, it wasn't the first time sex had turned into something more. He'd dated plenty of women for a month or two, even had a couple who'd lasted longer and who he'd actually thought of as his "girlfriend." But then, on both occasions, the woman in question had told him she loved him. And he hadn't wanted to hear that, hadn't felt the same way—he didn't think he'd ever been in love and had long since decided that his screwed-up upbringing had probably made it so he just wasn't cut out for that. So he'd ended the relationships and moved on.

As for Jenny, what they shared was . . . indefinable to him. She wasn't his girlfriend. But she wasn't just a quick lay, either. Although he hated the moments when words slipped out that might let her know that. *Wherever I am and whatever I'm doing, I'm wanting more of you?* He let out a sigh. Damn it, what had he been thinking?

He wasn't stupid—he understood how he felt for her. He felt . . . more needful of her than he should because she was the bright light in a world of darkness right now. He *got* that.

But he didn't want to let it show, because it would . . . make her think this was something it wasn't. By the end of the summer he'd be gone, *long* gone, and he never planned to look back. He didn't want Jenny to get hurt by that—because she'd been nothing but good to him, better than most people in his life had been, especially people from Destiny. *So you have to cool it, damn it, on saying shit like that. You have to keep this exactly what you told her it was: hot sex.*

"Hey," she whispered then, and he looked down to see her smiling sweetly up at him.

Despite his last thought, he smiled back. "Hey, pussycat."

She bit her lip, looking like a woman who had a secret she was about to tell. "That was . . . the best sex I've ever had."

He couldn't lie. "Me, too." *Aw shit—what happened to not telling her stuff like that?* She was just too open, too earnest, and ever since she'd found out about Wayne, he'd found her too easy to talk to.

She let her hand drift from his chest over to his arm, running her fingertips across his tattoo. "So about this—why'd you get it?"

She'd already asked him about this once. "Haven't we already discussed—"

"Besides wanting to be a bad-ass, I mean," she added with a laugh. "Why else?"

At first, he laughed, too—why did anyone get a tattoo?—but then he actually thought about the answer, and about the fact that Jenny seemed to know there was more to it. "Truthfully," he said, "I probably did it because Wayne got one. I was about nineteen or twenty, I guess, and Wayne made tattoos seem cool."

"He has more now," she commented quietly, a little sheepish—because she'd noticed that when peeking in the window of his house, he supposed.

"Mostly from prison."

"But you stopped at one," she pointed out.

He glanced down at her. "Guess I quit looking up to him so much after a while."

"Do you smoke?"

He flinched and gave her a look. That was kinda out of the blue.

"I just wondered because that day I met you when we were teenagers, you were smoking. Now I'm not around you enough to know, so I'm curious."

Oh. "No," he said. "Quit a long time ago." Another thing he'd probably started because his brother had.

"Do you drink?"

He laughed now at how inquisitive she'd suddenly gotten. "I'd take a beer if you offered me one, but . . . now that I think about it, I haven't had anything to drink since I came back to Destiny. What's with all the questions?"

She perched her chin atop her hands on his chest. "I don't know. I guess I've just started to . . . wonder things about you. I mean, we have sex like crazy animals—is it awful if I want to know a few things about you?"

Well, when she put it like that . . . "No, not awful. Just . . . new."

"Tell me more about your life in Cincinnati."

He tried to sum it up. "Like I told you, I work as a bricklayer and stonemason."

"So how'd you learn to do that?" She sounded truly interested, which for some reason caught him off guard.

He just shrugged. "When Wayne went to prison, I realized I needed to clean up my act, live better." As for why he'd picked that particular trade . . . "And I always just kind of . . . admired good brickwork and nice stone walls, you know? So I thought it would be a good thing to learn, and a job people would always need done."

"Do you enjoy it?"

He nodded against the pillow. "It makes me feel good to . . . build something I know is gonna be around awhile."

"Do you . . . have a girlfriend or anything?"

He looked at her in response to the pointed question. "Nobody special, pussycat. If I did, I wouldn't be here with you right now."

"Good," she said. "I don't like cheaters. For obvious reasons." Her cheating husband. When he'd first met her, he'd felt bad for her about that in a general sort of way. Now that he knew her better, he wanted to pound the guy into the ground.

"So, Miss Twenty Questions, what about *you*?"

"What *about* me?" She looked surprised he would ask, and he was surprised, too—but he could do this, talk to her like this, without saying romantic shit, so it would be okay.

What could he ask her? "You like being a teacher?"

She pursed her lips, looked undecided. "I like teaching a subject I love, like astronomy. But I never really planned on teaching middle-schoolers—it just worked out that way. And some of them are great—but it can be hard to hold their attention, and sometimes I feel more like a babysitter than a teacher."

Just then, he noticed a print on the wall, illuminated by the moonlight—an artsy-looking painting of a black cat with long whiskers and a curling tail. "Did you ever get another cat after that white one?" he asked, just because it popped into his head.

She shook her head, appearing a little dismayed by the question. "No. In fact, someone actually offered me one today and I turned it down. Why?"

"I don't know—you just seem . . . like a cat sort of girl."

She smiled softly, clearly pleased he could figure that out. "I am, actually—I love cats." Her smile faded just as quickly, though. "But they die."

In that moment, he could suddenly hear the silence

all around them—right before he reminded her, "Everything dies. Every*body* dies."

Their gazes met and he knew what they were both thinking about: Wayne. And her mother. They both knew about death coming. "But cats die faster," she whispered. "I couldn't help thinking about that today, when my friend offered me the cat. Maybe . . . that's why I like stars so much. They all eventually die, too, but it takes them billions of years."

"Stars die?" He guessed he'd heard of them exploding occasionally, but he didn't know much about what went on in space.

She nodded. "Yep. You were right when you said everything dies—even the very biggest things in the universe die sooner or later."

"So if you love the sky so much, why aren't you . . . some kind of fancy scientist or something?" He couldn't help thinking she'd probably be good at that sort of thing since she seemed pretty much *obsessed* with stars and planets.

What he hadn't expected was for the question to make her look . . . almost ashamed in some way. "I . . . wanted to be. I dreamed of being an astronomer, maybe even a physicist."

It left him to ask the obvious. "Why didn't you?"

She swallowed visibly and looked uncomfortable. "When I met Terrence, he thought being a teacher was more practical, more attainable. *He* wanted to be a teacher, so he kind of talked me into being one, too. I could kick myself for listening to him. And I feel angry at him for it sometimes. But I really have no one to blame but myself. I gave up on my dream. I let it get away from me."

"Show me," he said.

"Show you what?"

"Show me what's so great up there. What you look at with that telescope of yours." He couldn't believe he was saying it, because he wasn't even sure he really cared about seeing—but he'd rather be a guy who encouraged her dreams than one who took them away. And letting her show him seemed like a nice thing to do.

As for when he'd gotten to be such a nice guy—he had no idea.

"I'd love to, but I can't—here. Too many trees—they block too much of the sky."

"Let's go across the lake then."

Her eyes lit, even if a bit cautiously. "Really? Right now?"

He shrugged. "Sure, pussycat." She already knew his secrets, after all. And it had made him feel bad to think of her wanting to do something as simple as look at the sky but having it be sort of . . . just beyond her reach. That was how he'd felt about this side of the lake his whole life.

"Holy shit," he murmured when he spotted Saturn with its rings. He'd learned about the solar system a long time ago in grade school, of course, but . . . there was something about seeing it, another planet, with freaking *rings* around it, with his own eyes. It was just hard to believe he could be looking at something so far away—it was like sci-fi come to life.

"Now let's look deeper into space," Jenny said, stepping up to the telescope and starting to make adjustments to it, changing out the lens.

"You can look *deeper* into space?" he asked, astounded.

Her answer came matter-of-fact. "Oh *yeah. Much* deeper."

A moment later, after she used a dim, red-lensed flashlight to consult what looked to Mick like some kind of star map, she peered through the telescope, made more adjustments, then let out a heady-sounding sigh. "Got it," she said. Then backed away from the instrument and said, "Take a look. The Dumbbell Nebula."

Mick put his eye back to the lens and what he saw almost made his heart skip a beat. A huge, heavenly glow surrounded a darker shape that reminded him of an hourglass. "What the hell *is* that?"

"It's a planetary nebula. Which is basically a big blob of gases produced when a certain kind of star explodes."

"Wow," he murmured. "That's pretty damn cool."

"But the more common type of nebula is a big, gassy region where stars are actually *formed*."

He pulled back from the telescope. "Formed how?"

As she explained, she took back control of the telescope and played around with it a little more, until offering it back to him again. "Here—this is the Swan Nebula, a star-maker, but there aren't many stars visible. And you might have to use your imagination a little to see the swan."

He looked, and was amazed. "I see . . . more of a check mark," he admitted, but felt a little freaked out to think he was looking at the stuff that would turn into new stars.

"Ah. The short end of the check mark is the swan's head, and the long side is the body. Can you see it now?"

"Oh. Yeah. Kinda. So, how far away from us *is* this thing?"

"About five thousand light-years."

He pulled back, looked at her. He sort of remembered what a light-year was from school, too. But . . .

"You're saying it's so far away it takes five thousand years just for the *light* from it to travel here?"

"Yep. What we're looking at right now is actually how the nebula looked five thousand years ago. It'll take another five thousand for us to see how it looks tonight."

"Shit," he murmured. "That's . . . tough to wrap your brain around."

She smiled. "I know. It's a crazy world out there."

He laughed. "It can be a crazy world down here, too," he pointed out, but couldn't deny the world felt less crazy when he was with her.

And the thought made him stop, a little more taken with the girl before him than even the stuff stars were made of. He reached out and grabbed on to her hand, squeezing. "Thank you for showing me this, pussycat. You're right—it makes the bad things seem smaller."

She lowered her chin, cast a pretty smile. "Well, I kind of . . . loved showing you. I love that you get it and don't think I'm just a geeky girl with a telescope anymore."

"You, pussycat? Geeky? Never. You're too beautiful." Lifting his hand to her cheek, he gave her a soft, gentle kiss that was much more about just wanting to be close to her than about getting in her pants. And then one kiss beneath the stars turned into another, and another, their mouths lingering together, exploring—until he pulled back, stopped.

What the hell was he doing? He'd told Wayne it was just sex. He'd told himself that, too, a hundred times, that anything else he felt was just about need, comfort, about distracting him from the bad shit. But how did he make sense of this—of the weird, simple joy he'd just taken from looking at the damn stars with her?

"I should . . . take you home now," he told her, wondering if his sudden discomfort showed.

"I hope I haven't kept you away from your brother too long." Good, she just thought it was about Wayne.

He automatically shook his head. "It wasn't you—it was me." *Damn it—shut up already.* But in his head, he kept talking: *It was me just wanting to be with you.* And he knew he definitely *should* be quiet now, but there was one more thing he really needed to say, because it suddenly hit him that he wasn't sure he had. "Thank you, too, honey, for not telling your dad about Wayne."

"I wouldn't do that to you, Mick," she whispered, and his heart warmed.

There were moments when he still got fearful, wondering if she *could* still tell her dad about him and Wayne, but after tonight, he felt totally safe with Jenny knowing his secret.

Three things cannot be long hidden: the sun,
the moon, and the truth.

Buddha

Eleven

$\mathcal{D}$espite herself, Jenny walked into the Fourth of
July picnic at Betty and Ed's carrying her lemon bars
with a smile. She'd chosen a red-and-white polka-dot
sundress and flat red sandals for the occasion, and
had opted for a ponytail knowing that the day—and
night—would be long and hot. The heat wave hadn't
broken since she'd gotten home and wasn't expected
to anytime soon. And maybe she should still be worried over lots of things—but she wasn't.

She spent the next hour chatting with people, including Tessa and Amy—and Amy was quick to point
out Logan Whitaker across the meadow, who Jenny
couldn't deny *had* indeed grown up well. "He's a *fire-
man*," Amy pointed out—but Jenny didn't take her
bait.

"This is so great," Sue Ann said, stepping up to join

the other three girls. "All of us back together again. The only thing missing is Rachel."

And all of them sighed. Rachel had always been the outgoing one, the determined one—the one who'd gotten them in trouble a time or two. Well, except for Jenny, who had always refused to go along with whatever scheme was taking place. "So she doesn't even come home to Destiny to see her family?" Jenny asked, having wondered about that after their last conversation.

"Her family moved away, too," Amy said wistfully. "Only her grandma Edna and a few aunts and uncles are still here."

"I wish you'd reconsider going with us to Chicago in the fall. You, too, Sue Ann. Think of the fun we could have."

Jenny cleared her throat. "As I keep reminding everyone, I have no idea where I'll even be in September, although with any luck, I'll be busy teaching."

"Don't look now," Sue Ann said, "but Mike Romo at nine o'clock."

Since the girls stood in a circle, the other three weren't sure which way to look. "Which way *is* nine at the moment exactly?" Amy asked.

Sue Ann pursed her lips and looked irritated. "To my left."

Jenny indulged in a glimpse and, wow, when she spotted the dark-haired guy in a police uniform that matched her father's, she understood what all the fuss was about. "Holy crap."

Amy raised her eyebrows before even sneaking her peek. "Aha! So you *are* interested. One look at Mike Romo can make a girl more ready to get back in the dating pool than she thought."

"He's *so* snarly, though," Tessa said with a sneer.

"He was so mean to my Aunt Alice when he pulled her over that she ended up in tears."

"In his defense," Amy said, "your Aunt Alice drives like a nut."

Sue Ann cast Jenny a sideways glance and said, "Actually, sometimes Jenny *goes* for the scary type."

Both Tessa and Amy immediately zeroed in on this. "Do tell," Tessa said.

"That's so not like you," Amy added. "But I knew it—I just knew it. There *is* a mystery man in your life."

Dear God in heaven—what was Sue Ann *thinking*? A familiar warmth climbed Jenny's cheeks as she denied the whole thing—again. "Don't be silly, you guys. Sue Ann is just trying to be a troublemaker. *Aren't you?*" She glared at Sue Ann.

Her best friend looked almost as surprised by what she'd said as Jenny was—then nodded. "That's me, always making trouble. What can I say? It's a sickness."

Then Jenny changed the subject. "But speaking of the Romos, what relation is Mike to that Lucky Romo guy?" She was suddenly remembering that Lucky Romo had once hung out with Mick.

"Brother," Amy said. "But Lucky took off a long time ago—I don't think even Mike knows what became of him."

"Hmm," Jenny replied, beginning to realize that besides being a compulsive matchmaker, Amy truly had her finger on the pulse of the entire Destiny population, past and present.

"Time to eat, ladies," Ed, their host, poked his balding head into the small crowd to say, and Jenny was kind of relieved. She enjoyed seeing her old friends, but she was more than ready to tune out Amy's dating suggestions. Oh, and kill Sue Ann.

"I should murder you," she said under her breath as they broke away to go get in the food line.

Sue Ann looked appropriately guilty. "I agree. I don't know what came over me—it just popped out. Those girls are a bad influence on me. They make me feel like we're back at one of Rachel's pajama parties."

"I know what you mean. But if you can't control yourself, then no more guy-talk when we're around them. Remember, it's not just *my* secrets at stake here."

Sue Ann nodded obediently and lowered her voice further than she already had. "You're right. I keep forgetting you're aiding and abetting."

After which Jenny swallowed heavily. At moments, she forgot that, too. But she never forgot Mick's freedom was on the line.

And she felt a lot more relaxed when she finally settled in with Sue Ann's family at a picnic table, where she feasted on a fresh-off-the-grill burger, Mrs. Kinman's potato salad, Linda Sue's baked beans, and a couple of Lettie Gale's famous deviled eggs while listening to Sophie regale her with tales of Vacation Bible School. It was nice to focus on something besides her own dramas for a few minutes.

Not that it lasted long. When Jeff left the table with Sophie to watch her chase butterflies in the wide-open meadow behind Betty and Ed's house, Sue Ann said, "So, back to you and your scary type. What's new in the Jenny saga these days?"

After their lunch the other day, Sue Ann already knew the whole story about her taking down her mom's picture, yet she wasn't aware of the ongoing *new* guilt it had induced with her dad when he'd seen the room. "But he seems okay now," Jenny concluded after filling her in on the latest. "For the most part."

"Good. Only . . . that's not the part of the saga I was asking about. I asked about the *scary* guy in your life— remember?"

Jenny sighed. Oh yeah. But suddenly, this part was

. . . a little harder to talk about. Even with Sue Ann. So she fumbled through her thoughts aloud. "Okay, fine. The fact is . . . I'm feeling . . . pretty crazy about Mick."

In response, Sue Ann sucked in her breath and looked alarmed—just as Jenny had feared. "Wait a minute. I thought this was just sex."

"It is," Jenny assured her. "Mostly. Although, I mean, we've started . . . talking more lately. And he even rowed me across to his side of the lake so we could look at the stars together."

Sue Ann gritted her teeth as if to say, *Yikes.* "Jen—*hello*? That is not just sex, my friend."

Jenny shrugged. "Sure it is. Or, well, it's just something that goes *with* the sex and makes me more *comfortable* with the sex. Because it's just . . . nicer to *know* the guy you're getting wild with, you know?"

Just then, Mary Ann Davis from the Daisy Dress Shop wandered past, close to the table, with her husband and two children in tow, so Jenny and Sue Ann quieted until they were out of earshot. Then Sue Ann leaned close. "So no more dad guilt about"—she lowered her voice—"the wanted man across the lake?"

Jenny shook her head. "Not really. Maybe if I thought about it all the time, but I don't. I'm getting very . . . in control of myself lately. Ever since I realized Terrence was totally wrong about me, ever since I experienced the proof, I just feel more like I'm . . ."

"Woman-hear-me-roar?" Sue Ann suggested.

And Jenny giggled softly in reply. "Something like that."

"Hello, ladies."

Since they had their heads together, they both flinched, looking up—to see an older, still amazingly handsome version of Adam Becker, Jenny's one-time boyfriend, the guy everyone kept trying to fix her up with. "Adam?" she said, blinking.

"It's great to see you, Jenny," he answered, sounding much more masculine than she remembered. She was suddenly beginning to understand what everyone saw in him.

And, whoa, this was weird. Because once upon a time, she used to make out with him—rather intensely. And wow, he looked good. "You, too."

"I heard you were back in town, and I was hoping your dad would call me to mow the grass at your place, but he hasn't," he said on a slightly sheepish-yet-endearing laugh.

"Well, its hardly grown with the lack of rain."

"My loss. But I'm glad to finally bump into you."

Just then Sue Ann spoke up. "I'm gonna go . . . help Betty. I heard she's making homemade ice cream." But the look on Sue Ann's face very clearly said, *I still think Adam Becker is a much better rebound guy for you than Mick Brody.*

And as Adam sat down and they talked, Jenny couldn't deny that it made sense. Adam was still good-looking, well liked, prosperous, enterprising, and had somewhere along the way become pretty darn sexy. He told her he'd gotten divorced, then pointed out the little twin boys who'd joined Sophie in the butterfly chase. "Jacob and Joey," he said. "I get 'em three days a week and miss 'em like crazy when they're gone."

Jenny told Adam she'd gotten divorced, too, but kept it light, realizing that talking about it didn't bother her as much as it had just a couple of weeks ago. She explained about the teaching job she'd left and that she was here for the summer deciding what was next.

"*I* heard the Destiny School Board offered you a job,"

Adam said with one arched eyebrow. "We'd sure be happy to have you back here permanently, Jenny."

She tilted her head in surprise. "I forgot how quick news travels around here."

He shrugged. "The Destiny grapevine's alive and well. And I just put in some landscaping for Stan Goodman's wife," he concluded with a wink.

"Well, I haven't ruled it out, but I haven't given it a lot of thought, either," she explained. *I've been too busy keeping secrets and having covert sex.*

"Listen," he said, "I know your divorce is still fresh, but . . . let me take you out to dinner one night this week. There's a new Italian place over in Crestview."

Jenny's heart swelled. She loved Adam. In an old-times, first-passion kind of way. And if Mick hadn't been in the picture, who knew . . . maybe she'd have been more tempted. She could easily envision the big smile it would put on Sue Ann's face, and her dad's, too. She and Adam would make the perfect couple. He even came with the children she and Terrence had never produced.

But she really couldn't imagine going on a date with Adam—even for old times' sake—when she was feeling so . . . caught up in Mick. The other night with him had been amazingly freeing, and showing him the night skies had made her feel more . . . connected to him.

A little sadly, she reached out and took Adam's hand. "Thank you for asking me—but I don't think I'm ready to date yet." Because that sounded a lot better than, *Sorry, but I'm already having reckless casual sex with Mick Brody—you know, that guy who once robbed a liquor store in Crestview?*

Adam smiled in understanding and said, "No worries, Jenny. Maybe some other time—if you decide to stick around."

"Maybe," she told him. But even as smart as that sounded, especially since she knew Mick wouldn't be in her life for very long, it was hard to think of any other man right now.

After Adam left to check on his boys, Jenny made her way over to Miss Ellie, who sat in a lawn chair beneath a shade tree. Something about being around Miss Ellie always provided her with a sense of calm—even if she had to scream to be heard. "Hello, Miss Ellie!" she said loudly.

Miss Ellie looked up with a wrinkled smile. "Well, Jenny—hello, dear."

"What a pretty dress you're wearing!" Jenny yelled. It was decorated with butterflies in various pastel colors.

"It's nice and thin," she said. "Good for the hot weather, you know."

Just then, a pretty yellow butterfly fluttered up beneath the tree, flickered and flew around Miss Ellie for a moment, then alit on her lap. "Well, look at that," Miss Ellie said. "He thinks they're real."

Her almost childlike smile warmed Jenny's heart, and she suddenly understood what Miss Ellie's presence gave her: a reminder of the joys of a simpler life. The simpler life all around her in Destiny. *When she wasn't busy having ravenous sex with the liquor store robber, of course.* A thought which made her laugh out loud.

Miss Ellie looked up. "You seem in good spirits today, dear. I still can't believe that silly Terrence deserted you for a hippie, but I'm glad to see you smile."

"Don't worry, Miss Ellie, he's the last thing on my mind. Now, would you like me to go get you some ice cream?"

Miss Ellie put her hand to her ear—Jenny had forgotten to yell that time.

"Ice cream, Miss Ellie! Ice cream!"

Miss Ellie suddenly looked worried, her gray eyebrows knitting. "Oh, you shouldn't waste your time screaming over a man, dear." Then she looked cheerful again as she reached out to take Jenny's hand in hers. "But you know what would make you feel better? Some of Betty's homemade ice cream. Why don't you get us some?"

Jenny approached her father from behind at the picnic as he stood talking with Mike Romo—she planned to ask if he wanted to cook out at the cottage tomorrow evening. Maybe it would put any remaining tension about the pictures behind them.

That's when she heard him say, "Then I reckon I'll drive out to the Brody place one more time—and I'd better take off soon if I want to make it back in time for the fireworks."

Her heart nearly stopped. And despite the punishing heat of late afternoon, a cold chill raced up her spine. She couldn't have heard that correctly.

But she knew she had. *Oh God.* Oh God, what was going on here?

As soon as Mike walked away, she stepped up close, closing her hand tight over her father's arm. "Why would you drive out to the Brody place?" she asked pointedly.

He looked shocked at her tone and she realized her emotions had gotten the best of her. *Okay, calm down here.* She took a deep breath. *If you want to keep Mick safe, you have to play it cool.*

"Today of all days," she added, as if that was part of her concern. "I mean, it's the Fourth of July. And you love Betty and Ed's party—you look forward to it all summer. So why would you leave in the middle of it?"

He covered her hand with his own, patting it. "Relax,

Jennygirl. I'll be back for fireworks, and it'll likely be a wasted trip anyway."

She tried to breathe normally, though it was difficult. "But . . . why would you go *there*?"

At this, her father looked around to make sure they were alone, then lowered his voice. "Well, don't let this get around—we don't need folks scared and I'm sure it's nothin' to worry about—but . . . Wayne Brody broke out of prison a while back. The state authorities called me, seein's as Destiny was his last address, and I drove out there *then*, a couple of days after the escape, but the old place was quiet and untouched."

She figured that simply meant her dad had gotten there before Wayne or Mick had, thank goodness. "So why go again?"

"Well, he hasn't been caught yet, and the prison folks say he's sick, so they don't think he could've gotten far—they think he has to be holed up someplace. Then, just this mornin', Willie Hargis, who lives out on the highway close to the turnoff leadin' back to that side of the lake, mentioned to Mike that he's seen a pickup head back there a couple times lately. He assumed it was hunters, but I figure I should check it out."

"Does it have to be now? Today?" If she could get her father to wait, even just overnight, she could canoe across the lake and warn Mick. She didn't know if that would give him time to clear out completely, or if Wayne could even travel, but it would be better than nothing.

"Well, way I figure it, it does," her father said, crushing her hopes. "Never pays to wait with the law—I'd feel pretty foolish to get out there tomorrow and find out I'd just missed him." Her father narrowed his gaze on her then. "Somethin' eatin' you, Jennygirl? What's wrong?"

Jenny's heart beat nearly as hard as it had the night she'd first encountered Mick in the woods. "Nothing," she said, but knew she'd hesitated too long and probably sounded nervous.

"Don't *sound* like nothin'."

She sighed, feeling desperate, and not quite able to think straight. Oh God, Oh God, what should she do? Finally, she shook her head. "Everything's fine, Dad."

He gave her a long look, clearly trying to decide if he should believe her or not, then eventually said, "Well, all right then. I'm gonna head out there now. If anybody notices I'm gone, you tell 'em I'll be back by sundown and not to start those fireworks without me."

And then he started to walk away. And Jenny knew she couldn't let him. She just couldn't. She didn't know how the hell she was going to *stop* him, but she had to do *something*. So she followed quickly after him, then reached out and grabbed back onto his arm again, drawing him to a halt. "*Wait*."

Her dad looked quizzically over his shoulder. "What is it, Jenny?"

She felt like she would faint from the heat, like her legs were about to collapse beneath her. Her mind raced, but she could only think of one chance to save Mick and his brother.

"Well?" her father asked. "What's goin' on here? What aren't you tellin' me?"

She tried to form a plan, find words. Her skin prickled with uneasiness. Was she doing the right thing? Was she? But what else *could* she do? "Could we . . . go sit in your cruiser and talk? I'm feeling a little faint and could use some A/C."

Looking understandably confused, he said, "All right." Then he pressed a steadying hand to her back to guide her to the car, parked amid twenty or thirty others in a grassy area near the road.

Jenny tried to think as they walked, but nothing brilliant or new came to her. And once they were in the car, with the A/C blasting, her father said, "All right now, honey, what's this all about? What's wrong?"

She glanced up at him, but realized it was easier to look at the car's dashboard as they talked. *Oh God, please let this be the right thing to do.* "I . . . have something to tell you, Dad. But before I do, I need you to make me a promise." Her voice sounded unsteady to her own ears, and despite the cool air blowing across her face and neck, she still felt woozy, almost sick.

"What kinda promise?" he asked, his tone conveying that he suddenly realized this was something big.

She tried to swallow back the lump in her throat. *How could this be happening?* "I need you to promise me . . . to *swear* to me . . . that if you love me, you won't . . . *act* . . . on what I'm about to tell you."

He sat stunned for a moment, silent, but finally replied. "What on earth's goin' on here, Jenny?"

She had to stay strong, to insist. "Promise me," she said. "Promise me that if I tell you a secret, you won't act on it. Promise me that, for me, you'll pretend you don't know." Her heart felt like it was about to pound through her rib cage.

"This sounds serious," he said. "So how can I do that?"

She took a breath and forced herself to meet his gaze. "You just do it," she told him. "You just love me enough to do it."

When he sat there a minute longer, still quiet, she went on. "This is important to me, Dad—*so* important. Otherwise, I would never ask you to . . . to look the other way about something. But I know I'm right about this, so that's why I'm asking."

She knew she'd completely confused him when he said, "Are you in some kinda trouble?"

"No, it's not me," she snapped. "*Now just promise me! Please!*"

She'd raised her voice and knew it had shocked them both. Jenny had never yelled at her father in her life.

But apparently she'd picked a good time to do it, because it made him say, "Okay, Jenny, I promise. Calm down."

She drew in her breath, tried to relax. *This is awful, so awful.* "So I have your word that you won't act on what I tell you?"

"All right, yes—you have my word."

Okay. Good. Thank God. And now . . . she would have to break her father's heart.

She swallowed again, then began. "I've been . . . seeing someone—a man," she clarified, "since I got home."

Shock washed over her father's face, and she thought—*oh Daddy, you ain't heard nothin' yet.* But she had to press on. "I . . . canoed across the lake one night, because there's a rocky place up on the hill that's perfect for stargazing."

"How on earth did you know that?"

"Sue Ann and I used to sneak across to it when we were teenagers."

When he looked horrified, she said quickly, "Don't worry, that's the worst thing I ever did." *Until now.*

"Go on," he said.

She took another deep breath and hoped he wouldn't interrupt her so she could get this all out. "When I went across, I ran into . . . Mick Brody. And we started, um, seeing each other." *Rutting like animals.* "And . . . he's not as bad as you think, Dad, I promise. He's actually . . . a pretty good guy. But the thing is . . ."

"*Yeah?*" Maybe her dad could hear it coming. She tried to ignore how upset he already sounded.

Just spit it out. "The thing is, Wayne *is* there. But he's dying, Dad. He has a brain tumor and leukemia—

Mick said he won't last the summer. He only escaped because he didn't want to die in prison—he wanted to die at home. He asked Mick to take care of him until then."

When her father said nothing for a long moment, when the only sounds in the car were the *whoosh* of the A/C and the static of the police radio, she finally found the strength to look at him. And—oh God. She'd never felt so . . . disappointing. He stared at her like she was a stranger. She had to close her eyes a moment to block out the expression on his face.

"I'll honor my promise to you," he finally said, his voice uncharacteristically quiet, "but I can't understand why, *how*, you could keep somethin' like this from me." Then he shook his head, as if in disbelief. "My Jenny . . . with Mick Brody?" he muttered.

It was all she could do to hold back tears—but she had to be tough here, the tough new her.

And so she was. "If you knew him, you'd see he's not a bad person. And keeping it from you was really hard for me, but the reason I did was because, in my heart, I don't feel that Mick is doing anything wrong."

"You don't feel he's doin' anything wrong?" he yelled. "He's breakin' the law! They both are! How can that not be wrong? I thought I'd taught you better."

Jenny recoiled slightly at the outburst—but kept sticking up for herself. "You *did* teach me about right and wrong. But maybe I believe that right and wrong come in shades of gray."

Her father shook his head. "I've never seen shades of gray with the law."

"Well, that's because you're a cop and it's your job to uphold it. But that doesn't mean every law is right, and maybe being a cop makes you . . . narrow-minded. Because there *are* shades of gray, and arresting Mick and his brother would serve no purpose. He's just helping his brother die in peace, at home."

When he didn't answer, she added, quietly, "This whole thing has forced me to look at right and wrong in a whole new perspective. And what I've learned is that . . . maybe sometimes . . . doing the *wrong* thing . . . is the right thing to do."

Jenny sat by herself on a tablecloth spread on the ground in Ed and Betty's meadow watching neon bursts of red, white, and blue explode in the sky above her. She'd planned to share the spot with her father, but she'd last seen him talking with Ed and seeming grouchy. Understandably, she supposed.

All that matters is that he didn't go out to Mick's place. He'd made up some excuse to Mike Romo. *All that matters is that he promised to keep the same secret she was keeping, and even if he wasn't happy about it, Walter Tolliver never broke his word.*

But she still couldn't believe it had happened. She'd come here in such a good mood, too. Now, she'd been forced to tell her father something that had changed his whole opinion of her, for the worse, all for Mick Brody.

Why? She *had* to ask herself. *Why would you sacrifice your relationship with your father for Mick Brody?*

As the fireworks continued, she began to tick off reasons.

From the beginning, she just hadn't felt Mick's actions were wrong.

And . . . maybe this was just part of the process she was going through right now, part of learning to really be an adult, to take control of her life. Maybe being honest with her dad was a necessary step in that direction.

Or maybe you're falling in love with him.

She gasped. Where the hell had *that* come from? Because she was *not* in love with Mick Brody. She couldn't be. It was unthinkable. They were . . . so different. Like night and day. Black and white.

But hadn't she just told herself there were shades of gray everywhere?

She shook her head to clear away the confusion. None of that mattered—what mattered was that this was only an affair—not love. It had to be. Because she was just getting over Terrence and this was rebound sex. Because the very idea of "an affair" had made her feel so good, so strong inside, so . . . woman-hear-me-roar, just like Sue Ann had said.

But when you feared your dad would find out Mick's secret, you nearly crumbled. It felt like your world was dissolving, not Mick's. It felt like, if something bad happened to him, you'd fall apart.

She let out a sigh. That didn't sound much like an affair. Just like Sue Ann had also said.

But the very idea of loving Mick Brody made her feel . . . helpless inside. Like a vulnerable little girl. And she wasn't going to be that anymore—she just *wasn't*.

So this *wasn't* love. This was hot sex. Some summer companionship, that was all.

"What's up, Tolliver? You look like you lost your best friend."

She looked up to see Sue Ann, who now settled next to her on the cloth in a pretty summer skirt and red strappy top. She reached out and held on to Sue Ann's hand—tight. "No—thank God I still have *you*."

"What's *that* mean?" Sue Ann clearly, suddenly, grasped the magnitude of the situation.

Jenny looked at her friend beneath the lit-up sky and knew it must show in her eyes, but she had to say it anyway. "I had to tell my dad. He heard about Wayne's breakout and was going to drive out there. He's not going to now, but . . . I think he hates me."

Sue Ann's face fell. "Oh Jen," she said, "come here," then pulled Jenny into a hug.

"Worse yet," Jenny admitted, still in the embrace, "I've got this crazy fear in my head right now. I'm afraid . . . oh God . . . that I might actually be in love."

"Yeah, *that's* a newsflash—*not*," Sue Ann said, then patted her back and hugged her some more.

When Mick came in the back door a few nights later, Jenny's heart was in her throat. Her father had kept his promise, as she knew he would, because Walter Tolliver was a man of his word. But it still felt strange to see Mick for the first time after telling her father his secret.

Her thoughts shifted, though, when she realized he was carrying a long, narrow cylinder of cardboard. She pointed. "What's that?"

Glancing down at it, he looked . . . surprisingly sheepish. "Uh . . . nothing important. Just . . . something I thought you might like."

She narrowed her gaze on him slightly. Was she losing her mind or had Mick Brody actually brought her a present? She bit her lip to try to hold back her smile, but it didn't work very well. "So what is it?"

He held it out to her. "Here. But if you don't like it, that's okay. It's no big deal."

In fact, she *was* a little nervous opening it. What on earth would Mick give her as a gift? She couldn't imagine. What if she *didn't* like it? Could she fake a reaction?

But when she took the cap off one end and pulled out a poster of some sort, she unrolled it to see—oh wow, a print of Van Gogh's *Starry Night*. She gasped.

"For the wall," he said. "That spot looks pretty blank now."

"It's . . . amazing, Mick," she said, still studying Van Gogh's swirling blue-and-yellow impression of the night sky.

"Not *that* amazing," he said, trying to play it off as nothing. "I was just over in Crestview, doing laundry, and I walked past a shop window and saw this. You'll have to get a frame—I wasn't sure I could get one over here in the rowboat without dinging it, so I just got the print."

"I can't wait to hang it," she said, her heart near to bursting. "It's really perfect for the spot, and I love it. Thank you."

He started seeming more like his usual self then, taking the print from her hand, setting it aside on the coffee table, and saying, "Come here, pussycat," as he drew her into his arms.

She lifted her mouth to his for a warm, sweet kiss, and he said, "I didn't come all the way over here just to give you a picture of the sky, though."

"No?" she asked playfully.

"I mainly came to give you this." Then he pulled her body tight to his to let her feel the hard erection pressing at the crux of her thighs.

"Mmm, that's perfect, too," she promised him.

"Now that I'm not gonna argue with," he said with a sexy, arrogant glint in his eye that made her laugh softly even as she pooled with moisture below.

"Wanna go upstairs?" she asked. Because she could do that now. She was bold, aggressive Jenny now.

Once there, they undressed each other, and he pulled her on top of him and made her come. Then he kissed her between her legs and made her come again. After that, he entered her from behind while they lay on their sides, and he reached around to touch her until she came—wow—a third time! And by the time she reached her third orgasm, Jenny was pretty sure she'd died and gone to heaven—and yet, somehow, the *best* part for her was when *Mick* climaxed: listening to his groans, his sweet whispers, and knowing she'd taken him there.

As they lay snuggling afterward, she whispered to him, "How's Wayne?" She'd decided it would be crazy to tell him her father knew—knowing her dad would honor his word, she saw no reason to upset or worry Mick. He had enough to deal with already.

"He's . . . weaker lately," he replied.

"Is there anything I can do to help? I'd be happy to come over and cook, clean, take care of Wayne—whatever you need." She'd never asked before, not wanting to intrude, but she *was* "good Jenny," after all—she could only resist offering for so long.

"That's sweet," he said, "but no." Then shook his head softly. "Taking care of somebody who's dying is kind of . . ."

"Intimate?" she suggested after he trailed off.

"Yeah, maybe. But not intimate like *this*," he said, looking down at them, naked except for the covers. "I just . . . think it would be hard for Wayne to have anybody besides me seeing him the way he is right now."

She nodded. "I understand." Her mother had grown selective toward the end of her life, too, about who came into her room. She'd want to be remembered living, not dying.

"But when he's awake," Mick went on quietly, "we've been . . . talking. A lot. About old times—and other things, too. It's kinda nice."

They lay quietly then, Jenny thinking Mick had sounded more at peace just now than she'd ever heard him. But it also managed to remind her how *not* at peace she and her dad remained. She hated that she'd upset him. She hated that he truly saw her in a different light now. She hated that any of it was necessary. Yet it was. They hadn't spoken since the fireworks and it made her extra glad to see Mick tonight, to be close to him, to remind her why she'd done it.

He turned beneath the sheets then until they lay looking at each other, their faces close. His voice came out surprisingly soft. "Were you . . . with your mom when she died?"

Jenny drew in her breath and thought back over the years. "No. I knew it was almost the end, though, when my dad took me in to see her and she had a long talk with me—the kind you'd expect, about wanting me to be strong, and happy, and about how she was going to be watching me from heaven. Then they sent me to Sue Ann's for a while. It was strange. Part of me knew she was here dying the whole time, but another part of me was willing to be distracted by Sue Ann's mom taking us to see a movie at the Ambassador in town, playing in their swimming pool, and staying up late doing each other's hair."

"Do you still miss her?" he asked, faces still close.

She bit her lip, tried to compose an answer. "Yes. No. Sometimes." She let out a sigh. "The first years were hard—I was at an age when I really needed a mom. But after I moved away, life felt more normal—it was sort of like Mom and Dad were just somewhere I wasn't."

He cast a small, sympathetic sort of smile. "I'm not sure you really answered my question, pussycat. Do you still miss her? All these years later?"

She cast a similar smile in return. "Yes," she said again. "No," she added. "Sometimes." Then she reached up to touch the stubble on his cheek. "You're afraid you'll miss Wayne."

He didn't deny it, just looked kind of sad. "It's strange, 'cause he hasn't been around, you know? But

I'll just miss knowing he's *somewhere*. He's the only family I have."

"How did your mom and dad die?"

"Heart attacks," he said. "Both of them. A few years apart. They were only in their fifties, but they were both heavy smokers."

"Sorry," she said.

Yet Mick shook his head. "They weren't good parents. They treated us like . . . things that were in the way, things that cost them money. He drank a lot, and I think now that she was probably bi-polar or schizophrenic or something. I don't miss them. I only . . . miss what they could have been sometimes, miss what I wished they were."

Jenny kissed his mouth softly, leaned her forehead against his. "Why didn't you sell the land when you left?" She'd sort of wondered that ever since the night she'd found him there.

"Tried," he said. "It was on the market for about a year. I thought maybe a developer would buy it, put some houses around that side of the lake. But turns out the only thing my parents left me was land too steep and rocky and hard-to-get-to for anyone to want to live on it," he concluded with a cynical laugh.

"I'm sorry, Mick."

"For what?"

"I just . . . wish you'd had a happier life." She'd always felt sorry for herself for losing her mother so young, but she couldn't have *imagined* then what kind of life those two boys across the lake were enduring.

"Let's not talk anymore, pussycat," Mick said quietly. "Just kiss me."

An hour later, they'd made love again and Mick had gone, and Jenny stood naked, looking out the front window, able to make out the dark shadow of a rowboat moving slowly away from her across the lake. She felt like her heart was leaving *with* him.

But this isn't love, I don't love him. I can't. I just can't. Despite what she'd told Sue Ann at the fireworks, she'd decided she was wrong, that it couldn't be true. She'd just been overly emotional that night, after everything that had happened.

Why can't *you love him?* It was almost as if the question had come from somewhere other than her mind.

And she raised her gaze from the lake to the star-sprinkled sky above and wondered if she was under so much pressure here that she really was starting to lose it, because she could have sworn she'd just heard her mother's voice.

And that was crazy, but given how strange things suddenly felt between her and her dad, she found herself trying to imagine what her *mother* would think of her now—her actions, her feelings, her secret-keeping. She remembered so clearly those words her mother had imparted during that last big talk: *Be strong when I'm gone, and be brave enough to do what makes you happy, even when it's hard.*

But loving Mick Brody wouldn't make her happy.

He was so different than her, than anything she'd known. And even if thinking about Mick had done a lot to clear Terrence from her mind, Terrence had been her first love, her first sex, her *husband*, for heaven's sake. Distractions were nice, but it took awhile to get over that kind of loss, and didn't she need to give herself the time and space to do that?

And Mick would leave soon, after all. He'd leave Destiny, and her life.

And maybe the truth was that knowing Mick was temporary was . . . well, part of what had made it easier for Jenny to embrace the affair. Because she'd lost so much in her life, much of it just lately.

She'd lost her mother, she'd lost her dad's faith in her, she'd lost her marriage and her job and the life she'd built. Heck, after recent discussions, she wasn't even sure she'd ever really gotten over losing Snowball as a teenager—and she'd never owned a pet since.

So she'd lost a lot. And she might be woman-hear-her-roar, but that didn't mean she wanted to keep losing things she cared about.

And if she didn't love Mick, she couldn't lose him.

So she didn't love him. That simple. She just didn't.

Captain, I do not believe you realize the gravity of your situation.

Mr. Spock

Twelve

*B*eads of sweat rolled down Mick's chest, stomach, as he dipped the oars into the water, moving across the lake. The muscles in his arms were tired—he could feel the soreness with every stroke—but at least he'd finally finished digging.

Which was good, he feared, for more reasons than one. Wayne was getting sicker, weaker. The pain patches weren't lasting as long as they were supposed to anymore, and neither were the pills.

So he'd started changing the patches sooner than the instructions said. Because he didn't like seeing his brother in pain. Because he wasn't sure what else to do. He didn't exactly have a doctor or nurse handy to consult. He was winging it. And now he only hoped the medication lasted.

He'd been forced, just last night, to ask Wayne, "What if we run out?" He hadn't wanted to even *think* about that, but he'd counted the supply, and at the rate they were going, he'd be out of pain patches in a couple of weeks, out of oxycodone in three, tops.

"I know a guy you could call," Wayne had said, seeming not altogether coherent—but that's how it was lately. So Wayne was saying he knew where Mick could buy some illegal drugs. Great. That's just what he needed to do next to make his list of broken laws even longer.

Just please don't let us run out, please let them last.

He wasn't sure who he was even talking to, since he wasn't exactly a God-fearing man. And hell, it was like wishing for his brother to die—a hard thought to swallow.

Just quit thinking, dude, and row. He needed her tonight, bad. *Too* bad.

And he didn't care much anymore if it showed. He didn't care much anymore if it seemed an awful damn lot like he was in too deep here. Being with Wayne, watching him deteriorate, was getting harder. He *had* to have something else to hold on to now or he'd lose his fucking mind. If he hadn't met her, didn't have her, he didn't know how he'd be surviving this, what he'd do when he needed to get away for a little while. Go out into the woods and beat his fists on the ground like a caveman? Curl up in a ball like a little kid and cry? Thank God he didn't have to find out. Thank God he had Jenny to take away the hurt for a little while.

As he rowed the little boat up onto the shore next to her dock, his cock began to harden. He felt like one of Pavlov's dogs—coming here, anticipating her, had him conditioned to get excited the closer he got to her house.

He walked across the road in the dark, aware of lights on in other homes, but he'd noticed from the beginning that things were nearly as quiet on this side of the water at night as they were on his own—he'd yet to see a car pass during his comings and goings, or anyone even outside after dark. Even so, as he moved furtively up the driveway and around the back of the little yellow cottage, it still felt like he was doing something forbidden. The best damn forbidden thing he'd ever done.

He could have long since started going to the front door, but he *liked* the back door for some reason. He liked all the little details of being Jenny Tolliver's secret lover.

When he stepped up on the stoop, the inside door was wide open and through the old screen door he saw her walking toward him in the light echoing from the living room. And—*damn*—she wore only a flimsy, see-through pink bra and some kind of stretchy, lacy underwear that looked like tiny little shorts. Her hair was stacked up on her head in a messy, sexy knot. "Did you see me coming?" he asked, voice low from the instant lust coursing through him.

A pretty half smile lit her face. "No—it's just that the A/C's out, so I'm hot."

Stepping inside, he gave her a bold once-over, from the nipples he could see clearly through her bra down to her silky thighs. "You can say *that* again, pussycat," he murmured.

And she laughed, a soft, pretty trilling sound that moved all through him.

He reacted instinctually, lifting one hand to the side of her breast, stroking his thumb across that prettily beaded peak as he leaned in to kiss her. The way she looked tonight wasn't inspiring him to go slow. "Have you been walking around like this all day?" he couldn't help asking with a soft grin. It seemed like a waste to have a woman looking this sexual without anyone enjoying it.

She shook her head lightly, sighing from the kiss, the touch. "It just went out about an hour ago," she said, her voice dreamy, sultry, as she peered up into his eyes. "I didn't want to call my dad this late."

"Not that I want you to burn up, honey—but I'm kinda glad you didn't. I'd have hated to show up and not be able to come in."

She bit her lip, her face flushing with pleasure as he used both thumbs to stroke both nipples now. "Me, too."

"I wouldn't have been able to give you *this*," he said, low, then stepped closer, pressing his erection to her.

He kissed her again, this time lifting his hands to cup her face, and her palms rose to his chest. And then . . . some sort of weird practicality bit at him. He wasn't the type to rescue damsels in distress, but something made him say, "I could look at the A/C if you want. I'm pretty good with that sort of thing—worked for a heating-and-cooling guy for about six months when I first moved away.

"Thing is, though," even *more* practical concerns forced him to add, "I can't stay long tonight, so . . . afraid it's either that . . . or *this*." He backed her against a counter with his hips. "You choose."

She gave him a take-mercy-on-me smile. "So you either heat me up or cool me down?"

"Pretty much."

She bit her lip, looking semi-orgasmic already, then said, "Who needs air-conditioning anyway? Kiss me."

Thank God. Sweet relief rushed through his veins as he sank his mouth back to hers and curled his hands over her round ass. She arched against him, letting him feel how bad she wanted it tonight, and that only made his zipper strain tighter, made him want to get to her faster. So instead of bothering with the bed or the couch, he lifted her up onto the kitchen counter and stepped between her parted legs.

Damn, she looked good sweaty, and as he kissed her neck, her throat, her chest, he tasted the salt on her skin. When she yanked his T-shirt off and wrapped her legs around him, their flesh stuck together, and even with windows lifted wide at both sides of the galley-style kitchen, more than one kind of heat consumed him. "Wait a minute," he said.

"Huh?" she breathed, but he was already extracting himself from her shapely legs to turn around and open the doors on the fridge behind him, wide.

Cool air blasted out, from both the refrigerator and the freezer, and Jenny and Mick both let out a long, "Ahhhh." And while he was there, he reached in the ice bin and drew out a cube.

Turning back to her, he held the ice cube to her throat, listened to her feminine gasp at the cold sensation, then watched her close her eyes in pleasure and relief. He moved it slowly down, over her chest, between her breasts—then he pushed it into one cup of that flimsy bra, moving it over and around her pointed nipple. She made a startled sound at first, but it eased into a low, sultry moan. Their gazes met, and she looked wild as she ran both hands back through his hair.

Their eyes never parted as he withdrew the cube from the cup of her bra, then slipped it in the opposite side. She gasped again at the fresh sensation and he watched her nipple become harder and harder through the now-wet fabric. Her sexy sighs drove him to bend and suckle her other nipple through the damp bra, nibbling and biting, just a little—his need tonight less than gentle.

The ice cube was melting rapidly, so Mick soon tossed the remains in the sink and reached back into the freezer for another, which he glided slowly down her bare stomach, both of them watching the wet trail it left on her skin.

When he reached the v-shaped edge of her panties, just below her navel, he didn't hesitate to keep going, to slide the ice into the stretchy fabric and straight down between her legs. Another pretty gasp escaped her, followed by a few slightly strangled-sounding moans that made him a little crazy. She was biting her lower lip, whimpering hotly, watching his hand move inside her underwear, and his whole body burned with raw lust from touching her around the ice cube, stroking his fingertips through the folds, even wetter than usual right now from the ice.

She moved against him in jagged motions; she reached up overhead to grab on to the cabinets for balance. She looked more brazen and out-of-control than he'd ever seen her, and it only fueled him, turning his need more urgent.

"Lift your ass," he directed, voice low, but he had to help—because of her position on the counter—before he could pull down those sexy-as-sin panties and let them drop to the floor. Abandoning the ice again, he stepped between her legs and looked at her there and told her between hot, hungry breaths, "You're so beautiful, baby."

Her breath came just as ragged as his while, together, they fought past his belt and zipper until his cock burst free—and he couldn't wait another second before driving it into her moisture.

But a low, soft moan left him as he entered, and once there, he had to close his eyes. And maybe it was the open freezer door behind him, but despite the heat, a chill tingled down his spine. "So tight," he whispered to her. Warm. Safe. The best place he could imagine being in the whole damn world.

He held her at the edge of the counter and plunged into her, deep, slow, hard. He gazed into her eyes and drowned in the heat there. He bent to tongue her nipple, still covered with that teasing, transparent fabric, then bit it lightly, making her sob, making her flesh contract around him. After which he yanked down the cups of the bra so he could really *get* to her, really *feel* the turgid flesh tighten further in his mouth.

She arched into him, the agony of hot pleasure etched on her face—as he kissed both her breasts, as he gathered her body in his arms, as he thrust as deeply into her as he possibly could. And then the rhythm of her movements settled into something familiar—it was the way she moved when she was going to come.

He nibbled her shoulders, held her close, let her grind, growled his own pleasure. He whispered, "I want you to come *so* hard, baby—*so* hard."

Her jaw went slack and her lips looked swollen, her cheeks still pink from heat or sex or a combination of both. Tiny moans echoed from her. Then, "Please, more, almost."

"I'll give you all you want, pussycat," he whispered in her ear. "Everything I've got."

And then her breath caught, once, twice, and her body jerked slightly, a low sob leaving her as she moved against him, harder, harder—and he loved holding her while she came, loved feeling the orgasm vibrate through her body until it was all gone and they balanced there against the counter, embracing, bodies interlocked.

He kissed her then, and picked her up, still inside her. He thought of laying her across the kitchen table, but it was too damn hot over there, so he finally reclined her across the linoleum floor in front of the fridge, the cool air still pouring out, making the night better.

He knelt between her legs, pulling her torso up into his lap as she stretched naked but for the bra framing her breasts, and then he pounded into her. *God, yes.* That's what he needed tonight, to give it to her hard, to spill himself inside her. She cried out at each deep stroke, and for a moment he felt like he was in a dream, because this couldn't be little Jenny Tolliver, writhing on a kitchen floor, looking dirty and hot for him, taking his every rough thrust. But then she was saying his name—"Mick! Oh God, Mick!" her eyes shut, her arms stretched over her head in abandon, and sure enough, that was his sweet Jenny's voice, and he used two fingertips, rubbing them above where he entered her, rubbing until her breath caught again, until she was sobbing and moaning and coming again, her body convulsing around him.

"Aw . . . aw, God," he groaned, because that was all it took—he was coming, too, bursting inside her, driving deep, using his hands to pull her body tighter to his, shutting his eyes, getting lost, lost in the release, the consuming pleasure. Jesus God, *yes.*

And then they were quiet, still. He could hear crickets outside again, could feel the oppressive heat again battling the cool air at his back from the fridge. He could peer down on her again and see how amazing she looked lying there.

Slowly, he withdrew, and they both sighed at the disconnection, and he eased down next to her on the floor. They lay side by side, and he took in her body again, naked and wet and beautiful, as he slid one hand onto her hip. "That was *so* damn hot, honey. In the good way, I mean," he added with a grin, thinking of the warmth saturating the air.

The reminder of the heat made her glance up at the open window above their heads, and the look of ecstasy on her face turned to concern. "What if someone heard us?"

Maybe he should be worried, given his situation, but instead, he could only laugh. "Destiny," he said, "where no one has sex with the windows open."

Her eyes widened in distress and she pressed her palms to his chest. "Seriously—what if someone heard us?"

"*You*, you mean," he pointed out. She'd made a hell of a lot more noise than he had, which pleased the arrogant, lusty guy in him. In response to her question, though, he only shrugged. "Guess they'd probably think you have some company."

She still looked worried. "What if someone asks me about it, brings it up?"

He made a chiding face. "Get real, pussycat. Nobody in Destiny is gonna ask you who was making you scream your head off in passion."

She sighed in concession. "Okay, probably not. But still, it's kind of embarrassing."

"Only in Destiny," he insisted.

Next to him, she shook her pretty head. "No—for me, it would be embarrassing *anywhere*." She suddenly looked younger somehow, innocent, like that girl on the dock all those years ago. "I'm . . . not used to this. Being this wild."

Something about that tightened his chest and made him glad he'd come along when he had. Maybe he wasn't the only one getting something he needed here this summer. "Then it's about time somebody brought out that side of you."

"Agreed," she said. Then added, "Destiny isn't so bad, though. I never thought I'd enjoy being back, but . . . I'm actually thinking of staying."

He let his eyes widen in surprise. Nothing she'd told him before had made him think that was even a possibility. "Really?"

"I've been offered a job teaching at the high school. At first, I brushed it off—but today I ran into the principal, and he said I'd be teaching all upperclassmen, mostly elective courses, which means they choose to be there and aren't forced into it. I was thinking it might feel less like babysitting and more like really teaching. And fall is coming quick and I need a job. It's starting to seem appealing to stick around awhile, give it a try and see how it goes." She stopped then, sighed. "On the other hand, though, does coming home seem . . . too easy? Should I challenge myself more?" She looked up into his eyes, as if she truly expected him to have the answer.

He considered her words and replied with a shrug. "I don't weigh things too much these days by whether they seem easy or hard. I think more about what . . . feels right inside. The person I used to be . . . *never* really felt right inside, but I just didn't know any other way. Now I *know* when things feel right, and that's how I gauge them."

"Is it how you gauged it when Wayne called to ask for your help?"

He nodded briefly, sorry to be reminded of Wayne— and suffering an instant guilt for feeling that way.

"How *is* Wayne?" she asked gently.

He quietly sighed, then leaned his forehead over against hers. "Not good, pussycat."

"That's why you can't stay long."

"Yep."

"Are you sure there isn't anything I can do to help?"

His heart swelled, and all he could do in that moment was kiss her until he found his voice again. "You're sweet as hell, honey. And *this* helps. *Me and you* helps. But I just gotta ride this out. And, much as I'd rather stay here rolling around on the floor with you . . . ."

"You need to go."

He gave a short nod and knew they were both pretty bummed by it. Then he propped his head in his hand and let his eyes peruse her from head to toe, all sweaty, wet, and hot, with that bra still on but pulled down—and he didn't guard his words, since, with Jenny, it was beginning to feel like he didn't have to. "You look so naughty right now, pussycat, like a girl in a magazine," he concluded with a lascivious smile.

She flushed prettily, bit her lip, and said, "I thought you were . . . you know, reformed."

He laughed. "Not *that* reformed. If I ever get *that* reformed, shoot me."

The next morning, Jenny sat at her laptop, at a small desk in the living room, feeling a little giddy—about last night—and answering e-mail. She'd been keeping in touch with a few friends from Columbus that way, and Sue Ann and she had discovered it was an easy way to make plans. Plus Amy had e-mailed her some pictures from last autumn's Chicago trip.

But mainly, the giddy part was winning out over the practical e-mail part. It was all she could do not to type, *I had wild ice-cube sex last night!*

Until, that is, she was reminded of her father's presence in the next room when she heard him beating and clanging away on the air conditioner. Given that they'd barely spoken since the Fourth of July and that she was still sweating her brains out—and that sweating wasn't nearly as fun without Mick around—she found herself completely unable to focus on her replies and decided to go back to it later.

She was just about to click over to the Hubble telescope website when a new message arrived in her inbox—from Ralph Turley, the principal of Destiny High School. Despite the clanging and other distractions, she clicked to open it.

Just wanted to tell you what a pleasure it was talking with you yesterday, Jenny, and how much I hope you'll accept our offer and come back to your alma mater to teach. If you have any questions, just let me know.

Wow, they really wanted her. That was a nice feeling.

Was Mick right? About just trusting your heart and not worrying so much about the perceptions of a decision—your own or others'?

And as for Mick—oh God, her heart swelled just to think of him now. The things that man made her feel, both inside and out, were nearly overwhelming. And the way she'd felt when he'd left last night . . . hell, that had overwhelmed her, too. *Oh crap—it was a lot easier when I was just giddy about the sex.*

She'd tried to attribute her emotions last night to the heat, but she knew that was silly. *I love him,* she thought helplessly. She could try to deny it all she wanted, but that didn't change the facts. *Oh boy. Oh no. I really do. I really love him. I don't want to, but I just do.* Which was incredible and nightmarish all at once for a hundred different reasons. How the hell had this happened? When she'd promised herself nothing would get in the way of her pleasure, her wild affair, she'd never imagined the biggest obstacle would turn out to be falling in love with her lover.

Just then, her father ambled into the room, wiping his hands on the same rag he'd used every time he was here. "Think I got it workin' again—should cool down soon. But I wish you'd called me last night, or just come over to my place to sleep. D'you get any sleep at all in this miserable heat?" Despite his words, his tone was forced, and his eyes appeared sort of haunted when she met his gaze. Just looking at him that way tightened her chest.

"I slept . . . surprisingly well," she said. *A good orgasm or two can do that for you. Even amid the horror of admitting to yourself that you're in love with a guy you have no future with.* "I found an old fan and put it in the window above the bed, and it helped a lot."

Her father sighed. "Well . . . good."

It was then that she saw his eyes catch on the print Mick had given her, now hanging on the wall. She'd bought a nice frame and matting at McMillan's Hardware and framed it herself, just yesterday. "What's this?" he asked.

She swallowed back the lump in her throat, hating the tension between them. "A Van Gogh print—*Starry Night.*"

Her father pursed his lips and sighed. "It's nice," he admitted. "Not as nice as your mother's picture, but . . . it looks good with the yellow walls."

"Mick gave it to me," she said in a slightly hushed tone. Just to try that on for size. Even though she had no future with him—it was the principle of the thing; she didn't want her dad to hate the man she loved. And she should be able to say his name. *Even if he's technically a criminal?* Unfortunately, that made it a lot more complicated.

"Mick," her father repeated, judging, cynical, and clearly not liking the fact that she felt close enough to Mick to call him by only his first name. *Oh Daddy, if you only knew how close I feel to him.*

"Yes," she said. "He knows I like astronomy and that I haven't gotten to stargaze as much as I'd planned this summer."

He drew his eyes from the wall to her face, still critical. "I been thinkin' about this, Jenny, over and over again, and for the life of me, I can't understand how you could . . . cavort with someone like him."

Jenny blinked, shocked, offended. But wait, no, it was more than that—in fact, she was downright pissed off. She hadn't done everything right here, and she knew she'd put her father in a horrible position by telling him Mick's secret and asking him to keep it, but what he'd just said was more than she could stand. She'd been trying to smooth things over and keep their relationship on an even keel, but something in her snapped.

"Cavort?" she asked. "*Cavort*? I'm thirty-one years old, Dad!" Even if it didn't feel that way between them—she always felt younger in his presence.

"What does your age have to do with anything?" he asked, appearing confounded.

And she could only sigh. He *really* didn't get it. "Maybe I'm old enough to cavort with whomever I want to cavort with," she explained.

"But he's a criminal," her dad replied, the word slicing into her a lot deeper when *he* said it. "Did you know that? Never caught him, mind you, but I know he took part in at least one robbery."

Yeah, she knew that, and she hated it, but she'd also somehow gotten over it. "That's in the past," she insisted. "He's changed. He's not a criminal *anymore*."

"He sure as hell is."

Oh. Harboring a fugitive. *Damn it*. It was so easy to forget, even just a moment after it had come to mind, that he was breaking the law by caring for his brother. "Not by choice," she pointed out. "He's only honoring his brother's last request."

"You *always* have a choice," her father claimed.

And she let out a huff in reply. "Maybe so, but Mick did what he felt was right, and so did I. Why can't you drop this? Why can't you do what I said and just pretend you don't know?"

"Because now I'm technically breaking the law, too. For you," he reminded her softly.

Double damn it. *That* stopped her in her tracks.

Sighing, she stood up, walked over, and took her father's hands in hers. Hands that had rocked her as a baby. Hands that had held her when her mother had died. "I'm so deeply sorry about that part, Dad—I really am. You have no idea how I've struggled with this. But I'm asking you to trust in me, to believe in me enough to know I wouldn't have kept this from you, or asked of you what I did, if I didn't truly feel Mick is a good person." She squeezed his hands a little tighter and said, "Please, Daddy—believe in me."

The room was starting to cool now, but the air still felt stifling. She hated hurting him, hated knowing he truly thought less of her now somehow. And she was hoping and praying he'd say, *Okay, Jennygirl, I believe in you,* and give her a big hug.

Instead, though, he simply leaned over, kissed her on the forehead, then turned and walked out the door.

Later that day, Jenny and Sue Ann both stretched out in floating lounge chairs just off the dock. It was too hot to even think about being in the sun without staying cool.

"Ah, this is heaven," Sue Ann said, lifting a wine cooler to her lips, then leaning her head back to soak up the sun.

"Heaven's a stretch, I think," Jenny groused. Her mood hadn't improved much since the run-in with her father. "It's crazy hot out here. If we had any sense, we'd be in the nice, cool air-conditioning." A modern convenience a girl really appreciated after a night without it, even if she *had* found post-orgasmic sleep restful.

"Hot, schmot—this is nice. Two best friends basking away a lazy afternoon in the sun. I never really thought we'd get to hang out like this again, you know? So maybe that rat bastard's rattiness was good for *something*."

Jenny could only snarl. She loved hanging out with Sue Ann, too, but she was in no mood to actually acknowledge that Terrence's cheating could have any redeeming qualities.

"By the by," Sue Ann said, ignoring the snarl, "do you know anybody who wants to rent a house? My mom's Aunt Celia is moving in with Dinah and John. She's eighty-five now and really can't take care of herself anymore. But they don't want to sell the house, and figure it would be tough anyway right now with the new subdivision going in."

Jenny knew the house—a small, green, one-story cottage about half a mile past hers, farther up the lake. "Who would *I* know who'd want to rent a house?" she pointed out.

"Growl," Sue Ann said with playfully widened eyes. "Somebody's testy today."

"And *you're* unusually chipper. How was your weekend, by the way?"

"Magical, thank you," Sue Ann replied.

Jenny lowered her chin skeptically. "Magical?"

"Utterly. And if I seem cheerful today, it's because I'm still in the afterglow of a sex marathon."

Jenny raised her eyebrows, surprised. "Do tell." Since maybe they hadn't talked about sex all that much *before* her divorce, but they did now.

"My mother went on a trip to the Longaberger Basket factory this weekend. Have you ever seen it, by the way? The building is the world's largest basket and it's pretty darn impressive. Anyway, she took Sophie with her."

"Ah," Jenny said.

"Ah isn't the half of it," Sue Ann informed her. "And

much as I miss the little munchkin and much as I'm looking forward to picking her up when they get home this afternoon, I'm seriously thinking of trying to make this 'weekend with Grandma' thing a monthly event. It gave Jeff and me two entire nights of completely bliss-ful sex, which is two more than we've had in ages."

This actually did cheer Jenny up a little—she was happy for Sue Ann. "So was it . . . candles-and-wine blissful or urgent-and-heated blissful?"

A pleasant, easy smile graced Sue Ann's face. "A nice combo of both, actually. So how was *your* weekend? Are you still in love with Mick Brody?"

Jenny sighed. She really *had* given up denying it. Once she'd said the words out loud to Sue Ann during the fireworks, there'd really been no taking it back, no matter how she'd tried. "Yep," she said matter-of-factly, "and I don't think I like it."

Sue Ann raised her eyebrows. "Oh?"

"Example. He had to leave fairly quickly last night after we did it, and I *hated* it. And then I hated *myself* for hating it. I mean, he had a good *reason* to leave. And he'll leave for *good* soon, so I'd better get ready for that, right?"

"So you know for sure he's going to leave town again?"

Jenny nodded. "He's not a fan of Destiny. It sounds like Wayne's condition is deteriorating, and as soon as he dies, Mick'll be long gone."

Sue Ann made a sympathetic face. "That sucks."

"You know I never meant for this to happen—to get attached to the guy. Sometimes I still can't believe *any* of this—it feels surreal to me. But here I am, suddenly thinking about him all the time, all wrapped up in wondering when I'll see him again, and how good the sex will be, and what we'll talk about, and how long he'll stay. It's *awful*. It felt much better when I'd de-luded myself into believing it was just a wild affair."

"But even when love stinks," Sue Ann said, "it's pretty *amazing*, too, don't you think? I still remember when I fell for Jeff—back then, he thought of me as a friend, and I thought I was doomed, but at the same time . . ." She paused, looking all dreamy. ". . . I felt all glowy inside just thinking about him."

Jenny sighed, realizing the sad truth. "Yeah, I'm glowy, too. But I'd be glowier if . . . well, if everything was different."

"Yeah, the harboring-a-fugitive thing is kind of a bummer," Sue Ann said, now trying to play it off so lightly that Jenny couldn't help but laugh.

"And making my father *not* uphold the law, and destroying his faith in me and my judgment . . . all that stuff is a little bit of a downer, as well."

"So we should get back on a better subject," Sue Ann suggested. "Like how's the *sex* with Mr. Brody these days?"

Feeling instantly glowy again, Jenny let out a girlish sigh. "Fabulous, as usual. Last night when the A/C was out, he opened the refrigerator doors and we did it in the kitchen."

Sue Ann's jaw dropped. "God. Where at?"

"On the counter, then the floor," Jenny replied. "And there was ice involved."

"I'll be damned," Sue Ann said, slapping her palm down on the arm of her floating chair. "I have a sex marathon and *still* you trump me with that guy. I never even *thought* about the kitchen before. Maybe Jeff and I'll try that on the next grandma weekend."

Jenny held up one finger to temper Sue Ann's enthusiasm. "But I think the kitchen was only hot because we were, um, too urgent to go anywhere else. Otherwise, it just would have been hard and uncomfortable."

Yet Sue Ann's excitement would not be quelled.

"Well, don't forget the ice. The kitchen was also hot because of the ice."

Jenny could only shrug. "Point taken. The ice was . . . pretty phenomenal."

"That seals it," Sue Ann concluded with a nod. "I'm doing it with Jeff in the kitchen."

Given their conversation, Jenny couldn't resist asking the question on her mind. She took a sip of her berry cooler first, though, for courage. "So . . . you're no longer against me being with Mick?"

"I'm in an afterglow, remember? So maybe I won't feel so tolerant tomorrow." Yet then Sue Ann's voice softened. "Although it puts my mind at ease now that your dad knows."

Jenny rolled her eyes. "Well, that makes one of us. I'm really afraid I've created a rift between us that's not going to go away, even when Mick *does*."

Sue Ann tipped her own cooler back to her mouth, then tilted her head speculatively. "I guess the question then becomes—was it worth it? To damage a permanent relationship for a temporary one?"

And Jenny's stomach dropped. She pursed her lips and informed her friend, "You're supposed to say something like, 'Don't worry, your dad will get over this in time.'"

Sue Ann cringed, flashing an *oops!* look, then tried to correct herself. "Um, don't worry, your dad will get over this in time."

They kept talking—and not surprisingly, Sue Ann turned the conversation back to sex—but as the afternoon went on, Jenny's gaze repeatedly found its way across the lake, to the thick woods that hid the Brody cabin from view. *Was* it worth it? What she'd sacrificed to protect Mick?

The answer was complex—because it was so much

bigger than Mick. It was about right and wrong, and life and death and punishment, and how she'd been forced to think about all those things in new ways since the night she'd crossed the lake. But it was also about Mick himself, the dark and light of him, the good and bad, the better man she saw behind the bad-ass with the skull tattoo. And it was even about the joy and excitement he'd brought into her life when she'd felt depleted and alone.

And no matter how she sliced and diced it, no matter how she broke the situation up into pieces, issues, principles—when she asked herself Sue Ann's question, every time she came up with the same staggering answer.

Yes, it was worth it.

Sorry, Dad, but I just don't have any regrets about Mick, and I don't think I ever will.

Except for when he leaves.

That she would regret.

The sky was clear—remarkably clear—and
the twinkling of all the stars seemed to be
but throbs of one body, timed by a common
pulse.

Thomas Hardy

Thirteen

As Walter eased his cruiser off the highway and
into the gravel parking lot of the Dew Drop Inn, he realized he was breaking his own rule. But he was tired,
and thirsty, and he just wanted to unwind a little. He
was off duty, tired of this god-awful heat, and a beer
sounded good for a change.

That's the only reason you're here, he told himself as he
put the car in park. *Just for a beer.*

It was nearly eleven o'clock on a Tuesday, so the
place was quiet—only a few other patrons occupied
the bar, and most of them were gathered around the
pool table, laughing and boasting.

As he slid up onto the same stool he'd taken on his
previous visits, he found himself examining the faces

there, looking for Mick Brody. It had been a long time since he'd seen the Brody boy, but he didn't think any of the scruffy fellas shooting pool were him.

He'd listened carefully to every word of Jenny's story, but he wasn't convinced it was all true. She'd said she'd seen Wayne Brody lying in a bed, dying, but for all Walter knew, the guy was just strung out on drugs or something. The prison official he'd spoken to had said Wayne was real sick when he escaped, but he'd never said he was dying, so who knew where the truth lay.

And maybe it *was* true, every bit of it, but that didn't make him like it any better. Just because somebody was dying didn't make them a good person, didn't take back the bad things they'd done—and it sure didn't wipe Wayne Brody's crimes off the books.

He tried not to think about what he knew, tried to pretend Jenny had never told him—but it was practically *all* he could think about these days. He barely knew which made his gut clench more: knowing where an escaped convict was holed up and having promised his daughter he wouldn't do anything about it, or knowing Jenny was messing around with that kind of trouble, with a guy who Walter had never seen an ounce of good in. His Jennygirl. He'd thought he knew her. But suddenly it didn't feel that way. Suddenly it didn't feel like he knew her at all.

He'd nearly forgotten all about the beer by the time Anita Garey emerged from the ladies' room. She wore the same tight jeans as usual, and a purple tank top with lace around a low V-neck. It fit her tight, like most of the other clothes he'd seen her in, and just like before, he felt the very sight in his groin.

"Evening, Walter," she said as if they were old friends.

"Evenin'," he said, nodding.

"Sprite?" she asked, approaching him behind the bar.

"No—I'll take a beer tonight. Whatever ya got on tap."

"Comin' up," she said, reaching for a tall glass. "What's the occasion?"

He found himself perusing her shape again as she turned to fill the glass with foamy beer. Despite himself, he enjoyed the way she looked. She had a nice body—large, high breasts and an hourglass figure—and he supposed he couldn't blame her for not wanting to hide it under a bushel.

"Cat got your tongue?" she asked with a friendly grin as she set the beer on a napkin in front of him.

Damn—he'd gotten so caught up in looking at her that he hadn't answered. "Um, well . . . I reckon the occasion is . . . I'm under a lot of stress these days and just felt like unwindin' a little."

"Can't think of a better reason for a cold one than that," she said, and he smiled in return, a reflex, since she was so attractive. He had the odd impression of her getting more attractive each time he saw her, but he supposed he was just imagining that.

"Hear it might rain soon," she added, "and I don't know about you, but I say it's about damn time."

He found himself chuckling a little, but he wasn't sure why. Anita was just . . . herself. Genuine. Happy with who she was. He liked that. "I'll believe it when I see it," he said. "But yeah, a little rain would do a lot for my mood."

She crossed her arms, creating more cleavage where there was already plenty, but he didn't mind. He guessed the more he was around her, the less shocking it became—and the more pleasing to his male instincts, even if those had been in hibernation a good long while. "So what's got you stressed, Walter? If you need an ear, I don't mind listening."

Sighing, he confided, "More trouble with my daughter."

She lowered her chin as if to chide him. "Don't tell me you're still mad at her about those pictures?"

He shrugged. "Not really. But . . . turns out that was just the first sign that she's . . . well, not the girl I thought."

"No? Who is she then?" Behind the bar, Anita reached for a highball glass and started making herself some sort of mixed drink.

He wasn't sure how much to say, but she had helped him think more clearly the last time he'd talked to her, so he decided to tell her what he could. "Jenny's . . . gone and got herself involved with a no-good lowlife."

Anita tipped her head back, as if thinking, then resumed working on her drink as she said, "Let me ask you a question. This no-good lowlife—is he somebody you've had personal dealings with, someone whose character you're completely sure about? Or is he a lowlife . . . by reputation?"

Walter thought about it, sipped on his beer. "Little of both, I reckon. He was a bad seed when he was young. She tells me he's not that way anymore, but if thirty years as a cop has taught me anything, it's that, mostly, people don't change. They might *try* to change, they might *claim* they change, and they might even *change*— for a little while, but deep down, they mostly don't change."

"Fair enough," she said. "But you did say *mostly*."

"That's right," he replied. "Every now and then I'll see somebody who surprises me, who really straightens their life up and does better. But it's rare enough that I don't believe it until I see it, and until I see it last a while, too."

Finishing her colorful drink, she lifted it, took a sip, and said, "Mmm," in a way that made his pants a little tighter. Then she faced him again and looked like she was about to tell him a secret. "Maybe I shouldn't be this open with you since we just met, and since you're the local law and I'm new in town—but in our brief acquaintance I've come to think of us as friends, Walter. Would you agree?"

"I would," he said, curious now, and a little worried about what she was getting at. He took another long swallow of cold beer.

"Between you and me," she went on, "I like myself. I'm proud of who I am. Looking around this bar, it may not seem like I have much, but I've worked for what I've got, and I'm happy to have it. When I was young, see, I fell in with the wrong sort of people, and I made some regrettable decisions. But then one day it hit me that I'd stayed in those bad situations too long, that I was a full-fledged adult, and that this was it, my life, my one shot at it, and I didn't like where it was. So I finally got myself out of those circumstances, I went back to school and got my GED, and I even got a few credits from a community college to help me learn how to run a business. I turned it all around, Walter, and I'm a good person, and maybe more importantly, I'm living proof that people *can* change."

Walter found it shockingly easy not to judge her. He supposed she hadn't told him much he couldn't have guessed by looking. But from the moment he'd met her, he'd felt that good person inside her and overlooked the rest. "That's the thing," he said, starting to feel the beer a little. "You *are* livin' proof. You *are* a good person, I can tell that from talkin' to ya. But I haven't seen any proof or any good in this fella Jenny's mixed up with."

"Have you looked for it very hard?" she asked.

"Well, I haven't really seen the boy since he was young. But . . . I know for a fact that he's involved in somethin' right now that . . . well, he shouldn't be." He couldn't say "something illegal," because he was the *law,* damn it, and if he knew about something illegal, he should be putting a stop to it. And he liked Anita enough that he didn't want her to know he wasn't doing his duty just to keep a promise to Jenny.

"Listen," Anita said, shifting her weight from one foot to the other, "I obviously don't know this guy or your daughter or anything about the situation. But here's a few things I *do* know.

"People *can* change. And I'm willing to bet you brought your girl up right and that she's no dummy, so maybe you should be more open-minded about her faith in this boy. And even if it turns out he's bad to the bone and you were right all along, she's gotta learn that for herself. And she's gotta know her daddy's there for her, whatever happens."

He must have looked uncomfortable at that last part, because she added, "Take it from me, Walter—you let too many wedges get driven between you, and soon you and her'll be miles apart. That's what happened with me and my mother. To this day, I believe she wanted to forgive me for some of the things I did when I was young, but she couldn't bring herself to do it, and she died without us ever mending fences. You don't want to lose your daughter over this—or anything else, do you?"

"Of course not," he said, horrified at the very thought. He couldn't imagine his life without Jenny in it.

"Look, you told me she just came through a shitty divorce—and I can tell you from experience, that's a rough time for a woman. She's going through changes, trying to rebuild her life, trying to figure out what she's got to offer the world. Now you might not like the ways she's doin' that, but you gotta let her do it. Understand?"

Despite himself, Walter nodded. Anita spoke with such authority that it was hard to disagree with her.

Or maybe it was . . . wisdom, the hard-earned kind, that he heard in her voice. Either way, the stuff she said made sense. He just wished it made him feel better about Jenny's association with the Brodys.

Walter drained his beer, and when Anita asked if he wanted another, he was actually tempted. Just because he enjoyed her company and, given his mood, the idea of going home to a quiet, lonely house didn't appeal very much right now.

But the last thing he'd want to do was get drunk. He was the chief of police, after all, and he needed to keep folks' respect. He'd never lost it, but he'd also always lived carefully. To have another beer with Anita Garey because he was upset and lonely wasn't living carefully. "Nope, I'm done," he said. "How much do I owe ya?"

She flashed him a look he couldn't quite decipher—something like kindness, something like confidence, something like . . . flirtation? But no, he was surely imagining that last part. "It's on the house," she said.

"Why's that?"

"Gotta keep the local law happy," she joked, and he laughed. Actually laughed. It was the first time in a while. Probably since the Fourth of July. Which reminded him . . .

"Did you go to the park on the Fourth?"

She nodded. "Thought I might see you there, but I didn't."

"I . . . ended up goin' to a picnic."

She smiled, tilted her head slightly. "That sounds nice."

I should have asked her.

But then, no. That had been when Jenny had told him about Mick Brody and the whole day had been shot to hell. And besides, he still couldn't imagine what people around here would think if he showed up someplace with Anita. Because they wouldn't be able to see in her what *he* saw.

And he cared what people thought. A shameful truth—but there it was.

As he rose to go, the full measure of that shame struck, along with the full measure of how nice he felt it would be to just talk with her some more. In some . . . different setting, not a bar, not a place where he was the police chief, not a place where anybody else's opinion mattered. Someplace new.

"Anita," he said, looking back up, and realizing that he was suddenly nervous as hell.

"Yes, Walter?"

He pursed his lips, wished his throat didn't feel so dry, and tried to meet her bold, striking gaze. "I don't really know how to go about this, but . . . would you maybe want to come over to my house for dinner some night?"

He felt like he might throw up and wished he could blame it on the beer, but cold, stark fear was the only culprit. And he felt even sicker when he saw the surprise in her green eyes. Uh-oh. He was out of line here, the only one of them feeling this way. He felt the urge to fix it. "I shouldn't have asked—beer probably went to my head since I seldom drink. It's all right if you want to say no."

By the time he finished babbling, though, he realized her perplexed look had transformed back into one of confidence, and that now she was smiling at him. "Well then, I'm glad you had that beer, since I don't *want* to say no. In fact, Officer, that's the nicest offer I've had since I got to Destiny."

When Jenny first heard the noise, she couldn't place it. It was familiar, but . . .

And then she realized . . . it was raining outside!

Actually raining! For the first time since she'd come home. Finally! She walked to the front door and opened it wide, staring out to see the drops wetting the front walk and plopping into the lake in the distance.

And then the skies opened and it poured.

She could almost feel all of Destiny sighing in relief.

The weatherman had predicted rain for the next day or so, but had been unsure of how much, and this looked like a desperately needed soaker—thank goodness. She could stop watering the flowers incessantly, and the lawn would green up again, and the air would feel breathable for a little while. Ah . . .

Of course, after a few minutes, she got *used* to the rain and decided to do something constructive. But first, she put a stack of her mom's old albums on the stereo in the corner, having found she liked listening to music she knew her mother had enjoyed, and even finding some of it to be surprisingly hard rock, records Jenny hadn't known her mother owned. So even Judy Tolliver had a little bit of a secret side. That made Jenny smile, and hearing the music made her think about her mom living, thriving, being happy—as opposed to the shrine, which had only made her think about her mom dying.

While she listened to the records, she did some computer work—catching up on e-mail and doing some web-surfing. In particular, she found herself Googling topics she thought might be part of the curriculum she would create *if* she found herself teaching at the high school level this fall.

She still wasn't at all sure about staying—especially if her dad continued to be angry with her—but she found herself returning time and again to Mick's advice about doing what felt right.

She wasn't sure if Destiny would feel right to her forever, but in ways, it was starting to feel right for right now. Maybe a year, maybe more. Maybe sticking around would be the exact move that would fix things between her and her father. Maybe once Mick was gone, her dad would relax.

Ugh—once Mick was gone? She sighed, her stomach sinking to realize, once more, that he would be leaving soon—but then she went back to trying to concentrate on the lesson plan she was reading online. Not that it worked. Once she got Mick on the brain, he tended to stay there.

Just then, Night Ranger began to sing the rockin', "Don't Tell Me You Love Me," and Jenny's gut pinched.

Oh God, I wish I didn't love him. If only I'd truly kept it casual, like I planned. What a nightmare. But it was too late for that now.

Now all you can do is muddle through—and hope you don't fall apart once and for all when he goes.

Just after dark, Jenny sat curled up on the couch, rereading Stephen Hawking's *A Brief History of Time* and listening to the rain. After a few stop-and-start downpours earlier, the rain now fell in a steady rhythm, and she'd turned off the A/C to open the windows and let the fresh air inside. She knew "green" didn't have a scent, but that's always how she thought the air smelled after it rained in Destiny—green and fresh and fertile, like new life was emerging all around her.

She'd just begun to wonder if she'd heard movement outside, in the driveway, when a knock came on the back door, and her heart flip-flopped in her chest. She'd not expected him *tonight* of all nights, given the weather.

Stunned, she rushed to the door, pulled it open, and found him standing there, drenched and absolutely beautiful. In fact, the stark male beauty somehow just emanating from him struck her nearly senseless. "It's raining," she heard herself say dumbly.

He arched one eyebrow. "Thanks for the newsflash, pussycat."

Why couldn't she breathe suddenly? Then she figured it out. It was because he looked so good wet.

"So can I come in?" he asked expectantly.

Oh God—she was just standing there gaping at him getting rained on. "Oh—yeah—of course," she said, stepping back out of the way.

Mick walked past her, to the sink, where he smoothly stripped off his gray T-shirt and wrung it out. "Sorry for dripping all over your floor," he said.

But Jenny didn't answer—because if she'd been having a hard time breathing *before*, it had just gotten a lot worse. Because now he was wet *and* shirtless. Holy God.

When he raised his gaze to her, she realized she was standing there in her pajamas ogling him as if she'd never seen him before.

"What?" he said.

"Nothing," she managed. "You just look . . . um . . . good."

A hint of masculine arrogance transformed his expression as he dropped the shirt in the sink, then cast a wicked grin, reaching for her. "Bet I'll *feel* good, too."

And yep, no problem there—he definitely did. His skin was wet and hot and slippery, and as he pulled her close, his muscular arms wrapping around her, she didn't even mind the fact that he was getting *her* wet now. When he kissed her, even his mouth was wet, and she suffered the sensation of wanting to drown in him.

"Funny," he whispered in her ear then, "but I didn't think pussycats *liked* water."

She pulled back, looked up into his dark eyes. "Huh?"

Then she caught his teasing, seductive smile. "After the ice, and now this, I'm starting to think you've got a thing for water."

"Uh, no," she said automatically, because she really saw the ice and this as two different things—one had been about the contrast between cold and heat, and this was just about the way he looked. Which, when she glanced down at his slick stomach, made her bite her lip and suck in her breath.

"What do you mean, 'no'?" he asked with a playful smile, as if her denial was preposterous.

She smiled back into his eyes. "The fact is, Mr. Brody," she said, finally finding her voice, along with some teasing flirtation, "*everything* you do gets me hot. Water has nothing to do with it."

He looked pleased—but still playfully skeptical. Taking a step back, he took her hands in his and pulled her toward the door. "Let's go outside, pussycat, and I'll prove it."

Jenny let her eyes go wide. Was he serious? "Um, hello? It's raining out there. Why would we go out into the rain when we have a nice, dry house here?" Then she smiled. "Take off your jeans and I'll even put them in the dryer for you."

"Nice try," he quipped, "but I want to go out in the rain with you."

She simply tilted her head and gave him a look—one that still said, *No, you're crazy.*

"Don't you ever do anything impulsive?" he asked critically.

She gasped. Come on—how dare he? "Um, hello *again*? Sex in the woods? And don't forget the kitchen." She held one finger up in the air.

"Well, all that worked out pretty good," he reminded her. Then his voice deepened, with what sounded like a dare. "Do it again. Get wet with me, Jenny. Get messy."

The hair on Jenny's neck stood up as chills ran down her arms. Mick Brody got her hot in a way no other man could.

Apparently, her temptation showed on her face, since he prodded her some more, tugging her closer to the door. "Come outside with me, pussycat," he said, voice low, seductive. "Let me get you wet."

"Already did," she assured him breathily, thinking of what was going on in her panties right now.

A little sexy-as-sin smile curved the corners of his mouth. "Wetter then. Wetter than you've ever been before."

And after that, she couldn't protest anymore. Even as crazy as it felt to let Mick lead her out the door in a pale pink cami and pajama bottoms, she let him. Even though, despite the falling rain, it somehow felt like walking into fire, flames. Because it was one thing to be seduced by him, over and over again, and even to welcome it, to relish it. But this felt different. This felt like . . . final surrender. *Total* surrender. A man she would willingly follow out into the rain for sex was a man, she knew, who could make her do *anything*.

As they stepped out and the rain began to pelt her skin, she stopped, glanced up at the dark sky from which it fell, and said, "I'm gonna get drenched out here."

"That's the idea, honey," he said. And then he pulled her to him, kissed her like he was devouring her—and the rest just happened.

It was as if the rain . . . freed her somehow, as if it took away any last barriers, any last inhibitions inside her. One minute they stood in the wet grass making out, touching each other's faces, arms, shoulders—and the next he was lowering her top, taking the straps down, pushing it to her waist, baring her breasts to the rain, as well. When he sank his mouth to one nipple, she had the sensation that he drank of her, suckling off the wetness, making her whimper, before moving to the other breast. At the same time, he shoved down her p.j. bottoms, along with her underwear, and as the rain began to roll down her rear, legs, she realized that she *wanted* this now—she wanted to get wet with him, too.

She found herself pressing him down into the old wooden swing that hung from the big maple tree in the side yard. Found herself dropping to her knees in the wet grass and working at his zipper, freeing that part of him to the rain, as well. She heard her own gasp— why was she always a little surprised by how big and hard he was for her?—and then she found herself dipping down, taking him into her mouth.

When she'd done this before, she'd done it for him, wanting to pleasure him—but now she did it for her, too. She wanted to feel this—suddenly, she wanted to feel *everything* with him, *do* everything with him. And maybe the rain was washing away the barrier to that last little bit of herself she'd held back—the part of her that wanted to be aggressive and brazen, the part that still worried just a little what people would think if they knew, the part that harbored those last bits of guilt, about her mother's picture, about her father's ideas of who she should be. Because in that moment, suddenly, it was gone, all gone, completely. And nothing remained but her naked body and her desires and the man she wanted to be with.

"God, honey," he growled above her, his fingers threading through her hair, "aw, that's so damn nice— yeah." And his words fueled her, made her feel wild and good and like a skilled lover—until she wanted still more.

She rose to climb into his lap, straddling him in the swing, ready to have him inside her. He helped, his breath ragged and hot, using one hand to hold the chain at his side supporting the swing and the other to mold to her ass and push her downward.

They both moaned as he entered her, and she looked boldly into his eyes and breathed, "You feel amazing."

"You feel . . . just like I wanted you to," he said hotly. "Wetter than ever before."

She moved on him as she had many times, undulating rhythmically, finding her pleasure. But she never took her eyes off his, and his gaze on her never wavered, either. "Aw, baby, that's right," he rasped. "Ride me."

Again, the heated words spurred her on, made her feel wild and free as the rain sifted down through the tree branches onto them. "You make me live," she heard herself say without planning.

His breath still came hard as he thrust slowly inside her. "What, honey?" he murmured, their eyes still locked.

"You make me live, Mick. You force me to live. I came here to bury my head, but you make me live."

He kissed her then, hard and urgent, his fingers tangling in the wet hair at the nape of her neck. She twined her arms around his broad shoulders, took in everything about the moment—the darkness, the wetness, the wildness, the cool, moist air, how he filled her so deeply, and how everything inside her was starting to move in just the right way, coming together, taking her closer, closer—until she toppled into ecstasy with him one more glorious time, clinging to him, sobbing against his neck, loving the way his arms closed around her, holding her tight.

A few seconds later, Mick was pumping up into her again, harder now that she'd come, making her feel him way up inside. "More," she whispered, "more."

"You want more, pussycat—I'll give you more," he

growled, then drove still harder, harder. And then the world tumbled and they crashed to the ground—the swing had broken and they both let out small groans of shock, but they didn't stop moving together. He rolled her onto her back in the wet grass, plunging deeper, and she met each stroke, then rolled *him* onto *his* back.

She wasn't sure how many times they rolled that way, getting wetter and wetter, but finally she stopped and he towered above her and pinned her wrists to the ground as if to say, *I win.* And she thought—*no, we both win.* And she said between jagged breaths, "I want you to come in me," and he did.

When they finally went still, she realized the rain had stopped. But they were no less wet for it. They lay side by side in the grass, utterly soaked, his jeans at his knees, her cami in a wad at her waist—and she'd never felt better. She even heard a giddy trill of laughter escape her throat. Then she found Mick smiling at her, looking just as sexy and dangerous as ever. "What?" he asked.

"Nothing. This was just . . . pretty damn fun."

"Told you, pussycat."

But then she let her smile fade. Because her heart was beating so hard, pumping so much emotion through her veins. "I meant what I said before, about making me live."

He leaned closer, gave her a little kiss. "I'm glad."

Overhead, she could see dark clouds shifting, the light of the moon starting to peek through, a few stars twinkling in the background—and she decided she had to quit this, push back all she was feeling. *Say something simple, something . . . practical.* "That offer to dry your clothes still stands."

His expression changed—he looked a little distant, sad. "And I wish I could take you up on it, honey."

Oh. "But you have to go." Her heart pinched even as she said the words.

"Sorry," he murmured.

"So . . . Wayne's bad then?"

Next to her, he stiffened slightly. "Let's not talk about that, okay? It's a rule I have—when I'm with you . . . I'm just with you, not anywhere else."

She bit her lip and said, "I like that rule." But she was really thinking, *I love you, I love you, I love you. I'm doomed, but I love you.*

"Why don't we get dressed and maybe you can walk me down to the dock," he suggested.

And though she'd never done that before, she loved the idea of doing it now—it felt like the perfect ending to a liaison that had made her feel so . . . free to be with him. Finally. Well, wait, no, the perfect ending would be if he could stay. If they were like normal people, normal couples, without secrets or reputations. Maybe that offer to dry his clothes had been more emotional than practical, after all—an effort to extend his visit. But with Mick, she'd take what he could give her.

After they went in and toweled off, Jenny put on a fresh cami and a pair of gym shorts, and Mick didn't bother putting back on the wet tee he'd arrived in—he just carried it in his fist as they walked across the road and down onto the dock.

Once there, he lifted his palms to her face to kiss her, and she nearly melted from the fresh pleasure. With Mick, it seemed, she was insatiable—always wanting more. And as their kisses deepened in the first cool night air she'd felt since coming home, she realized he was pushing his hands up under her top—all the way, to her breasts—and then he was raising the fabric, peeling it upward, until she was on full display. Right there on the dock.

"Wh-what are you doing?" she asked.

Just before he lowered his mouth to one beaded peak, he whispered, "Making you live."

And she thought of protesting, because even though it was unlikely, one of her neighbors along the shore *could* see if they were looking out a window or came outside for anything—but she didn't, because it also felt *wild*. As wild as the woods. As wild as the rain. Mick gave her more freedom than she'd ever known she even wanted.

He kissed her breasts for a few blissful moments as she leaned her head back, basking in the pleasure, letting her gaze get lost in the stars now reappearing overhead.

Until he sweetly pulled her top back down into place, kissed her lips one last time, and said, "Bye, pussycat."

We have loved the stars too fondly to be fearful of the night.

Tombstone epitaph of two amateur astronomers

Fourteen

$\mathcal{T}$he blisters on Mick's hands had started to heal, but he knew more were coming. All the dirt he'd shoveled out of that hole had to go back in.

He sat next to Wayne's bed, watching him sleep fitfully, feeling his brother's pain in his gut. He thought of what Jenny had said to him the other night—that he was making her live. The irony burned inside him, the irony of making one person live while watching another die. Maybe that should make him think about the circle of life and all that profound shit, but mostly it just made him glad he was able to make *someone* happy. Wayne he could comfort, but there was no more happiness or sadness now—there was only sleep and pain and long nights and a knot in Mick's stomach that wouldn't go away.

The pain patches had quit working, and now Mick had to administer the other medicine—the stuff he had to inject, under Wayne's tongue. And he now had to crush up the oxycodone and put that under his brother's tongue, as well, because he could no longer swallow it.

Thank God it had rained. Thank God. Because it wasn't so hot in here now, and maybe that was a little thing, but it felt big at the moment. It had only rained for a day or so, on and off, and several more days had passed since then, but the temps had only climbed back into the mid-eighties and so far the humidity hadn't returned. He had to hang on to what he could to keep himself going now.

Darkness had just fallen, night had come, and pleasant, breathable air wafted in the open windows. He wondered if Wayne could feel that at all. He *wanted* his brother to feel it.

He watched him some more, pleased when his sleep slowly became more peaceful—probably the medicine he'd recently administered taking effect. And he watched his brother's face, gaunt now from not eating, and he tried to mentally prepare for what was to come. And then he turned his eyes on that photo Wayne had saved from their boyhood, and he cried, just a little.

But then he got disgusted with himself—this was no time for weakness—and he got up and walked outside, into the small clearing by the house. And he stared up into the stars, and he felt what Jenny had taught him the sky could make him feel: that in the hugeness of it all, his troubles weren't insurmountable, and in the vastness of time, these next few days were less than the blink of an eye and would be over soon.

Two days later, around noon, Wayne opened his eyes, looked up at Mick from his bed, and said, "Am I dead yet?"

For a second, Mick thought he was losing it—his

brother hadn't spoken in a long while. But he looked into Wayne's eyes, and behind the stark frailty, he saw a surprising lucidity that hadn't been there in days. "No," Mick said. "Not yet."

"I'm sorry I'm making you do this," Wayne said, his words slow, his voice dry and cracking. He didn't need to say more—they both knew how horrible this had gotten.

But Mick only shook his head. "No, it's okay," he promised.

Then Wayne started making a wheezing sound, so Mick hurried to grab a glass of water and stick a straw in it. He held it to Wayne's mouth and urged his brother to try to drink—and he choked a little, but got some down.

"Anything you want?" Mick asked when Wayne seemed calmer.

"Nah," Wayne said. And his eyes looked vacant for a moment, and Mick thought maybe he was "leaving" again as quickly as he'd arrived—but then he turned his head slightly toward Mick and said feebly, "Still seeing your girl across the lake?"

The question surprised Mick as much as Wayne's sudden clarity—it seemed like Mick's love life should be the last thing on Wayne's mind right now. "Yeah," he answered softly.

"What's it like?"

Mick blinked, confused. "What's what like?"

Wayne hesitated, then replied, his voice even weaker now. "Been a while . . . since I got laid. What's . . . the sex like?"

Mick drew in a deep breath. His brother wanted to remember what it was like to be with a woman. In any other situation, it might have felt like a betrayal to Jenny to talk about it, but this was . . . this was just one more way of helping his brother die. "It's . . .

warm," Mick said, more softly than he'd intended—then closed his eyes, tired and trying to come up with other ways to describe sex with Jenny. "Her skin is soft. Her curves are perfect . . . like they were made for my hands. When I'm inside her, I feel . . . safe. When she comes, she moans in a way I feel in my chest."

When Mick opened his eyes, Wayne's were shut, but he still replied. "Damn, bro . . . sounds nice."

"It is."

Wayne's breath came slow, shallow. "Can you . . . take me . . . outside? Into the sun?"

"All right," Mick said, without hesitation, anxious to honor any request his brother made now—despite the utter strangeness, and the finality that coursed through him, when he scooped his brother's depleted body up into his arms. Wayne was little more than skin and bones, and Mick felt that in a whole new, brutal way, holding him like this. But neither spoke as Mick carried him to one of the few sunny, grassy spots on their side of the lake—a little knoll, unshrouded by shade, that overlooked the water, which Mick thought especially pretty today with the sun shining on it. It was the same spot where he'd lain on his back with Jenny and looked at the stars on the night she'd found out about Wayne.

Wayne lay on the ground now, as well, too weak to sit up on his own, so Mick left him for a minute, returning with an old lounge chair from the shed that he was able to fold and set up on the ground like a backrest.

They sat quietly and he sensed Wayne soaking in the pretty day, soaking in . . . life, the last he would know of it. A bird sang somewhere nearby. Mick felt thankful again that the weather was nice, hot but not scorching—and then a soft breeze even wafted past, making the leaves in the trees *shush* together and the pine boughs sway. Everything about the moment felt surreal.

Mick saw Wayne's eyes skim the opposite shore, all

the pretty little houses perched there like pictures from a storybook. They used to sit here as boys sometimes, looking across the lake this way—but they'd never talked about it, about how much brighter the world appeared on the other side. Now, though, Wayne asked, "You ever wonder . . . what it's like . . . to live over there?"

"Yeah," Mick replied. He'd *always* wondered.

"Me, too."

"I've been . . . getting a taste of it lately, I guess. With Jenny."

Wayne slowly shifted his glance to Mick. "Yeah? What's . . . it like?"

"Nice. Just the way you'd expect. Nice . . . but dangerous." He looked across the lake again himself, remembering how far away it had seemed as a boy— sort of like The Emerald City across that wide field of poppies. "I'd almost rather not *know* what it's like, you know? Since I don't get to keep it."

"Maybe . . . you will," Wayne said, as if it were a real possibility.

And Mick knew better, but he wanted to let Wayne think cheerful thoughts, and he got the idea it made his brother happy to picture Mick over there amid the pastel cottages and colored canoes and hanging flowerpots. So he just said, "Maybe."

And then Wayne lifted his eyes skyward, up past the trees to the blue expanse above, dotted today with white, fluffy clouds. He stared intently, like someone watching a movie, mesmerized by what they saw on the screen, and he said, "Do you see that? Do you see it? Man, it's beautiful."

And then he closed his eyes, and he expelled a small puff of breath . . . and then he went still.

And Mick's chest tightened with a jolt because he knew Wayne was dead.

"Shit," he whispered to no one. "God." Because he'd known this was coming—but he just hadn't expected it right *now*, at this very moment, while they were talking, for Christ's sake.

And he didn't know if, with Wayne's last words, he'd simply been talking about the sky being beautiful—or if he'd seen a white light, or maybe the hand of God. And if the latter, if it was real or a hallucination. He only knew the strange starkness of death.

And as he looked at his brother's limp, lifeless body, he wondered who would remember Wayne—who would remember that he could be funny, that he'd been good at math, that he'd liked horses as a kid but had never ridden one. It would be like Wayne had never existed—and due to the circumstances of his death, Mick couldn't even give him a decent gravestone to mark his passing.

Despite the fact that Wayne couldn't hear him anymore, he heard himself say, "*I'll* remember you," just before the tears flowed down his face.

It had taken sheer will to put the lid on the simple wooden coffin Mick had built over the summer.

Sheer will to use the ropes-and-pulley system he'd set up to lower it into the ground.

Sheer will to shovel the dirt back over it.

A somehow numb-but-crushing pain had vibrated through his chest with every step he took, every move he made, to complete the grim task that he'd had to accomplish today.

Afterward, he sat next to the fresh grave for a long time, hours. He wasn't sure why.

Was he waiting for darkness to fall, for the day of his brother's death to come to an end? Was he avoiding going back into the house, feeling the fresh sense of loneliness that would surely fill the space? Maybe he just didn't want to leave Wayne alone there, in the ground. He knew Wayne was dead, but it felt strange, as if to walk away was to abandon him. He couldn't believe he'd just covered his brother with dirt—and his chest tightened all over again to remember it. Every fucking shovelful of it.

He's dead—it's okay that you covered him with dirt. It's okay.

He knew that—there was just something inside him having a hard time believing it right now.

As he sat with his knees pulled up to his chest, he reached down to run his fingers through the soft, rich soil atop the mound he'd created with it. He wondered if there was a God. He wondered if God had mercy on sinners like his brother when they died. And sinners like him.

Then he glanced up through the trees surrounding the little family cemetery only a stone's throw from the house to see Wayne's last blue sky beginning to turn just a little purple, like a pale bruise. Night was beginning to fall. Thank God. He wanted it to get dark now, dark, dark, dark—so he could finally go see Jenny. He guessed maybe *that* was what he'd been waiting for all this time, because it was the only thought in his head that held any goodness, any comfort, any relief.

Gravitation is not responsible for people falling in love.

Albert Einstein

Fifteen

*J*enny had spent the day doing the types of things all good Destinyites did. Mostly, because she was a little depressed. She hadn't heard from Mick in over a week. So she'd decided she needed to distract herself from thoughts of him. *I do not want to be the kind of woman who sits around pining over a man. No sirree.*

So she'd tried to cheer herself up that morning by baking muffins—both blueberry and apple. She'd taken a basket of them to the police station for her dad and the other officers, and when her dad had leaned over to give her a kiss on the forehead in thanks, he'd remained somewhat stiff but she could tell he was trying.

After that, she'd stopped by the Daisy Dress Shop and picked up a bold print sundress in shades of yellow and tangerine, along with a shrug to go over it, then dropped into the Destiny Properties office around the corner to ask Sue Ann to an impromptu lunch, her treat—and to Dolly's they went, stopping off for a quick hello to Amy at Under the Covers afterward.

On the way home, she'd stopped at Miss Ellie's with a second muffin basket, and Miss Ellie insisted they sit in her garden "for a spell" with tall glasses of iced tea. When Miss Ellie asked her if she'd decided what she was going to do at the end of the summer, which was fast approaching, she'd smiled and said across the small white round garden table, "I think I might stay."

"Well," Miss Ellie had said, "praying is always good for the soul."

"No," Jenny tried to correct herself, "I mean I think I might stay in Destiny and teach."

Miss Ellie had looked surprised. "Now, praying is one thing, dear, but I'm not sure you're cut out to preach. You best leave that to Reverend Marsh and decide what you want to do with your life."

Jenny had spent the late afternoon working in the yard. Rain had finally brought on the need for a light grass-cutting, so she'd called Becker Landscaping and had someone come out yesterday—but she'd made sure to be gone at the time just in case Adam himself showed up, because she didn't want to deal with any flirtation, even as attractive as Adam was. The receptionist at his company had asked if she wanted any other work done besides mowing, but she'd declined—since the weather was hot again now but not unbearable, and she still wanted to do it herself. Distraction, distraction, distraction, after all. So she pulled weeds in the flower gardens and tidied up the old rose bushes by the back fence. After which she'd stuffed the remnants of the old, broken swing into a garbage can.

But still, just like every night over the past week, when darkness fell, she was at home. She'd made a point of that. In case tonight was the night Mick came.

For heaven's sake—talk about sitting around pining over a man. If anyone else knew she was literally sitting there waiting for him, she'd have been mortally embarrassed. *You are in so freaking deep now—how the hell are you ever going to get out?*

She figured Mick's absence meant one of two things. Wayne was nearing death—or he'd died already and Mick had just *left* afterward, without even saying goodbye.

They'd never talked about that, about exactly how things would go after Wayne died—so what if he'd just gotten in that truck Willie Hargis had seen and gone back to Cincinnati already? What if she waited for him to knock on her back door every night for the rest of the summer and he *never* came?

You'll survive, that's what. You'll put it in its proper place, as the summer affair you meant it to be all along. She told herself this while rinsing her hands under the outdoor spigot, trying to breathe evenly, then stepping inside to grab a cold Diet Coke from the fridge.

But you love him now—you love him so much that you can barely think straight—so it's not that easy, she argued with herself.

Oh boy, wasn't *this* swell? Not only did he have her talking to herself, but he had *two* of her bickering back and forth between themselves now. Great.

And none of that even mattered. Because, love or not, *if he's gone, he's gone.*

She let out a weary sigh as she plopped in a kitchen chair. The air outside had turned dusky now, and the bright bulbs in the kitchen seemed to shine a light on her despair. The sad truth was, she couldn't imagine making peace with that, with him just "being gone." Ever.

She'd loved Terrence, but this was different. This had quickly gone soul deep. Terrence had been her first real passion, and the man who'd felt like the right, easy fit in her life, so right and easy that she'd given up her dreams for him without blinking. Mick was a much *harder* fit, a rough square peg into the smooth, round hole of her existence, but she longed for him as she'd never longed for anything or anyone—with a need she felt in her gut, a gnawing ache.

And she knew he'd leave Destiny one way or another soon, *but please let him at least say goodbye.* She needed that closure. She needed the chance to tell him he'd been special to her. And she even thought that maybe he needed to *hear* it. She wanted to think his life might somehow be just a little better for having known her.

She flinched when a light knock rattled the old back door—and her eyes rose to find the shadow and shape of Mick standing there. She drew in her breath sharply. *Nine days.* She'd been trying not to count, but it had been nine long days since she'd seen him. Her heart flooded with emotion as she pushed to her feet and went to open the door.

Elated, she yanked it wide.

Then took in the way he looked. His white T-shirt and jeans, as well as his face and arms, were soiled with dirt and grime, his skin damp with sweat. His eyes shone tired, haunted.

"God," she murmured. "Oh God, Mick." Reaching out, she found his hand and pulled him inside. "Come in."

"He's gone." She'd never heard Mick sound so hollow.

"I know," she whispered, drawing him gently deeper into the house. "Come in—come with me."

As she led him through the living room and up the stairs, she felt frightened for him, for what he'd been through. She'd been so silly, so selfish—sitting here thinking only of herself, her emotions. And never once had the brutal truth occurred to her that she now suddenly understood: Mick had had to do more than help his brother die, he'd also had to *bury* him. He'd just *buried* his *brother,* for God's sake, with his bare hands.

She'd never seen him look like this—so weakened, both in body and spirit. *I have to help him. I have to comfort him. I have to get him through this.* It was suddenly all that mattered. *I have to . . . to wash it away somehow.*

She led him without a word into the little bathroom in the hall that separated the two bedrooms upstairs, releasing his hand only to pull back the door on the tub/shower enclosure and turn the water on to let it warm. Then she quietly began to undress him.

When she pushed the tee up over his head, he raised his arms, even if a bit limply, like a child allowing her to take it off. And when she worked at his belt and zipper, it was much more loving than sexual. She unlaced his muddy workboots one by one, waiting as he stepped out of them, and when she pushed his jeans and underwear to the floor and he stepped free of those, too, he stood before her beautifully naked—but his eyes remained just as haunted and empty.

She shed her own clothes—shorts, a tank top, underwear—quickly and, stepping into the shower, urged Mick to follow. One sole intent drove her—*I have to clean him up, I have to wash all the dirt away, I have to make him forget what it felt like to bury his brother.*

Every muscle in Mick's body ached, and everything inside him felt listless. It was all he could do to move into the shower. It was like wading through a fog, and the truth was, he'd felt that way for a very long time, probably since the moment Wayne had died earlier that day. God, had it only been *that day*? It felt like . . . a week. Like he'd been putting his brother in the ground for days on end. Like the dirt had been caked and smudged on his arms that long.

Jenny stood in the shower with him, lovely and naked like some sort of water angel, and he yearned to want her like never before—but it was like being in a dream; he felt almost . . . paralyzed.

So when Jenny took charge, he let her. She situated his body under the spray and it cooled his skin. She reached for a bar of soap, something soft and girly and scented, and began to rub it over his chest, shoulders. He tried to feel her touch, but he kept seeing images from the day just past—images of Wayne, alive, dead, talking, silent, and then becoming just . . . a body, something lifeless that had to be put in the ground before the heat could decompose it.

Jenny moved the soap over other parts of him—his arms, then beneath them, his stomach, and lower. Nothing happened there, when she went lower, and he thought maybe he should be embarrassed, but he was too numb to care very much. He just kept seeing Wayne. And dirt. All that damn dirt.

When she took his hands and began to run the bar over his palms, he flinched in pain. "Blisters," he murmured, the water still sluicing down over his head, shoulders, back.

Their eyes met and she whispered, "Sorry."

And then she set the soap aside for a minute to study one of his palms—before she lifted it to her mouth for a tender kiss. And that was the moment when he began to see Jenny more than he saw Wayne.

As she continued to make him clean again, the strange numbness inside him began to fade—just a little. He let the rushing water begin to wash away the pain; he let Jenny's gentle *hands* begin to wash away the pain. When she reached up to wash his hair, he closed his eyes and tried hard to focus just on that and nothing else, on Jenny's hands in his hair, her fingers on his scalp, the physical sensation of it.

At some point, she stepped up behind him, wrapped her arms around his waist, and just held him that way—and kissed a spot on his back. He squeezed her soft hands in his—gingerly, because of the damn blisters—and since he still stood under the water, he decided it was a decent time to let a few more tears fall.

Jenny had never been much of a nurturing type, a caregiver. But that had changed the moment she'd opened the back door and seen Mick's eyes. Now they lay naked in her bed beneath cool sheets, and she held him while he slept. They hadn't made love—this just wasn't about that—she'd simply led him to the bed, pulled his body close, let him rest his head on her breast, and held him.

A shaft of moonlight arced through the window above, allowing her to study his face at rest. His long, dark lashes, the olive tones of his skin, the full, lush mouth. Even in pain, he was a beautiful man. She only hoped she'd done something to *ease* that pain—just a little.

Once she sensed he was sleeping soundly, though, she pulled carefully away from him and out of bed. She slipped into panties and a cami, then tiptoed to the bathroom to retrieve his clothes. Without turning on any upstairs lights, she gathered them and crept down to the laundry room. She set the washer to SOAK AND SCOUR mode, to be sure it got them clean, and while they washed, she wiped his belt and then his boots with a damp cloth to try to get the bulk of the dirt off those, as well. Checking the refrigerator, she was pleased to see she had eggs and even some bacon, which she set out to thaw—she wanted to make Mick a good, hearty breakfast in the morning since she suspected he probably hadn't eaten much the last day or so. Waiting for the washer to finish, she set out two plates and glasses, along with her mother's favorite old frying pan.

When finally the washer shut off, she found that the jeans, T-shirt, and boxers looked clean—the tee and boxers even appeared admirably white, given how dirty they'd been. She threw them all in the dryer and started them tumbling before turning out the downstairs lights and making her way back up to Mick.

As she eased back in beside him, he shifted, reached out an arm to curl it around her waist. She instinctively ran her fingertips lightly through his hair. He kissed her chest, rested his head there again, and this time she fell asleep, too, into a sleep so deep and comforting that she didn't stir again until the morning sun illuminated the room.

When she opened her eyes, Mick lay on the same pillow as her, watching her. She loved having had him in her bed all night, and now, in the morning—but she hated the reason why he was suddenly able to be here; Wayne didn't need him anymore. "How ya doin'?" she asked.

He nodded solemnly against the pillowcase. "Okay."

"Good."

Then he reached out to touch her face. "Thank you. For last night."

She simply shook her head. "Don't have to thank me," she said softly.

He swallowed visibly. His eyes looked less haunted now, but somehow seemed filled with truth, a stark honesty she'd never quite witnessed there before. "I *do*," he insisted. "Not many people have . . . been that good to me, Jenny."

"You *deserve* goodness, Mick," she whispered. "As much as anyone else."

He sighed, still looking unduly tired. "You're sweet."

"Are you hungry? I have bacon and eggs."

He nodded, hesitantly at first, but then more vigorously. "Yeah—yeah, that'd be nice." And it hit her—maybe even just an offer of breakfast seemed an unusual act of kindness, one he wasn't used to getting, or accepting. Then he looked down at himself, naked but for the sheet pulled to his waist—and tried for a small smile. "Better go find my clothes, though, or I might scare your neighbors if I walk past a window."

She grinned in return even if his smile hadn't quite reached his eyes. "They're all in the dryer downstairs."

He looked taken aback. "You washed them?"

She nodded.

"When?"

"In the night. I'm sneaky that way."

His eyes turned uncharacteristically gentle. "You never stop surprising me, pussycat."

She wanted to smile, but couldn't seem to make it happen. He was clearly trying to act normal, strong, yet he still looked so sad. "Is there . . . anything I can do to make this easier, Mick?"

"You're already doing it, honey," he said, reaching out to glide his hand onto her stomach over the polka-dot cami she wore. But then he sighed and glanced over his shoulder toward the lake—toward his old home, she supposed. "Things just . . . don't feel right, don't feel . . . finished."

"What do you mean?"

He gave his head a self-deprecating shake. "I just . . . put him in the ground and left him there. That was it. Guys a lot worse than him at least get . . . a funeral of some kind, you know?"

Jenny sucked in her breath. So many facets of this—of Mick helping his brother die—that she hadn't thought about. "Maybe . . . you and I could have one for him," she suggested.

His brows knit, and he looked slightly disbelieving. "We could?"

"Sure."

"How?"

She wasn't sure, either. And she hated funerals—because of the one she'd had to go to at thirteen. But for Mick, she would do this. "Well, let me think." She lay on her back, turning it over in her mind. "Did Wayne have . . . a favorite song?" Maybe she could get a copy of it and they could play it at the makeshift funeral.

Mick considered the question a minute, then replied. " 'Highway to Hell.' AC/DC."

And Jenny sighed. She might have her work cut out for her.

Shafts of sunlight angled down through the foliage above to shine like heavenly beams on Wayne's grave. Then Jenny hit a button on the boom box and the first hard-driving notes of "Highway to Hell" filled the air. A moment later, the unmistakable voice of the late Bon Scott joined in, and heaven and hell got a little closer to one another next to the grave in the woods by Blue Valley Lake.

After breakfast, she'd left Mick at the house to go to Sue Ann's to pick up an old cassette her friend had of the *Highway to Hell* album, which worked out fine since the boom box from the living room closet was old enough to have a working cassette player. She'd also dug up some flowers from the yard—a few clumps of bright pink dianthus and some of the white impatiens she'd planted back in June. Both were always labeled as annuals at the garden store, but in Jenny's experience, they grew back and spread nicely if you put them in rich soil—plus, it was the best she could come up with on short notice. After grabbing up the old Bible that had been a part of "the shrine" and adding it to the cardboard box of supplies she'd assembled, they'd taken Mick's rowboat across the lake, despite the possibility of being spotted. It was a quiet weekday morning, so the chances were blessedly slim, and she was pretty sure they'd made it unnoticed.

She'd wondered all her life—in a vague way—who was buried in the cemetery behind the Brody house, and now she knew. Looking around, she took in headstones, some crooked, others aging, all bearing the names of various Brodys going back to the turn of the last century. There were only a dozen or so graves other than the one they stood beside, but clearly a long line of Brodys had occupied this craggy, sunless land.

As she stood peering down at the rough-and-ready cross Mick had fashioned from pieces of two-by-four, feeling strange, somber—and a little surreal due to the music, she noticed a small grin playing about Mick's lips. The unexpected sight made her smile softly up at him. "What?" she whispered.

"I was just thinking how much Wayne would like this—having AC/DC blasting at his funeral."

She laughed a little, at the irony of it all. "Good—I'm glad."

When the song finished, Jenny stopped the music before the next song began, which, if she recalled, was one about having sex in a backseat.

"So, what now?" Mick asked.

She looked up at him. "Is . . . there anything you want to say?"

Mick thought briefly, then replied, "Wayne knows I loved him and I'll miss him. That's enough."

"I didn't know Wayne," she said, "but if you loved him, I'm sure he was a good guy."

He tilted his head. "Well, that might be a stretch. Let's say . . . he never meant to hurt anybody, and he did his best." He looked back down at the grave. "What now?"

"Do you want to . . . pray or anything?"

He looked completely out of his element, answering in a hushed tone. "I don't know. I don't know how. I never have."

And for some reason, that made her a little sad. "Want *me* to?"

He nodded slightly. "Okay."

So Jenny took Mick's hand in hers and bowed her head, closing her eyes. "Dear heavenly Father, we come here today to commit Wayne's spirit into Your loving arms. We ask that You give his brother, Mick, the strength and courage to leave him in Your care, confident in Your promise of eternal life through Jesus Christ our Lord. Amen."

She opened her eyes to find Mick staring at her in utter amazement. "*Damn*—that was *good*. Where'd you learn to do that, pussycat?"

"The Destiny Church of Christ."

"Ah."

"I"—she stooped down and reached into the box at her feet, into a tote bag she'd stuffed the Bible into— "thought I could read a little something, too." And after thumbing through to find what she was looking for, she recited the twenty-third Psalm.

Afterward, they both stayed quiet a minute, until Mick said, "That was real nice." Then, "What now?"

"Want to plant the flowers with me?"

He nodded, and together they knelt and put the dianthus and impatiens in the ground, atop the grave, in the loose dirt. "This'll help a lot," he said as they worked. "I mean, since there isn't a headstone. It'll kind of show . . . you know, that somebody's here, even after that cross falls over or rots away."

They worked in silence then, the only sounds a few

twitters from birds and the buzz of a passing honey-bee. Jenny tried not to think about what lay under all this fresh, dark earth—a coffin Mick had had to build himself, a body he'd had to lay there on his own. When all the flowers were planted, she said, "I brought a watering can, too—if you can show me to a faucet or spigot, I'll water these before we go."

She started to stand up, grabbing for the watering can in the box, but he suddenly said, "Wait," and she looked down to see him still kneeling over the burial spot.

She dropped back down onto her knees, too, across from him. "What?"

He peered down at the cross. "There's something else I want to say."

"Okay," she said on a nod.

She watched as Mick swallowed visibly, his eyes still on the grave. When he began to speak again, his voice had dropped an octave. "When I was little and I was scared of something in that house—noises outside, or my mom and dad yelling—Wayne would put his arm around me and tell me it was okay. He was a good big brother back then."

Jenny bit her lip and forced herself not to cry as she reached out across the fresh dirt to grasp Mick's hand—then she focused on the cross, too, to say, "Rest in peace, Wayne."

When Mick told Jenny he had some work to do inside the old cabin, he offered to take her back across the lake and return on his own, but she insisted on helping. Mainly, he told her, he wanted to pack up Wayne's clothes and used bedsheets in trash bags to haul away in his pickup the next time he went to town, along with some other things.

She was stunned at how small the cabin was inside,

and she tried not to think about what it must have been like to live here with parents who'd treated him badly. She also tried to ignore the ramshackle appearance of the place. Some of the interior walls were unfinished— not falling down from age and neglect, but had *never* been finished so that the beams and two-by-fours were bare. It made her family's small cottage look like a showplace, and also made her realize what a warm, pleasant little home it really was—something she'd perhaps taken for granted this summer.

None of that, though, was what made her begin to feel so hollow inside as they worked. As she held a trash bag for Mick while he cleaned food out of a mini-fridge that was either outdated or "Wayne's," she began to feel a little faint, short of breath. And she wished she could blame it on the heat—dear God, it must get overwhelmingly hot in here—but since the rain had come, almost two weeks ago now, the weather had been warm but quite tolerable, so . . . *Ugh, what the heck is making me feel this way?*

And as she stood across the rented hospital bed from Mick, helping him strip off the sheets, her chest tightened and she had the urge to cry. Oh brother—what was happening here? What was *wrong* with her?

It got even worse when she helped him stuff Wayne's clothes—mostly T-shirts and shorts, and one pair of jeans—into another garbage bag. "I'd give these to Goodwill," he said, "but he was . . . you know . . . sick in them. So I'm not sure anybody would want to wear them if they knew."

After that, he cleaned out a small pantry—shelves with a ragged curtain covering them. "Hate to throw out these peaches," Mick said over his shoulder. "But I don't ever want to see another peach again. You want 'em?" he asked. He explained that peaches were among the last foods Wayne had felt like eating.

"Maybe I can use them in pies or cobblers or something," she said, still fighting to hold back tears. "And if not, I'll put them in a food drive when the holidays roll around."

He turned to face her, saying, "I should've known you'd have some good idea like that, pussycat," but that's when he finally saw her distress. His eyes darkened. "What's wrong, honey? What is it?"

Oh hell. She still wasn't sure. So she said, "Funerals. They . . . get to me." It wasn't a lie.

His gaze softened in understanding. "Makes you think of your mom's, I guess."

She nodded. "And . . . and . . . I guess I just don't like the idea of you being alone in the world, without any family at all." Also not a lie. A stark, brutal truth, in fact.

He looked as strong and tough as usual, as strong and tough as he had before the last couple of days, and she was glad to see him starting to bounce back. "Wayne said something like that, too. But I've . . . *always* felt alone, mostly," he explained as if it were nothing.

She blinked, surprised. "What do you mean?"

He only shrugged. "Well, my mom and dad . . . I've told you about them. And I loved Wayne, but . . . he was different than me. He had a dark side. I followed him down that path for a while, because he was all I had, but we weren't all that much alike deep down inside. So . . . I've always sort of been on my own."

She swallowed back the tears that still threatened. "Well, I don't like that." She really didn't. She hated it, in fact.

Then his eyes changed, just a little. "I haven't been alone *lately*, honey," he said softly. "Since I met *you*. You've done a lot to help me through this."

"But now it's over." Oh Lord. *That* was it. *That* was the thing making her want to cry. *Oh God.*

"Don't worry about *me*, pussycat. I'm a big boy—I'll be fine."

But maybe I won't. Helping him pack up Wayne's things had felt so . . . final, made it so clear that his mission here was complete now, and this was . . . well, this was him getting ready to leave, plain and simple.

So she decided to open up to Mick a little more than she already had and tell him what was weighing on her heart right now. Not all of it. Not the part about him. But some of it. "Maybe . . . maybe this is hitting me . . . because *I* feel kind of alone in the world, too."

Mick's expression held comfort tempered with doubt. She could easily understand why. She had so much more than him. He set aside the can of peaches he'd been holding in his hand all this time and lifted his palms to her face. "How can you feel alone, honey? You've got your dad, and your friend, Sue Ann, and all those other people across the lake who care about you."

"You're right," she said, feeling a little silly. Compared to him, she had *tons* of people in her life. "But . . . I guess I feel like the people I love the most are always . . . abandoning me. Even if it's not their fault. My mother. Terrence. Snowball."

His indulgent smile held sympathy, too. "Pussycat, Snowball wasn't a person."

She sighed. "But I loved her so much at the time." She lowered her eyes, gave her head a short shake, and felt truly foolish now. Like the little girl her father had wanted to make of her ever since she'd come home. She supposed that on the inside, part of that girl really did remain. And she supposed it was getting clearer all the time, to both her and Mick, why she'd never gotten another cat.

But what it came down to was—now Mick was going to leave her, too. Mick Brody had become such a large part of her life that his absence was going to rip her heart out all over again. And she was feeling the rip already—the slow, painful tear—as he packed up this house and got ready to pull away from her.

Despite her best efforts, a tear finally snuck free, rolling down her cheek amid the shadowy confines of the little cabin in the woods. *Oh, for heaven's sake, stop this.*

But now, *Mick* was there for *her*, stepping forward to wrap her in his strong embrace. "Come here," he said. "Maybe I shouldn't have pulled you into this so much—Wayne dying, coming over last night the way I was."

Yet she immediately drew back enough to give her head a vehement shake. "No, Mick. I *wanted* to help you through it, any way I could. It's probably . . . one of the best things I've done for anyone in my life."

Their eyes met, held, and she melted in the light of his gaze until he softly brought his mouth down on hers.

Mmm, God, his kiss moved all through her, like energy, like pure electricity. And when it was over, he whispered in her ear, "It's the nicest thing anybody's done *for* me, pussycat. Thank you for that."

She worked to sniff back the rest of her tears. The kiss had helped. "Are you . . . coming back across the lake with me? Staying the night?" she asked—and she hoped like hell it didn't sound needy, but she'd suddenly found herself wondering if maybe he planned to leave immediately, *today*, now that Wayne was gone. Since they'd never talked about his precise plans, and the place *was* sort of a crime scene, after all.

When he nodded, relief flooded her body, especially when he said, "I liked sleeping with you. All night, I mean."

She smiled up at him. "I liked it, too."

"But tonight," he said, "I don't plan on just sleeping."

* * *

When Mick pushed his way into her slickness, it felt like . . . coming home. Which was kind of an alarming thought, but there it was. He'd grown accustomed to being with her. And he felt so damn safe with her. Hell—he didn't even know what safe really *felt* like, but he knew he felt it with *her*. "You're so hot, baby," he whispered. With Jenny, he could feel safe and totally turned-on at the same time.

She bit her lip, met his gaze, and lifted her body against his, taking him deeper. He groaned, his every muscle tensing with pleasure, his erection going even harder inside her.

As he moved in her warmth, he couldn't take his eyes off her face—her sweet eyes, glassy from arousal; her lush lips, looking lightly swollen from kisses. It made him kiss her *again*.

He was connected to her, more than just physically now. He was connected to her in a way he could barely fathom. He'd felt close to her already, but after what she'd done for him last night, and then today . . . He couldn't have let any other woman take care of him that way; he couldn't have let any other woman see him so . . . broken. But with her, he hadn't even weighed it— he'd just gone to her when he needed her. And she'd been there, with open arms.

She was different than any girl he'd known. So sweet and loving. So . . . giving. And sex, the real heat of it, usually faded for him after the first few times with a woman—but with Jenny, that hadn't happened. It just changed, just got hot in different ways.

As he drove into her tight, welcoming moisture again, again, his strokes growing harder, he just wanted . . . to make her feel them, feel *him*. He wanted to be tangled up in her, in her body, in her mind. He wanted her so much, in ways he couldn't even understand.

Except then—*oh God*—maybe he *did* understand. He'd just never felt it before.

But now it was hitting him hard, like a ton of bricks. "Aw . . . aw, baby," he groaned, "now. *Now.*" And then he came in her, hard, deep, eyes shut, teeth clenched, the orgasm stretching through every molecule of his being, delivering a pleasure so powerful it nearly swallowed him.

And as it finally passed, he peered down into her eyes, lifted one hand to her cheek, and said what he'd just figured out, what had just struck him with sudden and undeniable certainty. "I love you, Jenny."

Following the light of the sun, we left the Old World.

Inscription on Columbus's caravels

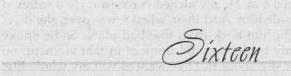

Sixteen

Lying beneath him, she looked stunned. *Shit*. What the hell had he just done?

So he quickly said, "Damn, I'm sorry if that's weird. I shouldn't have said it. Let's just pretend I didn't."

And then he rolled off her in the bed. He leaned his head back, to peer upward out the window overhead, trying to catch a glimpse of the moon or some stars. Already, that quickly, he'd started relying on that, relying on the stars to make his troubles feel small. What the hell had he been thinking to say that?

But then her hand was on his arm; she had turned on her side to gaze over at him. Her voice came hushed, pretty. "No, Mick—I've wanted to say it, too, but I was afraid."

Oh. Oh . . . God. That changed everything. His heartbeat slowed. The world felt right again. Except for one thing.

"I don't want you to be afraid of me anymore, pussy-cat."

Next to him, she bit her lip. "I'm not. I haven't been for a long time. I just thought . . . I thought if I said that, it would scare you away."

He simply shook his head. The truth was, maybe it would have, before now. But the last two days had changed him—no, no the whole last week had changed him. He'd watched Wayne die. He'd suffered alongside him. And then, when it was over, she'd . . . brought him back from that bad place. So he spoke the only truth he could think of in that moment, no longer shy about it. "I've wanted you my whole life, honey."

She sucked in her breath visibly, her eyes filling with some mixture of shock and joy. "You have?"

He simply nodded. Turned toward her in the bed and pulled her naked body close to his beneath the covers. "You were . . . the perfect girl I could never have. And it turns out that . . . you're so much more, more sweet, more hot, more everything, than I could have ever imagined back then. You're more than just a pretty face, Jenny. You're . . . everything a man could want in a woman."

Jenny could barely breathe. *Oh God.* Mick loved her, too. It was nothing short of astonishing. Big, tough, mean Mick Brody loved her. And in the blink of an eye, everything suddenly felt different, like she *wasn't* so alone, like crossing back over that lake tonight with him in the dusk, the stars just beginning to twinkle up above them, had meant more than it ever had before. It meant him moving deeper into her world. She could feel it.

"You can, uh, tell me, too, if you want," he suggested softly.

"Tell you?" She blinked, confused.

He looked her in the eye, even if his expression was a little sheepish. "What *I* just told *you*."

"Oh." She smiled, her heart warming. Had anyone ever said those words to him before and really meant it? Had he ever *wanted* a woman to say it before? Her heart told her no; her heart said she was the first, and that made it all the more special. "I love you, Mick," she whispered in the darkness, glad the moonlight allowed them to see each other. "I love you. I love you. I love you."

He gently closed his eyes—as if savoring it, she thought—and her whole body felt warmer.

"I want inside you again," he whispered against her neck.

She bit her lip and sighed, suddenly feeling like everything in her life was easier. "I could go for that."

"You'll have to help me get ready," he said. "It's only been a few minutes, and I'm good, but . . ."

"You're not that good," she said playfully.

He opened his eyes, flashing a chiding grin. "I was gonna say, 'I'm good, but I shoveled a shitload of dirt into a hole yesterday.'"

"Oh," she said, short, teasing.

"I'm definitely that good, pussycat, and don't you forget it."

"And if I do?"

His grin warmed. "I'll remind you. Over and over."

"Anytime you want to start, big guy," she said, and he laughed softly—then began to kiss her, her neck, her chest. She looped one leg over his hip.

"Have I ever told you my favorite things about your body?" he whispered between kisses.

She shook her head against the pillow. "Mmm mmm."

As he brushed his thumb over the peak of her breast, causing it to bead, he said, "I love the way your nipples get hard so easy."

It was true, they did—at least when Mick was around. "What else?"

"Your tummy is so soft," he said, running his palm over it. "And I love this mole next to your belly button."

She sucked in her breath slightly, pleased that something so small and inconsequential was worthy of notice to him.

Then he leaned closer to her ear, his breath warming it. "And I love how wet you get when I touch you."

She surged with moisture below and informed him, "Apparently just saying it works, too."

His eyes darkened with lust. "Good to know."

And then she spoke her *own* truth, a big truth, something that had been there from the beginning, but she'd never planned on telling him. "You make me . . . see myself differently. Better. In bed, I mean."

"You're *amazing* in bed, honey. The best. Ever."

The best. Ever. *Wow.*

And as Jenny gently pushed Mick to his back and began to kiss her way down his broad chest, over the muscles in his stomach, and lower, she wasn't sure if it was a reward for what he'd just said, if it was because she wanted to get him ready, or if it was just pure animal instinct. But when she took him in her mouth, the ministrations poured straight from her heart, her very soul. And then his hands were in her hair, stroking, massaging, and he began to murmur, "Aw, God. You're so good, Jenny . . . so, so good."

And when he entered her a moment later, as her body took him deep inside, she bit her lip, remembering those same words, how they'd tortured her, taunted her, when she'd first come home.

But suddenly being good didn't seem so bad. Turned out there were lots of ways to be "good Jenny."

* * *

The next morning, Jenny found her mom's old waffle iron on an upper shelf of a kitchen cabinet and discovered it still worked. Her hot, romantic night with Mick had inspired her to do something a little out-of-the-ordinary for breakfast.

Again, *still,* everything seemed fresh, changed, transformed. As if they'd entered a new, more certain, phase of their relationship. She couldn't be glad Wayne was dead, but she could sense how it had freed Mick—freed his time, freed his pain, freed his love.

She felt so merry that it didn't even get her down when, as they cleaned up the breakfast dishes together, she noticed it getting hot in the house and realized the A/C was on the fritz yet again. "Guess I'll have to call Dad," she said, almost cheerfully—her cheer fading only when she saw the look on Mick's face.

"I'm sure he'll be thrilled to see *me* here."

Oh. Good point. She pursed her lips, thinking, then announced, "Well, maybe it's time he *did* see you here. Maybe now that Wayne has . . . passed, it's not that big of a deal. After all, there's nothing to hide now. I mean, yeah, he probably doesn't have the best impression of you from the old days, but we no longer need to worry about you getting caught helping Wayne."

He shrugged. "Maybe. I still don't think it's a good idea, though, and it's probably risky for me to even *be* here in the daytime like this."

Of course, he couldn't know what *she* knew—that her dad was already well aware of the whole situation and had promised not to act on it. And she still had no plans to tell him—he just didn't need to know. It could only stress him out when, for the first time since they'd come together in the woods that night, he was starting to seem truly relaxed. "Whatever you think is best," she said. "But . . . I'm not worried."

"Yeah, well, you're not the one who committed a

crime, pussycat. So instead of calling your dad, why don't you let *me* look at the A/C?"

Oh yeah, he *had* told her he had experience with stuff like that—it had slipped her mind amid everything else. She motioned toward the laundry room and said, "Be my guest."

Five minutes later, as Jenny was drying the dishes, Mick reappeared in the kitchen and announced that he needed to get a part for the air conditioner.

"So you can see what's wrong?" she asked. "That fast?"

He nodded. "Just a little corrosion keeping some parts from connecting the way they should. It's hard to see if you don't know where to look." He wiped his hands on the front of his jeans. "I need to head out for a while today, anyway—I want to load the hospital bed and return it to the medical supply place north of Crestview, and I think there's a Home Depot near there, so I can stop and pick up what I need to fix the A/C."

"Want some company?" she offered.

He looked pleasantly surprised. "You want to drive around doing crappy errands with me? Have you ever actually *driven* the road that leads from my place out to the highway, pussycat? It's half an hour of curves and ruts each way."

She shrugged. "I'm not afraid of a few ruts. And maybe I . . . like spending time with you. Even on crappy errands."

A warm grin slowly unfurled on his face. "Well, the crappy errands sound a little less crappy now."

They spent the rest of the morning rowing back across the lake and loading the hospital bed in Mick's truck, a late-model Ford pickup that fit the description of the one Willie Hargis had seen. She found herself hoping Willie wouldn't notice it turning out onto the highway *today*, but reminded herself again that it didn't really matter—her dad had kept his word, and the worst worries were over now that Wayne could no longer be discovered.

Mick was right—the road to the highway was horrible—and now she understood why no one had wanted to build there when he'd tried to sell the land. The landscape stayed just as steep and craggy most of the way out as it was next to the lake. It was as if the Brody ancestors had picked the worst, most isolated spot they could find to make their home; the part of Destiny where Mick had grown up felt completely cut off from the rest of town.

As they drove together, she found herself feeling bolder, and more curious. About them. Her and Mick. They'd exchanged the big *I love you*s the night before, of course—and it had inspired waffles, a fluttering heart, and a warmth inside her so intense that she could barely fathom it. Part of her still couldn't believe it. *Mick loves me!*

But it left a huge question in the air, too. What did this mean for the future? She'd been happy as a clam all night and morning, but only as they'd rolled the heavy hospital bed up a plywood ramp into the truck had Jenny been reminded once more—Wayne was dead, and Mick's home was no longer here. Up to now, she'd resisted prying deeper into his plans, but after last night, she suddenly felt she could.

"So," she said as Mick swerved around a particularly deep hole in the dirt-and-gravel road, "now that Wayne is gone . . . what's next?"

He didn't ask her what she meant—he seemed to know. "I'm not quite sure, pussycat."

So she got bolder still. "There's . . . a house up the road from me for rent. Sue Ann's great-aunt's place. I could tell her I know someone who wants to look at it."

Mick slowly brought the truck to a halt on a flat

stretch of road with a steep embankment on one side, a jagged hill on the other, and gaped at her like she'd lost her mind. "Are you kidding? No way, pussycat. I could never live here again—people would run me out of town on a rail."

Maybe she should have expected that kind of reaction, but she hadn't. So she took a deep breath and simply said, "Maybe not. Just give them a chance. And there's a big new development going in near the edge of town—a hundred houses. *Brick* houses. Where they'll need brick*layers*. It . . . might make a lot of sense."

Across the console from her, Mick drew in his breath, looking pensive, doubtful—but not totally unmovable, either. "I don't know, honey. You know I never had any plans to stay here."

She bit her lip, thoughtfully, hopefully. "But isn't it fair to say that . . . things have changed?" Him and her, she meant.

He drew in his breath, met her gaze. Then said, "The best I can say is . . . I'll think about it."

He'd think about it. As opposed to, *no way in hell*. This was good. Promising. She held back her smile and said, "That's all I can ask."

And then, as he eased the truck forward again, as they rounded a sun-drenched bend, he said, softly, "What if . . . *you* came with *me*? To Cincinnati? Or . . . anywhere else?" He kept his eyes on the road as he spoke. "I know you're thinking about taking that job at the high school, but . . . maybe you could teach somewhere else. Someplace where people don't know me."

Jenny was utterly stunned, and touched. He was asking the same thing she was, but in a bigger way. He was saying he wanted to be with her, long term—wanted them to be someplace *together*. Of course, he'd said he loved her, so maybe she shouldn't be *so* surprised—but with Mick, she was. This had all happened so quickly, yet they both seemed so like-minded on it. At least on the wanting-to-be-together part. It felt amazing enough to make her say, "I guess I could consider that."

Mick still didn't quite look at her—she sensed this was something very new for him, this idea of building something lasting with a woman—but he silently reached out, grabbed her hand, and squeezed it, saying, "Thanks, pussycat."

And of course, for her, *his* suggestion was much scarier than hers—it meant going someplace entirely new, without much of a plan. But she quickly decided it would be unfair to rule it out. Mick Brody had shaken up her life, made her take chances, made her live. Maybe she should let him keep right on doing it.

After the errands and a nice lunch at a café in Crestview—the first time they'd ever eaten in a restaurant together—they headed back to Mick's cabin, where he still felt safer leaving the truck. Even though Jenny knew he didn't have to hide now, he seemed to think it wise to remain out of sight, and she could live with that for the time being. It was dusk by the time they rowed back across the lake, but he fixed the A/C while she grilled chicken breasts and corn on the cob on the back porch.

They made love in the freshly cooled house, in the living room this time, like when they'd first met—not for old times' sake, but because at that moment, the bedroom had just felt too far away. And as they lay mostly naked together on the couch beneath the old crocheted afghan, Jenny suggested yet one more trip back across the lake—to look at the stars.

"Woman, you must think I'm a machine," he groused

beneath his breath. "Digging graves, rowing boats, keeping you satisfied in bed—a man needs to rest once in a while, you know."

"I'll row," she volunteered. "And you *are* a machine. A *sex* machine."

He shrugged easily against a throw pillow. "Well, you got that part right." Then he kissed the tip of her nose. "And *I'll* row."

After climbing up on the same rocks that had brought them together in the first place, and without even setting up the telescope, Jenny leaned her head back and said, "Look up, Mick. Look at the sky."

When he did, she heard his sigh of awe. The night was particularly clear, and the hour was just right to see the Milky Way streaming across the cosmos in all its illuminating glory.

"The Milky Way," she informed him. Then explained how the galaxy was shaped like a disk and the Earth was near its outer edge. "So what you're seeing is . . . all the trillions of stars stretching across it to the other side."

"That's pretty amazing," he murmured. "How have I not seen this before?"

"Well, in the city, lights and pollution block it out. And you have to have a clear night at the right time of year. And you have to remember to look *up*, too," she teased him, since she was pretty sure he hadn't been very aware of the stars before she'd come along.

"I've been doing that a lot more lately," he confirmed. "You're right, about it making your worries seem less important. It helped sometimes, in those last days with Wayne."

He kissed her then, and she teased him that if he stayed in Destiny, they'd have this great view all the time. He teased her back that if she came to Cincinnati, he'd be keeping her too busy in bed for her to have any energy to go stargazing.

After finding Saturn and Venus and the Hercules Cluster through the telescope, they came back to her house and slept in her bed in their underwear, and Jenny wasn't sure about where to live—but she loved knowing that, one way or another, it was going to be with Mick. He wasn't going to leave her.

She'd spent all summer thinking that by now, August, she'd probably be alone, without a lover, and mourning the loss. Instead, she had a man who loved her, a man who she loved—and trusted. A man who made her feel wonderful about herself. A man who was going to stay in her life and not leave her feeling abandoned.

The following day, Jenny and Mick sat at her kitchen table nibbling at the last bits of breakfast—scrambled eggs and sausage links, with English muffins. She didn't normally make such hearty breakfasts every day, but having Mick around the house gave her the urge to . . . be domestic, and to keep their strength up after the workouts they gave each other in bed every night.

"I'm gonna head back across the lake for a while this morning, pussycat," he said after draining his glass of orange juice. "Got a little more work to do."

"I'd go with you again," Jenny replied, "but I have lunch plans with Sue Ann and some other friends today." The truth of it was, she was so deep in that "in love" stage that she wanted to spend every minute with him. But she was old enough to know you didn't throw your girlfriends over for a guy—no matter how hot and sexy he was.

"No problem," he said. "I'm just gonna do a little

more cleaning and load some more junk in the truck to be hauled away—stuff that should have been done years ago. And maybe I'll let the air out of the blow-up mattress I've been sleeping on there, since I . . . kind of have a new bed now." His eyes sparkled lecherously during those last words, turning her moist below—even this early in the morning.

"Speaking of your new bed," she ventured, "have you . . . been thinking? About the possibility of staying in Destiny?"

He leaned back in his chair and blew out a long breath. "If it was just you and me, honey, sure. But it's not. Have *you* thought about Cincinnati?"

She nodded. She had. And she wasn't opposed to the idea, except that *here* she had a job. And he probably did, too. And that mattered. She'd taken the summer off, but she wasn't made of money. "The thing is, school starts soon, so I doubt I'd find a teaching position this late in the summer other than the one I've been offered here. And despite the life of leisure I appear to live, my funds are getting a little depleted."

He shrugged knowingly. "I hear ya on that. I'm in the same boat after quitting my job in May to come out here and take care of Wayne. I had some money saved, but it's mostly gone now. Although"—he leaned forward toward her, his dark eyes pinning her in place—"I'd take care of you, pussycat, whether or not you find a job. You can count on that."

That touched her, deeply, because she suspected Mick had never wanted to take care of anyone else but himself before—and Wayne, this summer. But she wasn't the sort of woman who could be fulfilled letting a man take care of her. Okay, sexually maybe. And emotionally, too, even. But not financially. "Thank you for that. But it's important to me to . . . do something, you know? In fact, as much as I've enjoyed my leisure time this summer, I'm ready to get back to work, back to teaching."

And while part of her wanted to throw all that to the winds and say, 'Yes, Mick, I'll come to Cincinnati with you and we'll figure it all out,' another part of her wanted to do what *she* wanted for a change. She'd given up her dreams for Terrence, gone where he wanted, did what he wanted. So, no matter how much in love she was with Mick, she didn't want it to be the kind of love that required her to sacrifice everything she cared about. She needed to do things better, smarter, this time. She needed to take steps to make this solid, make it last.

And the truth was, she had more than just a job here. She had her father. And her friends. Things that mattered. Things that . . . well, things she was slowly starting to realize she wanted to *keep* in her life. On an everyday basis.

"Okay then," he said, pushing to his feet, "if you hate the idea of leaving, if you want to take this job, then . . . it's all right, pussycat."

She wasn't sure how to read his words. "And you would stay, too?"

He hesitated slightly. "I'm trying to work that out in my head right now. I'm trying to tell myself it would be okay."

She stood up next to him, took his hands. "It would. I promise. I would *make* it be okay."

"You can't control a whole town, Jenny."

She released his hands to point a teasing finger at him. "Don't sell me short, Brody—turns out I can do a *lot* of things I never thought I could."

A few minutes later, she walked him down to the dock. She'd truly quit caring if anyone saw at this point—maybe it really *was* time for people to see, to know, to find out there was more to Jenny Tolliver than the good girl they all saw, and more to Mick Brody than the guy they'd known years ago. And Mick was slowly beginning to seem less worried about being spotted, as well, which she figured was a good sign all the way around.

Nonetheless, it was another quiet, still summer morning as the sun began to burn hotly down on Blue Valley Lake, no neighbors in sight. Mick kissed Jenny goodbye, told her he'd be back later this afternoon, and she watched him row away from her. He kept his eyes on her the whole time and she found herself wishing she could capture the moment, how strong and sexy he looked in the morning light, his T-shirt stretched taut across the muscles in his chest, that wayward lock of hair drooping over his forehead.

She'd just started cleaning up the breakfast dishes a little while later when she heard a car in the driveway and looked out to see her father's cruiser. She opened the back door to greet him—realizing that Mick wasn't the only person who always entered this house through that particular door. "Morning, Dad," she said.

His smile didn't quite reach his eyes, but still, again, at least he was trying. "Jennygirl," he said in greeting.

"Want some eggs?" she asked as he stepped inside. A bowl of them still sat on the counter. "I can reheat them."

He shook his head. "That's nice, but no. Just thought I'd stop by before I head to work since I . . . haven't seen you much lately."

"Thanks," she whispered. He hadn't seen her much since he'd found out about Mick Brody. But since Mick wasn't going anywhere, wasn't leaving her life as she'd expected, she decided it was time to start . . . initiating her father to that idea.

So she put on a smile and said, "Guess what. Mick fixed the air conditioner. He used to work in heating and cooling. A small part needed to be replaced, and he says it's good as new now."

The look on her father's face told her he couldn't decide whether to be happy or sad—she knew it was definitely good news that the unit wouldn't have to be replaced, but that it was going to take a while before he got used to the idea of Mick being around, in her life, in *their* lives. "Well, reckon that's a relief," he said.

"And," she began cautiously, dropping her voice despite their being alone, "I may as well tell you—Wayne died a few days ago, so . . . there's no more secret to keep. It's done now, and no one ever has to know."

"Well, that," her father said pointedly, "is a *bigger* relief. Best news I've heard in a while."

She drew in her breath and stepped closer to him. "I'm really sorry, again, Dad, that I had to put you in that position. But at least it's over now, and we can just sort of . . . pretend it never happened."

He nodded, still looking troubled, uncertain, and it reminded her how much harder on him keeping such a secret had been than it had on her. He was a lawman, and she'd made him do something that went against his values, his very nature.

"And thank you again for . . . well, you know."

Another nod from her father, although she wished things felt more comfortable between them. She'd hoped the news about Wayne would make him relax. Maybe bringing Mick up so soon had been a mistake— but she just wanted to handle her life honestly. She was so tired of trying to please other people.

After that, they struggled to make small talk—about

her lunch with the girls later today, about school starting soon. Although he appeared happy when she said
she was probably going to take the job at the high
school and stay in town. How happy he'd be when he
found out Mick was most likely sticking around, too,
was another story, but she'd cross that bridge when
she came to it. She'd had enough drama surrounding
their relationship already and hadn't particularly been
prepared for more this morning.

So it felt almost like a reprieve when he said, "I'd
best be takin' off."

"Okay. Happy police chiefing," she said, trying for
some lightness. "Maybe we can . . . have lunch soon."

He nodded again, but this time didn't smile. "That'd
be nice."

And she didn't quite believe him.

Mick had watered the flowers on Wayne's grave and
spent a little time sitting on the ground next to the
wooden cross there, thinking about his brother, about
their past, about his future. He wasn't a guy who believed in talking to dead people, but something about
resting there in the morning shade had helped him
start sorting things out.

The truth was, he didn't know if he could live a
happy life in Destiny. The further truth was, he couldn't
quite fathom some of the stuff he'd said to Jenny over
the past couple of days. He'd heard the words leave
his mouth—all this talk about being together, staying
together—but it hadn't sounded like him.

The *most* surprising part, though, was that he'd
meant *all* of it. Every single word.

Even if, deep down inside, he wasn't sure about a
lot of things. All this had happened so damn quick. He
knew he loved her—that part wasn't in question—but

as he sat there beside his brother's resting place, the rich dirt slowly beginning to settle beneath the flowers planted there, he couldn't help asking himself: Was *Jenny* really ready for this? It was easy to forget sometimes that she'd just gotten divorced. As well as other things he'd come to know about her as they'd grown closer, too—like that Terrence had taken her virginity, and that made Mick only the second guy she'd ever had sex with.

In one way, that made him feel really special . . . and important. But in another way, he had to wonder: Was this one of those rebound things for her? Could a girl like Jenny really love *him*—Mick Brody—the way she *said*, the way she *thought*? Maybe it would all pass for her when the summer ended. Maybe he was just a Band-Aid on her heart right now.

But hell—what it came down to was that his worry didn't really change anything. Because for the first time in his life, he'd fallen in love. And he suddenly understood what a strange affliction it was—it made him happy and sad at the same time. He wasn't sure he liked suddenly feeling tied to someone—it was a little unsettling, and it was clearly going to make him do things he normally wouldn't. Yet despite all that, he couldn't imagine walking away.

So if Jenny wanted to stay here, he would try. And if Jenny wanted to love him, he would let her. She'd given him so much—he didn't want to be without her now. Life would feel empty.

And maybe his life had been *kind of* empty before her, but to go back to that after having her would be, well . . . hard, plain and simple. And maybe he'd rather take a chance *here* than be without her *there*.

Besides, when he looked at his life in Cincinnati, what did he really have to go back to, besides a place that had grown familiar to him. He wasn't the most open person in the world, so he didn't have a lot of friends—a few guys he didn't mind meeting for a beer or a ballgame, but that was about it. Jenny had people here, people who loved her, and it seemed selfish to try to tear her away from that.

So, for her, I'll try. I'll trust. I'll . . . open myself. I'll . . . be this guy I've never been before and don't even know how to be—this goofy "in love" guy, this guy who takes care of his woman, this guy who gives more than he takes. He found himself looking at the cross again as the words went through his mind. But that didn't mean he was talking to dead people.

After that, he did what he'd told her—he started cleaning up crap that had been left behind and neglected for years. He wasn't sure why it suddenly mattered to him since the place was going to be abandoned again soon, but maybe it had to do with Wayne's grave. He just didn't want a bunch of garbage around the place.

It was as he tossed a couple of trash bags into the bed of his truck that he heard something and looked up to see a police cruiser rambling up the road toward him. *A goddamn police cruiser.* Despite the heat of the day, his blood ran cold.

Son of a bitch. *Son. Of. A. Bitch.* What the fuck was *this* about?

His thoughts raced. Could he still go to jail for what he'd done? Was a fresh grave behind the old house of an escaped convict enough proof? Or—or would they do something awful like dig up Wayne's body to find out for sure? And was it going to be Chief Tolliver in that car or someone else?

Years ago, his first instinct at the sight of a cop car was to run. But he couldn't see that running right now would do much good—except to maybe make him look guilty of something. His heart hammered against his ribs, but he tried to take deep breaths and think how to deal with this.

Don't lose your cool, man. Just stand your ground. Play this smart. As smart as possible, anyway, under the circumstances. Shit, he wished Wayne's grave were less fresh, or that he'd dug it deeper in the woods, not right in the family cemetery. But it had made sense—and the truth was, by the time he'd started digging, he'd pretty much come to believe no one was ever going to find him back here. How had they found him *now*? Had someone seen him coming and going across the lake the last few days in the daylight, damn it?

As the police car pulled up nose to nose with his truck, which he'd backed up toward the house, Mick just kept tossing garbage bags, like nothing was wrong. In his heart, nothing *was* wrong. He'd done nothing here *he* considered a crime. But as Jenny's father stepped out of the car, Mick braced for the worst.

"Mick Brody," Tolliver said, his very tone disdainful—and unsurprised.

Mick stopped what he was doing and tried to stand a little taller than normal, tried to look just a little intimidating. "Chief Tolliver," he said in a similar timbre, not pretending he didn't know the man.

"Brody, I'll cut straight to it. I know what you're doing here—I know the whole damn story."

Shit. Mick's stomach sank. Still, he tried to act tough, crossing his arms across his chest, staring down his nose at the slightly smaller man—a gut reaction. "Yeah? What is it you think you know?"

Unfortunately, Tolliver didn't look the least bit worried. In fact, he looked downright cocky. "That your brother escaped from prison and came here to die."

Aw, Christ. Damn it to hell. Mick held his tongue—for perhaps a second too long—before saying, "Have a look around—you won't find anyone but me."

"I know that," the police chief shot back. "I know he died a few days ago. I know all about you and my daughter, too."

Mick said nothing in response to that, only shifted his weight from one foot to the other. Mainly because he was stunned. To the point of being light-headed—all the blood had drained from his brain. It was one thing for Tolliver to have somehow figured out about Wayne, but another to know Mick had been messing around with Jenny. Again, he thought of rowing across the lake in daylight—but the man knew a lot more than he could've figured out just from seeing Mick in a boat.

Tolliver went on, raising his voice. "Now listen to me, Brody, and listen damn good. I let all this slide—I let you stay out here harboring a wanted man, I gave you time to let him meet his maker. And I'm *still* gonna let it slide, even against my better judgment. But now it's time you clear out and not come back. Time for you to stay the hell away from my daughter, once and for all."

Mick took it all in, the threat, the knowledge Tolliver had, the surprising fact that he had indeed waited until now to come out here. But he couldn't quite wrap his mind around it all—it was a little too much when he hadn't been expecting it. There was mainly one thing he wanted to know. "You mind if I ask just how you got your information?"

"Jenny told me," Tolliver said.

And Mick's heart lurched in his chest as his stomach went hollow. He realized he'd started shaking his head. "No," he said simply. "She wouldn't do that."

"She *did*. How else would I know?"

God damn. Now Mick's heart physically *hurt*, felt like it was imploding upon itself. Could Tolliver be telling the truth? Mick couldn't believe it, but . . . shit, what he'd said made sense. How else *would* he know?

Mick sucked in his breath as anger slowly began to gather inside him, replacing the shock there. "How long?" he bit off. "How long have you known about this?"

" 'Bout since the Fourth of July," Tolliver said. "You got any other questions? 'Cause if you don't, you best get packin'. I want you out of town by the end of the day, and I don't want to see your face here again—ever. Am I makin' myself clear?"

Mick met the man's gaze through angry eyes. "Crystal."

He stood in the same place without moving until Jenny's father got back in his car, turned it around between some trees, and drove back down the rutty road, leaving a pale cloud of dirt to float behind the cruiser as he got farther away. He held on to the side of the truck as he tried to wrap his head around what had just happened.

Jenny had *told* her father? About him and Wayne? Being here? She'd told him *weeks* ago? Fucking *weeks*? He didn't *want* to believe it, but Tolliver had known too much, been too sure, too downright confident.

He'd *trusted* her. He'd fucking *believed* in her. In everything *about* her. He'd thought she was . . . *perfect*. Perfect enough to trust, perfect enough to love. And even if he'd had some worries over her flying into this fresh on the heels of her divorce—Jesus, that was a hell of a lot different than her willingly betraying him!

It didn't even really matter *why* Jenny had told her dad—guilt or being a daddy's girl or whatever half-ass reason, she'd put him at *risk*. Him *and* Wayne. She'd risked his freedom. She'd risked Wayne's prospect of having a peaceful death, free of steel bars and strangers. She'd risked every-fucking-thing that had mattered to him this summer.

And she'd never breathed a word about it.

If she'd told her father out of guilt—hell, couldn't she have at least *warned* Mick? Made him aware? Given him a chance to decide what to do, consider if he and Wayne should try to leave, or hide? *Shit. Shit, shit, shit.*

God *damn* her!

God damn her for fucking with his life.

God damn her for . . . fucking with his heart.

But hadn't he just been telling himself the hard truth he'd not quite wanted to believe? That Jenny couldn't love him *that* much, *enough,* so soon after her divorce? Hadn't he just been running all those doubts through his mind—how fast this had happened, how unsure he was about things. Shit—apparently he should have listened to himself. Apparently he'd had a lot more to worry about than Jenny being ready for a new relationship. But the not-loving-him-enough part—hell, he'd hit that one right on the nose.

When did you get so weak, Brody? So weak that you actually thought you could depend on somebody, open yourself up like this? It was because of Wayne, he knew—because watching his brother deteriorate had been the hardest thing he'd ever endured.

Only, at first, he'd *realized* what was happening— he'd understood that he went to her for comfort, that he wasn't as strong as usual right now. He'd understood the logic behind it.

It was after *that* when he'd messed up. It was when he'd been stupid enough to let himself fall for perfect Jenny Tolliver—who, it turned out, wasn't so perfect after all.

This is the way the world ends—not with a
bang but a whimper.

                                    T.S. Eliot

Seventeen

Jenny didn't worry when she got back from her
lunch with Sue Ann, Tessa, and Amy to find that Mick
wasn't there yet. It was still early in the day, after all.
But she couldn't wait to see him. To tell him that, after
Amy and Tessa had left the café to head back to the
bookstore, she'd arranged for Sue Ann to show him the
house tomorrow. To also tell him that, according to Sue
Ann, Bright Homes, in Crestview, had been contracted
to build the first section of houses in the new development, so now she knew who Mick could call about
getting hired on. Things were coming together—and
she just *knew* Mick could be happy here, that they *both*
could, *together*.

And it had been, well . . . just plain *fun* to fill Sue
Ann in on the latest. Okay, not so much about Wayne's
death and funeral, but about the *I love you*s that had
followed and the talks about staying together.

"He loves you?" Sue Ann had gasped, gaping at her across the little round table at Dolly's. The smothering heat they'd suffered most of the summer had, unfortunately, started to set back in today, so they'd eaten inside rather than on the patio, but that didn't encourage Sue Ann to keep her voice down until Jenny kicked her under the table.

Yet then she'd smiled and said, "Yes, he loves me, loves me, loves me."

Sue Ann had just sat there shaking her head in amazement. "Wow, Jen, do you know what this means? You're like . . . a lion tamer or something. You tamed the beast in big, bad Mick Brody."

Jenny couldn't resist playfully rolling her eyes upward and saying, "Well, not *too* much, I hope."

"So, you really think he'll stay? And you really think people will accept him?"

"Yes and yes." Then she'd pointed at Sue Ann across the table. "And *you* have to help me. You have to defend him when people say bad things. You have to remind them that people can change. You have to help him fit in."

Sue Ann bit her lip. "I can defend him and all that, but . . . forgive me for saying I have a hard time envisioning him, say, playing golf with Jeff or your dad."

"Maybe not, and my dad is going to be a superhard sell on this, but he can fit in other ways. He can go fishing with my dad. He can grill out with us."

"And you have no more doubts about him? You really think he's changed, deep down—that his past doesn't matter, that there's nothing to fear here?"

"I trust in that so completely, Sue Ann. I know it in my heart."

After that, Sue Ann had leaned forward slightly and smiled her best-friends-forever smile to say, "I'm truly happy for you, Jen. You deserve this—a guy who's really crazy about you. *And* who rocks your world in bed."

Just then, Mabel, a waitress who was seventy-five if she was a day, shot her head around, her eyes going as wide as the plates she carried.

"Keep it down, would ya?" Jenny grumbled.

But Sue Ann just shrugged it off. "Listen, from the way you've described him, once people get a look at him, they're gonna *know* he's rocking your world in bed—so, just FYI, you're gonna have to get used to people looking at you in a whole new way around here."

At first, that had caught Jenny off guard, brought up old feelings of worry and guilt—but then she'd just smiled and said, "So be it. And it's about time."

Jenny still didn't worry when the dinner hour came and Mick still wasn't there. He probably had a lot to do, and it had probably involved running errands to Crestview or beyond, given that he didn't feel he could shop for anything or even fill up on gas in Destiny. That would change soon—he'd keep getting more comfortable with the idea—but for now, even simple things probably took him a lot longer based on proximity alone.

So she grilled some hamburgers, hoping he'd show up while she was cooking, and then, later, she hoped he'd show up while she was eating. She kept his warm for a while, but then gave up on that and decided she could reheat it all in the microwave whenever he finally arrived.

Jenny still tried not to worry when darkness fell. She had no idea what was keeping him so busy, but whatever it was, maybe he just wanted to get it all done so he wouldn't need to go back over to the cabin anymore.

Yet as the hour grew later, as she changed into pajamas and watched a little TV to try to distract herself, she began to wonder where on earth he could be. What if . . . he'd had some sort of accident, on the road or otherwise? After all, despite his old reputation, Mick had proven to be pretty dependable in the time she'd known him.

It would be silly to go over there looking for him. Because there was surely some logical explanation. And what if she went canoeing across the lake and he showed up here in his truck? And while she was certainly no stranger to sneaking around his property by herself, she'd seldom gone over in the pitch-black darkness, and it suddenly sounded a little dangerous to her, especially given that there was no moon tonight, or stars, either, due to a hazy cloud cover she'd noticed at dusk when she'd been outside grilling. It was a truly dark night in Destiny, and it just seemed smarter to stay put and wait for him.

She thought about calling Sue Ann but decided against it. After all, what could her friend do but listen to her worries—and it was late, and Sue Ann had work tomorrow morning. And if she just went up to bed and fell asleep, surely she'd wake up soon to find him quietly coming in to lay down beside her and tell her where he'd been all day.

Of course, she couldn't sleep. She kept listening. For anything.

But he never came. The whole damn night passed, full of tossing and turning, and Mick never showed up.

By morning, Jenny felt sick. What did this mean? What if he really was hurt somewhere?

She didn't feel like eating, so she bypassed breakfast,

dressed in a tank top and khakis, and set out in the canoe. Her heart was in her throat the whole time she paddled, the whole while watching the shore for anything odd—but finding nothing.

When she reached the other side, Mick's rowboat rested on the sand, exactly where it should be. Okay, so he hadn't drowned in the lake—that was a good sign.

As she trudged up the steep hill to the house, she kept her eyes peeled, but didn't see anything unusual. Although his truck was gone—so he *had* left, and so far, hadn't come back. She took a deep breath. *Where are you, Mick? Where are you?*

God, it was hot—already, and it wasn't even 8:00 A.M. The brutal heat was back full force, that was for sure. And starting to sweat this early was doing nothing to help her mood.

Approaching the cabin, she peered through the window. Nothing looked especially different—except that the air mattress was gone. And she began to notice some changes outside the house, too. It was tidier—he'd picked up debris she'd noticed before—in particular, a rusted bicycle and some old, equally rusty clothesline poles.

And then she realized what else was missing outside. The generator. Mick had brought it with him rather than have the electricity turned back on, not wanting to create a trail to him and Wayne. He'd explained that he'd used it primarily during the day and turned it off most nights so as not to exceed its capacity. He'd also told her just a couple of days ago that he planned to leave it here for a while—since it belonged to him and he didn't particularly have anyplace to take it right now. And it was gone. Gone.

And somehow, she knew in her heart that it meant *he* was gone, too.

Gone from Destiny.

Gone from her life—just like she'd dreaded all summer. *Oh God.*

And sure, there could be some logical explanation for all this . . . but there wasn't. There just wasn't.

Except for one. He'd left her. Just like her mom. Just like Terrence. Just like the people she loved always did.

Jenny lay on the couch, hugging a pillow and trying not to cry. She *hated* crying—she hated everything about it. But she couldn't seem to stop. Crying made her feel so weak, so girlish, so . . . "good Jenny." She'd cried and cried when her mom had died, and she'd cried some more when Snowball had died, and she *hadn't* cried too terribly much over Terrence, thank God, but now she was crying her eyes out over Mick Brody.

Sue Ann sat in a chair across the room, eating ice cream and looking helpless. She'd brought the ice cream—strawberry cheesecake flavor—for Jenny, but Jenny had waved it off, still not in the mood to eat.

"I *hate* this," Jenny said through her tears. "I hate crying over him."

Sue Ann licked her spoon, then pursed her lips. "Well, Jen, you love the guy. It's natural to cry. Don't beat yourself up for it."

Jenny tried to swallow back her tears anyway. "Well then, maybe I hate that I was stupid enough to believe in him. My dad thought he was no good, and you thought the situation was scary, but did I listen? No."

"At least it's not worse. Since I guess it turns out that he's *not* scary—he's just a big fat jerk instead."

Jenny sniffed. "It still hurts just as bad. Why did I ever let this turn into more than just sex?"

"I'm not sure you had a choice—seemed like it was out of your control." Then Sue Ann tilted her head. "But at least . . . well, he brought a lot of happiness into your life at a time when you needed it. So it's like they say—it's better to have loved and lost than never to have loved at all."

Jenny sat up and flashed Sue Ann a disparaging look. "Spoken like someone who's never loved and lost."

Sue Ann shrugged. "Guilty. But isn't it true? I mean, at least you know the wonder of it, the passion, the hunger, the sweetness—all that stuff. Would you really be happier if you didn't know it?"

Jenny sighed in reply. "Well, that's the really annoying thing about love. I probably *would* be happier if I didn't know it, but once you *do* know it, once you feel those things for someone, you can't make yourself really wish it away. It's like wishing away . . . your soul."

"I have a suggestion," Sue Ann said through a mouthful of ice cream.

Jenny sucked in her breath, nervous. "And what might that be?"

"Adam Becker."

For a moment, Jenny actually considered it. Not that she wanted to fly into yet another relationship— that was the last thing she wanted. But it sounded so smart—Adam was a good guy, and he'd fit into her life so well, and her father would be so happy. And Adam would never just pack up his truck and drive away without a word. But finally she said, "I can't do it."

"Why not?"

"I'm in love with Mick."

Sue Ann leaned forward in her chair. "Have you not heard of rebound sex? In fact, in the beginning, wasn't *Mick* rebound sex?"

Jenny just shook her head. "Wouldn't be as good."

"How do you know?"

She had no doubts. "I just know. With Mick, things were . . . primal, animalistic. I don't feel like an animal when I think of Adam."

"Really? Because in case you failed to notice, he's pretty hot. What on earth *do* you feel like when you think of Adam?"

Jenny looked inside herself and replied, "Like a good Destiny girl who would only be going out with him because she wants to please everyone."

Sue Ann frowned. "Oh."

"And like that woman who Terrence thought couldn't be wild in bed. You can only be wild in bed—"

"Or the woods, or the kitchen," Sue Ann cut in.

"When you're inspired," Jenny finished. "And Adam Becker, hot as he may be, just doesn't inspire me anymore."

"Hmm, so what have we learned here?" Sue Ann mused. "We've learned that you are inspired to have wild sex with . . . hot, scary guys with tattoos." Then her eyebrows shot up and she pointed her spoon at Jenny. "Hey, maybe we could start hanging out at the jail, see what we could turn up for you."

At this, Jenny couldn't help smiling. "That's very funny." But then she felt glum again, that quickly. "Except that . . . like I've told you before, somewhere along the way Mick quit being scary."

"Okay, hot guys with tattoos, minus the scary. Hmm—I wonder if Mike Romo has any tattoos. He's kind of mean and rigid, but not scary. Well, either way, I'm sure we could find guys like that somewhere."

"Except for a couple of problems."

"Problem number one?"

"If I keep having rebound sex every time I get dumped, I'll turn into a slut."

Sue Ann shrugged and took a bite of ice cream. "There are worse things in life. Problem number two?"

"The idea of being touched by anyone other than Mick makes my skin crawl."

Across the room, Sue Ann only sighed, then held up the ice cream container. "You really should try this stuff—it's delicious, and it might help."

"Gaining five pounds will not help."

"I know," Sue Ann admitted. "But I'm out of ideas to make you feel better. And if you don't take this stuff away from me, *I'll* gain five pounds, and then, despite the fact that I've orchestrated another grandma weekend, neither *one* of us will be having any sex."

When a knock came on the back door the next day around noon, she leapt from the couch. Her first thought was that it was Mick, that he'd come back to her, that there was some crazy explanation for where he'd been the last few days.

But when she saw her father, her heart dropped all over again, and she felt angry at herself for thinking it could *possibly* be Mick. He was long gone, out of her life, never coming back, and she'd been a fool for him. She didn't believe Mick had used her to keep his secret or anything *that* awful, but what she did suspect was that he'd simply decided *love* was too big a word for him, that staying in Destiny for her was too big a commitment. In short, she figured he'd decided she wasn't worth sacrificing for. Even after all *she'd* sacrificed for *him* this summer.

"You're still in your pajamas," her dad said.

She looked down. "Oh, you're right. Guess I just . . . haven't gotten around to getting dressed yet." She'd actually been lying on the couch under the afghan, polishing off Sue Ann's ice cream. Oh boy—she suddenly felt pathetic.

Her dad looked duly concerned. "Are you . . . not feeling well?"

Jenny considered all the ways she could play this, but decided to just be completely straightforward.

"Mick left me," she informed him. "And I was in love with him." Then she plopped back down on the couch. "So no—I'm not feeling well."

As she stared at the empty ice cream container, she heard her father pull in a long, deep breath, then let it back out. "I'm sorry," he said.

"No you're not," she snapped suddenly, lifting her eyes to his. "You hated him. You didn't even *know* him, and you hated him. Well, it's your lucky day, Dad, because he's gone. Happy now?"

He lowered his gaze, hesitated a long moment, then said, "Honey, I just did what I thought was best."

And Jenny gasped, her eyes flying wide as the gravity of what he'd just said hit her full force. *Oh God!* "What did you do? What the hell did you do?"

Again, her father let out a sigh, and her heart beat too fast, and she thought she might lose her mind if he didn't spit it out—but then he finally answered. "Jenny, I just went and paid him a visit—that's all."

But she knew that *wasn't* all. "A visit? What kind of visit? Tell me what you did, Dad!"

He looked appropriately guilty now, only able to meet her gaze briefly as he said, "I told Mick that it was best he leave now, and . . ."

Oh God, she wanted to kill him. "And what?"

"And, well, without quite saying so, guess I implied that I'd charge him for harborin' a fugitive after the fact if he didn't." Now her father *did* finally look her in the eye—and she stared back at him, dumbfounded. "I kept my word to you, Jenny—I let his brother die in peace, I didn't make any trouble for 'em. But once his brother was dead, well . . . I thought it was time he move on."

Jenny couldn't believe it. She felt like someone was sucking the life from her body, from the inside out, like she was melting away to nothing. "How dare you!" she screamed. "How dare you do this to me!"

"Jenny, he's not the right guy for you and, deep down, you know that. You've been hurt by Terrence and along comes Mick Brody, but when all's said and done—"

"When all's said and done," she interrupted sharply, "you don't know anything about me. You don't know how I feel or what I want or what kind of man is right for me. And I'm not sure you really care—or you'd let me live my own life!" At some point she didn't realize, she'd pushed to her feet so that she and her father stood face to face. She clenched her fists at her side, waiting for him to answer, to defend himself, to argue—something.

So it surprised her when he looked sad, almost sympathetic, and spoke quietly. "Thing is . . . he left. Just like that. If he'd stayed, well then, maybe I'd have thought there was more to him, somethin' worth you hangin' on to. But he didn't even say goodbye, did he? Or you'd have already *known* why he left."

"No," she whispered, wondering why she felt so embarrassed, almost ashamed. Her chest ached. "He didn't say goodbye."

"I know that hurt you, but . . . if that's all it took to make him leave, he couldn't be much of a man."

And maybe her father was right about that—she couldn't figure it out right now, she couldn't be sure of anything at the moment. All she knew was that Mick was gone because her father had threatened him, and her happiness was gone *with* him. She'd thought this couldn't get any worse, but it had. Her heart was breaking all over again, just in a new way this time. "Maybe not," she finally said, feeling a whole new sort of wall being erected inside her, "but maybe the same is true of the guy who threatened him, too. Maybe neither *one* of you is worth my love."

* * *

Walter tried to feel happy as he checked the lasagna in the oven, but it wasn't working. He should probably at least feel nervous, or guilty for using Judy's recipe to feed another woman—but none of that was happening, either. He couldn't stop thinking about Jenny.

She'd looked so broken. He'd known she'd be upset, but he hadn't imagined she would take it quite *that* hard.

Still, it was best, wasn't it? No matter how he looked at it, Mick Brody wasn't the kind of guy his daughter should be with. And it'd been bad enough when he'd thought it was just a summer fling, but when he'd started getting the idea that Brody wasn't going to leave town, even after the death of his brother, he'd felt a call to action, like he had to do something to protect her, once and for all.

Just then, he heard a car in the driveway—kind of a loud one. He walked down the hall into the foyer and glanced out to see Anita getting out of . . . well, an old, piece-of-crap Dodge, one that apparently needed a muffler. He couldn't help letting it remind him that he'd . . . oh, Lordamercy—he'd begun to pursue a relationship with this woman, and it could damage the way people saw him.

It was a shame, because if people gave her a chance, if they looked beyond the beat-up car in the driveway and the tight tops she wore, he thought they'd have no choice but to like her. She wore another one tonight— this one tan with gold flecks in it that glittered as she moved up his walk and made his groin contract.

And then Walter drew in his breath as his own thought slapped him in the face. Was he a hypocrite? Was it possible? Could Mick Brody be like Anita? Could there somehow be more to him than Walter could see?

Naw—couldn't be. It was just like he'd told Anita— most people didn't change. And he'd seen nothing in his brief meeting with Mick Brody that had impressed him.

Anita—she was . . . a rare breed. Rare enough that he was willing to take a chance here and hope people knew him well enough to trust his opinion and not judge her too quickly. But Mick Brody—nope, he was nothing that special.

He opened the door as she stepped up on the front stoop. "Anita—hello. You find the place okay?"

She smiled, nodded. "You give good directions. Must be the policeman in you."

"You, uh, look real nice. Come on in."

"Thanks," she said, confident as ever. "You look nice, too." He'd worn a blue polo shirt and pleated khaki pants in an attempt to hide his expanding gut.

Walter showed Anita to the kitchen, and at first it was awkward, especially when she said, "Whatever's cooking smells good," and he stupidly said, "My wife's lasagna. I mean, late wife," and suffered the first stabs of guilt of the evening.

But then things got better. Because it seemed nothing much phased Anita. She'd simply replied, "She was a lucky lady," then quickly busied herself putting together the salad fixings he'd laid out while he sliced a loaf of Italian bread. That was another reason he liked her so much—no matter how nervous he got, she didn't seem to notice, and it put him right back at ease.

It was after they sat down to dinner that Anita asked him how Jenny was. "The last time we talked, you two were at odds. I hope that's gotten better now."

And Walter discovered he could barely swallow the bite of bread he'd just taken. He hadn't expected Jenny to come up—he'd resolved that *he* wouldn't bring her up tonight, because he didn't want to ruin the evening with how upset he was about her. "Afraid the truth is," he finally answered, "things are a lot worse. I sorta . . . talked to that fella she was seein' and . . . well, I told him to leave town."

"Walter, *no*," Anita said, sounding truly disappointed. It embarrassed him a little—apparently, when it came to this, Anita *wasn't* going to put him at ease.

"Now, I know I was buttin' in where I probably shouldn't have, but the boy left, and I'm glad. Only . . . now I don't know if Jenny'll ever forgive me. She said she was in love with him. I found her in her pajamas in the middle of the day. I've never seen her like this before, even after her divorce back in the spring. But I only did what I thought was right. The boy . . . well, the truth is, he's a criminal." He decided to go ahead and tell Anita that—mainly because it seemed like a good defense.

And it did seem to catch her attention. "Oh. Well, *bad* crimes?" she asked, tearing a bite of bread off the slice in her hand.

Walter replied, "Aren't any crimes bad?"

But across the table from him, Anita simply shrugged. "In my mind, everything's relative. If he's an ax murderer, yeah, get him away from her. But if he's got a speeding ticket or two, well . . . you see what I'm saying."

Walter thought for a moment on how to phrase this next part, then let down his defenses a little. "I can't really go into what he did, but the thing is—I'm not sure *what* I think about it. Jenny believed in her heart that it wasn't wrong, but I didn't see it that way." He shook his head a little, pondering it. "Only maybe that was the lawman in me—maybe I was narrow-minded, being too much an officer of the law and not enough of a . . . person."

Suddenly, Anita's eyes looked a little glassy, and awfully sad. Walter didn't know what to make of it. Lord, how had he upset her?

And when she spoke, her voice came out lower than usual. "Can I tell you a story, Walter?"

"Um, sure, of course."

"Well," she said, still sounding unlike her normal self—stiffer, and less confident, "I'm only going to talk about this once because I don't like thinking of it. But . . . once upon a time, I had myself a little child."

Walter was stunned. Anita hadn't seemed like the maternal type. "Oh," he murmured.

She swallowed visibly, then went on. "And that child's daddy was the spawn of the devil himself, I swear it. But the law said I had to let my child go with him even when I knew it wasn't safe. It was the hardest thing I ever did, and the worst thing I ever did. He took my child and he ran, Walter. That was twenty years ago, and I haven't seen either one of them since."

Walter's jaw dropped.

"I spend every night wondering where my child is, if he's healthy, if he's happy, if he's had any sort of decent life. I pray for him every night, too, although I don't know if God listens to prayers from a woman like me. And if I had it to do over again, you best believe I would have broken the law. I would have broken it a hundred times if it kept my child safe. So I'm just saying that . . . sometimes there are good reasons to break laws. Sometimes it's not all black-and-white."

Walter didn't know what to do, what to say. So he set down his bread and reached across the table and covered Anita's hand with his. "I'm real sorry about that, Anita. That's . . . well, just about one of the worst things I've ever heard. And . . . I reckon you're right—I wouldn't have blamed you if you'd been the one to run."

And then, just when Walter didn't know if he'd said

the right thing, or how on earth a man could console a mother on the loss of a child—Anita bounced back to her normal self and said, "Well, enough about that. I just . . . wanted to try to make you look at things from your Jenny's point of view a little bit, and from the view of this boy of hers."

He nodded—he got the point. He might not like it, but he got it.

"Now, let's talk about this lasagna," she said, more cheerful. "When you invited me over, I had no idea I'd be getting a gourmet meal. What's in it that makes it so tasty?"

Walter answered her as best he could, but her words stuck in his mind. Jenny had said the same thing about the world not always being black-and-white. But Anita's story dug down deep inside him. Even as they went on eating, chatting, he couldn't shake thinking about it. No wonder she was so strong— she'd *had* to be, for a long time now.

Was he wrong? About Mick Brody?

Seemed everywhere he turned, people said he was. First Jenny, now Anita.

But he tried to put it out of his mind so he could enjoy the rest of his evening—even if it kept gnawing at him beneath the surface. He'd invited Anita over for dinner—he wanted to be decent company.

By the time they finished eating, it had gotten dark out, so Walter suggested stepping onto his back deck. "My Jenny is an astronomer," he said, leaning his head back to peer up into a clear night sky—but this time he left out the next comment that came to mind, that Judy had enjoyed stargazing as well. "So I know a lot more about the stars than I would if she hadn't pretty much forced me to look through her telescope and learn all about them back when she was a girl."

"Do you have one?" Anita asked. "A telescope? I've never looked through one before."

" 'Fraid I don't," he said, sorry to have sparked her interest in something only to disappoint her. "But I'm sure we could borrow Jenny's some night if you like—once I figure out how to make her less mad at me, that is."

To his surprise, the lady next to him responded by locking her arm through his. "That'd be nice." And despite himself, he even found himself thinking maybe they could canoe over to that spot across the lake Jenny claimed was so good for stargazing. Or . . . maybe they could just go to the meadow at Betty and Ed's place. Maybe Betty and Ed would *like* Anita. Once they got past her tight clothes.

"Of course, there's plenty to look at in the sky even *without* a telescope," he told her. Then he gazed upward in the black expanse above and spotted a constellation he'd always liked, one that was, in fact, too large to study through a telescope and *had* to be viewed with the naked eye. He pointed it out—although they both had to lean around the branches of a sprawling maple tree to get a good view. "See that real bright star just below that longest branch? If you follow it down, you see another, and farther down"—he drew a line with one finger—"another. Now look out to the sides of the center star, and you're lookin' at the Northern Cross."

Next to him, Anita's eyes widened, her mouth dropping open in delight. "Oh—I see it! And my—it's so big. A big cross right up in the sky."

Then he showed her a couple of other major points of interest that could be seen in the summer sky with the naked eye as well, a little surprised he still remembered them: the Great Square of Pegasus, and then the Teapot—and he pointed out how that particular part of the Milky Way made it appear steam was coming from the Teapot's spout, pleased when she seemed transfixed by it.

"My, my, a man who knows about the stars," Anita said when he was done, turning to peer up at his face. "That's downright romantic, Officer Tolliver."

"It is?" he asked, his stomach twisting a little, in a good way.

Then she squeezed his hand and raised on her toes to give him a kiss, right on the mouth. It was a small kiss, but an *incredible* kiss—it was the first kiss Walter had gotten from a woman in nearly twenty years.

"That was . . . real nice," he told her. "Nicest thing to happen to me in a while."

She winked up at him in the dark. "Play your cards right, Officer, and there might be more where that came from."

A few days after Mick's departure, Jenny pulled herself together.

Specifically, she got up, got dressed, and called Stan Goodman on the phone to accept the offer to teach at Destiny High. Since school started in less than two weeks, she met with him and Principal Turley that very afternoon to fill out forms and work out her class schedule, which included Advanced Placement Science, Introduction to Physics, and her favorite, Introduction to Astronomy. She came home excited that Mr. Turley seemed so pleased with her curriculum ideas—he felt that the elective classes were going to make DHS much more competitive with science programs in other, larger schools.

After leaving the Board of Education, she stopped at Destiny Properties and told Sue Ann the news. Sue Ann had looked like she might climb up on top of her desk and dance until Jenny grabbed her arm and said, "Relax already. It isn't that big a deal."

"Not that big a deal?" Sue Ann said. "It's a *humongous* deal! It means our summer of hanging out together again will now also be at least an autumn, winter, and spring of hanging out, too. And it must mean that you're, well, bouncing back . . . *from Mick,*" she added in a whisper so her co-workers wouldn't hear.

Jenny kept her voice low. "Um, bouncing back—no. I'm still miserable, thanks. But I need to get back in the land of the living. And despite myself, I *have* enjoyed being home in Destiny. Somewhere along the way, I guess I realized I actually *like* it here."

Sue Ann shrugged, looking sorry to hear that Jenny was, indeed, still suffering. "Well, I'll take what I can get," she said. "And if you need me to, I'll cancel my plans with Jeff this weekend and hang out with you instead."

"You'd cancel a carefully planned sex marathon for me?" Jenny asked, truly touched.

"Are you kidding? Of course I would. Sex comes and goes, but a best friend is forever."

Jenny smiled softly, the most she could manage right now. "Well, lucky for you, I'm going to be knee-deep in lesson plans this weekend, so you can still break out the lingerie. But let's organize a swimming day next week, one afternoon when you're off work, so you can tell me all about it."

Sue Ann tilted her head, still speaking quietly. "You don't mind hearing about marathon sex when you're not having any?"

Jenny shrugged. "It'll be just like when *I* was having great sex and *you* weren't. I'll live vicariously."

What she'd told Sue Ann wasn't just her way of letting her friend off the hook—she really *would* need to spend most of the next two weeks preparing for her classes and getting mentally ready to jump back into the Destiny community in a much more prominent way. Which would be a great distraction from her broken heart, something she sorely needed.

Because, just as she'd implied to Sue Ann, she wasn't any less in love with Mick than she'd been a few days ago. In fact, her bones *ached* for him. Her skin longed for his touch. The only thing that had changed was that she'd quit moping around. She'd reminded herself that she hadn't come home to Destiny looking for a man, or love, or sex—she'd come here to retreat and make some decisions. And now, finally, she'd just made a few. *Move on with your life. Take this job where you can make a difference. Stay here where you have a few people who love you—at least for a while.*

Of course, while her *father* counted as one of those people, she was still mad as hell at him, and she wasn't sure she'd get over that anytime soon. Even though he came over that very evening with pork chops for the grill and a heartfelt apology.

"I had a dream about your mother last night," he told her.

She sat at the picnic table on the patio, despite the persisting heat, and grudgingly listened to him. "Oh?" It didn't surprise her—given the shrine, she suspected he dreamed about her mom all the time.

"In the dream, I was sitting on the glider on my front porch, and she walked right up and sat down beside me. And she said . . . that maybe we expected too much from you, put too many demands on you, and that it was hard to be perfect all the time. She said I had to let you find your own way. And it seemed . . . so *real*, like she was really there with me."

That part actually took Jenny aback. Because she'd

had dreams like that about her mother, too, dreams that seemed realer than real—but she hadn't had one for a long time now. Yet the message that her mother had delivered in this dream to her dad was . . . well, enough to make her wonder if somehow it *was* real, if her mom had looked down from somewhere above and seen into her heart—and was trying to make her dad see now, too.

And just then, Jenny remembered that recent night when she'd been thinking about Mick, and love, and trying to convince herself she wasn't in it, and how she'd heard her mother's voice in her mind—and now, combined with her father's dream, the very recollection sent a cold chill rippling down her spine despite the suffocating heat.

That was when her dad turned from the grill to face her, a big two-pronged fork in hand. "I know this doesn't make up for what I did, Jennygirl, but I know I was wrong, and I truly am sorry for causing you so much hurt. I hope you can find it in your heart to forgive me."

Jenny considered the words slowly, truly absorbing them. Her father sounded more like the dad she knew and loved than he had in weeks, and she could feel his sincerity, could feel his yearning to get back to the closeness they usually shared.

Her reply came from the heart. "I accept your apology, Dad." Then she took a deep breath and tried to say the rest. "And I'm trying to forgive you. But it might take a while. I know you can't understand this, but Mick was . . . the most amazing thing to ever happen to me. Everything before him, even Terrence, just . . . paled in comparison to the way he made me feel. So, yeah, like you said, maybe he *wasn't* the guy I thought if he left so easily, but on the other hand, you put him in an awful position, and he'd been under a tremendous strain all summer, and his brother just died a painful, horrible death, and Mick had to bury him with his own bare hands, so . . . I'm just not sure it's fair to judge him by that one choice."

"You're right," he said without missing a beat, shocking her. "And I wish like hell I could take that back, Jenny."

"Me, too."

Her dad looked even more troubled now and let out a sigh. "I reckon when you called me and said you'd taken the job and decided to stay, I thought it meant you were feeling better, and getting over him. But you're not, are you?"

She shook her head. "Taking the job and feeling better are two different things. And as for getting over Mick, I'm honestly not sure that I . . . ever will."

"Can I give you a hug?" he asked, looking nearly as glum as she felt.

"As long as you don't let the pork chops burn."

He flinched, turned, then flipped the chops on the grill. After which he put down his fork and crossed the patio toward her.

Despite her anger at him, putting her arms around her father's neck provided a familiar comfort she needed, so she hugged him tight and felt a little safer in the world, like the dad she'd known and loved all these years was back.

After he returned to the grill, taking up his big fork once more, he said, "Somethin' else I should tell you about."

"What's that?"

"I, uh, started seein' a woman."

At this, Jenny nearly fainted. "Wait—I didn't hear you correctly. It sounded like you said you'd started seeing a woman."

He turned to look at her. "I did. I mean, I am."

Her jaw dropped. Talk about a miracle. "Wow."

"Is that . . . okay with you?"

"It's . . . more than okay, Dad—it's great. It was even my suggestion if I recall."

He nodded in concession. "S'pose it was at that. Anyhow, her name is Anita, and she, uh, owns the Dew Drop Inn."

Jenny's jaw dropped still further. "Seriously?"

"Does that bother you? Me dating somebody who owns a bar?"

"*Me?* No. I'm just surprised it doesn't bother *you.*"

"Well, about that," he said. "Anita ain't the sort of woman—on the outside—who you might expect me to like. But she's got a real good heart, and I think once you get to know her a little that you'll like her, too."

The irony of the whole thing, that her father was dating a woman who apparently didn't meet normal Destiny standards, nearly made her burst into tears— but she didn't. She was done crying. She just said, "I'm sure I will. I think you'd have felt that way about Mick, too."

That night, around dusk, Jenny finished off her day by canoeing across the lake and taking her telescope up onto the rocks that had first lured her onto Mick's property. It felt strange to be walking back up that hill knowing he was nowhere around, and it reminded her—all too vividly—of that first night, of the unexpected, hot, urgent sex they'd shared. He'd been a stranger then, but it was almost hard to remember that, to think of him that way now.

As night fell around her, though, as the stars came out, as always, it made Jenny feel a little more at peace. She still hurt inside, but all those stars twinkling up above her reminded her how much more was going on out there, and that she was but an infinitesimal speck on a tiny blue planet on the edge of a galaxy that was one of trillions. And it would all be okay. She would survive this. It still hurt—it hurt so bad that it felt like something was clawing at her insides—but she would survive anyway.

And it was just as she was about to go searching for some deep-space objects that she glanced up in time to see a falling star go trailing downward, appearing to land on some distant hillside. Of course, she knew there was no such thing as a falling star, that what she'd just seen was actually a meteor, a piece of rock that had entered the earth's atmosphere and was burning up as it fell.

But the little girl inside her that had once believed in fairy tales and wishes upon stars quickly remembered that when you saw a falling star you were supposed to make a wish on it. And her first thought was to wish that she would get over Mick, that she would be strong and happy without him.

But it was just like she'd told Sue Ann; once you loved someone that way, you couldn't *really* wish for that love to end—it was too big a part of your soul. So instead she closed her eyes and made a wish for the man who had brought out such reckless abandon in her this summer: *I wish for Mick to find true happiness.*

Look, all I'm asking is for you to just have the tiniest bit of vision. You know, to just sit back for one minute and look at the big picture. To take a chance on something that just might end up being the most profoundly impactful moment for humanity, for the history . . . of history.

Carl Sagan

Eighteen

*M*ick stood in front of the bathroom mirror, shaving. He generally only did it every two or three days, but a glance at his reflection after getting out of the shower had reminded him it had been a while, almost a week. He scowled at himself slightly. *So you managed to keep yourself shaved and in clean clothes out at that shithole cabin while Wayne was dying, but you can't manage to do it here, where you have normal electricity and a normal life.* What the hell kind of sense did *that* make, besides none?

But he hadn't felt like doing much of *anything* since getting back to the city. He'd gotten a new apartment

in . . . well, kind of a crappy part of town, but it was
what he could afford right now. He'd gotten one truck-
load of stuff out of storage so far, but hadn't bothered
to haul the rest over yet. Hell, at the moment, he just
didn't really care if he had a bed to sleep on or a decent
place to watch TV. So far, he was sleeping on the same
blow-up mattress he'd used out at the cabin and eating
a lot of fast food.

It's the heat, he decided. It was hard to have much
energy when it was so damn hot. Never mind that he'd
had had plenty of energy in Destiny.

But you had to then, for Wayne.

*And you were getting laid. Getting laid can do a lot for a
guy's energy level.*

His gut clenched a little at the memory of Jenny
beneath him, eager and willing. He closed his eyes
for a second and shoved the vision aside. *This isn't
about Jenny. If anything, this is about Wayne; this is . . .
mourning.*

And he hadn't been a *total* lazy ass since coming back
to Cincinnati. He'd gotten his hair cut, which it had
needed. He'd gotten a new tattoo, something he'd been
thinking about since Wayne's death. And he'd gotten
his old job back with the same homebuilder who'd
employed him the last few years. His old boss wasn't
crazy about the fact that Mick had quit out of the blue
a few months ago and now suddenly shown back up,
but apparently the fact that the guy still needed a good
bricklayer outweighed that.

So Mick had started work again just this week, and
getting back into a routine and feeling a little bit useful
in the world . . . helped. To make him feel normal again.
Kind of. *This weekend you should get your shit out of storage, once and for all.*

As he left his building and crossed a pockmarked

parking lot to get in his truck and head to the job site where he was erecting a stone fireplace for someone with a lot more money than him, he decided maybe when he got off work tonight he'd wander down to the bar he'd seen a couple blocks away from his new place. It looked like the kind of place where a guy might meet a willing woman. The kind of place a guy could drown his sorrows in more ways than one. The idea of getting drunk and laid and not feeling anything when it was over appealed. *Then why haven't you done it yet?* That he couldn't quite answer.

He hadn't left Destiny because of Tolliver's threat. He'd left due to one thing and one thing only. Because there was no reason to stay anymore. The one reason he'd had up until then had betrayed him in the worst way he could imagine. He still didn't know why, and he couldn't understand it.

Had she not comprehended what was at stake? Had she just . . . not taken their relationship as seriously as he'd thought, as seriously as *he* had? Well, he'd feared that, hadn't he? Not that she'd hurt him, betrayed him, on purpose—but that she'd thought she felt more for him than she really did from being on the rebound from her asshole ex-husband. And if she didn't really love him, surely that had made telling her dad easier.

Of course, maybe she'd told her father back before . . . well, before it was serious, back when it was just sex. But even then, she'd *promised*, again and again. She'd made him feel so sure he could trust her. Over time, he'd come to trust her more than he'd ever trusted *anyone*, including his brother.

The reasons why, though, didn't really matter—all that mattered was that what he'd always suspected had turned out to be true: You couldn't trust anyone in this world. It had been his mistake for believing he could. His chest, stomach, felt hollow with thinking of her, and of how he'd felt when Tolliver had told Mick how he'd found out about Wayne.

But no, this isn't about Jenny. You're just . . . hungry or something.

So he pulled through a Burger King drive-thru and grabbed a breakfast sandwich and orange juice and scarfed it down on the way and tried to tell himself it made him feel better.

Practically speaking, after a few days of mulling over the situation, he'd almost quit being mad at her. Quit being mad, but not quit being . . . hurt. Feeling . . . let down. Deeply. She'd proven what he'd already known all along—that they were too different, that there was just too much standing between them for their relationship to be more than a summer of hot sex. Just as he'd told himself that last morning by the cabin, he should have listened to his instincts.

In a weird way, he was almost *glad* she'd done something to tip him off, to make him realize that what they had couldn't last—before it was too late. And as for all the shit he'd said to her those last couple of days, about loving her and taking care of her—well, even if he'd meant it, it wasn't a mistake he'd make again, with *any* woman. He was better off alone. As always, the only person he could really depend on was himself.

Although after he drove back through the winding streets of the under-construction neighborhood and pulled up along the curb of the house where he was working today, he quit feeling hollow—and started feeling *pissed as hell* when he saw a goddamn cop car sitting there, one that said DESTINY POLICE on the side.

God damn it—what the hell was *this* about?

Barely able to contain his fury, he slammed his door and marched past the other guys at the site to where none other than Walter Tolliver stood leaning against his cruiser. "Damn it," Mick snapped at him, "I did what you said, old man—and now you come here to make trouble for me?"

When Tolliver turned his head to face him, he looked . . . weirdly calm. Not at all like on the day he'd confronted Mick at the cabin. "It's not like that. I'm not here to make trouble."

Mick didn't know what to make of that, but said, "Yeah, well, that *car* makes trouble. That goddamn *car* tells everybody on this job site that I've got the law on my ass. I've worked long and hard to put my past behind me, and I sure as hell don't need you dredging it up." He was trying to keep his voice down so the two guys hauling cabinetry up the driveway right now wouldn't hear, but he had a feeling he wasn't doing a very good job.

"Relax, Brody," Tolliver said. "I told your boss and all those other fellas that I'm here on personal business, nothin' legal, and that's the truth."

Personal, huh? That blindsided Mick a little—and he wasn't altogether sure he believed it. "What could you and I have to talk about that's personal?"

The older man hesitated slightly, then looked Mick in the eye. "I'm here to apologize," he said.

And Mick narrowed his gaze, still not quite believing. "You're what?"

"I was wrong in what I said to you—it wasn't my business. You can go wherever you want."

"I know that," Mick replied simply, gruffly.

"And if you wanted to come back to Destiny, that'd be fine with me."

Mick couldn't have been more taken aback—so he just answered honestly. "Well, it wouldn't be fine with *me*. I was glad to see it disappear in my rearview mirror."

Tolliver narrowed his gaze on Mick. "That's funny, 'cause I thought you might be fixin' to stay."

Mick drew in his breath and decided to change the subject a little. "So why the change of heart? And what the hell brought you all the way to Cincinnati to tell me?"

Now it was the police chief who took a deep breath and blew it back out. "Truth is, Brody, I met a woman . . . who's made me start thinkin' maybe I judged you too harshly. Jenny told me you'd changed, but I didn't give you a chance. I try to be a good man, and I try to make up for my mistakes. I didn't treat you fairly, and I'm ownin' up to it, that's all."

Mick swallowed. Not many people had apologized to him for much in life. He thought through it a minute and spoke the truth, even if it was humbling. "The fact is, you treated me *more* than fair. I could be in jail right now, but I'm not. So if running me out of town is the worst you did to me, I'm not gonna fault you for it."

"Can you forgive Jenny, too? Because when you asked me how I found out about what you were doin', I didn't tell you *why* she told me. So I'll tell you now. I didn't give her much of a choice. I was gettin' ready to head out to your place 'cause I knew your brother had gone missin' and I'd had a tip somebody might be out at the cabin—and that's when Jenny stopped me. She told me in order to protect you. And she made me promise to leave you alone. It was real important to her. Otherwise, you probably *would* be in jail now. So by tellin' me, she pretty much . . . saved you. I hope you'll forgive her."

"I already forgave her," Mick admitted matter-of-factly.

"She doesn't know that."

Mick crossed his arms. "Well, that's probably best.

I think we all know that her and me . . ." He stopped, shook his head, glanced down at his dusty workboots. "Hell, when you have to sneak around to see somebody, it's never gonna work. It means there's a hell of a lot keeping you apart. I'm sorry I hurt her, but *you* know and *I* know that she's better off without somebody like me in her life."

"I didn't say that," Walter Tolliver replied, surprising him.

Still, Mick raised his gaze back to Jenny's father. "Nope, but I did. I appreciate you coming here, but you don't need to worry about me darkening Jenny's doorstep again. I got a life here, she's got a life there, and it'll be easier for everybody if we just keep it that way."

Mick didn't go to the bar up the street that night. Or the next night. Or the next.

Instead, he watched reality TV and decided that most of those people didn't know *anything* about reality. And he thought a lot about his visit from Walter Tolliver—because apparently, miracles *did* happen. He couldn't think of anyone on the planet he would be more surprised to get an apology from, and it gave him a grudging respect for the guy. He supposed that was why he'd gotten so honest with him before all was said and done.

As for Jenny, though . . . he didn't like to think of her hurting because of him, but he was hurting, too, and what he'd told her father was true: All of their lives were going to be easier with him here and her there. People in Destiny would never accept him. And once upon a time—hell, as recently as a couple of months ago—he hadn't cared what people thought of him, but somewhere along the way, he supposed that had changed. He'd started caring what Jenny thought of him. And now he supposed he cared what the people in Jenny's life thought of him. He just wasn't sure if that was a good thing or a bad one.

And it did weird things to his heart to realize, to wonder, if maybe he'd been wrong in the end, if maybe this was more than a rebound thing she'd gotten caught up in, if maybe it had been just as serious, just as real, as she'd made it sound at the time. Just as real as it had turned out to be for him.

Even if that was the case, though, it didn't alter the big picture. It was good he'd left when he did. In the end, she'd be happier without him—she'd be happier eventually settling down with somebody more *like* her, somebody who could give her more than he could.

It was Friday night when he brought home a Big Mac and some fries and ate at his old kitchen table while he watched the same television set he'd taken out to the cabin for Wayne. Local newscasters said the current heat emergency was still on and shelters were still open for people without air-conditioning. It was so hot now that it was killing people. The heat wave was finally supposed to break again tomorrow, but Mick decided he'd believe it when he felt it. And was thankful that at least he *did* have A/C. Not central air like at Jenny's house, but an old wall unit that kept the place comfortable enough.

When a knock came on the door, he flinched. Shit. Who would be knocking at *his* door? Almost panicking reflexively from his days of hiding out with Wayne, he glanced at the picture of him and his brother as boys— he'd picked up a frame for it and set it on a shelf on his TV stand, next to the arrowhead—then remembered Wayne was dead and that he wasn't doing anything illegal anymore.

So he decided it had to be somebody selling something and nearly didn't answer, but when the knock sounded again, louder and more annoying this time, he abandoned his last few fries and went to the door.

He opened it to see a scruffy-looking kid, probably eight or nine years old, holding a cardboard box. He glanced inside to see what the boy was selling—and flinched again at the sight of a miniature yellow cat. The cat looked up at him and said, "Meow!" It looked kind of desperate.

"You want this cat?" the kid asked.

Mick felt his eyebrows crinkle. "Uh, no."

"It's the last one. Started out with five. I have to give it away or my dad is going to drive it out in the country somewhere and dump it on the side of the road."

Damn—sounded like something *Mick's* dad would've done. Even so, Mick had never especially liked cats. Despite Jenny's affinity for them, he'd always thought they were sneaky, and clingy, and this one looked particularly needy. "Meow!" it said. "Meow, meow, meow!"

"Is something wrong with it? It looks . . . freaked-out."

The kid shrugged. "It just likes to meow a lot is all."

Swell. "Well, I don't need a cat. Sorry," he said, and started to close the door.

"Wait," the kid protested, so Mick stopped.

"What?"

"You're the last apartment. I've been through all three buildings and you're the last place to ask. So won't you please take this kitten, mister?"

"Meow! Meow!" the cat said. Like he knew what was going on. Like he was saying, *Save me, save me!*

Hell. Mick glanced down into the box again. He knew he was just imagining the cat looked afraid. He knew it wasn't his problem. He knew he shouldn't give a damn, or be picturing that cat meowing its fool head off on the side of a road someplace where no one would ever find it, like the long stretch of highway that led into Destiny.

Shit, I must be going soft. The whole damn summer had him feeling too much. He should slam the door in the kid's face once and for all. Instead, he said, "Does it come with the box?"

"Huh?"

"I don't have anyplace to keep a cat. Does it come with the box?"

"Mister, you don't keep a cat in a box. You let it walk around your apartment."

"Maybe *you* do," Mick said. "If I take the cat, I want the box."

"Okay," the kid replied with another shrug, handing the box over to Mick. Then he said, "Five dollars."

"*What?*"

"For the cat," the boy claimed.

Mick rolled his eyes and said, "You oughta be paying *me* five dollars—now get outta here." He shooed the kid away with his free hand and watched him go skidding down the hall on worn gym shoes, disappearing down the steps at the end.

Then Mick looked down into the box at the little yellow cat and thought, *What the hell did I just do?*

By the next morning, Mick wanted to do bodily harm to the cat. The damn thing had been meowing all damn night. He'd given it some milk and some chicken salad he'd had in the fridge—what the hell else did it want?

Pushing back a sheet and getting up from the air mattress in his underwear, he padded across the floor to where he'd left the box. "If you don't shut up soon, I'm gonna wring your little neck," he muttered—then glanced down to see that the bottom of the box was soaking wet. The cat had peed in it.

Not that Mick knew where else he'd expected the cat to pee—he hadn't thought about it. "Thing should've come with an owner's manual," he growled, peering down.

"Meow!" it said. "Meow!"

Mick just nodded at it in annoyance. "Yeah, I know, you're sitting in your own pee. Good enough reason to be pissed, I guess." Where *did* an inside cat pee anyway?

A litter box. Shit. This meant he actually had to get a damn *litter box*?

He *really* didn't want a cat. He'd never had one before—so why start now? Why the hell had he taken the damn thing? He just shook his head at the yellow kitten. "You're nothing but trouble."

Meandering back toward his mattress, he found a half-empty box of CDs he'd taken out of storage. He emptied the rest on the floor and carried the box over to where the cat's rested, near the front door, then reached inside, picking it up by the scruff of the neck. "Come on, trouble. Into your shiny new box."

"Meow! Meow! Meow!" the damn cat said.

"Aw, relax. It's bigger than your last place, and a hell of a lot dryer. For now, anyway. And at least I saved your little yellow ass from getting dumped. You oughta be thanking me."

But the kitten just kept on mewing like he was being severely mistreated.

"Never happy, are ya?" Mick groused. "Now I guess you want breakfast." Then he looked toward the kitchen. "Now I guess I gotta figure out what that's gonna be."

Just then, the phone rang, and Mick jumped. He'd clearly spent too long out in the woods without a phone of any kind. "Hello?"

"Hey there, Mr. Brody. This is Don from Winwood

Monuments—your gravestone is ready whenever you want to come pick it up." The call surprised him—he'd thought it would take longer.

"You open today?" he asked.

"Yes, sir. Until five."

Almost as soon as he'd departed from Destiny, Mick had decided he couldn't leave Wayne's grave without a marker. It had started eating at him, the idea that—even with Jenny's flowers—sooner or later there would be nothing to show that a body rested in that spot, a human being, his brother. And he'd decided that Cincinnati was far enough away that he could buy it here and take it out there himself. To avoid any suspicion, he'd explained it was for an old family cemetery out in the woods, and he'd had only w. brody, beloved brother engraved on it, no years.

It was Saturday—so despite his plans to haul some more stuff out of storage today, he guessed this meant he was making a trip to Destiny instead.

After hanging up the phone, he glanced down at the cat, thinking.

Hmm, maybe there was more than just one reason to go. He didn't hate Jenny—he'd gotten over the rest of his anger after her father's visit. And he still knew their lives, worlds, were too far apart to fit together. But . . . maybe he had some unfinished business to take care of in Destiny besides just the gravestone.

And maybe he could unload this damn cat while he was at it. "Pack your bags, Trouble," he said. "You're taking a trip."

For small creatures such as we, the vastness is bearable only through love.

Carl Sagan

Nineteen

To Mick's surprise, the weatherman had been right—the air outside felt better than it had in months. He even put his window down as he drove. Trouble meowed his head off for most of the trip, and Mick wondered if there was such a thing as kitty tranquilizers. As he headed toward Destiny, Eddie Vedder sang "Hard Sun" on the radio, and Mick thought about turning it off since the last thing he really wanted to think about was the hot, hard summer just past, but he ended up turning it louder instead in an attempt to drown out the racket from the box in the floor of the passenger seat.

First stop—he made the long, winding drive out to the cabin. Even with cool breezes sifting through the trees, he found he didn't like coming back here—too many bad memories, old and new—but he had to.

It felt both grim and . . . *right* to haul the weighty

headstone from the back of his truck to Wayne's grave. Fortunately, the flowers looked to be thriving—one good thing about all the tree cover, he supposed. Jenny had said the flowers would do well in the shade, but he guessed the trees must have somehow protected them from the heat, too, since they looked healthy as could be.

He yanked the wooden cross he'd built out of the ground and tossed it aside. Then, taking up the same shovel he'd used to dig the grave itself, he cleared a rectangular spot just beyond the top edge of the plot so the stone wouldn't shift as the soft soil settled. After that, he lowered the headstone into place, filled in and packed the dirt around the edges, and stood back to look.

And the sight—of his brother's grave being properly marked—left him feeling . . . well, much less grim than when he'd arrived. *This is better than it was before. This is a lot better.* Even having picked out one of the least expensive stones, it hadn't been cheap, especially at a time when his checking account was almost on "E," but Mick had known it would be a worthwhile investment.

Next, he made the long drive back out the rutted road to the highway, that damn kitten yapping all the way, and circled through town to the other side of the lake. As he reached the stretch of road that lined the water's edge, it felt odd—he hadn't driven on this road since he was a boy. He'd seldom had a reason to *then*, and more recently, well, he'd always taken the shorter water route to Jenny.

Now he was going to see her again, for the last time. Walter Tolliver had been a big enough man to correct his mistake; maybe that had inspired Mick to correct his own. Or maybe this just meant enough time had passed that he could see things more clearly now. He owed her an apology before he left her life for good.

And it was going to be pure hell to see her again, to see her again and then turn around and drive away—*but that's what you have to do.*

It occurred to him as he rounded a bend in the road that, from the very beginning of their relationship, neither one of them had been very good at keeping themselves in control when they were around each other. And for the first time, he wondered if he would see her today and just . . . fall on her, out of gut need. That's always how it was—he saw her and had to have her.

But that couldn't happen here. For so many reasons. No matter how good it sounded to him to be back inside her warm body, to move with her that way. Aw, damn—he was getting hard just thinking about it, remembering. It felt like it had been forever since he'd been with her.

He drew in a heavy breath, let it back out. *You can do this.*

This is just goodbye, just I'm sorry and goodbye.

He had to let her get on with her life, get back to living it with people who were more like her—and less like him.

He thought he was ready for this, ready for her, when he rounded another bend and the little yellow house came into view. Only—holy shit—it was surrounded by cars. Cars in the driveway, and more cars lining one side of the road.

Then he took in the people all standing around in the big side yard where they'd had sex in the rain—women in flowy dresses and guys in crisp-looking khaki shorts and polo shirts. A group of little kids, dressed the same way, ran around chasing each other and he could hear their laughter as he neared. Everyone smiled and held paper cups and plates, and a couple of guys were hammering horseshoe stakes into the ground with a mallet.

Taking it all in made him feel cold inside. Cold and stupidly lonely. "Shit," he muttered.

As he kept driving, he glanced down to the cat. "Maybe we should just keep on going." Then he sighed. "But then you'd have to live with me. And I don't see that going well for either one of us. *Damn it.*" He banged his hand on the steering wheel as the truck moved slowly past her house, past the row of cars taking up part of the road.

It was as the other side of the house came into view that he saw her—and his chest constricted as he heard that old Tommy Tutone song in his mind. *Can I still turn to you, Jenny?* Like all the other women at the party, she wore a pretty dress and stood with her dad and . . . damn, some woman who was built like a brick shithouse. Who the hell was *that*? The woman looked like she belonged here about as much as he did—and that gave him some unexpected courage.

So without letting himself weigh it very much, when he reached the end of the row of cars, he pulled over and parked. Like he was any other guest at her party. The idea of walking into the yard with all those people made his skin crawl, but since it was only her and her dad and that woman on this side of the house, he was just going to do it, get it the hell over with.

And . . . maybe it was *good* she was having a party. It reminded him how much he didn't fit in her life. And it made it pretty much impossible for him to put the moves on her, too.

As he reached down for the box, he realized the cat had finally gone quiet for a while. Maybe he'd lost his voice. But just in case that wasn't the reason, Mick said, "Listen, Trouble, act like you've got some sense here. Don't go meowing like you're dying or starving to death, and try to act quiet and likable or you might blow it. Got it?"

Trouble meowed in reply, but only once, so Mick said, "Good. But quit looking so needy, would ya?"

Then he got out, box in hand, and slammed the door. And as he started up through the yard toward her, he thought of the stars. *The universe is huge and your troubles are small. Five minutes and this will be over—for good.*

"Jenny, this is my friend, Anita. And Anita, here's my Jennygirl."

Jenny had to struggle to keep her eyes from popping out of her head. *Holy crap.* Anita was *not* what she'd expected—even with the warning her dad had given her—sporting long red, bouncing hair and poured into a summery dress that was perhaps a little young for her but fit her like a glove and made Jenny wish for such a body. "It's a pleasure to meet you," she said, and Anita reached around a covered Tupperware container with her free hand to clasp Jenny's.

"Well, you're just as pretty as your dad told me. Thanks so much for having me," Anita said with a smile, then glanced down to the Tupperware. "I hope deviled eggs are all right."

"Deviled eggs are perfect," Jenny said, not bothering to mention that Lettie Gale and at least two other people had already brought some.

"Walter," Betty called just then, peeking around the corner of the house, "can you come help Ed with the grill? He's not used to this newfangled kind, and I'm afraid he's gonna cause an explosion."

It was as Jenny's dad scurried off around the corner that Anita squarely met her gaze, in a way that surprised her, because it seemed filled with instant trust. "Just between you and me, Jenny, I'm a little nervous. I don't know anyone here but your dad, and I'm not too sure I'll fit in."

That fast, Jenny respected her genuine honesty and felt honored by how quickly Anita had confided in her, despite that they probably had little in common. So she made Anita the same promise she'd made Mick. "You will. I'll make sure of it."

Anita squeezed her hand again, her own accessorized with very long, red nails, and looked a little more at ease. "You're just as *sweet* as Walter said, too." Then she pointed toward the back of the house. "I'll go find a place for these eggs."

"I'll be right behind you as soon as I grab some lawn chairs from under the front porch," Jenny said with a smile. "In the meantime, just smile a lot, and say nice things about the weather and the town and everyone's food."

Anita gave a short nod, along with a conspiratorial wink. "Got it. Thanks." And they set off in opposite directions.

Jenny had decided to have a Labor Day Weekend picnic as her way of saying, *I'm back to stay, Destiny— at least for a while*. School had started and was going well—she'd been right, the older students took her classes because they *wanted* to and they enjoyed learning. She'd already planned a field trip to the rocks on the other side of the lake for one night next month, and she liked having a productive purpose in life again.

Of course, as recently as yesterday, she'd worried about the weather for the party, but this morning she'd woken up to a beautiful day filled with fresh air, cool breezes, and white fluffy clouds—a perfect end-of-summer day.

But then, of course, that wasn't true—it wasn't a

totally perfect day. To be totally perfect, Mick would have to be here.

As weeks passed, she was beginning to adapt back to life without him—she just wished she hadn't so quickly latched onto life *with* him. She came home from school each day with things she wished she could tell him. She often caught herself staring into the swirls of the Van Gogh print and wondering what he was doing. She felt lonely and achy in bed at night and tried to remember what it had felt like to sleep in his arms.

As Jenny knelt to pull away the lattice covering one side of the porch and dragged out extra lawn chairs, Lettie peeked around from the front. "Sue Ann wants to know if you want her baked beans in the house or on the picnic table."

"Picnic table if they're already warm—microwave if they're not," she said, then held out the sturdiest of the chairs to Lettie, who never minded lending a hand. "And could you take this to Miss Ellie and help Mary Katherine find her a nice spot in the shade?"

As Lettie disappeared, Jenny put the lattice back in place and gathered the remaining chairs in her arms. Then she looked up—and her heart nearly stopped. "Oh my God," she murmured, and let the chairs drop to the ground. The hottest, most rugged man she'd ever seen was walking toward her across the lawn—and it was Mick. Mick was *here.*

She sucked in her breath and tried to look normal, and confident, even though her womb contracted at the sight of him and she'd just dropped her chairs with a clatter and she realized instantly how very deeply in love with him she remained.

"Pussycat," he said, voice low, as his dark eyes found hers. The sun suddenly felt much hotter shining down on them and she began to sweat.

She struggled to find her voice. "Hello, Mick."

He looked uncertain, and maybe a little tired—but still good enough to eat. "I won't keep you long—I see you're having some kind of party."

"A Labor Day picnic. Even though it's only Saturday. I'm"—she swallowed—"surprised to see you."

He nodded in understanding, then pointed with his free hand across the lake—in the other hand he held a cardboard box, but she was so fixated on his face that she didn't even bother to wonder why. "I was just over at the cabin. I . . . bought a headstone. Figured it would be okay now."

She drew in her breath, thinking *what* a good brother he'd been to Wayne. "That's nice. I'm glad."

"You should see the flowers we planted. I figured they'd be withered by now, but they look great."

"I've been over to water them," she admitted.

And his eyes softened further, reminding her of times when he'd been . . . so surprisingly tender. "Damn, honey—that's sweet. Thank you."

She just shook her head and tried to stand up a little straighter and feel a little less emotional. "It's nothing."

"It's something," he insisted. "But to get to the reason why I'm here, I came to apologize."

Again, she sucked in her breath. "Oh."

"For leaving the way I did."

She wasn't gonna sugarcoat it. "Yeah, that was . . . pretty awful."

His gaze dropped, and she couldn't help feeling a charge of satisfaction to know the words wounded him. "I never wanted to hurt you, Jenny. You were the best thing that ever happened to me."

Oh. *God.* She was? Really? "Then why'd you go?"

He lifted his eyes back to hers. "Your dad kinda threatened me."

"Yeah, I heard. And that sucks." She narrowed her gaze on him, feeling bolder now. "But you never struck me as the kind of guy to run from a threat. And . . . you didn't even say goodbye. If that was the reason, you would've said goodbye."

He let out a heavy breath, stuffed his free hand in the front pocket of his blue jeans. "You're right. I left because I was mad at you. Because you told your dad I was here. And why. And I was pretty damn upset about that. I mean, I trusted you. But . . ." He shifted his weight from one foot to the other. "Now I get why you told him. And I know it was wrong to just leave like that, but . . . I guess I was at the end of my rope. I wasn't thinking straight anymore. It was a hellish summer. In *some* ways, I mean."

"I know," she whispered, despite the general hum of party noise coming from the other side of the house. "How are you doing?"

"Better. I guess."

He didn't sound too sure. "You guess?"

He shrugged, clearly not wanting to talk about it. "Getting by. More importantly, how are *you*, pussycat?"

Hearing the nickname again warmed her. "I'm . . . okay. I took the teaching job and it's going well."

"Good." He nodded.

Then she noticed a new tattoo—it peeked from under the sleeve of his T-shirt on the opposite arm from where the skull resided. Curiosity led her to reach out and lift his sleeve so she could see the whole thing. "What's this?" A thin cross descended over his biceps and at the top were the initials W. B., the W. on one side of the cross, the B. on the other.

"When Wayne died, I promised him I'd never forget him. Guess I figured this would be a good way to make sure I kept my promise."

Mick expressed his love in different ways than she did, in different ways than most people she'd known. But he expressed it strongly, and she felt herself falling for him even harder than she already had and wondering exactly what the hell she was going to do about it. She'd been aching to see him, but now that he was here . . . God, when he left, it was going to be like starting right back over again.

"Anyway," he said, "I also, uh . . . brought you this cat."

He motioned to the box and she looked down, unable to believe it was the first time she'd really noticed it. An incredibly cute tiger-striped kitten stood in the box looking up at her. "Oh my gosh, aren't you adorable," she cooed instinctively—before raising her gaze back to her ex-lover. "But . . . a cat? For me?"

"It needs a home," he explained. "And I figured . . . maybe it could replace Snowball . . . so you won't feel alone anymore. I've been calling it Trouble—but don't judge him by that, he's not all that bad."

Just then, the cat began to meow, over and over again.

"Shit," Mick muttered, then gave the cat a look, murmuring, "And you were doing so good, too." Peering back up at Jenny, he said, "He gets on these meowing jags, but otherwise, he seems okay to have around."

Jenny held in her smile, then reached in the box to scoop out the tiny kitten. It continued to mew, but she held its warm little body close to her chest, stroking its fur until it quieted. "He's just scared," she said to Mick, "but once he gets settled and starts to trust me, he'll be all right."

Their eyes met, and something so tender moved invisibly between them that she feared she'd start to weep.

Until finally Mick blinked, ending the moment, and saying, "So, does this mean you want the cat?"

She hadn't thought she wanted a cat when she got up this morning. But she was already instantly and undeniably in love with this one. And maybe it was about time she opened her heart this way. So . . . "Yeah, I want the cat."

"Good," he said. "He, uh . . . made me think of you. I knew you'd give him a good home and know how to take care of him."

"The him part," she said, trying for a smile, "is that official, or an assumption?"

He shrugged. "Looked like a guy to me, but I'm not a cat expert."

When she flipped the kitten over in her palm and spread his tiny legs to check, Mick looked taken aback. "Too young to be sure," she announced, "but as far as I can tell, you were right—he's a . . . guy." She smiled in conclusion, and so did Mick, just a little—and she wanted to touch him, but she didn't.

"Well, I better let you get back to your party."

"Okay," she whispered, her stomach in knots.

His voice dropped lower. "Take care of yourself, pussycat." Then he turned to go.

Jenny watched him walk across the yard as she hugged the kitten back to her chest, petting it some more. She felt like Mick was taking a part of her with him. The part that he'd taught to be wild, reckless, carefree. And the part that he'd taught lessons to about the black and white and gray of life, and standing up for what you thought was right even when it put you at risk.

And it was as he reached the edge of the yard . . . that she realized she couldn't let him go—not just yet. "Mick—wait," she called.

He stopped, looked over his shoulder, and her heart melted. *Now what?*

But it took only a second for her to find the answer. *Be wild, be reckless, be carefree. Just one more time.* So she stooped to place the kitten in the box Mick had left on the ground beside her and started walking toward him.

And when she reached him, she looked into his beautiful eyes and said, "I still love you like crazy. I . . . *ache* for you, Mick."

His eyes changed in an instant, and she knew—without doubt—that he ached for her, too. "Pussycat," he breathed, shaking his head, glancing at the ground for a long moment before looking back into her eyes. "I've been . . . lonely without you. Fucking miserable, if you want to know the truth. But I didn't come back here, even when I quit being mad at you, because . . . look at you. Look at *this*." He motioned first to her dress, then all around them, at the yard, the cars, the people laughing on the other side of the house, she supposed. "I don't fit here. And anywhere I *do* fit is . . . not a nice enough place for you to be. You deserve *this* kind of world, *this* kind of life."

"So do you," she insisted. "If you want it."

But Mick just shook his head, still unconvinced.

And it made Jenny angry, angry enough that she didn't try to hide it, clenching her fists and stomping one foot on the ground. "Damn it, Mick, what's really changed? Before my dad messed us up, you were . . . almost willing to stay here, to give it a try. What's changed since then?"

"I came to my senses," he said as if it were obvious. "I don't look like the people at your picnic, Jenny. I don't act like them."

"And I don't *want* you to. I just . . . want them to see in you the goodness *I* do. And I want you to see the same thing in them. And I know that can happen, if you just . . . trust me. Again."

When he didn't answer right away, Jenny reached out and took Mick's hands in hers. Then she looked down—at how his darker, work-roughened fingers twined with her lighter, softer ones. They looked good together, their hands, *felt* even better together. She squeezed tight and lifted her gaze to his. "Mick, I'm asking you—if you love me, stay with me. *You're* the best thing that ever happened to *me*, too."

And to Jenny's surprise, Mick looked positively stunned. "Me?"

And that's when she realized—he still didn't get it. He still didn't get how deep her love for him ran, how much she believed in him, how vital it felt to have him in her life.

She nodded profusely and said, "You love *all* of me. The good girl, the bad girl—even the girl who butts into your business when she shouldn't. Do you have any idea how rare that is? How special? No one has ever made me feel as . . . as *free* inside as you do, Mick.

"And since you left, I keep trying, really hard, to *be* free, to be the person I want to be, but . . . sometimes I feel like I can hardly breathe without you next to me, letting me just . . . be me." Then she dropped his hands and lifted her palms to his darkly stubbled face. "Give this a chance. Give *us* a chance. I love you, Mick. I love you, I love you, I love you." And then she kissed him.

It was a soft, slow, but utterly heated kiss—their mouths simply touched, lingered together, for a long, hot moment that allowed it to stretch all the way into her panties. She took in the musky, masculine scent of him that she'd missed so much and yearned to feel his hard body pressed against hers.

And then she waited. Because that kiss was all she had to give. It was the kind of kiss that held the world, and life, and promises, and if that wasn't enough to make him take a risk and stay here with her, she knew nothing *would* be.

And then, finally, he put his hand behind her head and drew their faces close once more, and breathed,

"Kiss me like that again, pussycat, and I'll do whatever you want."

So she did, over and over, until—with their faces still not more than an inch apart—whispered, raspy words began to spill out of him unexpectedly, like a dam breaking, like something he'd been storing up inside for a very long time. "I love you, Jenny Tolliver. I love you so damn much. I was a fool to ever leave you. I was a bigger fool to stay away. I don't care what these people think of me—I only care what *you* think of me. As long as you love me, honey, my life'll be better than I ever thought it could. You're all I need, pussycat. You're all I need."

After they kissed some more, until they were almost breathless, Jenny pulled back in his embrace to smile up into his eyes. "I guess the only question now is—can you live with Trouble?"

"I'm used to it, honey," he answered quite seriously.

She laughed. "No, I meant the cat."

A grin unfurled on his handsome face as he let his eyes fall half-shut, and he looked sexy as sin when he replied, "For you, pussycat, anything."

A few minutes later, Jenny led Mick by the hand around the back of the house and into the heart of his first Destiny picnic. The first person to spot them was her father, who came to greet them with a smile. "Wondered where you'd gotten off to," he said to Jenny, "but now I see. It's good to see you, Mick. Glad you're here."

Jenny saw the genuine surprise flash through Mick's eyes, just briefly, but then he held out his free hand to shake her father's and said, "Thanks—it's . . . nice to be here."

Just then, Anita arrived, looking far more comfortable already than Jenny might have expected. She said to Jenny, "I met your neighbor, Miss Ellie. She's something. Only she thinks I work in a car, instead of a bar."

"This is my dad's girlfriend, Anita," Jenny said to Mick. Then, "Anita, my . . . boyfriend, Mick Brody."

And as soon as her dad and Anita went on their way—back to help Ed with the grill, Mick turned to Jenny, wide-eyed, and said, "That's your dad's *girlfriend*? I'll be damned."

She laughed. "I know."

When Sue Ann hurriedly approached, stating that she feared there was going to be a paper plate shortage, and then mumbling under her breath, "Dear God, what's with all the deviled eggs?" she finally stopped, then flinched—clearly having just noticed that there was a totally hot man holding Jenny's hand. "Uh, hi," she said, clearly dumbstruck.

"This is Sue Ann," Jenny said. "Sue Ann, this is Mick."

"Uh-huh," Sue Ann murmured, clearly robbed of speech.

"He's . . . coming back to stay in Destiny—with me," Jenny added. And their eyes met and hers said silently to Sue Ann, *Did I lie about how sizzling hot he was?* and Sue Ann's replied, *No, girlfriend, you most definitely did not.*

"I'm . . . really glad to hear that," Sue Ann said, finally pulling herself together.

And Mick said, "I've heard a lot about you from Jenny. And I'm sure you probably have doubts about me, with good reason, but I hope you'll give me a chance to prove myself, to prove I'm good for her."

And when, a few minutes later, Mick was pulled into a conversation with her father and Ed about grills, Sue Ann said to Jenny, *still* utterly stunned, "You, uh, didn't mention that he was debonair and knew exactly the right thing to say."

Jenny shook her head, just as shocked. "I didn't know. Trust me, he's full of surprises."

"Like suddenly showing up here today?"

Jenny nodded, then bit her lip to hide the grin. "It would seem that he was a fool to ever leave me and I'm all he needs."

Sue Ann pressed a palm to her chest, looking all aflutter. "Oh my God, that's amazing. And I know this means you're going to be trumping my sex again, but that's okay—I just want you to be happy."

After they'd eaten, but before the game of horseshoes Sue Ann's husband talked him into, Jenny introduced Mick around to Tessa and Amy and Lettie Gale, among others, who all behaved politely and tried to hide their shock—and awe.

"I knew it—I knew there was a secret man!" Jenny heard Amy say softly to Tessa as they walked away.

And Tessa replied with, "You know, when we were young, I always secretly thought he was sexy, but I just never told anyone."

After which Jenny drew Mick up under the maple tree to introduce him to Miss Ellie. "*Miss Ellie,*" she screamed, "*this is Mick Brody! He's my boyfriend!*"

And she stood there waiting to hear how dear, sweet Miss Ellie would twist her words this time, but instead the old woman just said, "Oh my—he's a big improvement over Terrence."

"*Why do you say that, Miss Ellie?*" she yelled.

"Well, are you blind, dear?" Miss Ellie asked. "Look at him. He's *hot.*"

Epilogue

The following summer

Jenny and Mick headed across the lake in the green canoe, her telescope resting between them. "Pretty soon," he said, "we won't have to paddle over here every time you want to look at the stars." By day, he did masonry work at the new development on the edge of town, but by night, he was busy building a balcony above the front porch, where the trees wouldn't get in the way. They'd bought the house from her father, so they felt free to remodel and redecorate at will now. And as for the shrine to her mother, it was all packed away somewhere at her dad's house, as it should be. Anita was an understanding woman, but not so understanding that she wanted a life-size portrait of her boyfriend's late wife hanging in the house—and to Jenny's dad's credit, he finally seemed to "get it."

"You know I can't wait 'til my balcony's done," she said to Mick, "but I'll still want to keep coming over *here* sometimes, too." The canoe glided smoothly across the water, nearing the southern shore, and crickets sang in the trees.

He grinned. "You just like what happens in the woods on the way up the hill." They never planned it, but sometimes, when they passed by the spot where they'd first bumped into each other, they found themselves reliving that first meeting.

"Maybe," she said, aloof, teasing.

He arched one eyebrow in doubt. "*Maybe*, pussycat?"

She smiled in concession. "All right, *definitely*. But it's about more than just sex. I never would have met you—again—if I hadn't come over here to look at the stars. And we wouldn't have had that lovely wedding in Miss Ellie's English garden, and you wouldn't be the unofficial horseshoe champion of Destiny. I didn't even know you *played* horseshoes until you beat the socks off of everybody at my Labor Day picnic."

He shrugged. "What can I say? I'm a man of hidden talents."

She let a wicked grin sneak onto her face. "I won't argue with you on *that*." He still rocked her world in bed like no other guy could. "Besides, you'll like coming over to this side better once the cabin is knocked down and the cemetery is enclosed." That was the plan for next summer—Mick wanted to make a nicer resting place for his brother, and there was nothing about life in the old house he cared to remember.

"Probably, but . . . don't forget what I told you about school. I like it here a lot now, but if you decide to go back to school, do your astronomy thing full-time, I'm on board. I still hate knowing that bastard stole your dream," he growled.

And Jenny only sighed. The truth was, she'd never been happier than she was right now, and she loved

her job and being close to her father and her friends,
and she suspected her old dreams were best left in the
past—yet she *also* loved that Mick valued them so much
on her behalf. Then she asked him something that had
somehow never come up between them before. "What
was *your* dream, Mick? Back when we were young?"

An uncharacteristic look of contentment washed
over his face. "To live on *your* side of the lake. And
. . . to fit in there." He raised teasing eyebrows. "So
I'm livin' the dream, baby." But she knew he was also
being serious.

When the canoe glided up onto the sand, they stepped
out and Mick grabbed the waterproof bag holding her
equipment. She trudged ahead of him into the woods,
but as the trees closed in around them, blocking out
the remaining light of the day, Jenny slowed her pace
to maneuver the hill.

That's when she felt Mick's hand slide around her
waist, up under her tank top. Her whole body warmed
as his touch grazed her skin, and a sigh of pleasure escaped her even as she looked over her shoulder to say,
"What're you doing?"

He leaned in behind her to kiss her neck. "Thinking
. . . the stars can wait."

Jenny bit her lip as Mick's sweet kisses moved
through her like hot liquid—but still protested. "The
sky is *perfect* right now, Mick. And the weatherman
said there'll be clouds later, rain by midnight. And I
want to try out my new lens."

"Too bad—I want you," he rasped in her ear. "Right
here, where I first *had* you."

Okay, that made her a little wet, but still . . . "Mick—
come on. Stars first, sex later—I promise."

"Sex now," he argued, sounding just a little like a
caveman and pressing against her until she felt the full
effect of his erection at her rear.

"Mmm," she heard herself moan in response. "But . . . come on, let's go." She reached for his hand, took it in her own, then proceeded to draw him up the steep landscape.

Until he stopped her again, with his body. Just like the first time—he stepped in front of her on the trail and said familiar-sounding words, but they came out more seductive than menacing this time. "Listen, honey, you're not going up that hill."

"Oh yes I am." She tried to push past him, but he stepped in her way again, molding his big hands to her shoulders.

"You don't want to mess with me, pussycat," he warned.

"And if I do?"

He crossed his arms, arched one eyebrow. "I might have to . . . have my way with you."

To which she teasingly rolled her eyes and said, "Promises, promises."

In reply, Mick pinned her to a tree. And the playful look on his face quickly transformed into something much more feral and hot, burning her up from the inside out.

And the rest was history, one more reckless, urgent encounter with Mick Brody in the woods across Blue Valley Lake. Only now he was the love of her life.